The Secret of the Kindred Spirit

by

Jacqueline DeGroot

Joyce &
Charlotte:
Enjoy Cassie
& Michael!

Jacky
DeGroot

ISBN: 1-4033-0407-6 (Ebook)
ISBN: 0-9747374-9-6 (Softcover)

This book is printed on acid free paper.

Disclaimer

This is a fictional story set in the Town of Sunset Beach. It takes place while the much-discussed and highly controversial 65-foot high-rise span bridge is being built. The author has taken leave to write about an event that may or may not happen, although, she does feel that its construction is inevitable. All characters in this book have no existence outside the imagination of the author and have no relation whatsoever to anyone bearing the same name or names. They are not even distantly inspired by any individual known or unknown to the author and all incidents are pure fiction.

Acknowledgement

A very big THANK YOU to my proof readers:
Kathy Blaine, Arlene Cook, Bill DeGroot, Jack Echard, Deanna Eirtle, Cliff and Lynn Errickson, Debra Fenton, Peggy Grich and Barbara Scott-Cannon. I can never thank you enough for your interest and your time. I also want to thank all the people who read my first book, "Climax," and encouraged me to continue writing.

A special thank you to Jim Grich, my IMAC guru. How is it you are able to have such a good attitude and be so helpful and patient anytime I call, day or night? You are truly one in a million.

Other Books By Jacqueline DeGroot:

Climax
What Dreams Are Made Of

Chapter 1

August 2001

As Cassie turned the kayak away from the marshy shoreline toward the bridge pilings, she looked closely at their crusty coatings trying to see signs of the tide markings. She'd been floating aimlessly around the Intracoastal, close to the bridge, for the better part of an hour, hoping to familiarize herself with the area around the old bridge and also the area where she'd be building the new bridge.

Oh, she liked the sound of that. *She'd* be building the new bridge. It would actually be her father's company that built it, but she was the designer, the architect, and unless she screwed up big time, she'd be the master contractor in charge. It would be her first chance to prove herself, not only to her dad, but to the crew she'd been working with ever since her summers in high school.

As the sun beat down on her head, she remembered the baseball cap she'd left in her GMC Jimmy. Thank God she'd remembered her sunglasses; the sun glinting off the water was enough to blind her with its shiny glare. She paddled over to the small bridge tender's house that was attached to the bascule part of the bridge. It was low tide right now, so the house was a good fifteen feet above her. This truly was a unique bridge, one of the last of its type, consisting of an apparatus that relied on one end to counterbalance the other by weights, very much like a seesaw. It was a design remarkable in its simplicity.

1

She marveled at the quaintness of the old bridge and at the same time, she tsk-tsked the condition of it as her tongue repeatedly clicked against the roof of her crimson-lined mouth. Deplorable. It was truly amazing that the state still allowed it to be used. She was under the last swing bridge on the east coast; the bridge connecting the mainland of Brunswick County to the island of Sunset Beach. Sunset Beach was about an hour's drive south of Wilmington, North Carolina and an hour's drive north of Myrtle Beach in South Carolina—in fact, it was Sunset Beach and the attached 39 acres of Bird Island that separated the two states.

Cassie knew the history of the bridge well. Her father had insisted she know the local history before coming down the first time, almost two years earlier, before they had put in a bid for the job of replacing bridge number 198 on SR 1172 over the Intracoastal Waterway at Sunset Beach, North Carolina. The first bridge to cross to the island of Sunset Beach was finished in 1958 by a local developer named Mannon C. Gore. It was a cable swing drawbridge controlled by a three-drum winch. It was replaced in 1961 by the North Carolina Department of Transportation and then again in 1973. The bridge maintenance crews of Wilmington replaced it a fourth time in 1984, and here it stood in all its decaying glory—all 508 feet 6 inches of it. Oh sure, there'd been a lot of repairs done over the years, but it had been time for a new one a long time ago. And that in itself was an interesting story. Some of the locals had literally been fighting City Hall for over twelve years to keep the Town of Sunset Beach from having a high span bridge built that

2

wouldn't require hourly openings and closings for the boat traffic on the Intracoastal.

As she looked up at all the toreutic worm holes left by those damnably proliferate sea leeches on the underside of the bridge, she could hear the thumping, creaking and metal-on-metal grating noises as the cars above her drove over to the island. The greedy little marine worms had bored holes everywhere, infesting every plank. She quickly looked down and shook her head trying to shake off the small wood and dust particles that were settling down and embedding themselves in her thick, short, black curls.

It was then that she saw it. There, floating and bobbing against a pylon. What the hell was that? It looked like some kind of a hat bill sticking up out of the murky, green water. Then it flipped over and she screamed with an eerily shrill voice she didn't even know she'd had inside her.

A man's grizzled head was bobbing up and down with the currents caused from the last boat's wake. A graying old man's head, with a baseball cap still attached to it was spinning around and around as it came closer and closer to her kayak, with one eye open, seemingly staring at her, and the other entirely missing from its socket. His nose was oddly pocked with bite marks and his lips gaped open, appearing to be bleeding where the corners met a deep gash from his cheek. She screamed again, this time louder but not quite so piercing as she frantically paddled and then finally pushed her small boat away from the slimy, creosote-covered timber. When she was finally out from under the shade of the bridge and back in the bright sunlight, she squinted up at the tiny yellow house and shouted and waved until a middle-aged man came out of the house and looked down at her.

"What's all the hollerin' about?" he called over the side of the railing.

"There . . . there's a head! A man's head!" she was finally able to get the horrible words out.

"What?"

"A man! His head! Just his head is here in the water under the bridge!" she hollered back up at him.

"No shit?"

"Look mister, I'm not a kid playing a joke!" Although she knew that to a lot of people she looked like she could be. Her short unruly mop, coupled with her freckled nose and tanned, slender build gave her the look of a seventeen-year-old camp counselor rather than the 24-year-old construction worker that she fancied herself to be. "Call the police! And hurry, before it disappears!"

He leaned over the side of the railing trying to see where she was pointing, but it was too far under the bridge.

"Hurry!"

"All right. All right. I'm goin'," he said as he turned around and went back into the bridge tender's house.

Cassie kept trying to fight the currents that wanted to send her back under the bridge. Using her two-sided paddle, she leveraged it so she could stay in the sun, well away from the head she could still see bobbing over in the shadows. The writing and symbol on the bill of the hat told her that he had apparently been a Duke fan. The blue and white of the Blue Devil mascot smiling at her added an even more menacing element to the gruesome scene just ten feet in front of her.

She heard the siren in the distance and her head immediately looked up, as if her rescuers would already be there. As the sound of the siren came closer, she shuddered. How was she going to get away from here? The strength in her arms was all but gone as she diligently held fast to the paddle pushed up against the piling. She could feel her arms starting to tremble and she knew that soon they would give out from the tenseness of her muscles. They would be rendered useless while she floated helplessly over to the dismembered head.

She heard people running across the bridge, a series of loud footsteps pounding furiously on the old rotting wood. Then she looked up and saw a uniformed police officer leaning over the railing. Her rescuer. Her charging knight. Her Adonis.

The stark contrast between the man's complexion and his hair coloring was startling. His short hair was so black and thickly sculpted around his face that her eyes were irresistibly drawn to his prominent widow's peak. His beard, even though she was pretty certain he must've shaved it this morning, was perpetually visible beneath his lightly tanned face. The coarse dark hairs were probably a problem he hated to contend with everyday, but she found evidence of his heavy beard quite virile. He was astonishingly handsome with his classical features and sharply defined good looks. He could have been a model, in fact, he reminded her of several she had seen in glossy, department store catalogues. Piercing eyes under dark, winged brows met hers and it took her an extra moment after drinking him in to remember why he was even there.

"Are you okay?" he called down to her. She noticed that his steely blue eyes were filled with concern, but also with interest.

"Yeah. I think so. But I can't get off these pylons or I'll run right into that thing again."

"What exactly is it? Pete said you found a head?"

"That's what it is all right. A man's head," she called back up to him.

"Well, hold on, we've got a boat coming. Should be here in a few minutes. We had to get it from Ocean Isle."

"I'll hold on as long as I can and then you're going to hear the loudest scream of your life!"

"Okay, okay. Take it easy! We'll get you away from it. Just don't panic."

She heard another siren and they both turned their head toward the whelping sound that intensified with each second.

"They're here. It'll take a few minutes to get the boat into the water and get to you. But someone's coming, hang in there."

The paddle suddenly slipped from her hand and fell into the water and she groaned aloud as she realized what she had done. She knew if she reached for it, she'd unbalance herself and tip the kayak; so she just watched it drift away, under the bridge to the Duke hat. With her hand she pushed against the pylon hoping to hold on and to keep the kayak from moving behind it, but she slipped and dislodged herself. As she started floating away from the pylon, she hollered, "I can't hold on. I'm going to swim for the shore."

"No! Don't do that!" He quickly looked around for something he could use to help her and spotted a coiled rope attached to a life preserver by the door of the control house. He grabbed it and went back to the railing. "Here, grab the float as I lower it down to you, then I'll tow you to shore."

He lowered the round styrofoam circle down to her and she looped her arm through the center of it.

"Okay, now just hold on to that and try to stay centered in the kayak while I pull you in."

"Okay."

"Ready?"

"Yeah."

He walked backward off the bridge, staying close to the railing and keeping his eye on her as he moved her through the water by tugging on the rope and reeling it in. The kayak started moving away from the bridge and toward the shore. When he reached the shoreline and reeled her in, he could see the relief flooding her face. And what a nice face it was. He couldn't quite gauge her age, but he was hoping that she was at least 21. My, my, what a beauty, he thought as he continued pulling on the rope until the kayak touched the sodden shore. Then he stepped down into the murky water, seemingly oblivious that his shoes were getting wet as he offered her his hand.

She looked into his face and smiled, and in that second, his whole world shifted. She lifted her sunglasses and set them on top of her head among thick black curls, and it was then that he first saw her eyes; eyes the color of grape hyacinths. Mesmerized for a few seconds, he stared into them, marveling at their bright, violet-blue clarity. Combined with her honeyed tan, her high cheek bones and her full, red lips, her eyes made her face friendly somehow—and gorgeous.

She took his hand as she gingerly tried to step out of the kayak. He sensed her awkwardness and unbalanced condition and grabbed her forearm to steady her before reaching under her arms and pulling her up and out of the kayak as if she was no heavier than a small child. He lifted her right over the kayak and to the edge of the shore where he set her down just long enough to put his arm under her knees before he carried her up the long slope to the top of the bank.

She was held tightly against his hard chest and, as there didn't seem to be anything to do with her hands, she wrapped them around his neck and then self-consciously lowered them to his shoulders.

"You can keep them there," he murmured softly into her hair.

And she wished she had. The hard muscles of his pecs and shoulders were doing something to her insides, something strange and unsettling, but kind of incredible. "It was nice of you to see me ashore," she said as he gently set her on her feet at the top of the small rise.

"Not all that nice, it's my job," he said with a grin. "But I would have done it anyway, even out of uniform."

Not one to be shy in front of strange men, Cassie wondered what her blushing was all about, so she hid her face with her hands as she shielded it from the sun and looked over to where the other officers were putting the inflatable rescue boat into the water.

8

"You could've saved them the trouble, if you'd just brought the head back with you in your kayak," he teased.

Her instant recollection of the gruesome sight caused her to shudder and then she had absolutely no idea why, but she suddenly started crying. Sobbing and crying and stuttering, "It . . . it was awful. Awwful. That poor man. And he even lost his eye!" she wailed.

He pulled her into his arms and let her dampen the front of his uniform with her tears while he waited to introduce himself. He tried to keep his mind focused away from the wonderful feeling her ample breasts created as they were crushed against his chest. When she pulled away from him, he could see her nipples as they strained against her tank top. "I'm Michael Troy and I'm sorry you had to find it." He offered her his handkerchief and she dried her eyes before they walked over to the shore where the rescue boat would be landing.

"I'm Cassie. Cassie Andrews. It looks like they found it."

"Yes." He had seen them take it out of the water and put it into the boat. Even from this distance he knew who it was. He muttered, "Jesus Christ," and gave a big sigh.

They walked over to the boat as it was being pulled up onto the bank and they were both able to see the head sitting on a tarp in the bottom of the boat.

Cassie spun away from it and collided with Michael's chest, and again he comforted her by encircling her shoulders within his arms. Even though she was quite upset, she couldn't help enjoying the warmth and masculine feel of him. There was a pleasant scent to him, like a forest of pine trees moments after a drenching summer rain.

"Who is it?" she asked quietly, somehow knowing from Michael's reaction that he knew whose head it was.

"It's D. Duke."

"Who's he?"

"Actually his last name is Ellington, that's why everyone calls him Duke."

"What's the 'D' for?"

"Damn. Damn Duke is what everybody called him."

"Why?"

"It's a long story and I have a hunch it's the reason somebody killed him. I wonder where the hell the rest of him is?"

"I'd like to hear the story sometime. Will you tell it to me?" she asked, hopeful that maybe she wouldn't be seeing the last of him.

"Yeah, sure. Meanwhile, I guess I'd better get the coroner out here. It'll probably take him the better part of an hour even if I can track him down right away."

"Well, I'll get out of your way. You don't need me hanging around, looks like you've got plenty of other people showing up to do that for you." She motioned to the people lining up at the bridge railing and others standing at the top of the bank.

"Yeah. And I guess I'd better call for some help. Looks like traffic at the bridge is backing up as well." He whipped a small, black pad out of his front shirt pocket and smiled when he noticed the cover was a little damp. "I need to get your name, address and phone number for my report."

"Sure. Cassie Andrews."

"Address?"

"I'm staying with some friends in Sea Trail while I look for a place to live."

"Do you know their address?"

"No, I'm sorry. But I know their phone number."

She rattled it off and he wrote it down. "Single?"

"Pardon?"

"Are you single?"

"Yes," she answered and watched as he wrote that down also.

"Seeing anybody?"

"No," she replied with a huge grin as he stopped writing.

"Want to?"

"Want to what?"

"See somebody?"

"Maybe. You got somebody in mind, a friend or a brother or somethin'?" she asked with a sideways, knowing smile.

"No. Just me. I'll call you. Would that be okay?"

"Sure. I want to hear the story about D. Duke."

"Are you okay now?"

"Yeah. I'm fine. It was just a shock. That's the last thing you expect to find floating in the Intracoastal."

"I can imagine. Where's your car? I'll get somebody to help me load your kayak."

"It's over on the causeway at the boat ramp. But I can carry my kayak, it's not that heavy."

He waved her off and turned and motioned to a fellow officer. Together they brought the kayak up and carried it over the bridge to the top of the boat ramp and her Jimmy.

They loaded her short, stubby kayak into the back, along with the two-piece paddle the other officers had retrieved for her. Then he walked her around to the driver's side and opened the door for her. As soon as she was settled in, he placed his hand over hers as it rested on the steering wheel.

"You're sure you're okay?"

"Yes. I'm sure."

"Well, I'm not."

"What's the matter?" she asked with concern.

"My heart's been racing ever since I laid eyes on you."

She laughed. "That's about one of the best lines I think I've ever heard."

He smiled and winked at her and then quickly turned away and went back to his cruiser.

Cassie started the Jimmy and pulled into the line of traffic waiting to cross the bridge back to the mainland. *Wait 'til Jenny hears about this! She'll never believe it!*

Cassie had been one of Jenny's customers when Jenny sold cars and trucks in Virginia. Cassie's family lived and operated their construction business in McLean and Jenny had earned Cassie's father's loyalty many years ago when she had shown him how he could save money by buying a more heavy duty series than he usually did, allowing the company to keep their trucks on the road for three to five years instead of one. Since she sold them all the trucks the business used, it was a move certain to cut into her commissions since they wouldn't be trading them in as often, but it didn't. Their business took off and the next year they needed three more; the second year, five more; the third year, fifteen more; and now, almost twenty years later, they bought almost a hundred new units a year to add to their fleet. In addition to that, all of the family's personal vehicles were handled through her too, which is how Cassie and Jenny had become such good friends, even though Jenny was almost twice Cassie's age. Jenny had sold Cassie her very first car, a sporty firebird that had seen her all the way through college. But Jenny was no longer at Royal Pontiac GMC to handle the huge fleet account she'd amassed over the years. She had retired in her mid-forties to Sunset Beach and met and married the man of her dreams, Colin.

Colin and Jenny were very much in love. One only had to look at them together or watch one or the other as they walked into a room and spotted the other after being separated for several hours, to see the instant sparkle of devotion and passion on their faces. They had been married a few years now and Cassie didn't think the bloom of new love was ever going to fade for them. If anything, they looked more in love every day. She was living with them temporarily, until she and Jenny could find her a suitable place that was inexpensive enough for her to buy for the three years she would be living here building the new bridge to the island of Sunset Beach.

Cassie drove into Sea Trail Plantation, a large coastal community less than a mile from the bridge site. The plantation was so close to the bridge that parts of two golf holes on their Dan Maple's course were going to have to be redesigned because the footings for the bridge span were going to start right about where their sand traps were now situated. Jenny, Colin and Paisley, Jenny's teenaged daughter, lived in a house central to the pools and tennis courts; and Cassie was finding their hospitality and the resort amenities of the plantation not too hard to take at all. Aside from setting up meetings with the North Carolina Department of Transportation, the Federal Highway Administration, various Sunset Beach officials and a slew of local contractors, she almost felt like she was on vacation.

She pulled her Jimmy onto the right spur of the driveway and parked beneath a huge flowering Crepe Myrtle. She used her key to get in through the front door and stopped at the end of the foyer when she realized she had caught Colin and Jenny on the sofa enjoying a little afternoon delight.

"Oops!" she called out as she quickly shielded her eyes and broke off to the right side of the house where the guest room and Paisley's room were. Just before she closed the door to her room she called out, "Nice buns, Colin."

He gave a light chuckle and Jenny gasped with embarrassment before Colin stood up with her in his arms, her legs wrapped tightly around his hips and carried her to their bedroom for a little more privacy. He knew Paisley was in school but he should have remembered that they had a house guest. It didn't bother him any that they had been caught in the act, but he knew Jenny was going to be mortified the next time she saw Cassie.

Chapter 2

An hour later, Jenny was in the kitchen making a cake when Cassie asked if she wanted to see her new bathing suit.

"Sure. I certainly don't want to hear anymore about that poor man's head."

Colin had left to go to the driving range, so Cassie shimmied out of her shorts and pulled the tank top she was wearing over her head. As her shorts and top fell to the floor, she adjusted the straps of her top.

"Geez, Cass, you're practically falling out of that thing. If it weren't for the fact that your nipples are covered, you'd be topless. It looks like you've got diagonally folded post-it notes taped to just the very center of your breasts."

"I'm only trying to do the barest coverage allowed, just enough to be legal."

"Well, if that's all you care about, just walk over to Bird Island and take the whole thing off. Nude bathing is done over there with tacit permission all the time."

"Really?" Cassie asked, suddenly very interested in Bird Island as she turned around to show the just-barely-there, no-more-than-a-thong bottom.

Jenny had a moment of envy as she eyed Cassie's completely undimpled and unpuckered, rounded buns. The two-inch swath of cloth going up the dividing center probably concealed the only area on Cassie's body that wasn't a golden tan color. In her mid-forties, Jenny knew she had a body that Colin adored, but still

15

it would have been nice if he could have seen it when she was Cassie's age.

"Yeah. It's a privately owned island. Part of it is in South Carolina, no one can figure out who has jurisdiction. The City of Sunset Beach closes its eyes as long as you don't cross the line back into Sunset Beach unclothed, and the county doesn't interfere unless you litter or walk on the dunes."

"Well, then that's where I'm going to work on my tan."

"Well, just be careful. Usually it's just gay couples who hang out there, but you never know."

"Okay, see ya at dinner time. What are we havin'?"

"Steaks on the grill, salad, corn on the cob and this pineapple macadamia nut cake."

"Umm, sounds good. Jen, you're too good to me. Honestly, I don't know what I did to deserve such a good friend."

"You were born into the right family. It's your father I'm doing this for. You . . . you're spoiled rotten," she said with an affectionate grin.

"I know. But I'm not such a bad kid."

"Yeah, I know, you're not such a bad kid. In fact, I suspect that your reputation is not at all earned, care to enlighten me someday?"

Cassie shook her head 'no,' picked up her clothes, put them back on and went to grab a beach towel from the linen closet, calling after her, "Remember, I'm expecting a call from that gorgeous cop, Michael something or other."

"I won't forget. It would do you good to date someone who at least has some respect for the law this time."

Cassie closed the door a little harder than she had meant to. Was anybody ever going to forgive her for getting hooked up with that sleazeball drug dealer? Honestly, she'd had no idea he even used drugs let alone sold them. Again, her father had had to bail her out of trouble when her boyfriend got arrested with her in his car, along with his whole inventory of hash. She was still doing penance for that one.

Jenny was making the icing for the cake when the phone rang forty minutes later.

"Hello?"

"Cassie?"

"No, This is Jenny. Cassie's not here right now, may I take a message?"

"Yeah. This is Officer Michael Troy with the Sunset Beach Police Department, I'm just calling to see if she's all right after this afternoon's ordeal."

"Yes, she's fine. In fact, she's over on Bird Island sunbathing. What an awful thing. Do they know anymore about what happened yet?"

"No, not really. The coroner was here about half an hour ago. We'll have to wait and see what he comes up with."

"Yeah. How awful. Well, Cassie should be home around six. Can I take your number?"

"Sure. It's 555-2151, just tell her to ask for me. I should be here 'til seven or so."

"Okay."

Michael hung up the phone and stared at the wall. So, she was sunbathing. On Bird Island. There was only one reason to walk an extra mile or two to sunbathe on Bird Island. He wondered. Was she the type?

17

He thought about it for a few minutes, then his imagination got the better of him. He had to go see. The single-minded thought of the breasts that had been pressed into his chest earlier today, being uncovered, was doing incredible things to him. He checked out for an hour, drove across the bridge, parked close to the gazebo and went looking for Matt, one of his friends on the Beach Patrol. He started walking west and after only a few minutes he saw him on his four-wheeler and waved him over.

"Hey, mind if I borrow your ride for fifteen or twenty minutes? I've got a complaint I need to check out on Bird Island."

"Sure, Mike. Here ya go," he said as he hopped off, leaving it running for him. "D'ya get a complaint about a nude bather?" he asked with a lecherous leer.

"No. Should I have?" he asked almost too quickly.

"Well, I did see a fine-looking tuna walking down that way 'bout half an hour ago. But I haven't made it back that way to check 'er out yet."

"You still carry those field glasses in the saddlebags?"

"Sure, right side I think."

"Okay, thanks. I'll check her out while I'm there for you," he said as he sped off down the hard-packed sand close to the water's edge.

"Gee, thanks," Matt said halfheartedly.

Just a few years ago, Sunset Beach was separated from Bird Island by Madd Inlet, but a summer storm in 1998 filled in the inlet and now the only thing separating the two was a small sign advising that it was unlawful to come back onto Sunset Beach nude.

When he got to the small dry gully that used to be the inlet, which was now a relatively permanent sand bridge to the other island, he stopped the four-wheeler and found the binoculars. There were a few walkers on the west end, but they appeared to be two couples in their sixties. He drove a little further until he thought he spotted a bather on a towel halfway down the beach, about three hundred yards away. Again, he hoisted the glasses to his eyes and scanned the horizon. The beach was deserted except for that one lone bather, and as his eyes locked onto her image and he adjusted the focus, he swore softly to himself. *Holy shit! There she was. Oh my God. She was naked. She was splendidly, gloriously naked!* There was no mistaking the woman; it was definitely Cassie. Those shiny, black, corkscrew curls were a dead giveaway. She was on her stomach, on a towel with her face turned away from him and she had the sweetest, loveliest, sloping curve going from her delectably rounded derriere past the small of her back to her smooth, soft shoulders. He moved the binoculars around until he could see where the side of her breast was exposed as she laid her head on top of her folded arms.

He felt himself harden and he licked his lips as he slowly followed the path of her silhouette all the way down her back again, past her raised hips, her ass, her thighs and her calves, all the way down to her trim ankles and to the toes buried in the sand at the edge of the towel. As he moved the glasses to the right, starting their slow assent back up again, he reached down to adjust himself. He was hot and it wasn't just because the late summer sun was shining so brightly. When his eyes got back up to her head, he wondered how long he'd have to sit there in the scorching sun in his dark navy blue uniform before she sat up and he'd get a view of her breasts. He was sure it would be worth it, but would it be the right thing to do? No, of course not, he knew that.

He put the field glasses away and started the four-wheeler moving again, making sure to keep it throttled down so it wouldn't warn her of his approach too soon.

Cassie was practically asleep. This was the most relaxed she'd been in weeks. She was doing something she had never done before, she was actually on a beach in the all together, enjoying the solitude and the sun's rays beating down on her. She never would have thought to do this if Jenny hadn't mentioned it, but once she had walked all the way down here and seen how isolated it was, she'd felt safe, even comfortable with the idea of tanning naked. And she felt deliciously wicked. For all her reputation, she was really not the party girl everybody thought she was. Getting up every morning at five a.m. would've squelched that even if her hidden morality hadn't. She had to be on the job with her crews by six a.m. And she absolutely had to have eight hours sleep, so that meant she had to be in bed by nine. Hell, most of the parties she was invited to didn't even start 'til ten! Still, she enjoyed her reputation; it made her feel older, somehow.

God, this was the life. Nothing to do but lie on the beach listening to the waves lapping on the shore and the birds squawking overhead. Now there was the steady drone of an airplane, and it was reverberating through the sand into her ear, getting louder, maybe closer? How was it doing that? She rolled over just as the noise became deafening and at exactly that moment, she felt the slight spray of sand that was flung onto her.

Ohmygod! she thought as she saw the four-wheeler with the male rider on top, not ten feet from her. She grabbed for her towel but it was under her. She scrambled off of it and onto the hot sand, her already heated body instantly feeling the super-heated sand burning her flesh. She had to get up, she was burning her skin. She did think to grab her towel as she stood up and finally managed to cover herself.

She looked up and over at the man who had been on a mission to ogle her. "You!" she spat out.

He gave her a big wide grin as he adjusted himself on the seat. *Yup, he thought. Nice tits, too.*

"You! You . . . Peeping Tom!"

"Hey, hey! Whoa! This is a public area, I wasn't doing anything I wasn't supposed to be doing. In fact, I *am* supposed to be patrolling the beaches."

"I thought I was alone."

"I can see that."

"Well, it's not illegal."

"No, it's not legal or illegal, there's sort of a gray area down here about that."

"Jenny said it was okay if I sunbathed in the nude here."

"Honey, it's more than okay with me. Just let me know the next time you plan on coming out."

"Yeah, I'll be sure to do that!" she snapped at him. "Now would you please be kind enough to turn your back so I can put my suit back on?"

"Sure." He maneuvered the four-wheeler in a little circle and waited. Finally, he asked, "Aren't you finished yet?"

"Yeah."

He spun back around and whistled. "Boy, that's not much better for coverage, but my, you do look fine."

She blushed furiously and then wrapped the towel around her, starting it under her arms.

"Hey! That's not fair!"

"I think you've seen enough."

"Now that's where you're wrong, I haven't seen nearly enough of you. How about dinner tonight?"

"Sorry, I can't. My friend, Jenny, is making a special dinner for me tonight."

"Well, can I pick you up after dinner and maybe we can take a walk on the beach?"

"Which beach?"

"Does it matter?"

"Yeah. I plan on keeping my clothes on this time."

"Damn!" He gave her a big smile. "We'll see."

"There's no 'we'll see' about it! Just because you've seen me naked doesn't mean anything."

"Oh yes, it does."

"Oh yeah, what?"

"It means if you'll take your clothes off for just anybody, maybe you'll take them off for me again if I ask real nice."

"I didn't take my clothes off for just anybody! There was nobody here! You snuck up on me!"

"Anybody could've."

She thought for a minute. "Yeah. I guess you're right. I guess I'd better not do this anymore."

"That's not what I wanted to hear."

"What did you want to hear?"

"Never mind. How about that walk tonight?"

"Sure. Why don't you pick me up around eight? That'll give me time to help Jenny with the dishes. I still don't know the address though."

"I do. I got it from the cross-reference on the computer."

"Boy, you already know a lot about me."

He smiled. "Uh huh. Yep, I do. You've got a small, strawberry birthmark on your right cheek."

Instantly her hand went to her bottom to where her birthmark was and her face went beet red. "Hhhow?" she stammered.

His hand went to the open saddlebag and he pulled out the field glasses. "I could have looked at you all day." Then he nonchalantly dropped the glasses back into the box, placed both of his hands on the handle bars, revved the throttle and made a wide arc before tearing down the beach, heading back in the direction from where he'd come.

Cassie stood there, rubbing her right cheek and holding her towel around her. Maybe this hadn't been such a good idea after all, she thought.

Chapter 3

Michael came to pick up Cassie at exactly eight o'clock, and after Cassie introduced him to Colin, Jenny and Paisley, they left to go for their walk on the beach.

Michael settled her into the passenger seat of his fairly new Pontiac Grand Prix then walked around the front of his car to the driver's side.

"So, you're a Pontiac man huh?" she asked.

"Just this time, I had a Chevy Camaro before."

"That's interesting. I had a Pontiac Firebird before I got the company Jimmy."

"Your company provides your wheels?"

"Yeah. Actually it's my dad's company. I work for him."

"Yeah? What do you do?"

She watched his big hands as he steered the car around the curves in the road, and she remembered how they'd felt when he'd held her and comforted her that afternoon. "We build bridges and tunnels and dams. We also contract out for subways and els. My division handles bridges over estuaries, and I specialize in design, structure and staging."

"Really?" he asked, incredibly impressed.

"Really," she answered with a big, knowing grin. People always doubted her capabilities; construction work, especially from the brain end, was always considered men's work. Now he was probably going to ask her whose secretary she was. "In fact, that's why

I'm here. My company is building the new bridge over the island."

"You're kidding!"

"Nope. That's why I was out in the Intracoastal. I was checking things out from the water's perspective, getting to know the shoreline and the marshy areas a little."

He stopped at the light before the bridge and looked over at her, "So what is it you do for the company? Work the cranes? Operate the backhoes and bulldozers? Surveying? Diving?"

Finally a man who gave women a little credit. "Actually, I can do all of that, but my job is master contractor and job foreman."

"You're shitting me! I was only joking about you doing all that stuff."

Instantly he noticed her expression change as she turned away from him and stared out the windshield. A moment later she coolly replied, "I would prefer you not use that type of language around me and no, I'm not *joshing* you. I have been formally educated to design and construct bridges and, even if I don't look like I know the difference between a caisson and a coffer, let me assure you that indeed, I do. *And*, I am fully capable of maneuvering a reinforced concrete beam off a truck, up into the air and down onto your head! All without the help of one testosterone-pumped up male!"

"Hey! I don't know exactly what I said to rile you so, but whatever it was, I'm sorry. I didn't mean to doubt you. It's just unusual to find a girl who likes to work with life-sized tinker toys."

"No, it's not. There are lots of us. And unfortunately lots of guys like you who are just too macho to think women can't do much more than breast feed and vacuum up your messes."

The light turned and he started over the bridge. As they bounced along, going way down one ramp and then all the way up another as the pontoon part of the bridge reflected the low tide, Michael blew out a big, heavy breath. "I am really sorry I upset you, but you have absolutely the wrong idea about me. I know that women can do anything they set their minds to. Hell, my sister's a tug boat pilot on the St. Lawrence Seaway."

"Really?"

"See! There you go doing it! So don't accuse me of stereotyping! And no, she's not. I don't even have a sister." He smiled at her, giving her a lopsided grin that said, *Aha, I caught you at your own game.*

She didn't say anything, she just stuck her tongue out at him.

"Don't stick that out unless you plan on using it," he admonished in a low, sexy voice.

Cassie quickly turned back to the front, her emotions calming but with a new kind of heat seeping through her from hearing his husky reprimand.

He pulled into a space in the parking lot that led to the gazebo. "Listen, I'm sorry I said something that offended you. I don't want us to get off on the wrong foot here, please accept my apologies. I think women are wonderful and capable and they rule the world. Sometimes they're stupid for putting up with jerks like us, but really what choice do they have? We're cute and cuddly and we help them make babies." He lifted

26

his sculpted eyebrows in question and gave her a big devastating smile. "Can't we be friends, my cute little Tonka Toy demolisher?"

She smiled at his cute contriteness, but it was mostly his flashing eyes and beguiling smile that won her over. "Friends, but you don't get to play with my crane."

"Sweetheart, there are lots of things you have that I'd like to play with, but your crane isn't one of them."

Again, she thought she'd melt from the erotic message he insinuated with those huskily spoken words. The man was hot. Sexy and hot, hot, hot. She'd do good to remember that. 'Too hot to handle' should be her mantra here, this man had the power to hurt, she could feel it deep down inside. The power that emanated from him was raw and sensual, she could feel his magnetism pulling on her as he exerted it on her defenses. But while her mind warned her that he could be trouble, her body was finding avenues to open to him to entice him to do just that; to break through her defenses.

He came around to her side of the car, but not in time to keep her from letting herself out. He should have known that a woman who owned her own fleet of Caterpillars wouldn't need the assistance of any man to get out of a car.

They walked side by side through the parking lot, and then he indicated for her to proceed him up the wooden walkway to the gazebo. His eyes followed her as she walked in front of him. Ooh la la. He would have to remember to always let this woman go first, her walk was something no man could possibly ignore. It was an absolute pleasure to watch her hips sway and catch as she moved forward in front of him through the gazebo and down the beach access to the sand. He had visions of her jumping off the seat of a high bulldozer, into his arms, her legs grabbing him around the waist as he caught her. And he knew he was in trouble. For the second time that day, she'd caused his whole world to shift and he was having a hard time trying to calm the sensations.

She went ahead of him to the water's edge while he watched her. He noticed that all the men on the beach were also watching her. No doubt about it, she was hot. She was dressed simply in khaki hiking shorts with a white, sleeveless, button-up shirt, but she was definitely hot. Very hot. He watched her long tanned legs as she kicked off her white and gold sandals. Her ankles were trim, her calves were quite shapely and her thighs were remarkably lean. Whether she kept her athletic good looks up by climbing up and down off of heavy construction equipment or by regular workouts, he didn't care, he just hoped she'd keep it up. It would be a shame for any woman to lose perfectly toned legs like hers.

She turned back to him with a questioning look and he realized that he'd been staring. He walked down to the water's edge to join her after discarding his deck shoes at the base of the cross that stood near the gazebo. Not that anybody would think to take them, but it didn't hurt to have a reminder that this was where people gathered for services every Sunday, just in case his $85 Rockports appealed to someone. His eyes were focused on Cassie and he couldn't help the thought that instantly came to him; this one would have to grace his bed sheets soon. He was suddenly very curious about

28

her bedroom nature. Just how spirited was this impetuous woman anyway?

When he was just a foot away from her, she started walking along the shore towards Tubbs Inlet; the inlet between Sunset Beach and the next beach up the coast, Ocean Isle. He reached to take her hand but she pulled it away.

"C'mon, surely we can at least hold hands? I've seen your butt, your booty and your boobs."

"Well, I didn't have any choice in that, I do in this," she said as she wrapped her arms around her waist causing her breasts to lift in a most delicious manner.

"Well if you think I'm going to apologize for that, you're wrong. That was the absolute highlight of my day."

She looked over at him and saw the last light of day sparkling in his dark blue eyes. She wondered if he would mind repaying the favor and letting her ogle his hard, muscular body.

"Believe it or not, I'm usually a pretty modest and private person."

"Honey, I saw your bathing suit, remember? The only thing left to the imagination is what kind of earrings you're wearing, because I guarantee you, nobody will ever think to look at your ears."

"It's a brand new bathing suit and that was the first time I wore it. I wanted to minimize my tan lines."

"That's a shame."

"Why?"

"Because I *like* tan lines."

"I don't believe I was thinking of you when I bought it."

29

"No, I guess not." There was silence for a moment and then he asked, "Were you thinking of someone else?"

She looked over at him and simply shook her head. A moment later, she added, "No. There is no someone else. I've been told to cool it for a while."

"By whom?"

"My father. It seems the last candidate for a boyfriend wasn't very well researched. I've been told to concentrate on other things for the time being, namely my job down here."

"Care to talk about it?"

"No, not really. Suffice it to say, I was a real jerk. But at least I've learned my lesson."

"And what's that?"

"Know the one you're with."

"Hmm. I guess that means it's not too likely that I'm going to get to sleep with you tonight?"

She laughed a delightful and almost hysterical laugh. "I guess you could say that!" she replied, still laughing.

"Unless you're up for a crash course. I could teach you all you need to know about me in just a few short hours."

She flashed a bright smile at him, "Thanks, but I think I'll pass this time."

"You don't know what you're missing . . . "

"Neither do you."

"Unfortunately, I think I do."

"Let's talk about you for a while. All we've talked about is me. Isn't there a girlfriend waiting for your call?"

"Several."

"Oh." They walked in silence for a few minutes and then she tentatively asked, "Nothing serious?"

"No, nothing serious."

"Has there ever been?"

"Yeah. I was engaged once."

"Really?"

"Yup."

"What happened?"

"I pushed her to have sex."

"So?"

"So we did, and it was awful—she hated it. Didn't want to do it again at all."

"Wow. So what did you do?"

"Well, we went for counseling."

"Did that help?"

"No. It didn't. Well, not much anyway. She finally agreed that after we were married, we'd have sex on a schedule if I insisted we had to have it."

"So you broke up."

"Yup."

"Didn't you love her?"

"Of course I loved her, but I was 20, I also loved sex. I wanted it on the table, then under the table, against the fridge, then in the fridge, on a chair, on the steps, in the car. I couldn't agree to every third Thursday night between seven and eight. I didn't think we had enough to make marriage work under those conditions."

"So, do you still want to have sex in all those places?"

"Nah. In the refrigerator doesn't really appeal to me anymore."

She laughed and he looked over at her. She was so beautiful and she had a laugh that made his belly warm.

He reached for her hand and this time she didn't pull away. They walked hand-in-hand up the beach enjoying the feel of each other's pulsing tingle against their skin.

"So, sex is more important than love?" she asked.

"No," he said thoughtfully. "Sex is *as* important as love though. It's the way a man shows a woman he loves her and it's the way a woman shows a man she loves him."

"What about people who have sex who aren't in love?"

"They're in love with sex. Once you fall in love, you're in love with both."

They felt the cool water as it rushed up to cover their feet. The sun was almost all the way down, and the only lights were the lights from the beach houses behind them.

"So, tell me about D. Duke. What's his story?"

He reached over with one arm and grabbed her around the shoulders and gave her a light squeeze. "Sure know how to move the conversation along don't ya?"

"Well, you were getting a bit melancholy."

"Sorry." He took a big breath and then started. "D. Duke, as he was popularly known, has lived on this island almost all his life." He gestured with his hand over to the left towards a large grouping of houses. "Way up there on the left is his house. It was his grandfather's and after that his father's. No one knows

32

whatever became of the women, they must've run 'em off at an early age with their strange behavior.

"D. Duke was never a really bright kid but he got along with everyone; and to hear him tell it, he had the most wonderful childhood growing up on this isolated island. He never married, never even had a girlfriend so far as anybody can remember. And when his father died, he lived alone in that clapboard siding house with its gray slate roof. You'd see him fishing on the pier, digging for worms after a rain, and picking up trash. Wherever he went, he was always picking up trash." He stopped for a minute, recollecting, then continued. "I'd almost forgotten that part. I bet he collected over a ton of trash over the years; the beach will probably never be as clean again with him gone."

She squeezed his hand encouraging him to continue.

"Well, about twelve years ago, the town started thinking about getting a new bridge. This one was always breaking down. Not too seriously, just enough to be a nuisance and unsafe in people's minds. Once, a barge hit it and they couldn't get it fixed for two days. The people stranded on the island were terribly inconvenienced and the talks escalated. Well, D. Duke, who was just Duke back then, started to get pretty verbal. He didn't want a new bridge. He liked the old one just fine.

"He started coming to the meetings at the town hall, standing up and talking forever, drowning out what everyone else was saying and generally being outspoken and belligerent. Along about that time, a small group of homeowners banded together to oppose the new bridge also. They thought that all a new bridge would give them was more tourists and day-trippers and a more commercially viable beach. So they took matters into their own hands, hired an attorney, and petitioned the courts using the premise that a new bridge would adversely effect the environment. A study was ordered by Judge Earl Britt. A study that ended up costing the state over two million dollars, a study that should have taken less than five years but ended up taking close to ten. In the meantime, Duke tried to join the faction opposing the bridge. No one ever knew if he had actually ever become a member because the group always denied his affiliation, but he thought he was a member, regardless of what they said. So he became their self-appointed harassment instigator. Over the years, you would not believe the complaints we had about him.

"While the tourists were in the grocery store stocking up on food for the week, he would empty their baskets of the toilet paper they had selected and substitute it with a septic-safe, unscented brand. While he was doing this, he gave them a long-winded lecture about the fragile sewage system on the island, causing many to fear that if they flushed one too many times, they were going to cause the waste of the whole island to come backing up into their condos.

"He would walk along the beach grabbing glass bottles out of people's hands and directly depositing them and their contents into his ever-handy bag of trash. Which was kind of okay, since you aren't supposed to have glass of any kind on the beach anyway, but he was never polite, and it caused quite a few problems and even a few fights.

"If people had floodlights on the back of their houses that shone on the beach at night, he would trespass on their property and take the light bulbs out and discard them. He was a fanatic about the turtles and their nests."

"He doesn't sound so bad to me, sounds like he was just trying to make people obey the laws," she said.

"Wait. It gets better, or worse I should say." He stopped, walked her back to a raised area of dry sand and pulled her down to sit beside him on the beach. Then, as they both stared off into the waters of the Atlantic illuminated by the moon, he continued. "He hated wind chimes, especially the really loud ones, so he would sneak onto the decks and duct tape the chimes together or cut the strings to silence them. He would look in people's trash cans and then go knock on their doors and berate them for not setting aside their recyclables and taking them to the recycling center. He told anybody who would listen that the new bridge would make their rent go up by hundreds of dollars a week because the homeowners would have to pass the assessment they'd be getting on to them. He told them there were sharks and jellyfish in the water when there weren't. He would scream at a little kid like a banshee if he or she happened to go over the dunes to retrieve a downed kite. And we suspect he let stray kittens into people's houses when they left them open while they were on the beach. I can't remember everything he did right now, but there was a lot, and over the years there were hundreds of things he was accused of that we don't know if he did or not.

Anyway, that's where the name Damned Duke came from, hence D. Duke."

"So you think somebody might have killed him because he ticked them off?"

"Could be. Let's face it, he was not the best ambassador of goodwill for the homeowners whose incomes depend on their rental properties."

"So he was a staunch opponent of the new bridge?"

"To the extreme. I'm afraid you and he would not have been on good terms and Lord only knows what kind of havoc he could have made for you while you were building the bridge."

"Well, then I guess I should be grateful to whoever did this."

"Grateful to someone who lopped a man's head off?"

"Well, I guess you're right. No one deserves that."

"And besides, at this point we don't know if he was killed because someone blew a gasket over some asinine prank. He could have been killed for any number of reasons."

"Could it have been an accident? Maybe he fell off a boat and a propeller got him."

"The coroner says no, the cut is not that clean. He thinks it was hacked off by something that wasn't all that sharp."

"Ugh. I hope he was at least already dead before that happened to him."

"All indications are that he was, but we'll know more about all that in a few days. Right now they're out trying to find the rest of him before an unsuspecting tourist does."

"Yeah, like me."

"Yeah, like you." He smiled, "I probably wouldn't have met you if D. Duke hadn't lost his head. Wish I could thank him for that."

"You sound like you liked him."

"He wasn't a bad sort. He just loved his island, hated the tourists, and didn't mind letting them know it. He didn't want progress. He wanted things to stay the way they were forever. There are a lot of people like that. He was a curmudgeon, an old man who lived for what you see in front of you and all around you, the pristine beauty of this paradise."

They were quiet for quite a while, each lost in their own thoughts. Then Michael pulled her close, turned her to face him, and looked into her eyes.

"I will never forget this day."

"Why? Because of D. Duke?"

"No, because of you. I have thoroughly enjoyed meeting you, ogling you, talking to you and kissing you."

"You haven't . . ."

"Mmmhmm . . . ," he said as his mouth closed over hers.

Chapter 4

His firm, yet pliant lips moved slowly over hers savoring the feel of her lips molding to his. He kept moving them very lightly over hers, renewing the wonderful tingling sensations the contact caused. He stretched his lips over hers again and again as he captured them with his, feeling their soft fullness against his mouth. The tip of his tongue licked her ripe, plump bottom lip and then it moved to trace the distinct bow at the center of her upper lip. As he kissed her, his hand moved to the back of her neck and he caressed the smooth skin as he felt her soft curls fan over the back of his hand.

With his other hand, his fingertips traced the curve of her jaw and then his thumb grazed the column of her throat as his hand made its way down to her chest to cover her breast. Her hand met his there and she opened it against his, imprisoning it to keep it from its intended target.

Slowly she pulled away from him and stared, mesmerized, into his eyes. "I can't. I don't know you."

"Michael Troy. Six foot two, two hundred and five pounds . . . "

She interrupted him by placing her palm against his freshly shaven cheek, her eyes still focused on his, "Hair as black as coal, eyes the color of aquamarines shimmering in a blue sea . . . "

He leaned over to touch her lips with his again before adding, "Caucasian, born and raised in Raleigh, father Italian, mother Greek, one brother, raised Catholic . . . "

She lifted their entwined hands, then splayed her palm open against his, his fingers extending over her fingertips by at least an inch, "Well endowed, if this is any indication," referring to the old adage that a man's sex organ corresponded to the size of his hands.

"It is," he said as he brought their hands to the center of his lap and placed hers over his arousal, sufficiently answering her unasked question.

She blushed as she realized how incredibly forward she had been. And vulgar. Since when had size ever mattered to her? She knew she had just given him the impression that she'd been around and that she was looking for a stud. As if to confirm this, his hand closed over hers and encouraged it to stroke him.

She jerked her hand away. "I'm sorry. I've given you the wrong idea, I didn't mean to."

"No, I don't think you did," he said as he took her lips again, this time quickly deepening the kiss with his tongue.

As soon as she felt his tongue glide along her lips, she gave a small moan that allowed him entry. That was all the encouragement he needed. He grabbed her to him, pulled her hard against his chest and plundered her mouth wildly with his tongue. The passion that ignited between them was raw and primal. As his lips moved hungrily over hers, her hands captured his head to hold him closer. Over and over, as she ran her hands through his thick hair, his tongue thrust into her and he savored her sweet, slick moistness.

Cassie had never been so swept away by a man's kiss before and this man's kisses were threatening to undo her, just as he was now undoing the front of her shirt. He had all three buttons undone and his hand insinuated into her bra, pulling her breast free before she could stop him. By then she didn't want to stop him, but she made a feeble attempt to anyway. He captured her hand, brought his lips down to it and kissed it. Then he turned it over and licked the pad below her thumb before going on to lick each finger, all the while feasting his eyes on the breast he had just uncovered.

As good as this was feeling, she knew she couldn't let it continue. Right now he seemed ravenous and she wasn't sure she could stop him or if she could even convince herself she wanted to. But she knew she had to. She just couldn't let herself go, not with a man she had just met, no matter how wonderful he was making her feel.

She reluctantly pulled her hand away and moved it to hide her bared breast. His hand met hers and he softly covered it, the palm of his hand overlapping the back of hers. Then ever so slowly, he lifted her hand and placed the center of her palm over the center of her breast. He forced it in small circles over her nipple, causing her to visibly tremor with the sensation. Then he brought her fingertips together and made her pinch her own nipple. He encouraged her to pull on it by holding her fingers with his and gently tugging on them. In the darkening twilight he could vaguely see her blushing as she looked down to see what he was making her do to herself and he didn't know when he'd ever been so aroused.

Watching her while he manipulated her hand to do what he was dying to do to her himself was probably one of the most erotic things he'd ever done with a woman and he was shaking as he tried to control himself. With deft fingers, he slipped her bra strap down off her shoulder and exposed her other breast. Taking her other hand from her lap, he placed it, palm open, over the newly-bared breast and then, completely covering her hand with his, he hefted the weight of it. Even with her hand as a barrier, he could feel that it was substantial and as soft and fleshy a mound as any man could want. He yearned to taste it. Gently, he pried her hand away from the tip where he was forcing her to pinch her own nipple and leaned forward to taste the tight, hardened bud with his tongue.

The jolt was electrifying to them both as his wet tongue touched her and his eager lips surrounded her nipple. He sucked and laved it with his tongue while he listened to the soft crooning sounds escaping her lips. His erection was straining against his shorts and he wanted her so badly he couldn't stop himself. Sitting there on the ledge of sand, he lifted her up by her bottom and positioned her crotch between his legs, high up on his thighs so he could feel her right up against him. Tightly gripping her ass he rubbed her up and down the length of his erection as it stood up against his groin, straining toward the waistband on his shorts. He groaned with intense pleasure as he blatantly and silently issued his entreaty to her by pressing his fullness into the cleft he was making in her shorts.

She moved with him, pressing just as fervently against him as he was pressing against her before suddenly pulling away and crying out, "Damn you

Michael! You're driving me crazy. But we have to stop. Please, please. We have to stop."

Very reluctantly he did stop, and he numbly watched her as she pulled her shirt plackets together. "You have beautiful breasts," he whispered huskily as she managed to fasten her bra together.

"Thank you," she answered politely, just as if he'd just told her he liked her shoes.

He turned her face to his and gave her a small, quick kiss. Then, looking into her dark, blue, sultry eyes he asked her a question that caused something in her stomach to drop. "Would you let me feel you where you're wet for me? I want to feel what I've done to you. I want to touch your hot, steamy core, to feel how much you want me." His voice was so low and so husky that, coupled with his words, she shivered.

He didn't wait for her answer, just drew her back onto his lap, parted her thighs and eased a fingertip up under her shorts and under the elastic of her panties. When he felt her heat and her dampness, he let out a long sigh and then mercilessly shoved his middle finger deep inside her. Her sudden gasp along with her head falling softly onto his shoulder told him he was welcome here, at least for a few moments. Using his thumb he caressed her labial lips and then slowly extracting his finger, he found her aroused nub and massaged it with great care, circling it over and over until he felt her breathing quicken and her clitoris spasm under his finger. He held it there enjoying each trembling jolt as she convulsed and shook in his arms. Then he withdrew his hand from her panties, lifted her chin from his chest and softly kissed her. When her eyes opened and she was looking dazedly into his face, he took his middle finger, put it into his mouth and slowly and oh so sensuously licked it clean.

As she watched him, she darn near swooned. The man was just too good to be true—too sexy, too erotic, and too damn confident. She was awed by him, by his good looks, his arrogant demeanor, and his superb sexual technique. Never had she been treated so delicately, so reverently and so cavalierly, all at the same time. And she knew this was trouble. This was a love 'em and leave 'em kind of guy if she ever saw one. One just didn't get that good without lots of practice—practice with lots of different women, lots of overcome, mesmerized women, and she reluctantly realized that she'd just joined their ranks.

She was incredibly surprised when he stood up taking her with him and started adjusting his clothes. "We should probably be heading back now, the tide's coming in and I believe we walked about two miles to get here, so it's the same two miles back."

"Yyyes, I guess you're right," she stammered as she finished patting the sand off of her shorts. She turned her back to him and nervously ruffled her hands through her hair, trying to fluff it up and to let the wind get at it to loosen some of the curl.

He laughed and pulled her into his arms for a big hug. "Please don't go getting all nervous and fidgety on me. I like you being open with me and I enjoy being open with you, don't mess up what we're starting by being self-conscious about all this."

She looked up into his smiling face, "What exactly are we starting, if you don't mind me being so open to ask?"

"I don't know. But I want to see you again."

"I think you've seen plenty of me already, considering we've only known each other for one day."

"Not hardly. You're not the type of girl a man's eyes can easily get enough of. I imagine a man taking his ease in your body would find it hard to get enough of you that way, too."

"Just what will be left when you've had enough of me?"

"Not even a crumb for anybody else, if I can help it."

"That's what I'm afraid of."

"Don't be. I won't hurt you. I promise."

"How can you promise that to anyone?"

"Because it's true. *I* won't ever hurt you. I didn't say that you couldn't be hurt, just that *I* wouldn't be the one doing it."

They started walking back and she thought about that for a minute. "So you're saying that if I get hurt, it's because of something *I* do or don't do. That's very interesting because that's exactly what happened between Mark and me. I didn't do something I should have done."

"What's that?"

"Get to know him better before I got involved with him."

"Oh. I just shot myself in the foot, right?"

"Right."

"Just wondering why I suddenly developed a limp," he said as he started dragging his foot in the sand behind him.

She laughed at his antics and at his woebegone expression until tears were streaming from her eyes.

44

She used the back of her hands to swipe at them and that's when he noticed that those thick, dark lashes fringing her dark sapphire eyes were all hers. In fact, he noticed as he gazed at her lovely face, except for the lipstick he'd managed to kiss off, she was quite a natural beauty—something pretty rare these days.

"So, care to clue me in on what happened between you and 'Mark?' "

"I don't want to talk about it."

"So, there's no heads up for me? I could easily find myself in the same situation?"

"Not likely. But I'll find out soon enough."

"Oh, really? How?"

She thought for a minute, then stopped and with absolute dead seriousness she asked, "Would you mind filling out a questionnaire for me?"

He looked back at her completely stunned. "What?"

"A questionnaire. If I ask you some questions, would you answer them for me, honestly?"

He laughed a deep, full, hearty laugh, then after catching his breath, he answered, "Of course, I would. I'd be happy to. When shall we do all this?"

"Well, let's see. Saturday is Jenny and Colin's anniversary. They've been so wonderful to me that I want to do something extra special for them. I was thinking about making them a cake. Maybe you could come for dinner and afterward we can go for a drive or something and you could answer my list of questions."

"Sounds good. And a cake sounds like a good idea. That would be very nice."

"Yeah. I know," she said dejectedly.

"What's the matter?"

"I don't know how to cook."

"Bake," he corrected. "Making a cake is baking, not cooking."

"Great. So I don't know how to bake, either."

"Well, you're in luck. I do."

"You do?"

"Well if you can know how to drive a dump truck, why can't I know how to bake?"

"Sorry. I did it again, huh?"

"Yeah, Miss-don't-put-my-round-luscious-body-into-a-square-hole feminist."

"Thanks for the compliment and I'll try not to do it again. So, back to the baking. You know how to make a cake?"

"Yeah. It's easy. I used to love to watch my mother in the kitchen. I'd be glad to help you if you like."

"You would?"

"Sure. I'll try to keep the cost reasonable."

"The cost?"

"Yeah. I do something for you, you do something for me."

"Uh oh. This doesn't sound so good. What's it going to cost me?"

He thought for a minute, then turned to her. "You have to help me find something in the back seat of my car."

"What did you lose in the back seat of your car?"

"Nothing yet. But by Saturday, I will have."

She shook her head and smiled, "You're incorrigible."

"I know, but I also know how to bake a big, scrumptious, chocolate cake with thick, creamy, chocolate frosting—all from scratch. Deal?"

"How long do we have to 'look' for this missing item?"

"Oh, say about twenty to thirty minutes."

"Jenny just loves chocolate."

"We'll do it even one better. How about a Buttermilk Chocolate Cake with a Macaroon filling with Real Chocolate Frosting and a Raspberry Coulis on the side?"

"Deal."

"Did I say we would be looking for your bra and panties?"

"No, you did not and no we will not. Better find something else to lose."

"Well, it was an idea."

"A bad one."

"I didn't think so."

"I did."

"Guess you're the one who counts."

"Remember that."

"You'll keep reminding me, right?"

"Right."

"When we get to the gazebo, will you let me kiss you?"

"I think it's dangerous for me to be kissing you right about now."

Encouraged by this, he smiled, "Really? Why is that?"

"Well, if I get kissed just exactly the right way, I'm liable to lose all my senses and before you know it, I've got your zipper down, your cock in my hand and my lips just dying to kiss it."

"Oh, my God," he said as he immediately sunk to his knees in the sand.

Cassie looked over at him and laughed, "Serves you right. C'mon, I'll race you to the gazebo." She started running while he slowly managed to get himself up to join her. He overtook her when they were just twenty yards away and they both arrived at the gazebo panting.

As he was bent over, his hands cupping his knees, trying to catch his breath, he asked, "Do I get any extra credit for winning?"

"No. Now, if you'd shown some compassion for all the down-trodden women and let me win . . ."

"Now, you tell me. C'mere."

He stood up and pulled her into his arms. Searching her face for any sign of resistance, he gathered her against him and slanted his lips over hers. The heat and desire that unfurled in her belly at the touch of his lips to hers astounded her. This man must never know the power his kisses had over her. This was the headiest sensation she'd ever had without alcohol and, as his fingers clasped her head tightly against his, she snaked her arms around his neck and arched her aroused body into his.

When the kiss ended, he asked her if he had kissed her the exact right way and she lied to him. He smiled down at her and winked at her smoldering, half-lidded eyes. He knew she was lying but he just swatted her on the butt and said, "Well, I guess, I'll just have to keep practicing 'til I get it right."

"Yeah," she said halfheartedly as she practically stumbled through an erotic haze to get to his car.

He smiled as he watched her. There was something about her, something different from any woman he'd ever been with, something exciting and fresh, and something else. Whatever it was, he thought as he drove her home, he didn't want to be without it. Somehow, it was quieting a restlessness he'd always been afraid to name.

Chapter 5

Cassie spent the next morning at the site mentally planning the staging area and matching up the survey points. Tomorrow the equipment would start arriving and so would the members of her team. The port-a-johns had already been ordered along with the work trailers and the storage sheds, and two days from now the trucks with the fill dirt and gravel would be arriving. Then, they would be in business; the project would begin.

Bridge replacement project number B-682 for the North Carolina Department of Transportation was the subject of a US District Court case. In response to some concerned citizens, who did not want their quaint bridge replaced, the court ordered the preparation of an environmental impact statement. That was done on November 19, 1990. The comprehensive study, involving no less than fifty government and private agencies, was finally signed off on seven years later in October of 1997. The government agencies involved studied the feasibility and impact of several alternatives, including a no-build alternative, and recommended the W1R initiative—a two lane, high-level fixed span over the 90 foot wide channel maintained by the US Army Corps of Engineers. The alternative, to be built 150 feet west of the existing pontoon bridge, would offer uninterrupted vessel travel along the Atlantic Intracoastal Waterway as well as providing direct and continual access to the island.

The homeowners on the island were outnumbered four to one at the onset of the court battles, but by the time the study was completed, they were outnumbered by almost six to one because of annexations on the mainland and new development. The only recourse for the homeowners who opposed a new bridge, who wanted to stop the construction of what they felt was going to be an "ugly concrete gateway" to their island, was litigation, and they were very good at it. Even as Cassie's company was being awarded the project last April, they were being advised that legally, things were still not yet resolved. The fact that they were actually now in start up mode, was nothing short of miraculous according to the people at Town Hall. Within the community, emotions were still running high and protests of one sort or another were continuing and probably would long after the dedication ceremony. Undaunted, Cassie was excited with her new project, all 2,372 feet of it.

After lunch, she was going to go back to Holden Beach to take a few more pictures of the bridge that should have been Sunset's. Ten years ago, the Sunset Beach bridge had been designed and the funds approved and set aside when the big brouhaha over the coastal environment had erupted, instigated by the handful of taxpayers opposing the bridge.

When the judge who heard the case approved the study, effectively blocking the project, the Department of Transportation shifted the available funds and the existing bridge plans to the next city on the list that had requested one. That city was Holden Beach, approximately twenty miles north of Sunset Beach. The plans hadn't even needed to be altered other than reversing them. Now, Cassie would be building pretty much the exact same bridge that had been designed and approved for Sunset Beach well over a decade ago. It would be nice to have a few pictures of the completed bridge as inspiration on the walls of her office in the work trailer.

After that, she was meeting with Jenny and a real estate agent to check out a few of the condos that were for sale in the area. The time allocated for the project from start to finish was three years. So Cassie decided, that in light of the increasing values of real estate in the area, it would probably make sense to buy something and either keep it or sell it a few years from now, rather than pay rent and have nothing to show for it.

She had just folded up all of her plats and plans and was heading back to her Jimmy when she saw the white and blue markings of a Sunset Beach police car out of the corner of her eye. She turned and smiled as she recognized Michael behind the wheel urging the car off of the road and onto the grass field that would soon become part of the construction site.

"Hi!" he called to her from the open window as he propped his hand on the large chrome floodlight attached to the door frame. Man, she looked good. She was wearing tight jeans, a white T-shirt with her company logo on it and hiking boots that had seen better days, but she looked good enough to eat—every inch of her.

"Hey," she said as she walked over to where he stopped the car.

"Figured it all out yet?"

"Yeah, just waitin' for the Tonka trucks to get here." She looked into his crystal-clear blue eyes and couldn't help smiling. It did something strange to her just to look at him. Something that made her almost giddy.

"When's that gonna be?"

"Tomorrow, if all goes well. I've got a meeting first thing in the morning with your chief to work out all the traffic problems."

"Yeah, I know. We've been advised," he said with a grimace.

"Sorry. At least we're starting when it's off season."

"Yeah, that's a blessing. Got time for breakfast tomorrow before you get to work?"

"Only if there's a place that's open at six. I've got to be on site by seven tomorrow. After that, it'll be six a.m. every morning except Sunday.

"There are several places open by six: Big Nell's on 179, Sunrise Pancake House in Calabash and the Dawg House at Ocean Isle. Take your pick, I'm kinda partial to Big Nell's 'cause it's on my way to work and Etta treats me real nice, but you pick—I go there all the time."

"I'll meet you at Sunrise, I could go for a meat lover's omelet. How's that?"

"Great. See you then," he said and with a wave of his hand he turned the car back onto the road and was gone.

Cassie drove back to Jenny's house to get her camera and to grab a peanut butter and jelly sandwich, which she ate as she drove to Holden Beach. When she got there half an hour later, she drove back and forth over the bridge several times enjoying the spectacular view from the high span as it came down over the Intracoastal.

The citizens of Sunset Beach were going to have an exceptional vista from the center of their bridge, even the fuddy-duddy opposing taxpayers were going to be sorry they hadn't built it sooner. It was going to be picture-postcard perfect and she could hardly contain her excitement. It would be a view well worth waiting for; the marshes would be so much more visually accessible and the wildlife living there would be brought to the forefront. The coastal birds in their natural habitat would put on a performing show all hours of the day and night as cars drove over the bridge. The waters of the Intracoastal would reflect as blue green from high above instead of the greenish brown color they appeared to have from up close. Yes, it would all be worth it when it was done.

She found a place under the bridge to park and then walked around under the high piers taking pictures. When she had taken the closeups she wanted, she walked a quarter of a mile away and took a panoramic snapshot of as much of the span as she could fit into her viewfinder.

Gathering her photographic equipment together, she set out to find an ice cream shop. Something about the beautiful late summer day demanded ice cream, and she gave into the craving in a little shop in the Cheers Plaza in the town of Shallotte.

She was going to love living here. Everything was somehow slower and friendlier. Maybe it was because there was no traffic to contend with, no long lines at the grocery stores, or just maybe it was because the spirit of being on vacation pervaded, working wasn't the major focus for the people living here. Getting the work done so you could go out on your boat, over to the beaches, or out on the golf courses was the goal here. You didn't even want to go to a business on a Friday afternoon without calling to see if they were still open. It was not at all unusual for people to unexpectantly close up shop for the weekend around two on a beautiful, sunny day in this coastal community where the banks weren't open at all on Saturdays.

Licking her pistachio almond ice cream cone, Cassie sat in her Jimmy with the windows down enjoying the warm breeze and the sun on her face as her thoughts reverted back to Michael. What was it about that guy? It seemed like she couldn't go a full ten minutes without thinking about him in one way or another. She had started working on the questionnaire in her spare time. She wrote the questions on several loose leaf pieces of paper she kept in a folder. She also carried a notebook in her purse so she could jot down thoughts as they came to her, even the more blatant and outlandish thoughts that occurred to her she recorded, knowing that some of the questions would never make it to the final write up. The questions that had really been bothering her that she'd never have the courage to actually ask him, like: What position is your favorite? When you make love to a woman, do you make love to her as thoroughly with your tongue in her nether lips as you do with it in her mouth? What are the things that turn you on the most? Are you capable of falling madly, passionately and irrevocably in love? And, what would your all-time dream woman be like?

She added that last question to her secret list and then closed the notebook and slid it into a side pocket of her purse so it would be handy for her next impulsive thought. It was time to meet Jenny and the realtor, so she popped the last bite of the cone into her mouth, put the Jimmy in gear, and headed back to Sunset Beach.

She spent the next few hours with Jenny and Harley, her real estate agent, looking at condos in the area. She looked at several in the Colony section of Oyster Bay, a few called Royal Poste Road Villas in Sea Trail Plantation, and one at Sandpiper Bay off of Georgetown Road. They were all very nice and quite reasonably priced, but none of them felt right to her. So she set up another appointment to look at some more.

The next morning as she drove along Beach Drive looking out over the waters of the Intracoastal to the back side of Sunset Beach and Bird Island, she marveled yet again at the serenity and the beauty of this out of the way Brunswick County island. She could see the elegant white egrets soaring in and out of the marshy waters that made up the banks of the Intracoastal in this region. She watched as a Golden Book image of an old-time tugboat pushed a large barge toward the bridge and she automatically checked the clock on the dash to see how long he'd have to wait before remembering that the bridge opened on demand for commercial traffic. He wouldn't have to wait at all—the cars would.

She was on her way to Calabash to meet Michael for breakfast and she was more than aware that she was very anxious to see him. The excitement of seeing

56

him again brought a flush to her face and a warmth to the blood flowing in her veins and she couldn't help but smile. She was immensely enjoying her new life down here. Her hand went to her curls, still damp from her shower and she absentmindedly fluffed them, trying to get rid of some of the stiffness caused by the styling gel she'd used.

Michael was already seated at a table in the non-smoking section when she arrived. He stood up when he saw her and remained standing until she took her seat. He had been raised with good manners she thought as she remembered the night he tried to tell her about himself in between his hot kisses.

"Hi!" he said brightly, his smile wide in a face that looked freshly shaved and scrubbed. Something about the contrasting colors of his skin made her want to stroke his cheeks. He had just shaved, you could see how smooth his skin was, yet you could still see the beard he had under his skin and you just knew that by two o'clock this afternoon he'd need another shave if he didn't want to feel scratchy. His hair was also still wet and he had combed it back off of his forehead letting his prominent widow's peak have the focal part of his rugged face. Later, when it dried, it would fall forward a bit, softening his features slightly.

"Good morning," she said as she adjusted herself in the booth. The vinyl of the bench was cold against her bare thighs.

"Coffee?" he asked as he lifted the carafe to pour her some.

"Yes, please."

She picked up the mug and wrapped both her hands around it as she sipped at the fragrant brew.

"Black?" he asked.

"Is there any other way?"

He indicated his mug with the tan-colored liquid in it. "Apparently."

"Wuss."

"Hey, hey. No aspersions against my manhood before ten o'clock in the morning."

The waitress came over and they ordered. Michael was having the banana nut pancakes and Cassie was having the meat lover's omelet with grits and a biscuit. She knew she'd probably never get lunch today so she was filling up with protein and carbs for the long first day on the site.

"So how'd it go yesterday?" he asked.

"Fine. I reviewed the surveys, went to Holden to take some pictures, and then met Jenny to look at some condos."

"Really? Did you find anything you liked?"

"Yeah, a few. There was a really nice place over at the Colony, a darling unit over at Sandpiper and several at Sea Trail. Where do you live?"

"I have a place at Shallotte Point. I bought it a few years ago as a fixer-upper for a pretty good price. Now, after much time and many dollars, it's a nice little cottage that I like to come home to. It now boasts a rear deck that has more square footage than the whole house and I just finished building a small dock for my boat."

"Oh? What kind of boat?"

"Just a little Chris Craft, something to go out in and catch fish."

"What kind of fish?"

"Spot, drum, grouper, the occasional tuna, things like that. Do you fish?"

"I used to, haven't had much time for it the past few years."

"Well, we'll have to go sometime."

"I'd like that."

"I'd like that, too. I'd like to see that bathing suit again," he said with a big grin.

She blushed slightly, then turned to face the waitress as she delivered their food.

"Everything looks great," she commented.

"It always is here. It's one of the most consistently good restaurants I've found around here. Jeff runs a tight ship and the locals really appreciate it—you mess up my breakfast and it can ruin my whole day!"

She smiled at that and asked, "When did you move here?"

"Oh, about five years ago."

"Then how do you know so much about the history of the island and D. Duke?"

"My family has owned property here since the early sixties. We used to spend the whole summer here when I was a kid."

"Wow. You must be from a pretty well-to-do family."

"Not really. My father owned a travel agency and it was just easier to ship my mother, my brother, and I out here for the summer while he worked in Raleigh. He came out to stay with us almost every weekend. He taught us to fish, to golf, and to walk."

"To walk?"

"Walk. My dad loved to walk. We walked everywhere. I'll bet there's not a place on that whole island that my foot hasn't touched at one time or another."

"Sounds like a nice man."

"Yeah. How 'bout your dad?"

"He taught me to build bridges."

"Why?"

"Because I asked him to."

"Why did you want to?"

"Because I wanted to be with him."

"Yeah. I understand that. How about your Mom? What's she like?"

"She's gone. She died when I was nine. Leukemia."

"Oh, I'm sorry. It must have been very hard for you."

"Yeah. Hard for my dad too. I think that's why he works so hard, he doesn't want to come home to an empty house. And speaking of houses," she said, trying to change the subject, "maybe I should do what you did and look for a little cottage."

"It doesn't sound like you're going to have the time to take care of a place of your own, especially if it needs some work."

"Yeah, you're probably right. A condo will allow me a lot more freedom and the time that I do get off, I won't have to spend doing yard work and stuff."

"Who's your realtor?"

"A guy named Harley something."

"Harley Ransom."

"Yeah. That's him."

"How'd you get hooked up with him?"

"You know him?"

"Yeah. Everybody knows him. His father's one of the largest developers in Brunswick County."

"You don't sound like you like him."

"I don't."

"Why?"

"He's too full of himself. Always has been. What did you think of him?" he asked warily, undeniably aware of Harley's appeal to women because of his bank account balance and his cocky good looks.

"He was nice. He took his time with us and answered all our questions and he offered to take me out again on my next day off to look at a few more places."

"Yeah. I'll just bet he did."

"What's that supposed to mean?"

"It means, of course he did. That's what realtors do isn't it?" he back peddled.

"As much as I'm enjoying your company, I need to 'git,' " she said mimicking a southern colloquialism.

They fought over the check. He won by agreeing to let her pay the next time and then he walked her out to her Jimmy.

"So, I'll see you Saturday. What say I pick you up around eleven, we head to the grocery store to buy the ingredients for the cake and then we'll hightail it to my place to bake it so Jenny and Colin will be surprised?"

"Sounds like a good plan."

"Well, good luck on your first day on the job."

"Thanks. And thanks for breakfast."

"You're quite welcome." He wanted to kiss her, but he didn't think it would be appropriate, here in the parking lot that faced the main drag through Calabash.

He watched her pull out and head back up Beach Drive toward Sunset before getting into his Grand Prix and heading to work. Saturday seemed like light years away.

Chapter 6

Michael picked Cassie up promptly at eleven. She told Jenny that she and Michael were going to drive around to look at some condos. And since she didn't want Michael to talk to Jenny, because he didn't know about the fabrication she had made involving him to hide what they were really going to be doing today, she met him as he pulled into the driveway and quickly got into his car.

"In a hurry are we?" he asked with a comical smile on his face.

"Yeah, I just wanted to get away before Jenny asked me one more time about what I was doing today."

"Did you tell her that we were going to be all alone at my place all afternoon, getting hot and steamy while we cooked up something?"

"Baked. Remember? And don't get any ideas. You have yet to answer my questionnaire."

"Yeah. I can hardly wait."

"You have a list of the ingredients we need?"

He tapped the front pocket on his light blue chambray shirt. "Got it right here."

"How about the pans? Do we need to get some pans?"

"No, I have all that. In fact I have most of the ingredients at home, we only need a few things."

"You don't know how much I appreciate this."

"You can show me later," he said with a lecherous leer.

She smiled wickedly back at him, "That depends on your answers."

"Am I being graded on this?"

"Yup."

"Good thing I've always been good at taking tests, among other things," he said as he turned and focused on her lips while waiting for traffic to clear before making the turn into the parking lot in front of the Food Lion.

Cassie felt the heat in her belly as his implied meaning sunk in. A whole afternoon in what was probably going to be a pretty confined area. How was she going to keep her distance from this man who turned her on just by saying "hello?"

"All we need is cake flour, unsweetened cocoa powder and some good quality unsweetened chocolate."

"That's all?"

"Oh, yeah, we probably should get some wine coolers for you. All I have at home is beer." When he saw her questioning look, he added, "Might as well relax and enjoy your day off."

"I don't plan on *relaxing*."

"Now, I didn't mean it that way."

"Sure you didn't," she said with a snide smile as they walked through the automatic doors. He bought some wine coolers anyway and insisted on paying for everything.

In the car she fumbled through her purse and found the exact amount he had spent and dropped it into his console saying, "How can I give this cake to them as a gift if you pay for it and bake it too?"

He didn't say anything, just took her hand, brought it to his lips, and kissed it. They talked about the upcoming Labor Day holiday and both of them bemoaned the fact that they had to work part of the holiday weekend.

"It's actually not a bad weekend to pull duty— every place is so crowded it's hard to go anywhere or do anything, anyway. I don't dare take my boat out. There are so many inexperienced boaters out on the holidays, but after Labor Day—what a difference. No lines anywhere and you can go for miles down the Intracoastal sometimes before seeing another boat.

"We're really lucky to live where the weather's like summertime until the middle of November. In fact, I think October is my favorite month here."

"It's my favorite month anywhere," she said.

A few minutes later they turned down Pigott Drive, followed it all the way down until it came to a dead end and then turned right onto Village Point Road, the road that lead to Shallotte Point, where he pulled into the driveway of a cute little house.

"Here it is, my mini castle by the sea."

"It's adorable," she said as she took it in. It was a small building with ribbed slate siding painted white. The front door was a heavily varnished light oak color, and the functional shutters were wedgwood blue. Under each window was a mature, flowering Oleander bush. The front yard was neat and trim with little flower beds here and there around several gnarled oak trees. The grass looked freshly mowed and she was sure that he must have done it this morning before coming to get her.

He led her up the gray slate flagstones to the front door and let them in. It was not at all what Cassie had expected. Somehow she had envisioned bold stripes, earth tone colors and heavy, masculine furniture. She was pleasantly surprised to find a living room furnished in coordinating floral prints with oyster white carpeting and light blonde furniture. There even seemed to be the faint smell of potpourri or maybe that flowery, cinnamon smell had come from one of the candles grouped together on the coffee table.

"Very nice," she said.

"Thank you, but I can't take credit. I had some help."

When he didn't elaborate, she knew the answer. Whatever woman had been in his life at the time must have helped him decorate. She wondered briefly if the woman he had been engaged to had had a hand in this.

He led her through the short hallway to the back of the house to the kitchen. The appliances were all fairly new, so were the counters, the tile floor and the cabinets. He had certainly done a lot to fix up the place. Everything was white except the cabinets which were a honey oak color. They were probably the original cabinets that he had refinished. It was a nice, homey kitchen. And she was right, they would be very close all afternoon.

He put the grocery bags on the counter next to the ingredients he had taken out earlier. "Okay. Let's get crackin'. You're the assistant. That means you do as I say and you clean up the mess. Got it?"

"Okay. What's first?"

"Preheat the oven to 350 degrees." He pointed to the oven and she marched right over and turned the dials. He turned back to the recipe after watching her trim body lean over the top of the stove as she reached for the upper knobs.

"Next, grease and flour three round, eight-inch cake pans. Here," he handed her a spray can of Baker's Joy. "Spray them with this, it's a great short cut."

After she finished, he continued reading: "Stir together the flour, cocoa powder, baking powder, baking soda and salt. Here, I've got everything already measured, just put it all into this bowl." He put a large stainless steel bowl on the counter in front of her, and then as he called out each ingredient, she dumped it in: "Two cups cake flour, half a cup unsweetened cocoa powder, half a teaspoon baking powder, half a teaspoon baking soda, one teaspoon salt. Okay, put that aside." He took it from her and grabbing both shoulders from the back, he walked her over to the other counter where he had already set up an electric stand mixer.

"Okay, now you need to put one and three-fourths cups of sugar into that bowl and then add these eggs, one at a time, beating until fluffy. Got it?"

"I'm not a simpleton you know. I can crack eggs."

"Okay, here they are," he indicated the three eggs sitting in a bowl on the counter, "make sure you don't get any shell in there," he admonished sternly.

As soon as he turned his back on her she turned and stuck her tongue out at him, but he saw her reflection in the glass over the stove. "Now what did I say about not doing that unless you had plans to use it?"

She quickly spun back around and busied herself with the task of beating and cracking eggs. Lord help her if she lost a piece of shell, he'd probably paddle her. she thought and was surprised when just the thought of that weakened her at the knees.

"Finished?" he asked from the other side of the counter.

"Yes . . ."

"Okay beat in the vanilla, there's a teaspoon there, just measure out one and be careful, it comes out of the bottle quickly."

"Yes sir!" she said in her best military voice.

"Very funny."

"Okay, now add the flour mixture alternating with the buttermilk I just made."

"You *made* buttermilk?"

"Yeah. It's easy and it's a lot cheaper than buying a whole half gallon when I only need a cup."

"Pray tell, how does one *make* buttermilk?"

"You take regular milk and sour it."

"Sour it?"

"Yeah. You use either a tablespoon of lemon juice or a tablespoon of vinegar. I usually use vinegar, it gives it a slightly mellower taste."

"Oh, you do, do you?" she said making fun of his seriousness over this mundane kitchen topic.

He walked over to where she stood in her flat sandals and it was immediately brought to her attention that he positively loomed over her as he stared down into her up-turned face. "Yes, I do," he said softly as he leaned down and captured her lips with his. It was a stop-the-world-from-spining, I-gotta-get-off, kind of kiss. One that left her shattered with its abrupt withdrawal and floored by its intensity. Her lips were still humming from the pressure of his lips on hers when he turned back around and said, "I don't hear the mixer . . . are you wool gathering?"

He knew damn well what she was doing! She was trying to recover, trying to get her equilibrium back. With the flick of her fingers, she started the mixer, completely forgetting that she hadn't added any of the buttermilk. Flour went everywhere. He quickly hit the switch then his hand immediately covered hers and she stiffened, ready for his verbal attack.

"I didn't realize I'd affected you so," he said softly in his deepest, huskiest voice.

She just stood there stammering something that sounded like "Nnnnnooo."

He wrapped his flour-covered hand around her neck and pulled her face toward his, murmuring softly as he pulled her closer, "Yesss," just before taking her mouth with his. His hard lips moved over her soft ones and she could feel the slight stubble of his beard as he pressed them into hers and she could feel the pulse in her neck beating a wild cadence under his thumb as he held her to him.

His lips released hers and his eyes focused on her moistened lips. "I bother you," he said as he bent to kiss her again.

"Admit it," he said before taking her mouth once again.

She answered by returning his kiss and running her hands up through his hair.

Both of his hands immediately went around her, pulling her body close to his. When his hands moved down to her denim-clad ass, he dug his fingers into her tight cheeks and pulled her hard up against his blatant arousal. He moaned into her mouth when he felt her pushing back against him. He lifted her off of her feet and walked back with her until they were up against the edge of the counter on the other side of the tiny kitchen, then put his hand on her outer thigh and lifted her leg over his hip. Jamming the large bulge in front of him into her crotch, he moaned her name into her ear, "Cassie, Cassie . . . Oh, God, you feel so good." He trailed kisses down the column of her throat, stopping long enough at the small vee-shaped hollow to meet his hand as he started unbuttoning her shirt.

Just as soon as he finally managed to unbutton the top three buttons using his left, less-coordinated hand, a bell went off. He recognized it as what it was, simply the oven letting him know it was now preheated. She, unaccustomed to the sound, pulled away, using the distraction as an opportunity to cool things off. "What was that?"

"Just the oven," he said as he tried to pull her face back to his.

"I think we'd better get back to the cake," she said softly.

"I don't."

She smiled up at him, "No, I guess, you wouldn't."

Reluctantly, he let her go, his hands dropping to his sides.

She walked over to the counter and started cleaning up the mess the flour had made. "Do we have to add more flour now?"

"No, we'll just use a little less of the buttermilk," he said as he walked over to where she was and looked into the bowl. He added some buttermilk and turned the mixer on low, watching as it blended the batter.

When all the buttermilk and flour mixture had been added and thoroughly blended, he turned the mixer off and instructed her to divide the batter between the three pans while he started cleaning up the mess they'd made. When she was finished, he took the pans and put them in the oven and set the timer for 25 minutes. He walked over to the refrigerator, took out a bottle of beer and a wine cooler. She was over at the sink washing the dishes. Putting the beer on the counter, he stealthily moved behind her. With one hand, he moved the hair away from the nape of her neck while he bent to kiss her there. With the other, he took the cold bottle and slid it down the front of her shirt. Wet, soapy hands instantly grabbed at the bottle as her skin reacted to the cold. He laughed at her reaction, then set the bottle beside her on the counter.

"C'mon let's go out back and relax while the cake is baking."

She turned to face him and he chuckled, "Wow, your shirt is all wet. You sure are sloppy."

He didn't know she still had the wet dish rag in her hand. She brought it up and let it go, right into his face.

"Well, your face is all wet. You sure are sloppy," she parroted back as she side stepped him, grabbed the wine cooler off the counter, and marched out the back door. She heard him chuckling as she unintentionally slammed the screen door and walked out onto the deck.

Wow. He was right about the size of this deck. It could easily have been attached to one of the more luxurious manor houses that dotted Beach Drive along the banks of the Intracoastal. It was quite impressive to say the least. On one side was a wrought iron table

71

with matching chairs and a colorful umbrella sticking through the center of the glass. A large covered grill was a few feet away. The rest of the deck area consisted of wooden lounge chairs with padded cushions and potted plants. This was definitely set up with the idea of entertaining in mind. Not too many people would fit inside the house, but plenty would fit out here on the deck and on the surrounding patio area below.

Michael joined her, taking her elbow lightly as he led her to the edge of the deck where they could look out at the waters of the Shallotte River. A few jet skis were just passing by and the riders waved as if they knew Michael.

"It's beautiful out here."

"Yeah. It's the whole reason I bought this house."

She looked off to the right and saw a long pier stretching out at least seventy-five feet from the edge of the patio below them. Its wooden planking crossing a marshy area until it reached a section that would allow free passage. At the end of the pier was a large boat with the name "Grecian Paradise" written in script across the back.

"That's your boat, huh?"

"That's it."

"Well, it looks like you've got it all here."

"It's more than enough to keep me busy. C'mon, let's go down. I'll show you my garden." He took her arm again and led her over to the steps that led down to the patio and the terraced lawn that lay below.

He had staked off an area to the right where he was growing tomatoes, cucumbers and peppers. "I make my own pickles, relish and salsa," he said proudly.

"Wow, I am incredibly impressed," she said as she bent down to finger a few cucumber vines trailing along on the ground. She walked over to a grouping of painted white Adirondack chairs that sat on the lawn just a few feet away from the sloping hill leading to the railroad-tie terraces. She sat down in one and opened her drink.

"What a spectacular backyard. It's perfect for almost anything. Well, except maybe children. I guess it could be pretty dangerous if you had kids."

"That never seemed to be a worry. It wasn't likely I was ever going to get Jeanette pregnant boinking her once a month."

"Wow. You sound bitter. How long ago did this happen?"

"Two years ago," he said as he took the seat beside her. "And no, I'm not bitter. I think things worked out for the best. I wouldn't be sitting here with you, otherwise."

"Where's Jeanette now?"

"In Charlotte. She married some geek from the electric company."

"Why do I get the feeling that you're not over this?"

"Oh, I most certainly am. I guess I'm just at that age where I'm watching all my friends marry and have children, and I wonder what I'm missing. I'm not used to playing catch up."

A large sailboat glided by and they both watched it in silence. A soft breeze lifted the branch of the tree limb hanging overhead and Cassie laid her head back and stared up at it. "How can you stand it here when everything is always so pristine and beautiful?"

He laughed and it was a throaty, masculine boom of delight before taking a big swallow of his beer. "Believe me, it's not always this serene. We have hurricanes, remember? And every ten years we do get a little snow. And D. Duke isn't the first murder we've had here. So far, it's the only unsolved one, but it's by no means the first." He tilted his head slightly, "I think I hear the timer." He took another swig and stood up, "I'll check them. You just stay here and relax."

"Okay, I think I will."

She sat and sipped her wine cooler as she watched the boats go by. Then she stood up and walked over to the edge of the lawn and looked down the river toward the inlet. She could just make out the widening area of the inlet. Michael had done very well for himself when he had selected this property. She was sure that the land was worth at least five times the value of the house. It gave pause to her idea of buying a condo instead of some land, but even she had to admit, Harriet Homeowner she definitely wasn't.

Michael looked out of the kitchen window and watched Cassie as she strolled along the river bank. Hot prickles of fire leapt through his body and settled in the area of his groin, and not for the first time that day, he wondered how it would feel to be inside her, to feel her clamped around him, urging him closer. She did strange things to his insides and he was having a devil of a time keeping his hands off of her.

She turned and smiled up at him, though he doubted that she could actually see him through the reflection of the afternoon sun on the glass. She practically took his breath away with her quiet, elegant beauty. He would have her. Of this he was certain.

74

There hadn't been a woman yet that he'd desired that he hadn't been able to have.

He tested the cakes, took them out of the oven, ran a knife blade around the inside edge of each pan and placed them on cooling racks. He set the timer for ten minutes and started getting the ingredients together for the icing, the macaroon filling and the raspberry sauce. When he heard her coming up the deck steps, he smiled to himself. No, there hadn't been a woman yet.

"Mmm. Smells delicious in here," she said as soon as she was through the back door. "Mmmm. Chocolate. Jenny is going to be so surprised."

He smiled at her. "Well, get over here and let's get this frosting made. And this time, try not to make a complete shambles out of my kitchen."

She smiled back at him and stuck out her tongue.

"One of these days, I'm going to make you use that."

She blushed progressively darker shades of pink while she looked around for a trash can to throw her empty bottle into.

"Under the sink," he said while he whisked together a cup of sugar, three and a half tablespoons of cornstarch, a pinch of salt and two ounces of finely chopped unsweetened chocolate in a Calphalon saucepan. The tea kettle on the stove started to whistle and he asked her to bring the one cup measure over to him. He poured a cup of the boiling water into the mixture then whisked everything together while he brought it to a boil. When it was boiling, he turned the burner down and whisked it for another two minutes as it simmered.

"Would you mind filling the bowl in the sink with ice?" he asked while he removed the mixture from the stove and poured it into a small stainless steel mixing bowl. He added a little vanilla extract and a touch of orange-flavored liqueur then he set the bowl inside the bowl full of ice. He disengaged the top half of the electric mixer from the stand and beat in two tablespoons of soft butter until the frosting was light and fluffy and held its peaks.

Then he put some on his finger and beckoned for her to come sample it. Her eyes stayed focused on his the whole time it took for her to cross the kitchen, then they lowered to his outstretched finger and she licked it.

"Ahhh," he said, positively dying from the erotic sensation.

"Ummm. Wonderful. It's so chocolately and smooth."

"Here," he said, dipping another finger back into the bowl. "Have some more."

She didn't deny him, or herself. She licked his finger clean.

"My, my, my . . ." he said as he watched her, then he took his index finger, swiped the edge of the bowl and coated her lips. "My turn," he said as he bent to kiss and lick the frosting from her lips.

Her tongue snaked into his mouth trying to steal the frosting his tongue had on it and he groaned his extreme pleasure. Before she knew what was happening he had her in his arms carrying her to the sofa. He laid her down, placing her head on a throw cushion while his other hand quickly removed her sandals and let them drop to the floor.

As soon as their lips parted, she managed to get the word, "No" out.

He laid his body directly on top of hers, saying simply, "Yes."

His mouth greedily took hers, suctioning her lips while his tongue plundered and thrust repeatedly into her mouth, grazing her teeth with its tip.

His hand went to her midriff where he lifted her shirt and grabbed the smooth, bare skin of her waist. He forced his legs between hers and positioned his pulsing arousal at their juncture, easing himself off of her and then pressing himself firmly back into her over and over again. His breathing was harsh and ragged now and he really wasn't paying all that much attention to her sudden stillness until her hands moved to his shoulders and she gave a shove. Breathily, she gasped, "Michael, Michael, no, no, we can't."

"Yes, yes, we can. I'm aching for you. Feel me." He took her hand from his shoulder and shifting his weight he placed it over his swollen manhood.

"Michael. I can feel that you want me. But I can't. Not just yet. I can't."

"Are you sure?"

"Yes, I'm very sure."

"This gives a new meaning to the words from the song, 'I'm blue over you.' "

She laughed and tried to sit up while he slowly eased his way off of her. "I'm highly aroused by you myself, if it's any consolation."

"Not much, but hey, you're the one calling the shots. I'm ready whenever you are."

"I think we'd better finish that cake."

An hour later the cake was assembled with the chocolate macaroon filling between each layer and it was frosted and even decorated with a shell border and piped flowers. The raspberry sauce was in a container ready to take with them to pool onto the serving plates alongside the pieces of cake. Cassie stood back to admire it. "I've got to hand it to you Michael, you sure know your way around a kitchen."

"Wait 'til you see what I can do in the bedroom," he said with a wink in her direction.

She just shook her head as she went back to the sink to finish cleaning up.

"What did you make the filling with?" she asked as she sampled some that was left in the bowl.

He looked up towards the ceiling as he remembered the ingredients, "One cup of shredded coconut, mixed with one teaspoon of vanilla and one-eighth of a teaspoon of salt. Combine with enough sweetened condensed milk to make a paste then stir in two tablespoons of cocoa powder."

"And the raspberry sauce?"

"Oh, that's even easier, press a pint of raspberries through a sieve, add a tablespoon of raspberry liqueur, then add just enough confectioner's sugar to make it thick, heat over low heat until it almost boils, then pour through a sieve again."

After all traces of the messy afternoon were disposed of, Cassie turned to Michael, who was leaning against the counter watching her. "Why don't you take me back home now and then come back for dinner at seven? We can surprise them when you show up with the cake. Will you be able to transport it okay without messing it up?"

"Sure. I've got a box I can use to put it in."

"Great."

"How 'bout a good-bye kiss?"

"Oh, no! Your kisses don't say good-bye. They say stay a while longer."

"Figured that out all by yourself, huh?"

"Yes! It took a while, but I figured it out."

"You're too smart for your own britches," he said as he patted her rump on the way out the door to his car. "And mighty fine britches they are too," he said as he stepped back, tilted his head and unabashedly admired her rear end.

On the way back, he chuckled at her excitement over the cake. She was like a little kid, waiting to present her little, hand-made gift that she'd made at school.

He dropped her off saying that he'd be back with the cake at seven. She ran up the stairs and into the house and he smiled. What an imp.

He drove back to his house and was just about to get out of the car when he spotted something sticking out from under the front seat. He bent over to see what it was and pulled a little notebook out from the bottom corner of the seat. He looked at it questioningly, trying to place it. It didn't look familiar to him, so he assumed it must be Cassie's. It must have fallen from her purse. He was ready to just toss it onto the passenger seat, so he could return it later, when he noticed his name as a page flipped open.

He picked it up again and thumbed through it. It was blank, except for two pages. The heading on the first page that had any writing on it was: *Questions for*

Michael. Leaving the door open, he sat back down in the driver's seat to read what she'd written.

What is your favorite position? When you make love to a woman do you make love to her as thoroughly with your mouth in her nether lips as you do with it in her mouth? What are the things that turn you on the most? Are you capable of falling, madly, passionately and irrevocably in love? What would your all-time dream woman be like?

Whoa! He read them all again and then sat stunned for a minute, imperceptibly shaking his head. This couldn't be. She needed to know the answers to these questions so she could get to know him better? This wasn't getting to know him, this *was* knowing him, quite intimately, in fact.

He got out of the car, taking the notebook with him, still staring down at the questions as he closed the car door and walked into the house.

He walked over to the small table in the eat-in part of the kitchen and sat down. Then he got back up to go get a pen. Hell, if she wanted answers, he'd give them to her.

Number one: *What is your favorite position?* He held the pen to his lip while he stared at the ceiling. No doubt about it. He wrote his answer, "Doggy style."

Number two: *When you make love to a woman, do you make love to her as thoroughly with your tongue in her nether lips as you do with it in her mouth?* "Most definitely."

Number three: *What are the things that turn you on the most?* He sat back in his chair for a minute, then sat forward again and hunched over as he wrote, as if someone was going to cheat and steal his answers.

"French kissing, a woman licking my nipples, my balls and my cock, especially the underside. I also like having the area under my balls stroked, it does incredible things to me."

Number four: *Are you capable of falling madly, passionately and irrevocably in love?* "I would like to think so."

Number five: *What would your all-time dream woman be like?* "You. That's the right answer, right?"

He checked his answers, making sure there wasn't anything he wanted to change, and then he closed the notebook and stood up. God, he could use a shower. A nice cold one. This woman was completely in charge of the direction his blood was flowing lately.

After his shower, he took a short nap before dressing and carrying the cake to the car. He was almost to the end of his road when he remembered the notebook, so he went back to get it. They needed to get past this part about the questionnaire and the sooner the better.

Cassie opened the door when he rang the bell and he couldn't help licking his lips as he followed her into the house. That question number two was somehow now foremost in his mind. He handed her the cake so she could present it.

Colin and Jenny welcomed him and together they oohed and aahed over the cake. Michael sat in the family room with Colin watching a golf match while Jenny and Cassie finished getting dinner ready. Paisley set the table and then they all sat down to eat. Jenny and Cassie had been cooking all afternoon according to Colin, but Michael suspected that Cassie had been more prep chef than sous chef when he saw what they were having: Stuffed Pork Medallions, Asparagus Soufflé, Caramelized Onions and Carrots and Twice-Baked, Garlic Mashed Potatoes with a loaf of freshly baked bread, something Jenny called Hawaiian Sugar Loaf.

Everything was superb and Michael was so stuffed that he had no idea where he was going to put his piece of cake when it was served. But once it was in front of him, he found a place for it just like everyone else. Cassie and Michael got elaborate praise for their efforts and, after a second cup of coffee, they both got up to help with the dishes. They were shooed off by both Colin and Jenny who said they should run along and enjoy what was left of the evening. Not needing to be told twice, they walked out the front door to Michael's car.

As soon as they were behind closed doors, Michael took the small notebook out of his pocket and threw it into Cassie's lap. "There you go, I answered all your questions. And let me tell you, if you don't know me after all that, I don't suppose you ever will. That's some pretty intimate stuff you've asked there."

Cassie looked down at the notebook in her lap and as soon as she recognized it, her whole face went completely red. "Where did you get that?" she hissed.

"You left it in my car this afternoon," he answered, not understanding what she was so upset about.

"Oh, no."

"What's the matter, you wanted me to answer your questions. I did. See?" he said as he flipped open to the page where he answered them.

"This isn't the questionnaire." She pulled a few pieces of paper out of her purse. "This is the questionnaire."

"Well then, what's this?"

"Private. Meant for my eyes only. I didn't mean for you to see this. I am so embarrassed." She hid her face in her hands and breathed like she hadn't taken a breath all night.

"Well, I have to admit, I was pretty stunned by your questions."

"Yeah. I'm sure you were."

"But I answered them all, just like I thought I was supposed to."

"I can't wait to read the answers," she deadpanned.

"C'mon, cheer up, it's not that bad. So I've seen your extremely horny side, so what? You've seen mine several times."

She gave him a weak smile. "Well let's not sit here in the driveway, let's go somewhere so you can answer the real questionnaire I made for you."

He groaned, "Another test? Man, I thought I did all right on the other one, what if I fail this one?"

"Somehow, I don't think you will."

He drove to a secluded area underneath the Ocean Isle Bridge and parked the car. It was getting dark, but there was still light enough to read by with the map light on. "Okay, shoot."

"What's your favorite movie?"

"Roadhouse."

"What's your favorite book?"

He thought for a moment, "I'll read anything by Martini or Patterson."

"Color?"

"Blue."

"Food?"

"Steak."

And so it continued for almost half an hour.

"This is the last one."

"Thank God. My SATs weren't this long."

She sent him a smirk that he could barely make out in the near darkness.

"If you could eradicate one bad thing in the world, what would it be? These are your choices: Drugs, Rap Music, Drinking, Prostitution, Prejudice, Cancer."

"Ooh, that's a toughie. I think Rap Music, I'd be lost without my prostitute."

"C'mon Michael, seriously."

He let out a long, heavy sigh, enough to temporarily dislodge a lock of his dark, thick hair. "Cancer."

"Why?"

"Now I have to justify my answer, too?"

"Why?" she repeated.

"Because that's the only one that doesn't give people a choice."

"Good answer."

"Thank you. Now am I done?"

"Yes, you've answered all the questions."

"Okay, now you answer one for me."

"What?"

"Why did we do this? Do you seriously think you know me any better now that you know I prefer steak to pasta and that I hang the toilet paper roll with the paper coming from the front instead of the back?"

She thought for a minute. "No, I guess I don't. There was only one question I really wanted an answer to anyway."

"Which one was that?"

"Do you do drugs?"

"Well, why didn't you just ask me that one?"

"I don't know. Maybe I didn't think you'd tell me the truth."

"What makes you think I am now?"

"I don't know. I just think you are."

"Why?"

"Because of the time we've spent together."

"And that's exactly how you're going to learn all about me, just as it's exactly how I'm going to learn about you, from spending time together. Time just being together, getting to know one another. It's what dating is all about."

"You're right. I don't know why I was trying to rush things."

"I do. Judging from your other questions, you're a horny little bitch!" he said as he put his arm around her and pulled her to him for a ravenous kiss.

His hands tangled in her hair as his lips sought hers, trying to taste every part of them. When he pulled away for a minute, he murmured low in her ear, "Let's get in the back seat, I just lost my mind."

Chapter 7

Cassie sat in the middle of her bed with her legs tucked under her looking at the notebook that Michael had returned to her earlier this evening. She had forgotten all about it until now, and had even gotten up out of bed to retrieve it from her purse when she'd remembered it, just so she could read what he had written for his answers.

She looked at his answer to the first question. "Doggy style." *Holy moly. Yikes!* The image of him kneeling behind her, his hands on her hips as he repeatedly rammed into her came quickly to mind and she shuddered with the unexpected heat of it. Her eyes flew down the page to the second question, his answer to that: "Most definitely." *Oh, my my my.* Continuing on down the page, her eyes stopped and riveted on his answer to the third question: "French kissing, a woman licking my nipples, my balls and my cock, especially the underside. I also like having the area under my balls stroked, it does incredible things to me." *Man this was way more than she had wanted to know about the man!* But with a strange kind of fascination and curiosity she continued. "I would like to think so." *Well, that was certainly a nice answer.* "You. That's the right answer, right?"

The heat in her belly and regions even lower prompted her to scoot back to the headboard, and oblivious to the late hour, she picked up the phone on her nightstand. Her uncanny memory for numbers didn't fail her and she punched in his home phone number.

A sleepy male voice answered and she waited a moment before saying, "Doggy style, huh?"

She heard a throaty chuckle come over the wire then a deep sigh. "Well, if you must know there's only one position that's not my favorite."

"And what's that?"

"The one where I have to stand on my head."

"Is there really one like that?"

"You tell me."

"How the heck am I supposed to know?"

"You're the educated one."

"Not like that I'm not."

"A babe in the woods, huh?"

"Well, let's just say I've only experienced things in the most conventional of ways."

"Well, we've got some work ahead of us then, don't we?"

"I don't know, do we?"

"As soon as you give me the go ahead, I'll start your lessons."

"That's very sweet of you."

"No problem. Glad I can help."

"What's this thing about licking your nipples, balls and cock?" She heard his sudden gasp and she smiled. She knew that the only reason she was purposefully and flagrantly teasing him like this was because there was a safe distance between them.

"Memorize it and all power and glory can be yours."

"Pretty strong stuff, huh?" she quipped.

"Not any stronger than 'my tongue in your nether lips.' "

"Touché."

"Did you wake me up just to give me a hard on for any particular reason?"

"Just to see if I could," she said with a smile she was sure he could sense even over the phone.

"Oh, you can. No two ways about it, you can. Come see."

"I'll take your word for it."

"Chicken."

"No, that's not it. I'm just suddenly very, very sleepy." She made loud yawning noises. "Gotta go now, got to get some sleep."

"Hey! That's not fair! You wake me up, get me horny as hell, and then you hang up on me so you can get to sleep?"

"Sorry. I just can't stay up any longer." Again she over-exaggerated some yawning sounds.

"Just wait 'til I get my hands on you."

"Yeah. Then what'll you do?"

"Well let's just say that you might as well start going by the name of Lassie," he said as he rolled over and cradled the phone.

Cassie sat back against the headboard smiling. What a night! What a day and a night, in fact. She thought back to the time they had spent in the back seat of his car. He had somehow convinced her that twenty minutes of making out in the back seat of his car wouldn't lead to anything they couldn't handle. Yeah, right. Well, she had promised and a deal was a deal.

She'd handled it though, by letting him know at just about the crucial time that this was not a good time of the month for him to be intimate with her, that is, if he valued his upholstery. She had started her period just minutes before he had arrived for dinner. That had dampened things quite a bit, and she had half expected him to set her aside; but instead, he sat up in a corner and pulled her under the crook of his arm. With his arm wrapped around her shoulders, he showed concern for how she was feeling by gently rubbing her belly.

They'd had a really good time just talking and laughing. She had ended up in fits of laughter over his attempts to get situated in the back seat of his car. He was a pretty big guy with broad shoulders and long legs and there was no way he could stretch out or get comfortable. At one point, when he had been trying to maneuver her body under his while still trying to stay prone, he had whispered humorously into her ear, "You do know that I have a house we can do this in?"

She'd answered, "What's the fun in that?" before she'd struggled to unseat him.

Looking back down at the notebook she still held in her hand, she focused her eyes on his answer to the fourth question. "I would like to think so." She would like to think so, too. What would it be like to have a man like Michael madly, passionately and irrevocably in love with her?

She reached over to turn off the lamp. As she turned onto her stomach and fluffed her pillow, she remembered his answer to the fifth question— "You." Her head hit the pillow and the word kept reverberating in her head. *You. You. You.*

Chapter 8

The rest of D. Duke's body was found on Sunday morning, and it hadn't been at all pleasant for the vacationer who found it. He was at Sunset Beach with his wife and sons and their extended families for a reunion. One of the activities for this boisterous, fun-loving group was a daily sand sculpture contest. Several of the kids, and quite a few of the adults, fancied themselves to be quite artistic so the challenges were met very seriously. To this end, Tom Lancaster was diligently digging a very deep hole. He and his sons were going to create a version of Atlantis at the bottom of it whenever he finally had it all dug out.

His shovel hit something that made a scraping sound like metal on metal and he looked down to see what he had struck. It appeared to be some sort of buckle, he thought, bending down to pick it up. When he did that, he realized it was not loose, it was somehow embedded, so he pulled harder. His hand now held the buckle along with an inch or two of the attached belt and it still wasn't giving. He pulled again, harder this time, and with both hands. As his hands lifted and the sand fell away, he saw the torso of a man covered with hundreds of scurrying crabs. More crabs than he had ever seen in his life, fell off of the body as he dropped it. Then they started spreading out in all directions, many of them coming right for his feet. He clumsily scrambled up one side of his hole, causing some of it to collapse in, while he sobbed out something unintelligible.

Climbing up and out of the hole, he looked for his wife and their two sons. The boys were walking back up to the shore with the water-filled buckets he had requested. His wife's beach chair was empty, she had probably walked down the beach to their access walkway and gone inside their rental for something. He ran down to where the boys were, determined not to let them get anywhere near the hole. He was gasping and trembling as he took the buckets from them and setting the buckets down, he knelt and gathered his boys close.

"Boys, I need you to get on your bikes," he indicated the yellow recumbent bikes they had rented for the week, parked over by an umbrella, "and go find the guy on the four-wheeler, the beach patrol guy we saw riding by earlier." He pointed in the direction he was going the last time they had seen him ride by. "Tell him it's an emergency, to call the police and tell them to get here right away."

"Why dad?"

"Don't ask any questions now, just do it. And hurry." He swatted them both lightly on their butts, encouraging them to move off quickly. Then he watched them run over to their bikes and take off down the beach toward Bird Island. They weren't far from the dry gully separating the two beaches. Their rented beach house was on 40th Street, on the west end of the beach. And, since Tom didn't like an audience while he worked, they had lugged all of their gear even further down the beach in an attempt to find an unoccupied, pristine area of sand.

He cautiously crept back to where the hole was, and keeping a safe distance from the crumbling edge, he looked down into it. He had to immediately turn his head away. When he saw the remnants of what appeared to be a man's body that had been picked and chewed on by the scavengers of the sea, he felt his stomach lurch and he made it up to the dunes just in time to lose his breakfast. His mind had vaguely registered that there hadn't been a head attached to the torso, but he forced himself not to think about that. It was just too awful. He saw his wife walking down the beach toward him with the forgotten book in her hand and he ran to head her off. While he was talking to her, he heard the low rumble of the four-wheeler as it approached from the other side. Leaving her with strict instructions to get the boys who were following well behind the officer and take them way down the beach toward the pier, he quickly kissed her on the cheek and ran to meet the officer.

The police were called, and by the time Michael arrived, quite a crowd had gathered. He set about disbanding the group of curious onlookers. He had already notified the chief who was trying to find out which church the coroner belonged to. It was just barely eleven, so unless he found him now, it could be hours before he would return home—the southern tradition being to have a huge supper after church on Sundays, which often turned into long, lazy afternoons on someone's front porch.

Michael had been sent to secure the scene and to preserve as much area untouched as possible until the coroner and the crime scene guys could get there. It was a hot, hot day and as he shooed the birds that kept angling in, trying to get at the rotting flesh in the hole, he was overcome many times by the stench.

How the hell did his body get way out here? It was probably close to two miles from his house on the opposite side of the island on the canal between Dolphin and Sailfish. Who would've brought him this far to bury him and why? Why drag or carry a heavy body all this way when there were so many places a lot closer to bury it? He looked around trying to figure it out. Then it occurred to him that from this vantage point on the beach, no one would be likely to see you at night. There were no houses close enough for the lights from them to illuminate the area. And it should have been far enough away from the nearest beach access that the body might never have been discovered. When he'd questioned Mr. Lancaster about his selection of this particular site for his sand project, he had explained that his desire for privacy while constructing his underwater city was his impetus for digging here. If Mr. Lancaster felt out of the way here, he supposed the person who had murdered D. Duke did also.

He saw some police vehicles making their way down the crowded beach toward him. Thank God. He was sweating big time, everywhere, and he needed to get out of the sun and away from this awful smell.

While his cohorts looked around for anything that might have been left by the murderer, and still survived a dozen or so high tides and a quick, gully-washer storm, he stared at D. Duke's body as it was put into a body bag and loaded into the back of a police truck. Nobody deserved to die this way just because they couldn't stand the confusion of their life changing all around them. He had just wanted things to stay the way they were, the way they'd been all his life. But somebody, somebody evil, had wanted him to stop being so vocal about it. Who could that have been? By the time he was relieved and sent back to the station, he had a head spinning with questions.

The crime team had scoured D. Duke's house and even he had gone over there twice, trying to find anything that might give a clue about what went on or who could've been there. The coroner had determined that he had died sometime between seven and ten p.m. Tuesday night. The bones in his neck, the few that were there, were crushed. And the surrounding tissue that hadn't been eaten by fish was torn so raggedly that there was no doubt he had been violently beheaded. Without the rest of the body, it had been hard to tell exactly how he had died, although there was a slight depression in the base of his skull that could have been the cause of death. But he still could have had a heart attack or been shot to death before he became detached from his head. Without the rest of him, it was just impossible to say for sure how he was murdered or if, in fact, he had been murdered. But everybody suspected that he had been, his head wouldn't have been detached like that naturally.

Well, now they had the rest of him and maybe they could learn more about what had happened to him on that Tuesday night. He went to the locker room to wash up and change into a fresh uniform. The shirt he was wearing was drenched with sweat and sticking to his chest and back like a piece of wet cellophane.

The excitement on the beach had aroused a lot of attention at the station and Michael was glad to just get back out on patrol. He drove by Jenny and Colin's house, hoping to catch a glimpse of Cassie out front playing basketball with Paisley or tossing the ball down the driveway to their little dog, Taffy, but her Jimmy wasn't even there. It was interesting how many times he patrolled this particular street now, looking not for anything out of the norm, like a workman out of place or a group of unruly kids, but for a short, curvaceous, bombshell with hair that reminded him of a Bobbsey twin.

When his shift was over, he went home to shower and call her. Colin told him that Cassie, Jenny and Paisley had gone shopping at the mall and then they were going to see a movie, some girlie, chic flick he said. He invited him to come over to watch an exhibition game with him on TV, but Michael declined, saying that if he couldn't see Cassie, he might just as well mow the lawn. Colin understood, having been under the powerful spell of undeniable attraction to an incredibly, fetching female himself when he'd first met Jenny. Sometimes he still thought he was under that spell.

Chapter 9

Cassie sat at her small desk in the cramped trailer fidgeting with a new set of walkie-talkies trying to test them out before giving one to her construction manager. There was nothing but static as she tried to tune one in before setting the channel on the other one. As she flipped the dial, she reached for the other one, but stopped when she heard a clear male voice coming through on the other end.

She listened for a minute as she thought she recognized Michael's voice. It was Michael's voice! And from the gist of the conversation, he was talking to another cop. She felt a little guilty about eavesdropping, but her curiosity got the better of her and when they decided to change to a different frequency, she moved her dial to join them. She didn't know who the first man talking was, but she knew without a doubt that the man answering him was Michael.

"Yeah, this is the best place to live. We got a pretty easy job compared to the city cops, and then we have an unlimited amount of new pussy each week from the Myrtle Beach tourists."

"You must be kidding! How can you keep taking the chances you do with all those different women? Aren't you afraid of catching something?" She could hear the incredulity in Michael's voice.

"Nah! I got a program I follow. Religiously."

"Oh yeah? And what's that?"

"I go to a bar and I find a real attractive woman accompanied by a not-so-attractive one. And believe me, they pair up that way all the time."

"Okay. Then what?" Michael asked.

"I latch onto the homely one."

"You must be nuts. Why in the world would you do that?"

"Easy. The attractive one always gets picked up, the not-so-cute one doesn't."

"So you like 'em ugly?"

"No. Just inexperienced. I get to break them in. And they are so grateful to have a guy paying attention to them, that I get to do damn near anything I want to do to them."

"What the hell are you talking about? You fuck 'em right?" It was strange hearing Michael talk like this, but she wasn't about to tune this conversation out.

"Oh, yeah. I fuck 'em all right. I fuck 'em everywhere. The cunt, the ass and the mouth. As many times as I want to."

"The ass?"

"Oh, yeah. That's the best place of all."

"Now I know you're kidding."

"No, I'm not. Seriously, you don't own a woman, you don't possess her soul 'til you bottom-fuck her."

"You mean put your cock where she shits?"

"Well, you use a condom you jerk! None of it touches you."

"Doesn't it hurt her?"

"Hell, yes! That's the part that turns me on so much. But you'd be surprised—once you've done it to them once, they actually ask you to do it again. And I think it's a hell of a lot safer. First of all you've got the ugly chick who's either a virgin or practically one instead of the looker who's givin' it to everybody; second, they almost always have virgin assholes; and third, forget the faces, they're turned the other way. And even the ugly girls have sweet tits, pussies and bum holes. Nothin' says you have to kiss 'em for cryin' out loud!"

"Ray, remind me to accompany you next time you head south."

Just then the walkie-talkie started crackling in Cassie's ear and she couldn't hear the rest of the conversation. She frantically changed channels, shook the damned thing and even slammed it on the desk, all to no avail, she didn't hear the rest of what was said:

"Why? You want to try my program?"

"No. I want to warn those unsuspecting women."

"Hey! You wouldn't want to ruin all my fun now would ya?"

"I think you're making this up."

"You do, do you? Remember last year when the captain told me I couldn't give my business card and work number out anymore?"

"Yeah."

"Well that's because I was getting too many personal calls from Myrtle Beach. Too many women wanting to spread their ass cheeks for me again," he said as he arched his body out and using his hand he cupped his balls. "Once they get it there, they gotta have it again. Nothing is quite like it. Take my word for it. Try it some time. It's the tightest little hole on even the loosest of women."

"We better get back to work. They're going to be lookin' for us."

"Yeah. Let's go check out the island. Maybe there's a fat, lonely co-ed. You know, they're never fat there. No matter how big the cheeks, the opening is tight, tight, tight."

"You are sick, sick, sick."

Ray laughed. "You may be right, right, right!"

Cassie could not believe what she had heard! Michael! Michael saying he wanted to go with this Ray whoever he was to Myrtle Beach to abuse and debase lonely women. God! And she thought he was such a nice guy! Man, you just never really knew someone, did you, she thought to herself. Well, it was good that she found out now just what kind of guy he truly was, because the way things had been going with them, she was sure they would have been doing the hot and heavy any day now.

She would have been just another out-of-towner spreading her legs for a rutting jerk who thought he was hot stuff. Well, she'd show him. She wouldn't even talk to him anymore. She wouldn't even think about him anymore!

The door to the trailer opened and her construction manager poked his head in. "Ain't ya got those things working yet?"

"Yeah, here ya go. Just stay away from channel 19."

"Why?"

"'Cause I don't need you traipsing off to Myrtle Beach, too."

"What?"

"Forget it. Just take this and go. How's it going out there?"

"Chaotic as one might expect for the set up. But we're movin' dirt."

"Good. I'm running home for a minute. I forgot to bring my supplier's file. I'll be right back."

"You okay?"

"Yeah. Just the wrong things on my mind. I'll be fine. Don't worry about me."

"I never do."

She smiled at Lou's confidence in her. He was in his fifties and he should have been one of the hardest to win over when she came back from college and tried to take over a part of her dad's business, but he wasn't. He had been the first person to give her a full vote of confidence, and he had been a loyal friend to her ever since.

Cassie swiped at a tear of anger as she drove along the winding road back to Jenny's house. She pulled into the driveway a bit too fast and then jerked the transmission into park, sending everything she had piled into the front seat onto the floor. "Great!"

Jenny was dusting the piano by the foyer when Cassie let herself in and stomped through the house murmuring to herself, "What a jerk!" Then a few moments later, "Glad I found out now what a cad he is before I made a complete imbecile out of myself." Followed by, "I can't believe I was so taken in by him!"

"What or who are you talking about, if I might ask?"

"Michael! I never want to see him again!"

"What happened?"

"I don't want to talk about it! And if he calls, you can tell him to go to hell!" With that, she slammed out of the house and burned rubber backing out of the driveway.

She spent the rest of the day supervising the dump trucks as they came onto the site and questioned each and every movement the ground crew was making until Lou came over to her and said, "Everything is fine, don't be so nervous. We all know what we're doing, give the guys a break. They've done all this before, you know."

"Yeah. I'm sorry. There's just so much riding on this for me."

"Honey, we all know that. Most of us have worked for your dad, remember? Go find something else to do, we've got this covered."

"Okay. You're right. I'll be in the trailer. Call me if you need me."

"Sure thing."

She grabbed her clipboard off the hood of her Jimmy and went back into the trailer. They'd only been here a few days and already the inside of the new trailer was coated with dust from all the dirt they were moving.

She sat down at her desk and called all the suppliers, making sure everything was going to arrive as needed. Then she called her dad as she had promised. One call every single day, or he would come down. That was the last thing she needed now, so she made sure to check in as directed.

Michael called twice but both times she put him off saying she was too busy to talk. He'd get the message soon. He was a pretty smart guy.

For the next two days, she either hung up on him or declined his phone calls. Then on the third night, he chanced to see her getting into Harley's 'vette when he randomly and constantly drove by Jenny and Colin's house.

He couldn't remember ever being so angry or so jealous. Just what the hell was going on here? They looked like they were going out for a night on the town, not looking at real estate. He thought about following them but thought better of it. What did he care where she was going? Obviously, she didn't care to see him anymore, so he might as well get on with it.

The call for assistance at the Quick Mart pulled his thoughts back and he flipped the siren and lights on just as he pulled out onto route 179.

He took the report on a gas-and-go case, and after getting the description and tag number from the security camera, he headed out in the same direction the car had gone. He checked the computer and found the address for the owner, and driving slightly faster than he should have, he took a shortcut and beat the guy to his driveway. The arrest and detainment took up the last hour of his shift and after driving by Cassie's one more time, he went home.

It was two o'clock in the morning and he couldn't sleep. He'd had enough. He had to find out what the hell was going on. He got up and paced back and forth before deciding that he would just have to chance Colin's wrath. He got dressed, drove over to their house and rang the doorbell. A very rumpled Colin answered and opened the door wide, mumbling "What took you so long? I figured you'd have been here by now."

Michael didn't answer him, he just stepped inside the foyer. Colin pointed in the direction of Cassie's bedroom and closed the front door before mumbling something about going back to bed.

Michael went into the darkened hallway, and not even bothering to knock, he opened her door.

"Who is it? Jenny?" he heard Cassie mumble.

He closed the door behind him and tried to make out her sleeping form in the dark room.

"It's me, Michael," he whispered.

"Michael? What are you doing here?"

"I had to see you."

"Now?"

"Well, it didn't seem like you wanted to see me any other time," he said as he felt his way around the room to come sit on the edge of the bed.

Cassie sat up and stretched her hand out to the touch lamp on the night stand, brushing it once to softly illuminate the room.

Michael thought she had never looked more beautiful. In her sleep-tousled state, she looked warm and inviting. She raised her hand and ran her fingers through her hair, lifting her curls from her forehead. He could smell the sweet honeysuckle fragrance coming from her.

Cassie looked at Michael's serious face and gave a big sigh. "Michael, I don't want to see you anymore. We're just not right for each other."

"Just how did you figure that out from Saturday night to Monday afternoon? When you called me late Saturday night, everything was fine. What's happened?"

"I just realized we weren't right for each other."

"Bullshit! Now I'm not leaving until you tell me what's going on. We can sit here all night, but I'm not budging one inch until you tell me."

"Can't I just decide I don't want to be involved with you without this turning into a circus?"

"No. Something happened to make you shut me out and I want to know what it was." He took her hands in his and stroked the undersides of them. "Cassie, honey, we have something special here. I feel it, you feel it, I know you do. Don't throw it away because of some kind of misunderstanding."

"There's nothing between us."

"The hell there's not. There's never been this kind of chemistry between you and anybody else. I'd bet my life on it. There sure as hell hasn't ever been anything like this before for me. And I'm not going to just let it go without knowing why. So tell me."

"I think you assume too much."

"Like what?"

"Like we're going to sleep together."

"Well, we are."

"No, we're not."

"The chemistry's there. I know you can feel it. Don't even try to tell me you don't feel it."

"I don't feel it. Sorry."

With his hand he cupped the back of her head and leaned in to kiss her, letting his lips softly play over hers before roughly pulling her into his chest and deepening the kiss. It was an extraordinary kiss. It was all at once commanding and resolute and it spoke volumes to her about his need and hunger.

When he finally lifted his lips from hers, his eyes fell to the moist, soft flesh, and the heat from his eyes devoured them now as his lips had done just moments before.

"I am falling for you. And I think you're falling for me, too. And there's nothing you can say that will convince me otherwise."

He bent and kissed her lightly on her parted lips, then putting his hands firmly on her shoulders, he set her away from him. "Spill it. Now," he commanded.

His voice held a firmness that put him in control, and she lifted her eyes to see the fierce determination in them. Here was a man fighting for what he wanted, and he wasn't going to leave this room until he was a victor, she knew that.

"I chanced to overhear a conversation you had with somebody."

"Who?"

"A man named Ray, I think he's an officer."

"Ray? Ray Cooper?"

"I don't know his last name."

"Well what were we saying that upset you so?"

"You were talking about picking up unattractive girls in Myrtle Beach."

He looked totally confused for a moment and then it dawned on him what conversation she meant.

"How the hell did you overhear that?"

"On one of my walkie-talkies."

"Well, there shouldn't have been anything about that conversation that would have made you mad at *me*."

"You must be kidding!"

"Would you mind telling me exactly what I said that upset you."

"You said you wanted to know next time he went there," just recalling the conversation was bringing tears to her eyes and she was softly sobbing now.

"Yeah? And then I said . . ."

"I don't know what you said next. All I got was static after that."

"Oh. So you're mad at me about a conversation you overheard and you didn't even hear the whole conversation."

"What difference would it make? You wanted to join him in his debauchery."

"I most certainly did not! If you had heard the rest of what I said to him, you would have heard me say that I wanted to know the next time he went so I could go with him and warn the unsuspecting women."

"Really?"

"Of course. You thought I wanted to go pick up lonely, unattractive girls and hump them in their rears?" he asked incredulously. "What kind of guy do you think I am anyway? Do I strike you as the kind of guy who can't do any better than that?" he was angry now and she knew it.

"No. No, of course not. It's just that . . ."

"That what?"

"Well, you seemed so interested and you said you wanted to go . . ."

"Jesus, Cass. I thought we had more going for us than that. Haven't you learned anything about me from all those questionnaires?"

She cringed. "I'm sorry. I didn't want it to be true and I shouldn't have believed it was true."

"Well, let that be a lesson. Next time, hear the whole conversation or better yet, don't listen to any part of it."

"Okay," she said sheepishly.

He cupped her face with both palms and drew her toward him. But before their lips could touch, he abruptly released her.

She sat stunned, looking at his face. "What's wrong?"

"I saw you going out tonight with Harley. What was that all about?"

"He asked me out. We went shagging at Fat Harold's."

"Did you let him kiss you?"

She had a guilty look on her face, and he immediately knew the answer.

He hit the bed between them with his fist. Then he abruptly stood up and walked to the door.

He had his hand on the knob, turning it when she whispered, "I wanted to see if another man could kiss me like you. If I could enjoy someone else's kisses as much as yours."

He stopped, his back to her, his hand still on the knob. "And?"

"I only let him kiss me once and I used half a bottle of mouthwash trying to get rid of the taste of it."

He turned back to face her. "That bad, huh?"

"Well, maybe not to somebody else, somebody who hasn't had one of yours."

He came back to sit beside her on the bed and taking her into his arms, he held her to him, her head resting on his shoulder. "Promise me you won't be so eager to mistrust me again."

"I promise."

"And promise me you'll always come to me if there's any kind of problem between us."

"I promise."

"And promise me, you'll sleep with me tomorrow night."

She hesitated for just a moment. "I promise."

His eyes widened with surprise then he gathered her even closer and lifting her face up at his, he captured her mouth with his.

Ten minutes later, he softly closed the door to her room and tiptoed to the foyer. "Good night, Colin," he said to the stony silhouette outlined by the moonlight sitting over on the sofa.

"Good night, Michael."

He heard the door being locked behind him as he jogged down the front steps. He felt like singing, "Tonight, Tonight," as he walked to his car because it was already tomorrow, and tonight he would take his ease inside her. He certainly hoped that Colin wasn't reading his thoughts.

Chapter 10

Cassie hadn't been able to get fully back to sleep. So, at five o'clock, she tumbled out of bed, put her workout clothes on and grabbed the keys to her Jimmy. She drove through Sea Trail, out the south gate and turned left onto Beach Drive. She stopped and waited at the stop sign even though she could see that there were no cars coming for at least as far as the curving bend in the road at the east entrance to the development. Turning right at Shark's Beachwear, she drove down the little incline to wait at the light before the bridge. As soon as she pulled up to it, it turned green and she drove over. It was low tide and her Jimmy rattled and bounced a little more than usual before leveling out on the other side. She drove down the long causeway, marveling at the peaceful vista of the faintly lit marshes and the dotted lights of the beach houses lining the horizon ahead of her.

The sunrise would still be an hour or so away. Cassie was filled with a sense of well being just knowing she was going to be here to see it as it came up from the left side of the island. She never took the beauty of this island for granted. Almost everyone here lived in fear that something like a hurricane would come along one day and destroy it. This was just such a beautiful place, too beautiful to be believed at times.

A line she had memorized from the Brunswick Beacon's Letters to the Editor, written by a homeowner opposed to the new bridge, sprang to mind: "The spirit of Sunset Beach is nurtured in the isolation created by the bridge." There were many who believed that the old bridge offered just enough difficulty and inconvenience to keep Sunset Beach exclusive. She knew her new bridge was very controversial for that very same reason, and that a lot of the people who would be watching as it went up, would not be in favor of it. And at times like these, she was on their side, opposed to any change that would alter this tranquil, little island. And she wondered just what impact her two-lane, high span would have on their lives.

Cassie parked her car in the parking lot in front of the gazebo and walked up the decking to the wood-planked gazebo. A lanky old man sat on a bench staring at his hands as she walked by him. He looked up and smiled and said, "Morning." She smiled back at him and said, "Aren't we both up before the roosters?" His friendly nod followed her form as she made her way down the decking, over the dunes and to the sand.

She stretched for a few minutes and then started jogging toward Bird Island. She looked up at the pier as she ran under it and she could hear the footsteps of the people above her as they headed out onto the long pier for a day of fishing. As expected, the beach was deserted. She'd probably make it to the island before seeing another jogger, but there would be plenty on her way back. Trying to get her breathing and her body into a comfortable rhythm, she focused on the waves as they lapped the shore. The sand at the water's edge was hard-packed, easy to run on—firm, yet giving. Later today, bike and stroller tire tread marks would join the tread patterns of the runners' shoes.

There was an energy bursting inside her and she could only hope that it would sustain her through her long day and night. She reflected then on her promise to Michael. Had she been just a tad too hasty? Was she really ready to take their relationship to the next level? What if, like his ex-fiance, they found sex with each other lacking? Somehow, she didn't think that was going to happen though, judging by the way her heart hammered when he was anywhere around. She doubted that she would have any trouble being intimate with him. Just the thought of his arousing caresses stroking her body made something inside her belly coil. And the idea that she would soon be accepting the most virile part of his body into the center of hers was already causing her to flush and get weak at the knees. Maybe she was ready for this after all. It was a cinch that even if her mind wasn't, at least her body sure was.

She saw the dunes of Bird Island looming ahead just to her right and she drew on her reserves to sprint for a little while. When she had made it halfway down the island, she started looking for the black and white mailbox through the graying mists shrouding the dunes.

There, there it was, up in the dune line, surrounded by little tufts of sea oats. She walked up the beach to where the mailbox poked out of a dune, pulled open the door, and removed a spiral notebook and a ballpoint pen. Then she walked a few feet further into the shelter of the dunes and sat on the edge of the partially-covered driftwood bench.

The letters on the U.S. regulation mailbox indicated that this was where the mail for the "Kindred

Spirit" was to be delivered. And for twenty years that is exactly what people had been doing, coming here to write letters baring their hearts and their souls and then posting them in the box.

The pages of the notebook Cassie opened were heavy and warped from the humidity of the salt air, but they were dry—dry and crinkly like parchment, because of the protection the mailbox offered.

People from all over the world came here to get an answer to a problem, to share a secret, to express their joy over a new love or their grief over a lost one, or to simply remark on the beauty and tranquility that they found here. The tender thoughts can be read by anyone who has the desire and the time. Once a month, the journals are collected by the anonymous Kindred Spirit, and fresh ones left in their place. Supposedly, no one knows who the spirit is and that in itself lends to the charm and mystique that has sent many a vacationer on their long pilgrimage down the beach to the rusted box and weathered bench, many visiting year after year to write in the journals before the vast ocean. She was in awe of the respect and honor the participants had for each other's writings, like an unspoken bond between strangers as they dealt with their heart-wrenching emotions by writing about them. Pictures and mementos attached to the pages were never disturbed, pages never destroyed or removed as the notebooks filled up month after month and year after year with poignant messages from people who knew that their muddled ramblings were going to be read and saved and whispered to the wind.

Cassie wrote quickly in her neat, fluid cursive style about her joy to be here, her trepidations about her job and her excitement about Michael, intimating that 'ready or not, here we go' was how she was feeling right now and that she hoped he was as sincere in his feelings for her as she was in her feelings for him. Then she signed it with a big fancy 'C' and dated it. She was flipping through the last few pages looking at the entries, when her eyes fastened on a small paragraph written just yesterday: "I know who did it. I didn't mean for anything to happen to D. Duke. I know it's all my fault and I'm sick over it. They need to ask about the cats." It too, was dated, but not signed.

Cassie read it over several times, but it didn't make a lot of sense to her. She put the notebook back, jogged in place for a moment to loosen up, and then sprinted back down the beach to the firmer sand.

This sure was puzzling, but apparently somebody knew who the murderer was, and they were either afraid to tell the police or they were guilty for their part in it. Or, just maybe, that message had been left by the murderer himself. Cassie shivered as she ran and suddenly, self-conscious of how isolated she was, she searched the horizon in front of her and the dunes beside her, uncertain and suddenly fearful that she was being watched.

The sun was cresting the marsh and rising above the roofs of the houses on the other end of the island. As soon as she approached the dry gully leading back to Sunset Beach, she saw other joggers and walkers coming toward her. She took a deep breath and slowed her pace, realizing now that she had actually been doing a lot more running than jogging.

As soon as she got home, she told herself she'd call Michael and tell him about the journal entry she'd seen. And then she realized that in doing that, she would be practically inviting him to read the one *she'd* written. Wonderful! Well, there was no help for it, that cryptic message might be the only clue they'd get in this case. Maybe he wouldn't read hers, maybe he wouldn't know it was hers if he did, maybe she'd better not hope for that.

She ran up the wooden walkway, through the center of the gazebo where the old man from before was nodding off, and down the ramp to the parking lot to her Jimmy. Everything was starting to brighten up now and this little coastal community was slowly rousing itself as she left the island and drove back home.

As soon as she walked through the door she punched in Michael's number, hoping to catch him before he made it into the shower.

"Yeah?" a sleepy male voice answered.

"Michael. It's me, Cassie."

"Hi, sweetheart. What's the matter?"

Was he already that in tune to her that he could tell when she was upset about something? "Michael, I just came from the Kindred Spirit mailbox. There's a journal entry from yesterday left by someone who says they know who killed D. Duke."

Michael sat up and scratched his head. "Really?"

"Yes. I just came from there and I thought that maybe you should go see it before someone, maybe even the murderer sees it and takes that page."

"Why didn't you take it?"

"Michael! I couldn't do that! That would be like taking an offertory candle from the church!"

He chuckled at her. "Okay, okay, I'll get dressed and go over there."

"And Michael?"

"Yeah?"

"I'd appreciate it if you didn't read anything dated today, written in kind of a parochial-style writing."

"Not a chance babe. If you've written something there, it's free game."

"Well you wouldn't ever have thought to read it if I hadn't had to tell you about this other thing."

"True. Maybe I'll cut you some slack."

"No, you won't."

"Yeah, you're right. No, I won't." He snickered a little then asked in a low, sexy voice, "Just what did you say?"

"I said . . . never mind. It doesn't matter. I've got to go get a shower and get to work. Call me later, okay?"

"Sure thing. And thanks."

"You're welcome, I hope it helps."

Later that day, Michael stopped by the construction site just as Cassie was climbing down from a bulldozer.

"You really do play with Tonka toys, huh?"

"That's a CAT, I don't think the Caterpillar Company would like you calling their machine a Tonka toy." She pushed her hard hat further back on her head and looked up at him.

God, she was just so cute, he thought. He took all of her in, from her heavy, camel-colored work boots, to her dusty, faded and very tight jeans with the partially ripped off pocket, to the ribbed tank top covered by a ragged old denim-colored shirt with rolled up sleeves that was held on only by the knot at her waist. Her mahogany-hued curls poked out all round her yellow hard hat. She looked like a miniature version of Construction Barbie, all rounded curves tucked into what could have been Ken's work clothes.

"Is there a place we can go that's private?"

"The only private place around here is the port-a-john, and sometimes that's not even a hundred percent."

"How about your office in the trailer?"

"My office is everybody's office."

"Well, it'll have to do. I need to talk to you."

They walked over to the trailer and Michael held the door open for her. Once inside, he closed the door and leaned back against it.

"What's up? Why the serious expression on your face?" she asked.

"I won't be able to see you tonight. I'm being sent to Hope Mills."

She didn't know whether to be relieved or disappointed, and as soon as she looked over at him, he acknowledged that with a wry smile. "I read your entry, maybe it's just as well." The defeated look on his face tore into her, and she suddenly knew that she wanted him, more than she'd ever wanted any man. Even though she knew he would never believe her if she told him that now, she tried anyway. "Michael, despite what I wrote earlier, I am ready now."

"What's happened to change things?"

"I don't exactly know. I just know that the next time you get me in your back seat, you're going to have a hard time getting me out."

He smiled at her. "Well, that's nice to hear, but I'm afraid I don't know when that's going to be."

"Why? And why are you being sent to Hope Mills, wherever that is?"

"Well, it's actually all your fault. The police chief wants me to try to find out who wrote that journal entry. He thinks that message could have been left by the murderer. So, since our police force consists of only twelve officers, we each have to double as detectives when the need arises. He's sending me to Hope Mills so I can meet the man who has the rest of the journals. The chief wants me to try to match up the handwriting to see if there was anything else written prior to today that would lead us to whoever it was that left that message yesterday."

"I thought nobody knew who the Kindred Spirit was."

"A few people know. Cliff down at the Sunset Beach Trading Company knows, he knows everything. I have to go see him now, get sworn to secrecy and get the address."

"His? I thought it was a woman?"

"Look, I've already told you more than you should know. Stop asking questions, okay?"

"No. I want to know more. Like when are you coming back?"

"Don't know. Probably tonight, could be tomorrow or even the next day. It depends. I won't be able to borrow the journals, I have to use them there."

"Sounds like a lot of work. Are you a handwriting expert or have you had some training in this? How are you supposed to match up the writing style?"

"I've never done anything like this before, but one of the guys at the community college gave me a few things to look for. For instance, did you notice that all the e's were like c's with diagonal vertical lines drawn through them sort of like cent signs? And that all the t's are crossed diagonally, too?"

"No, I didn't really notice. Sounds like you've got a hell of a tiresome job in front of you though."

"Yeah. Nothing like the plans I originally had for tonight. C'mere," he said opening his arms for her.

Without hesitation she walked right into them and hugged him around the waist. When she looked up into his face, she saw the desire he had for her burning in his eyes. "Let me know the second you get back."

"Yeah, right. You'll probably be on the ground somewhere under a backhoe trying to change a hydraulic shock or something."

"Well, even if I am, let me know."

"I will." He leaned down to kiss her and was amazed at the intensity with which she returned his kiss.

He felt the door being opened behind him, and even though there was no way the intruder could push him out of the way, he let her go and stepped aside.

"Well, I have to get going. I'll try to call you whenever I can."

She looked up into his face and smiled, "Good luck with your search. Wouldn't it be great if you could crack the case? I, for one, would like to know that the waters around here are safe before I put my kayak back in them."

He smiled back at her. "I'll do my best, you get busy with this bridge. I expect to see you at least halfway to the island by the time I get back."

She chuckled, "That's not likely, unless you plan on being away 'til Christmas 2003."

"No. I don't. I don't think I could stand to be away from you that long."

A throat being cleared behind him alerted them to the fact that they were not alone, still he leaned forward and kissed her on the lips. "I'll call you," he reiterated as he turned and side-stepped Lou before he opened the door to leave the trailer.

The bright sun flashed in his face as he made his way down the rickety wooden stairs, across the construction yard and to his cruiser. Why did he have that empty hollow feeling in the pit of his stomach? The feeling that he was going off to war, uncertain if he would ever see her again or that when he did, she might belong to somebody else. Christ, he was only going to be gone for a day or two at most! Why should he even care so much? Because it was new, he told himself. Because these feelings for her were new, and new feelings were so emotional, so much more intense than feelings that were allowed to be desensitized by time and familiarity. That's exactly what it was. Once he'd had her a time or two, these feelings would go away. They would simply go away.

Chapter 11
Hope Mills

It was two a.m. and still he couldn't sleep. Michael sat at a small table by the door in his motel room. He looked at the pages of notes scattered in front of him and for the fortieth time, ran his fingers through his hair. He had done it so many times now that it was oily and sticking almost straight up instead of smoothed back from his forehead.

He'd ended up going back five years, two years back from the last entry he'd found. He'd been lucky in one aspect, the distinctive style of printing coupled with those distinctive e's and t's and he'd also noticed the s'es had a slight hook to the bottom curve, had stood out in the journals after only a few hours.

It had been very hard at first as he sat going through the first stack of journals. First of all, the journals were all different. Most were spiral, but they were different sizes, different thicknesses and even the spaces between the lines were different. The same color of ink was seldom used for more than a few entries in a row. This, he knew from his own experiences, was because the pens available were either plentiful or scarce in the mailbox. After ten hours of searching, he was sure he'd found all the entries written by someone who had the style of writing he had managed to commit to memory.

There had been three years that she had written in the journals. The reasons he thought the person he was looking for was a 'she' instead of a 'he' were: (a) the writing looked more on the feminine side to him, although he knew that didn't necessarily mean anything; and (b) the flowery things that were written about the island, the beach and life in general seemed more like the thoughts of a woman than those of a man. Again, it didn't necessarily mean anything, but in his mind, he'd already named this woman Lady Kit—for her reference to the cats.

There were 18 entries—most of them occurring between the 8th and the 15th of the month. Most of them were short, usually just four or five lines. He had copied each one onto an index card because he knew he wouldn't be able to take the journals with him, unless he wanted to obtain a search warrant and force the issue, which he definitely did not. Now he was checking the order they were in, making sure they were in chronological order. Next he would read them again to see if he could add to the list of clues he had written on the yellow legal pad balanced on his knee.

So far, all he had was: something about cats; probably doesn't live here all the time; definitely has a home somewhere else; must surely be able to walk at least two miles to get to the mailbox; knew D. Duke or knew of him; knew the island well; liked tourists—maybe because she rented her house out; didn't particularly care for teenagers or college kids; worried about the hurricanes. Hell, who didn't? Drinks alcohol—okay, well that narrows it down. And the biggest clue of all was that she probably lived or stayed on the east end of the island. On the bay side. On the side that had more evidence of frat parties and Atlantic Coast Conference spirit parties. And, she cooks.

121

He reread the first card: "What a lovely day. I could sit here for hours and maybe I shall. Now that the inlet is gone, I don't have to worry about when I head back home. It used to scare me that I could get stuck on this side, so I rarely ventured down this far. The birds are so beautiful as they skim in single file over the water's edge, one day I must remember to bring my camera. September 9, 1998."

Nothing new there. He was going to add 'likes birds' to his list but then he thought, who doesn't? And she isn't a very strong swimmer or she doesn't have confidence in herself. The inlet, even at its worst could usually be traversed, except maybe at high tide during the days of a full moon. The inlet wasn't an issue anymore that's for certain. He remembered it fondly and sometimes even thought about taking a shovel out there in the middle of the night and digging a trench so that it would open up again and start flowing like it used to. But, of course, that was against the law and it wouldn't do his career any favors if he was caught doing it.

He turned the card over on the table in front of him and read the second one: "Just a tad nippy today, glad I remembered to bring my good jersey jacket. Buried a friend back home. It's sad to think that she'll never see the waves lapping on the shore or the sun setting over the bay while sipping on a vodka tonic. This is a melancholy visit for me today, I guess I'll go home and make a pot of Mulligatawny Stew. October 14, 1998."

I wonder what nationality you'd have to be to have grown up with Mulligatawny Stew—Irish? Scottish? Of course that really didn't matter very much anymore. People were quite culturally diverse these days, even in

Brunswick County, *if* you could find the ingredients. He recalled the many times he had driven all the way into Wilmington to Harris Teeter to get the ingredients he needed for his Thai cooking. So she cooked. He felt an affinity with her—to like to cook was to like to nurture. She seemed like such a nice person. He wondered who she was and if he'd ever seen her in the Food Lion or at CVS. Maybe he'd even pulled her over and given her a ticket. Now that would be something helpful. Why didn't she write about her car and what the license tag number was?

He flipped that card on top of the other one and continued reading: "Tis the season! Started decorating, I hope the garland I bought smells this good by the time the holiday gets here. This time of the year reminds me so much of my childhood. I miss my mother. I never did understand what she saw in my father though. December 9, 1998." Nothing there was probably going to help him. She liked the smell of evergreen and didn't like her father. Those weren't things you could recognize on one's face. Now if he could do a survey . . .

Another card was added to the pile, and he read the next one: "It is so cold, I wish I'd worn my gloves. I think this pen is going to freeze in my hand. The waves look forbidding or is that foreboding? Anyway, I sure don't want to get near them. Men who work in ships out to sea this time of the year surely have a rough life. I see one way out there now. The price for good seafood. I'll never complain about the prices again! February 10, 1999."

He felt himself shiver slightly just from reading her words. Baby it's cold outside! He flipped over the card.

"The magnificence of spring! Everything is blooming. The azaleas are stunning. I must have missed the forsythia this year though, I don't remember seeing any at all. How nice to discard the layers of clothing on this warm spring day. Somebody left a wine bottle here, can't they read the signs? No glass on the beach!!! April 14, 1999."

Likes flowers. All right, what woman doesn't? Doesn't like litter. Okay, we aren't making any great strides here. He dropped the card and ran his fingers though his hair, then he stood up and stretched. He needed to get some sleep. He left the piles of cards on the table and took off his clothes. Just before his head hit the pillow, he realized he'd spent the night getting to know a woman quite different from the woman he'd planned on getting to know tonight. He wondered if Cassie missed him; if she'd thought about him at all since he'd left her at the construction site.

Chapter 12

The next morning Michael gathered up his collection of index cards, his notes and his overnight bag and checked out of the motel. There wasn't anything more he could do here. He'd painstakingly copied each journal entry that he had instantly known was from Lady Kit and satisfied himself that there weren't any he'd missed before leaving the home of the anonymous Kindred Spirit late last night. He could go over the cards as many times as he needed to when he got back to Sunset Beach.

After checking in at the station, he called the coroner to see what information the rest of D. Duke's body had yielded. He was told that a report was being faxed and that unless Spaghettios or Whiskas had any significance to him, there were no more leads.

He went over to the fax machine and watched as the report incrementally slid out of the lighted slot. As soon as it dropped, he picked it up and read it.

As originally thought, he died by major trauma to the head followed shortly thereafter by decapitation. He was a reasonably healthy man for his age and nothing else unusual was noted. His last meal, only partially digested in his stomach was Spaghettios.

There was exactly $1.32 in one front pant pocket. The other one contained the top tear strip from a cello bag of Whiskas cat food. His wallet had been found in his back pocket, it contained an almost expired NCDMV ID card. D. Duke didn't drive, so this was his form of identification, although why he needed it on the island was anybody's guess. It wasn't like he was an unknown, and it wasn't like he was going to write a check anywhere. He didn't even have a checking account that anyone could find. It seemed that he paid for everything with cash. The wallet also contained the original ID card that came with the wallet; it had been filled out by hand. The emergency contact number was his home phone number and the medical emergency number was for a doctor in Shallotte. There were two ticket stubs from the movie theater at Briarcliffe Mall where he and somebody else had seen the "Star Wars" sequel a few summers ago. Michael supposed the somebody else had been whomever D. Duke had managed to talk into driving him all the way down to the mall in South Carolina.

There was a plastic comb between two of the empty cellophane sleeves that had apparently been there so long that it was settled into the imprint it had caused. All of the other sleeves were empty; there were no charge cards and there were no pictures. And there was no money in the billfold section. But somehow, this did not smack of a murder committed during a robbery. It was more likely that this was the normal state of D. Duke's wallet—empty. He probably only carried one because he always had.

There was only one other thing found on his body. A key. A key to a safe deposit box according to the report. It had been the only thing in his buttoned-up front shirt pocket. A picture had been taken of it and faxed over with the report. Michael turned the page sideways to read the number. Sixty-four, and unless he was mistaken it was to a box at the BB&T at Ocean Isle. He had a box there and the key looked just like his, but maybe they all looked alike. That would be something he'd have to go get from the coroner's office so he could track down the box that it fit. This could be their biggest clue yet. It was odd that a safety deposit key was the only key found on him, people usually didn't carry that one around. Michael couldn't decide whether the fact that he hadn't had his house key on him was unusual or not, a lot of people on the island didn't bother to lock up despite warnings from the police, especially the older homeowners who had no concept of the ever-so-slowly encroaching criminal element. Then again, maybe it had gotten lost somewhere, but apparently not in the muirky waters of the salt marsh; according to the report, the lower portion of his body had not been submerged in fresh or salt water.

He went to catch the chief up on what he was doing. And, after the unsettling feeling of disappointing the chief with his meager findings, he was told to stick with it, to follow every lead until he came up with something. The file for the case was on the corner of the chief's desk and he indicated that he should take it and read it. "It's probably better that one of you work on this. You've got a logical mind, run with it and see if you can figure something out. Start with D. Duke's house and go from there. There's a key in an envelope in the file."

Michael wasn't thrilled to be taken off of his regular duties to work on this, but the chief always knew the best way to utilize his small force. The crime of murder wasn't something they had a task force for, they'd only had three in the last decade and it had been obvious in each case who'd done it. A girlfriend for one and a family member for the other two. The surrounding areas had had a few more, but even so, the homicide rate was negligible in the lower Brunswick Islands.

It was, therefore, unsettling for this small community to know that there was a murderer in its midst: a murderer who was not only stealthy but brutally violent. Michael was honored that he was given the case, but not at all confident that he could handle it. The police academy where he'd taken all his courses hadn't stressed homicide investigating in their curriculum. How to deal with unruly teenagers, drunk drivers and drug trafficking were skills he had mastered instead. He picked up the folder, nodded his acceptance of the duty assigned to him and left the chief's office.

He had no idea what to do now, how to even get started, or more started than he already was with eighteen index cards from a witness or possibly the murderer. Then the chief's words came to back to him. "Start at D. Duke's house and go from there."

He opened the folder, scanned each page as he turned it, and when he found the envelope with the house key in it, he stuck it in his pocket. Before he headed over to the island, he called Cassie at the number she had given him for the phone in the trailer.

There was no answer, and after six rings he assumed there was no answering machine. He tried her home number and Jenny answered. He was told that Cassie was looking at a townhouse on the plantation, one she'd seen twice before. She was considering putting an offer on it. He asked her if she would take a message. Then he drove over to the island. When he reached the stop sign at Main Street, he turned left heading to the east side of the island.

Michael purposely drove the long way, all the way down Main Street where the front row houses were, before back tracking after the road looped around and heading west behind the second row houses. He turned onto a side street and pulled into the yard in front of an unobtrusive dull brown beach house that sat high up on stilts. It was as nondescript as D. Duke had been. The gravel driveway was almost empty of gravel; after so many years of being washed away by hurricanes and not being replenished, all that was left was a chalky gray dust that matched the barren gray spots on the front lawn where grass no longer grew. It was one of the older beach houses on the island and its years of neglect were starkly noticeable next to the newer pastel houses with their nicely landscaped lawns and healthy, trimmed bushes. D. Duke's bushes were sparse, scrawny, and badly in need of mulching. Looking up at the house, he decided that wasn't all that needed to be done around here.

Michael climbed the steep wooden stairs to the front door, and using the key from his pocket, he unlocked it and entered the house. The first thing that assailed him was the smell. It was an old man's smell, and it brought with it a strong reminder of his past as thoughts of his grandfather came to his mind. He breathed in deeply as he stood there, just over the threshold. What did that old man's smell consist of anyway? Musty wood? A lingering trace of Bay Rum or Old Spice? Some kind of powder or residue from shaving cream? He really couldn't define it, but he'd smelled it on himself once. Once, just after he'd finished making homemade vegetable soup. He'd smelled it on his hands, the hands that had just cut up celery and onion and tomatoes. So he knew the old man smell had something to do with food, too. Old men fooled around with tomatoes, maybe that was the connection. Every old man worth his salt, planted tomatoes, tended to the tomatoes, harvested the tomatoes, and then gave the tomatoes away. He shook his head and closed the door, then he looked around.

The living room was the front room and it was filled with heavy, durable furniture, the kind where you could see the wooden frames on the sides and under the front cushions. The sofa and a matching chair were upholstered in faux leather, something his father used to call Naugahyde. There was an old corduroy recliner in the corner facing the 25-inch TV. Beside that was a TV tray table with lighthouses lacquered under the finish. There was a bronze sculpted American Eagle on the top shelf of the bookcase under the window. He walked over and read the names of the books. They were all Reader's Digest Condensed Books and the titles he had heard of, but he didn't believe he'd ever read a single one. Novels like: "Seven Days in May," "Ring of Bright Water," "The Judas Tree" and "The Wind at Morning."

He walked into the dining room that was separated from the kitchen by a low counter that had two vinyl covered stools tucked under it. The only thing on the dining room table was a ballpoint pen resting atop the mustard-colored plastic, felt-backed tablecloth. It was an ugly room; everything was drab. The walls were paneled with dark oak, maybe that was why.

As he entered the kitchen his eyes were drawn to the window over the sink. The view from here was of the canal and the bay and it was a nice, restful view. There were a few boats docked at the neighboring houses and he could tell that the tide was partially out. Anybody going out with any kind of a draft would probably have to wait a few hours before getting back in.

His eyes dropped to the white porcelain sink and he saw a bowl soaking there with a spoon in it. He looked closer. Yes, it had been a bowl of Spaghettios. He was reminded just why he was here and he started to look around in earnest. The trash can under the sink had not been emptied and some flies were paying a lot of attention to the empty Spaghettios can. Rummaging through the rest of the trash, he found nothing he could attribute any significance to: an empty sleeve for a 60-watt light bulb, a Kool-aid packet that prompted him to check out the refrigerator and sure enough, the man drank Kool-aid! A wad of paper towels was the only other trash, apparently D. Duke had taken his trash out just before fixing his dinner.

Michael took inventory of the refrigerator contents. The bright red Kool-aid was in a tall clear pitcher with a picture of a sailboat on it. There was a package of baloney, some pimento loaf, a loaf of no count white bread, a carton of milk, the usual condiments, and some blackberry seedless preserves.

Everything was neat and clean and nothing seemed out of place. He continued on through the hallway to check out the two bedrooms and the bathroom. Clean, normal, if you considered a crocheted toilet paper cover with a doll's body stuck into the hole—normal.

The bedrooms had remarkably few furnishings and the room that Michael figured to be D. Duke's had a closet with just six hangers—three pants, three shirts. The dresser was a huge cherry thing that came to the center of his chest. On top of it was a long white lace runner, and on top of that were several bottles of men's cologne. Ah, that old man smell. He was curious so he walked over and read the labels. Hai-Karate? Did they still make that? Brut 33 and Stetson. Boy, who felt like an old man now?

He turned around and looked at the made-up bed. The linens consisted of a yellow chenille bedspread with the chenille threads worn off in several places, lumpy looking pillows and a needlepoint pillow of the American flag. He walked around the house slowly, trying to observe and spot any incongruities, but that was pretty hard in a house like this where everything was a little 'off' as far as he was concerned.

He opened the double doors in the dining room that led to the back deck and to the steps that led down to D. Duke's private dock. He stood by the railing looking down at the canal and the bay. This was really an awesome view of the island. Turning to his left, he could see the blue of the ocean over the roofs of the first and second row houses. Nice place. It could stand coming into the 21st century though.

He leaned on the wide porch railing and watched the birds, the tide, and the neighbors as they came and went. And then it occurred to him that there was no boat tied up below. He was sure he had read something in one of the reports that said D.Duke had owned a small boat. He saw a man across the canal putting up some lattice work and decided to go talk to him. He went down the stairs, noting that they could stand a good power washing, and walked to the bank of the canal. He called over and the man stopped what he was doing and walked over to his side of the bank. There was only about forty feet separating them so it was easy to call back and forth.

"Didn't D. Duke have a boat?" he asked.

"Yeah. It was a john boat with a small motor."

"Do you know where it is?"

"Haven't seen it since I found out he died."

"Was it there before he died?"

"Yeah, I guess so. I never really noticed exactly when it wasn't there anymore."

"Did he use it a lot?"

"No. Not anymore. I hear he used to though. We've only been here for two years. I've seen him out in it once or twice."

"So I gather you didn't see anything unusual?"

"The police asked everybody on both sides of the canal; hardly anybody's been home. Some of the places were rented. But as far as I know, nobody saw or heard anything. He was a quiet kind of fella. He walked everywhere he went. I hardly ever saw him since he was up and out long before I even got up most mornings."

"Well, thanks. I guess I need to see if I can find that boat."

"Good luck," the man said as he waved before turning back to his project.

Michael climbed the stairs and stood on the weathered deck a few minutes longer, enjoying the view of the interior part of the island. It was very tranquil here. His eyes followed the lines of the horizon and from this vantage point he could just about make out the other side of the Intracoastal. He couldn't quite make out the bridge, the old one or the new one Cassie was building, but he could see the water tower which would be very close to the base of it, just a few hundred feet short of the approach to the high span. The words to Louie Armstrong's song came to him, "I see skies of blue . . ." he hummed for a while before finishing with, "and I think to myself, what a wonderful world."

He went back through the house turning off lights as he went. When he put his hand on the front door knob he hesitated as he stared at the black powder residue left on the light switch and door frame from the fingerprinting that had been done. He had already opened the door a little, now he closed it firmly and went back into the kitchen. He washed and dried the bowl and spoon in the sink and took out the liner from the trash can wedged under the sink. While he was putting the empty trash can back under the sink, he spotted an assortment of cat food behind some cleaning supplies on the other side of the cabinet. He knelt to read the labels: Nine Lives, Meow Mix and Whiskas.

This was very odd. He had found no evidence of a cat living here at all—no cat dish or water bowl, no toys or scratching post, no cat hairs that would have had him sneezing almost from the git go when he came in. Maybe he had a friend who visited with a cat? There was something about cats he kept remembering from the journal entry. "Ask about the cats." Ask *who* about the cats? Why did people have to be so cryptic, anyway?

He was headed back to the front door when he spotted the old-fashioned princess phone attached to the wall. It also was still covered with black dust from fingerprinting. It was a shame they hadn't found anything but D. Duke's prints. He reached for the phone and punched in Cassie's number at the trailer. This time she answered.

" 'Bout time I tracked you down."

"Hi," she said in a soft, sexy voice.

"What cha doin'?"

"Tryin' to talk the CAT company into sending somebody out here tonight to fix the big earth mover."

"There's somethin' you can't fix?"

"There's a lot I can fix, but I definitely can't fix a burned-up motor."

"They can fix that kind of stuff on site?"

"Yeah, usually. I sure hope they can. It costs a small fortune to haul these things around."

"So when will you know?"

"Know what?"

"Know if you have to wait around for this guy?"

"Why do you assume it's going to be a guy?"

"All right, all right. When will you know if you have to wait around for a repair person?"

"Oh, I won't have to wait. They don't need anyone here, they have their own keys and the maintenance trucks are equipped with big lights. They'll either make it tonight as I've begged and pleaded with them to, or they won't, and we'll lose another day tomorrow."

"Well, I hope for your sake, that they drop whatever they're doing and get out here tonight."

"Thank you."

135

"In the meantime . . ."

"Yes?"

"How would you feel about doing a little kayaking by moonlight?"

"Why do I get the feeling that this is not exactly a romantic overture?"

"Because it's not. Well, I guess it could be though. We can take a picnic dinner and a blanket over to the backside of Bird Island."

"What's the real reason that I'm only an afterthought?"

"I need to see if I can find a boat, D. Duke's boat. It's not docked at his house like it should be. And I didn't want to go out looking for it by myself."

"Scared of the dark?" she taunted.

"No. Scared I won't see it. I have awful night vision."

"Okay, I'll go. Do you have your own kayak?"

"Yeah. I haven't used it for awhile, but I have one. It's in my shed. I usually just put it in from my dock, but that's way too far from the area we need to search. Do you think you can come get me and my kayak with your Jimmy?"

"Sure. What time?"

"I'm heading home now, just show up whenever you can."

"Okay, probably be about an hour."

"Fine. And Cass?"

"Yeah?"

"Slather on the bug spray, you'll need it."

"This is a wonderful date you're taking me on. I expect you want me to pack the dinner, too?"

"No, I'll take care of that. You're in for a treat."

"Oh? What's that?"

"Me."

"I thought you'd forgotten."

"Not in a million years. Tell Jenny *and Colin* not to expect you home until late."

"All right . . . see you soon."

He hung up the phone, and taking the trash with him, he locked the front door and went out to his cruiser.

He stopped by the station to check out then hurried home to get his kayak out of the shed and to get their picnic dinner ready. He hoped she liked his favorite sandwich, peanut butter and jelly with bacon on his own homemade bread.

Cassie arrived at 6:30 and they packed up the kayak with the bag containing their dinner and a small cooler. As soon as Michael was sitting beside her in the Jimmy, he reached over and pulled her up against the center console. One hand went around her shoulders while the other cupped her cheek and throat.

"I've missed you," he said huskily as his lips descended to hers.

His face tilted sideways and his lips covered hers, lightly caressing her full bottom lip before slipping his tongue under her upper one.

"Yuck!" he said as he pulled away.

"You told me slather myself with bug spray."

"I didn't mean for you to DEET your lips!"

"Oh, so bugs know the difference between lips and other skin?"

"No, I guess you're right. Be careful you don't lick that stuff, it can't possibly be good for you; it sure doesn't taste good," he said as he wiped his mouth with his handkerchief. "When we get back, I'm going to have to hose you down before I can kiss you."

"This date is becoming more romantic by the minute," she said sarcastically as she started the Jimmy and put it in gear.

He chuckled and reached over to touch her cheek. "Now really, how many guys have ever asked you to go out to look for a dead man's boat with the promise of mosquito bites and Gatorade wine?"

"Gatorade wine?"

"It's my own concoction. You'll love it. It's like a sweet Sangria, only with a bit more of a kick. If it gets chilly out there, it'll warm us up."

"Alcohol doesn't really warm you up you know."

"Yes, I know. But it has a way of heating things up," he said with a grin, "if you know what I mean."

She smiled over at him, "I know what you mean."

It was still light when they drove over the bridge and unloaded their gear at the boat ramp. You could see the sun over the west side of the island as it prepared to disappear into the edges of the marsh. They had maybe an hour of daylight followed by an hour of a twilight dusk before night would fall and the moon would be their only source of light.

They donned their life vests and crawled into their slightly elevated seats in the center of their kayaks. And, using their double-sided paddles, pushed off from the shore and paddled away from the bridge making their way into the waters of the Intracoastal. They stayed close to the marshy shore on the left side, each quietly concentrating on getting a comfortable rhythm going.

"Never thought I'd get back in this water and so close to the bridge this soon," she commented.

"Well, I appreciate you coming with me. Once it gets dark, I'll be at a loss to even find our way back."

"How can you be a cop if you can't see at night?"

"Oh, I can see to drive at night. But sometimes I have to use the bright lights in the communities that don't have street lamps."

"Which is almost all of them," she interjected.

He gave her a wry smile, "And I take a big flashlight everywhere I go." He produced a huge black flashlight that was about as long as three regular ones taped together.

"And then of course I use Braille."

"Braille?"

"Yeah, I reach out and touch everything 'til I find what I want. I'll show you later how that works." She looked over at him and he winked at her. She felt the flush of heat from her neck down to the tops of her thighs and something zinged in the pit of her stomach.

He pointed to a beautiful snowy egret standing perfectly still not ten feet from them. They both stopped paddling and just let their kayaks glide. The lone big eye facing them stared as they went by but the bird never moved a muscle. It was as if it was a plastic lawn ornament, until all at once, a fish entered its territory. Then, it swooped soundlessly down and deftly caught the fish in its beak. It was a special moment in time, like a first-hand glimpse into the world of Wild Kingdom, a chance to see nature in its most preserved and unbreeched state. They both looked at each other and smiled. No words were needed.

They paddled against the current for almost half an hour before they came to an area that opened up to the marshy fingers behind Sunset Beach and Bird Island. Here there were many options—little meandering branches that lead to sheltered coves and docks stretching out longer than football fields.

Michael had concluded that the only reason D. Duke's boat would be missing was if whoever took it had used it to transport himself and D. Duke's remains over to the area of the island where the lower part of his body had been found. If D. Duke had gone out in it by himself, his life vest wouldn't have been left in the wooden box at the end of his dock. He would have made sure he was wearing it. All of his neighbors had mentioned that D. Duke never went out on the water without it.

If what he suspected was true, that person would not have wanted to take it back. Why chance being seen returning it? And, forensically speaking, it could have a wealth of clues. No, whoever it was would probably have tried to hide it. The most likely way to dispose of it so it wouldn't easily be found would be to pull it up onto a marshy shore on the back side of one of these islands. Most john boats were either green or brown so they would blend in with the environment. And, unless somebody spotted it from the air, it could be years before it was found if it didn't get washed off the shore and trapped back in the currents of the coastal waters by a storm or hurricane.

Yes, he was convinced that if he had used the boat to take a body to the beach to bury it, he would have ditched the boat, possibly upside down to anchor it better, in the tall, thick reeds of the marshes. But where? There were so many places to look, and it wouldn't be easy in the dark, especially from the extremely low vantage point that the kayaks offered. He had an idea though.

"Hey, let's head over to the back of the island. We'll follow the path of the old burned up bridge over to the where the lagoon from Madd Inlet used to be."

"I have no idea what you're talking about, but lead on."

He paddled closer to her. "Many years ago there was a bridge connecting Bird Island to Sunset Beach. It burned down and the county or state, I forget which, wouldn't let them rebuild it. Some of the old pilings are still visible at low or mid tide. It started over near the end of Bay Street, you know where that is?"

"Is that the road that connects at the end of fortieth?"

"Yeah."

"Okay, I think I know where that is."

"Well, let's go around there and pull in behind where Madd Inlet used to be."

"Okay. Lead the way. It all looks like the same marsh to me from here."

Fifteen minutes later they were making their approach to the sandy shore just a few minutes walk from where the majority of D. Duke's body had been found.

Michael reached shore first and pulled his kayak up onto the shore. Then he walked into the water and yanked hers up beside his. He offered her his hand and she took it. They looked into each other's eyes while he slowly pulled her out of the kayak. Then, when they were both standing, only the width of the kayak

141

separating the two, he reached his other arm out, circled her waist and brought her up against his chest.

"I'm going to chance it," he whispered into the hair beside her ear.

"Chance what?"

"DEET," he said as his lips found hers and he thoroughly kissed her. His hands went from around her waist to around her bottom as he lifted her higher onto his chest. By the time the kiss was ended, her elbows were on his shoulders and she was looking down into his smiling face.

"What are you all smiles about?" she asked playfully.

"Just thinking about tonight."

"What about tonight?"

"You know, tonight's the night."

"Oh, no. Tonight's not the night. The other night was the night. You missed it."

"You said you were ready."

"That was then."

"You said to let you know as soon as I got back."

"Yeah, that was so I could find out how you did."

"No it wasn't."

"Yes it was. So tell me, how'd it go."

"I'll tell you how it went, but this conversation is not over. You gave me a rain check."

"You talking about golf?"

She grabbed the bag, and he grabbed the cooler and blanket. Then, as they walked up the beach, he reached out and squeezed her buttock, "No, I'm not talkin' about golf! What happened to the 'next time you get me in the back seat of your car, you'll have a hard time getting me out' speech?"

142

"Boy, you don't forget anything do you?"

"Not when it concerns you."

She smiled over at him and his heart melted. Was there ever a smile that was so seductive?

They found a flat spot to spread the blanket. As Michael knelt to straighten the corners he looked around. This was the area he used to come to to watch the mullets chase the shadows when the inlet was full with the tide. He was saddened that would never be again. He remembered the sun-warmed water filled with tiny, silver-flecked fish, and all the birds lined up from the ocean almost back to the Intracoastal, as the water rushed passed them, like a carryout line, while the lagoon filled and emptied twice each day. Things in nature changed, he had to remember that. And that wasn't always a bad thing. D. Duke's adamant feelings to see things stay the same, his desire to continually live in the past, came to mind, and he was reminded yet once again how very much alike they were in that regard.

"Hey, Morose Face, what's for dinner?" Cassie called from the other side of the blanket as she removed her water shoes and stretched her toes.

Michael did the same thing, using his to hold down the opposite corners of the blanket. "Was it that obvious what I was thinking?"

"I have no idea what you were thinking. But whatever it was, it wasn't good."

"I've been thinking about D. Duke a lot lately. Let's start eating and I'll fill you in on where I've been and what I've found out. And we're having PB and J fluffer-nutters with bacon, original Frito's, Hardees coleslaw, 'cause I didn't have the time to make it myself, fresh peach slices and Aunt Jemima's Easy Bake Coffee Cake, along with my very special, and-don't-even-bother-asking-me-for-the-recipe-cause-I-won't-give-it-to-you-Gatorgria."

They ate and talked and drank several glasses each of Michael's strange but very delicious concoction. Cassie could feel herself getting light-headed, but decided that wasn't such a bad feeling to have right now as she sat listening to Michael talk about the journal, D. Duke's house, and the clues that didn't add up to solve the mystery of his death.

The sandwich was surprisingly good for its simplicity and she told him so. He attributed it to his very own homemade peanut butter and the fresh strawberry preserves he'd bought at Holden Brothers as well as the fresh, no preservatives-added homemade bread he had baked a few days ago. She hadn't had marshmallow fluff in years and the bacon was a good quality, maple-smoked variety, cooked just as she like it, nice and crisp. What a novel thing this was, to have a boyfriend who actually liked to cook.

The sun was practically all the way down now on this side of the island and the rioting colors fanning out in front of them, as they faced west, were absolutely beautiful. It was a sunset worthy of painting. He grabbed her hand and stood up, pulling her up with him. "Before it gets dark, let's see if we can spot that boat. C'mon. Just leave everything here, we'll come back."

He pulled her behind him as he raced up a dune on the Bird Island side.

"Hey! Nobody's allowed on the dunes!"

"This is police business. We need to find the highest vantage point. C'mon," he said as he pulled her up to join him. The sand crumbled under their feet as they dug into the side of the dune, trying to get to the top. When they finally reached the summit, they gazed at the vista. Cassie was the first to speak, "It's magnificent."

And it truly was. The sun was setting and the colors were spreading out and diminishing all across the horizon. From the top of the dune they had a back drop of soft pastels: mauves, violets, and rosy pinks with streaks of vivid orange against the sandy white color of the dunes with their off-white feathery plumes, set one behind the other throughout the interior of the island. On the outer edges of the island, emerald green strips where interspersed over the marshes and beyond them was the greenish-blue of the ocean where it met the Intracoastal at Little River Inlet. A few boats were in the inlet, splashing the white foam of their wakes onto the large gray boulders of the jetty. It was a perfect picture, and as they both stood there absorbing it, Michael put his arm around Cassie's shoulder. "It just does not get any better than this," he whispered. "A gorgeous sunset on a picturesque island with a beautiful woman by my side."

"Yeah," she murmured, "a wonderful peanut butter and jelly dinner, all you-can-drink kick-a-poo juice..."

"Kick-a-poo juice!" he exclaimed, then tousled her already wind-blown hair. "How dare you?" he asked as he bent low and picked her up. His mouth claimed hers before he had her snuggled firmly up against his chest. His kiss was passionate and demanding as he tasted the wine and peanut butter flavors still lingering in her mouth. He loved peanut butter and he couldn't get enough of the taste as his tongue licked and sampled her mouth. Or was it the taste of her that he just couldn't get enough of? He lowered her until her face was inches from his then he met her eyes with his dark smoldering ones. He was in the process of setting her back on her feet when something caught the corner of his eye. He turned his head quickly to catch it again. There on the right, way over to the right, on the opposite side from where they were, something was glinting in the last rays of the sun. Just a tiny spark of silver, he squinted and looked closer.

"Eureka," he murmured softly. "I think we found it."

Cassie, still mesmerized by his deep kiss, turned to look where he was looking. At first, she didn't see anything but sand and marsh, and then she saw it too. There, jutting out from under what looked from here like a thick strip of green, was the underside of a boat. The silver-gray of an aluminum boat that had been painted green, but not recently enough to keep it camouflaged against the reflecting rays of the setting sun, was barely visible in the faint light.

"Well, I'll be. You are detective material after all," she said solicitously as she patted him on the arm.

He gave her a crooked grin. "Gee thanks, that means so much coming from you."

"You'd better be nice to me . . . it's getting dark."

His voice became very husky, "You'd better be nice to *me*... it's getting dark."

They stood looking into each other's eyes for what could have been minutes or seconds as time seemed to stand still before he almost savagely pulled her to him and crushed her lips under his with such fervor that she felt her knees waffle. His powerful arms held her tight against his chest while his lips ravished hers, arousing them both to an undeniable passion.

"Cassie . . ." the word was slurred as his mouth left hers and moved to her jaw where his tongue started to trace a pathway to her ear. He found that he had become immune to the taste of her bug spray. Either that, or he already had so much on his tongue, that it didn't matter anymore.

Once his tongue reached her ear, the heat from his mouth, joined with the probing tip of his tongue in her small whorl, caused her senses to reel and she felt herself melting right into his arms.

He felt it too, and it gave him renewed energy and a feeling of raw power just knowing she was overcome by him, that she was not as invincible as she seemed to be to his touch, to his lips. He groaned from the sheer pleasure of having her here, melting against him like she was just so much hot wax. As her body softened to his, his hardened to hers and even as his hands moved to her shoulders to separate them, he knew their bodies would soon be joining together.

His breath was harsh and raspy as he propelled her down off the dune and back to the blanket. Looking deeply into her eyes, as he led her backwards towards the blanket, he purred, Speak now, before I get you on that blanket, if you've changed your mind."

Cassie's eyes opened wide because there was no denying what he was talking about doing. And he was going to be doing it right here and right now, unless she stopped him.

"Last chance, Cass," he said as her heel touched the edge of the blanket. His eyes were hot and penetrating and he was totally focused on her face as he stood next to her and began unbuttoning her shirt.

She swallowed and looked back into his face, seeing the determination in his tightly clenched jaw, defying her to deny him.

But she didn't want to deny him. She took her hand and caressed the hardened planes of his face, trying to soothe the dam of passion he was holding back, until he knew it was safe to let it go. That single soft touch of her palm against his rough-hewn cheek told him he could let go now, he could have her. And have her, he would. A guttural groan escaped his lips as her shirt fell open. The lacy bra she was wearing covered only the bottom curves of her breasts, the top portion was scalloped to cover just the very center, where the hardened nipples were just visible beneath the lace. They were jutting against the open eyelet of the lacy pattern.

He'd seen her breasts before, but only fleetingly and never like this. His hands covered the material, cupping her while his thumbs delved under and pulled the material away from the tips. As soon as the cooling night air hit them, they shriveled into even harder and tighter buds. Then she moaned, and he was lost.

He pulled her shirt off and reached behind her for the fasteners to her bra. He popped both eyelets off the hooks and gently dragging his hands up to her shoulders, he pulled the straps down and off of her arms. He tossed her bra on the blanket where he'd already tossed her shirt.

She stood looking up at him while he stood looking down at her. It unnerved her to have him staring at her like this, but it was quite obvious he wasn't going to stop. The look on his face was intense, like he was studying something complicated, something that had his complete and undivided attention.

"You are so beautiful, so perfectly formed," he whispered.

She didn't know whether she was supposed to say thank you or not. After all, that was a compliment. But she didn't want to interrupt him; he seemed so lost in thought, almost like she wasn't even there. But of course she was there—he was staring at her bared chest and she was unabashedly letting him!

It was then that he reached for her hand and carried it up to his bared throat. "Undress me," he said simply as he continued to stare at her, and not her exactly, just her chest.

She started with the top button and with each one she undid, she exposed more and more of his thickly-matted chest. When she reached his navel, and had to pull the shirt out of his pants, there was only one button left. She undid it and opened his shirt all the way.

"Remove it."

She slid her hands up his chest and over his shoulders, removing his shirt as her hands came down his arms. As soon as he was shirtless too, he put his hands on her shoulders and pulled her into his chest. The sensation arcing through her at the touch of his naked chest against her bared breasts was of a torch fire being touched to a dry haystack. Flames went everywhere as their bodies clung. He reached between them and took a hardened peak between his thumb and forefinger and lightly pinching it together, he rubbed her engorged nipple over his flat one. His throaty, uncontrolled groan of extreme pleasure sent ripples of pleasure through her and she moved with her hand to do the same with her other nipple and his other nipple. She could tell by his reaction that he was no longer in his right mind. He fell to his knees on the edge of the blanket, taking her with him. Then, as they knelt together, he took her mouth with his as his hands felt for and found the closure for her jeans. He had them unbuttoned, unzipped and shucked down to her knees before she had a chance to catch her breath. He then insinuated his hand between her thighs, separating them slightly as he groped with his other hand to pull down her panties.

She was kneeling in front of him, her breasts mingling with his chest hairs, her lips being sucked and licked by his and now his hand was between her thighs, spreading them so he could have access to her womanhood. And he wasn't going fast enough for her. She wanted to be prone on the blanket, her thighs wide, her knees bent with him lying between them, his hardness thrusting repeatedly into her softness. When she felt a finger spread her lips and enter her, she gasped and collapsed onto his hand. Her knees did not want to support her anymore, they wanted to be spread wide, facing the stars that were just starting to come out.

"Oh, honey," he crooned, "you feel so good. Ahhh, you're so wet."

His lips dragged down the column of her throat to her chest and then latched onto a nipple. As he sucked and tongued it, she grasped his head and held it there. She arched herself into the hand that was cupping her and even though his finger was still deeply embedded in her, it wasn't enough. She needed more. And she needed it now. She removed a hand from the back of his head and moved it down feeling for his belt buckle and zipper. He made some more moaning sounds while he continued to suckle her but didn't stop her. When she kept fumbling with the belt buckle, his hand joined hers there and he softly moved it aside. While he quickly undid the buckle and then unzipped his pants, he was still pulling on a nipple with his mouth and thrusting a finger in and out of her.

As soon as he had freed himself, his hand found hers again and he covered his erection with her hand. She timidly stroked it with her fingertips and he made a sound akin to sobbing. He was practically mewling by the time she had worked her hand lower and cupped his balls. His sizable erection was thick and pulsing and when she used her other hand to caress his swaying sacs at the same time, he keened and pushed her down onto the blanket.

"You remember your journal entry, 'ready or not, here I come?' " he asked as he stood up, fished around in a pocket and then removed his pants.

"Yes," she said looking up at him as he looked down at her while she took her pants and panties all the way off.

"Well, ready or not, let's come together."

She admired his ruggedly handsome face and then turned her attention to his big hands while he unrolled the condom over his breathtaking erection.

He knelt between her legs, placed the tip of his penis against her opening and pushed. She readily accepted him into her body as he settled himself on top of her.

For several moments neither one moved, they just stared into each other's eyes, the light of the slow-rising moon just enough to see by. "You feel good wrapped around me," he murmured into her ear just before he started thrusting into her. Gently, he moved in and out, trying different angles, until he could tell by her breathing that he'd found one that she liked. Then he reached under her and gripped her buttocks, and as he thrust into her he pulled her even closer to him. He seated himself deeply into her, rubbing the length of him up and down her smooth, slick welcoming shaft as he pressed the rest of his body up against hers. He felt her quicken and start to arch then she frantically pulled him up against her, her fingers deeply embedding themselves into his buttocks and her legs climbing high on his back. With the beginnings of a small shudder, she surrendered herself to him and he took her the rest of the way, holding himself tightly against her as she pulsed and quivered away from him before resignedly fluttering back. The whole time he had been watching the expressions change on her face and now he could not contain his own explosion as he saw the twisted agony on her face instantly change to one of incredible, awed wonder and it sent him jettisoning out of the universe. And when it was over, he didn't know how he'd get back. It had taken so much out of him.

His head fell beside hers on the blanket and for several moments she thought he'd fallen asleep. She was staring up at the stars, listening to his breathing as it evened out when he finally lifted his head and smiled down at her.

"Ahhh. You northern girls who like to play with toys in the sand. This southern boy, just can't keep up with you."

She smiled up at him. "I think you kept up just fine."

He leaned down and kissed her on the shoulder. "I think I'd do a lot better if you wouldn't keep trying to poison me with DEET." He brushed his lips against the hairs on his forearm, "I can sure see why the bugs don't like that stuff."

He gingerly lifted himself off of her and went to discreetly dispose of the condom. It was completely dark now, and even though the moon was out, it wasn't full and clouds were passing in and out of the moonbeams.

"I guess we'd better head back, I think we've accomplished all we're going to tonight."

"Gee, thanks!"

"I didn't mean it like that! I meant the boat."

"Oh yeah, the boat."

"Yeah, the reason we came all the way out here, remember?"

"Well, I got a little distracted."

"Like I didn't?"

"Well, actually, you started it."

"You're not going to get me to regret that."

"Well, that's nice to know."

He came over and wrapped his arms around her, "No, *you're* nice to know."

She blushed and turned away to button up her shirt. "So what about the boat?"

"I'll get somebody to pick it up tomorrow. It's too buggy now and besides I'd like to see if we can preserve as much evidence as possible. There should be fingerprints, hair, clothing threads, any number of things we can use if we don't contaminate the field too much."

Cassie picked up all their things and folded the blanket while he finished dressing.

"I had a wonderful time here; it's beautiful. Can we come back again, sometime?" she asked.

"Count on it." He walked over and softly stroked her cheek, "I had a most marvelous time, too," he said as he leaned down and lightly kissed her.

She reached up and rubbed his cheek, "I'm glad you shaved before I came over."

He grimaced, "Have to, unless you need an exfoliating or dermabrasion treatment."

She smiled back at him, "No thank you, I'd prefer to come out of our love making sessions with my skin still intact."

"Hmm . . . our love making sessions? That means there'll be more?"

"Oh, I wouldn't force you or anything," she teased.

"That's good, 'cause I wouldn't want to be forced into that kind of thing," he dead panned.

"Yeah, I'll just bet."

He chuckled as he bent to pick up their things, "Just wear something leather next time we come back."

She followed along behind him carrying the blanket, "Yeah, I'll be sure to do that."

Michael helped her into her kayak and pushed her off. She waited for him to come alongside and then together they paddled along the marshy edges until they were back in the slow, breeze-driven currents of the Intracoastal.

Chapter 13

Cassie sat on the pastel-striped sectional sofa and looked out to the Carolina room and beyond, to the view of the sixth hole of the Maples course. She had been sitting here for the better part of an hour trying to make up her mind. But she found that her mind kept wandering back to last night, to Bird Island, and the blanket on the beach, and Michael. She had taken him home and he had kissed her good night after unloading his kayak. He hadn't said when he'd see her again and he hadn't said anything about what he was feeling. She felt almost like a conquest. A project conquered. A few nights ago, he'd told her that he thought he was falling in love with her. What had happened? Had he stopped falling? Had he caught himself before he'd actually fallen into it?

She shook her head and forced herself to think of the matter at hand. After all, how long could she stall Harley, who was in the kitchen making a few calls. This was the third time she'd asked to see this particular unit and they both knew that out of all the places he'd shown her, this one had touched something in her. From the moment they'd pulled up to the front door the very first time, she'd felt at home here.

She was sitting in the living room of a townhouse in a small section of Sea Trail called The Woods, unit D4 to be exact. The Woods was a cluster of townhouses stuck right in the middle of the Live Oaks section, which was all single family homes. Jenny and Colin lived in Live Oaks; their house was just a short

156

walk away. There was something quaint about the private, little community bordered on all sides by homes three times the size of the townhouses. Cassie had immediately liked the secluded "cottage in the woods" feeling that the landscaping provided. Fully mature trees had been left everywhere. There were even a few in the middle of the parking lot that had red reflectors sunk into their bark so you wouldn't hit them as you drove around them at night.

Inside, this end unit was surprisingly roomy. There was a nice size kitchen with practically new looking appliances and cabinets. The tile floor sparkled in the light coming in from the window over the sink. A small table with two chairs sat in a little alcove in front of shuttered closet doors that housed the washer and dryer. There was a long counter separating the kitchen from the dining room and then there was the living room with its cathedral ceiling where she now sat staring into space. She stood up and opened the sliding glass doors that separated the living room from the glassed-in Carolina room. She stepped out into the sunny room with its gorgeous view of the golf course.

The unit was being sold as is, completely furnished. The owners were living in New Jersey and didn't even want to bother with coming down to pack what few personal items there were. So everything would be hers: the beachy rattan furniture her fingers were now stroking, the beautiful massive cherry bedroom furniture in the master bedroom, the books on the three-piece honey oak wall unit in the living room, all the dishes, pots and pans; everything down to the box of Cheerios in the well-stocked pantry. There were more spice jars than she knew what to do with, but she had no doubt that Michael was familiar with each and every one. She'd only need to bring her clothes. It was perfect for her and she knew it. So why was she hesitating?

She knew the answer—it was a permanent commitment to a place. Even though she'd spent four years settled into an apartment on campus when she'd been in college—then she'd only been renting, she could have left at anytime. This time she would be buying, owning her own home that she'd be responsible for maintaining. She would be here for at least three years. Would she be happy here? She looked around one more time and then went to join Harley in the kitchen.

"Okay. I'll take it."

He looked up from the cell phone that he was punching buttons on, "Really?" he asked with a big smile.

She smiled back at him, "Really. Don't you think it's about time? You must've shown me twenty places."

"I didn't mind one single bit. Let's go back to my office. I'll get a contract drawn up and then we can go out on the town to celebrate."

"I can't. I have to get back. I have some work I have to do tonight." She was lying to him. There was no work, but she couldn't very well tell him that she had to get back home to wait for a call that she might not get—Michael's call.

"Okay, I guess I'll have to take another rain check, but now that you're going to be a resident of North Carolina, you're gonna have to switch your priorities around a little bit. All work and no play is no good.

158

You're too fine a woman to be workin' day and night. The nights should be reserved for playin', and I want you to play with me a little." He tried to gather her up into his arms, but she turned away. "Harley, it's not that way with us."

"Well, it sure could be if you'd just give me a chance!" he wailed.

"I'm not interested in getting into a relationship right now." What the hell was she saying? She damn sure was, it just wasn't with him.

He looked at her quizzically for a moment and then arched an eyebrow at her, "You ain't gay or anything are ya? I ain't never seen a woman shy away from my advances like you do."

She laughed heartily and went back to the Carolina room to close the jalousied windows she'd opened and to lock the sliding door. "No, I'm not a lesbian." Then, not wanting to hurt his feelings by telling him that his advances turned her off, she added, "I think we should just remain friends until all our business dealings are over with and then we'll go from there. My daddy always says that you shouldn't mix business with pleasure."

Well, that seemed to appease him. He smiled and nodded, "My daddy told me that, too. Course I never listen to him, and he never listens to himself. He's on his fourth wife now, and all of them were agents for him before he married 'em."

"Whoa. That's not a good track record."

"No. It's probably why I haven't settled down with anybody by now. But I'm thinkin' that you could be a good candidate."

She feigned a smile for him, "Thanks."

"No, I'm serious. You and me, we could have a real good thing."

She shook her head, "I think I'd better listen to my daddy. Let's just wait 'til after we've closed on this townhouse, then we'll go out and celebrate."

"Yeah," he said with a lascivious grin, "then we'll celebrate."

Good God, where did this guy get all his gall from? It was everything she could do to keep from laughing in his face. She walked out of the townhouse and got into her Jimmy. Thank God, she'd insisted that they meet here. "Harley, I'll stop by your office tomorrow to sign the contract."

"Don't you want to negotiate?"

"I think what they're asking is a fair price. The unit is immaculate and they've kept up on all the maintenance. They should be rewarded for that. Just try to get a settlement date as soon as you can, I'm already pre-approved for a loan."

"You sure make it easy for a guy."

Yeah, she thought, I sure made it easy for Michael. What was she going to do if he didn't call? " 'Night Harley," she said as she started the Jimmy.

"See ya tomorrow at the office, Cass."

Cass. Michael was the only one she wanted to call her Cass.

When Cassie came around the curve to pull into the driveway, she realized that she hadn't needed to worry quite so much about getting a phone call from Michael. There he was in the center of the driveway playing basketball with Paisley and Colin. Jenny was sitting on the top porch step idly stroking Taffy who was flipped over onto her back enjoying a belly rub. As soon as she

160

stepped out of the Jimmy, Taffy leapt off the porch and came to investigate. Cassie bent low to pet her as Michael walked over to her.

"Where ya been?"

"Didn't Jenny tell you?"

"No, I was just told that you weren't here but they were expecting you at any minute, so I didn't ask. I just saw Harley's 'vette go by, so I can only assume you were somewhere with him."

"Yup. Just bought a townhouse with a gorgeous view of the Maples sixth hole."

Michael just stared at her with consternation written all over his face. He was having a hard time deciding exactly how he felt about all this. On the one hand, he should be happy that she was, in effect, making Sunset Beach her permanent home. But on the other hand, her making such a big decision without even talking it over with him, made their budding relationship seem trivial. What if, after a few months, he decided to ask her to come live with him, what then?

He summoned a small smile, "Oh that's nice. Where?"

"Just around the corner," she pointed in the direction she had just come from, "at the bottom of this street, take a left, and I'm just about in the middle of The Woods section."

"Well, congratulations. You seem very happy about it."

"I am. It's a nice little place, wait 'til you see it."

"And when will that be?"

"Just a few weeks, I hope."

"I'll help you move in."

"Well, I really won't need much help. It's already completely furnished. And, I didn't bring very much down with me, just a few suitcases and some books."

"Oh," he said sounding a little under appreciated.

Cassie picked up on his feelings of rejection right away and said, "But there is something you can do to help."

"Yeah? What's that?"

She stood on tiptoe and whispered into his ear, "You could fix the first dinner in my new house and then help me check out the bed springs of my new mattress."

He gave her a big grin and all the uncertainty of her completely independent decision was wiped out of his eyes. "Now that's something I can look forward to."

Cassie took in his sweat-soaked T-shirt that was outlining his well formed muscles and the tight jeans molding to his thighs, "Yeah, me too."

"Did they get D. Duke's boat today?"

"Yup. I got a fax this afternoon from I.D. in Bolivia, one of the guys wants to know if he can get it for a good price when they're done with it."

"What'd you tell him?"

"It's evidence. It could be years before it's released and even then, I have no idea who it will belong to."

Cassie looked over at the small group playing one-on-one under the basketball hoop, "So who's winning?" she asked, tilting her head over at Colin who was chugging down a large glass of water.

Sheepishly, he ducked his head and murmured, "Paisley."

Cassie laughed and walked up to join the others on the porch. After telling everybody about her new place, she ran inside to change before joining the basketball game. When the mosquitoes were out in full force, and they couldn't manage to move off of a tied score, they called it quits. Cassie was hungry and so was Paisley, so Jenny and Michael whipped up a homemade pizza using a Bobboli crust. Then they all sat around the low country dining room table and played Phase Ten until it was finished baking. Michael had to explain to Cassie that they were indeed baking the pizza, not cooking it as she had said. After all, it was a pizza *pie*. She had stuck her tongue out at him and he had dramatically raised one eyebrow at her, reminding her he had a use for that tongue. After they had all eaten their fill, Cassie walked Michael out to the front porch to say good night.

He placed her chin in the palm of his hand and he huskily murmured, "I want to see you again."

"You're seeing me now," she said coyly.

"I mean *see* you."

"*See* me?"

"All right, it's more like I want to *feel* you, rather than *see* you then."

"*Feel* me?" she asked innocently.

He bent and kissed her adorable lips. "Yes, I want to feel you, every part of you."

"Any places in particular?"

"Oh yes. Several places in particular."

"Care to name them?" she asked as she returned his light kisses.

"Let's just say those parts that make you feminine instead of masculine."

"Oh, you want to stroke my superior brain."

He reached down between their bodies and cupped her womanhood. "If that's what you call this."

"Well, it is the part that rules my thoughts sometimes."

His hands went around to her bottom and he pulled her in close to him. She could feel the swell of him against her hip, "I see your thoughts are being taken over by your lower brain, too."

"I have only one brain when you're around."

"Single-minded, huh?"

"I am right now." He kissed her along the line of her jaw until he reached her ear, where he breathily whispered, "I want to sheath myself with you. I want to feel my cock buried deep inside you. In short, I want to fuck you. Have I made myself clear yet?"

She drew in a deep breath, his words causing her to tremble inside. "Quite clear."

"When, then?"

"Saturday."

"Too long. I can't wait that long."

"Is tomorrow night soon enough?"

"Not really, but I guess it'll have to do," he said as he slowly released her.

"I probably won't leave the site until late."

"I don't care. Just come over to my house when you're done."

"I'll have to clean up first."

"I have soap. I have water. I'll clean you." The dark intensity of his eyes burned into her and as she envisioned him ministering to her in his shower, she felt the heat in her core melt her upper thighs.

"Ohhh," she said as she grabbed for his shoulders to keep from swooning backward.

He held her up and chuckled, "In fact, I'll lick you clean," he said then bent to kiss her softly on her parted lips, "starting here." His tongue traced her jaw line to her ear then he proceeded to lick the whorls of her ear. All Cassie could do was softly moan as he caressed her little canal with his pointed, warm tongue and steamy breath.

When he was sure she couldn't stand up on her own, he propped her up against the door and backed away from her.

"Tomorrow," he said simply.

"Tomorrow," she agreed and watched him as he got into his car and backed out of the driveway.

Chapter 14

Michael was driving back from D. Duke's bank, the bank that D. Duke had used for his savings account, mortgage loan, and safety deposit box when the call came out, the call that was the most dreaded. Fire on the island. He was just leaving the light at Ocean Isle Beach, about three miles away from the Seaside intersection and the main shopping area of Sunset Beach, which was another two miles from the bridge. He switched on his siren and bar light and strained to hear the crackling conversation as the dispatcher relayed the situation at the bridge. He listened helplessly as he heard the dispatcher report that the bridge was open to boat traffic. He heard the anguish in the man's voice as he alerted them to the fact that the bridge tender couldn't close it yet, that there was a huge barge carrying an old drawbridge for a resort being built further south. And it wasn't anywhere near clear of the fenders yet.

Michael could hear the sirens from the fire trucks both through the radio and from outside his window as he sped by the town hall on his way to the island. Behind him, he could see the fire truck for Ocean Isle as it responded. He moved out of the way, knowing that it wouldn't do any good to let it pass. From the frantic sounds on the radio it sounded like it would be a good ten minutes before the engines could get over to the island and everyone was in an uproar. The noise from the air horn was still vibrating in his ears when he joined the motorcade waiting for the bridge to swing closed behind the slow moving barge.

The bridge operator was making the small control house chase the big wake being made by the barge. It wasn't a safe distance but you could see that every effort was being made to make the connection as soon as physically possible. As soon as the bridge swung in line with the road, the gates went up and the fire trucks rumbled over. It was high tide and the usual caution taken in the center was abandoned for the scant seconds it would ultimately save.

As soon as the fire fighting equipment was on its way down the causeway, Michael followed. He knew exactly where the house was that was burning. He'd driven by it many times over the years. It was front row on the east end, maybe eight or nine years old. He could picture the intricately carved plaque attached to the creamy beige paint that proclaimed this piece of paradise too good to be believed, hence it was dubbed, "Virtual Reality."

By the time he pulled his cruiser in line behind all the other emergency vehicles on the narrow grass shoulder, he knew they'd lost the chance that they'd had to contain it. The first few minutes in a fire are the most important, and these first few minutes had been wasted waiting to get over to the island. The house that was on fire was a duplex, one side being the mirror image of the other. The right side was completely engulfed with flames coming out of the windows and through the roof, the left side had smoke pouring out. Within minutes, high walls of water were cascading down in huge streams, seemingly doing little to appease the hungry, lapping tongues. Voices crackled over loudspeakers and hoses were turned to houses bordering on either side. Michael could hear the splintering sounds of wood being cleaved and pulled apart as the firemen tried to collapse a wall.

Six firemen had immediately entered the burning building, hopping off the trucks as they'd pulled up and now they were all returning, four of them with their arms full.

Over by an ambulance a small bundle in a blanket was being unwrapped by two paramedics as a sobbing and screaming mother looked on. Her husband was trying to hold onto her but she was fighting him to get away. On the ground were two other small bodies, now covered with blankets.

Two hours later they finally had the fire out. They had lost the two buildings on either side. But the worst horror of all was that they had lost three children, their twenty-three-year-old nanny, and the family's beloved Yorkshire terrier. The parents of the children had been walking on the pier while their nanny was fixing lunch for the children. She was frying bacon for BLTs on the stove when the grease caught fire. She panicked and tried to carry the burning pan to the sink. She dropped it, spreading the flaming grease to the cabinets and wooden floor and from there to the stairs leading to the bedrooms where the children were playing. The nanny spent too much time trying to put the fire out before calling 911. Then it was too late to get the children or herself out. In typical rental fashion, the unit has been rented to two families. But in this case, a unit designed to sleep eight, was actually housing twelve. Two sisters with their husbands and their parents, five children, one nanny and a forbidden pet—pets were not allowed in the rental units, but people sneaked them in all the time. The two other children had accompanied their parents and grandparents to Southport for the day or they might have perished also.

When Michael was asked to help fingerprint the dead children for identification records, he was so overcome with grief for the youngsters that he could not control his tears. The gut wrenching sobs coming from the parents tore into his soul, and he knew that he would never be the same. The memory of this day would haunt him forever; it caused the blood in his veins to feel like ice. These parents had done nothing wrong. They had made sure their children had adult supervision. They had taken them to a family-oriented beach for a wholesome vacation. They had done everything possible to ensure their safety except they hadn't counted on the "quaint" bridge at Sunset Beach to let them down when they needed it most.

Later, Michael would find out that the barge carrying the bridge section had been scheduled to go through the Sunset Beach swing bridge during the night, but it had run aground on a shoal in the middle of the Intracoastal at low tide so they'd had to wait for high tide to get it moving again. The ten minutes the fire trucks had waited at the bridge could be blamed on the tide, but as Michael recited the three children's names in his head, he amended that thought. The children's deaths and that of their nanny could really only be blamed on one thing, and that was the bridge. For the first time, he wished that things had been different a decade ago, and that the people who had opposed the new bridge had had the experience of holding a dead baby in their arms, one that had died from smoke inhalation, before presenting their petitions.

Then his thoughts reverted to Cassie and he remembered that without the old bridge, he might never have met her. As those thoughts surfaced, he quickly banished them. Hell, as much as he liked her and desired her, he would certainly have traded the opportunity to ever get to know her for those four innocent lives. Maybe he could have met her some other way, he thought with a grin. Surely that could have happened. A lot of people from Virginia come down here all the time. But it was moot; all his thinking wouldn't change a damn thing. And now, there were four lives that would never see the new bridge, never love or be loved, never worry about whether it was high or low tide.

Since he was on the island, he went to D. Duke's house to find the papers the lady at the bank had talked about. He had been right about the key. It did belong to a safety deposit box at BB&T. But there had been nothing in it. Nothing except a ten dollar bill that had the rare 'Silver Certificate' embossed at the top instead of the typical 'Federal Reserve Note.' He found out that the exact same amount of money was deposited into D. Duke's savings account every month, and the bank had verified that it was from Social Security. There was over forty thousand dollars in a money market account. It had been explained to him by the banker, that D. Duke had signed a reverse mortgage almost ten years ago and that he was still living off of the proceeds when he'd died. Nothing really unusual here, except that the woman had insisted that D. Duke took some official looking papers out of his safety deposit box the day he died. She showed Michael D. Duke's signature card, and sure enough, he had been there that day. She hadn't seen what the papers were, but she thought they looked legal somehow. So here he was, back at D. Duke's, looking for papers that could be anything, or knowing D. Duke, nothing.

Using the key he kept in his cruiser, he let himself in. Again, he was confronted with that 'old man' smell, and again, he smiled and thought of his late grandfather. After fifteen minutes of looking everywhere he could think of, he still hadn't found any papers having any significance to anything. He did find a stack of old newsletters from the property owners opposing the bridge in the bottom of a closet, and he mentally made a note to go see some of the people who had been opposed to the new bridge from the very beginning. But he knew that today was not the day he should talk to anybody who had been pivotal in halting the construction of the bridge ten years ago.

He walked around the beach house trying to put his brain on auto pilot, to see if maybe his subconscious could pick up on something his conscious mind was rejecting or overlooking. He walked out on the back deck and looked out over the island. He wondered how much time D. Duke had spent out here over the years, admiring the view, watching the waves lapping against the shore and seeing the boats go by. He looked down at the yard below and, slanting his head to the left, he tried to figure out just what it was he was seeing directly below. He moved back and forth along the rail until he finally figured out what it was. Grabbing the wooden handrail he ran down the steps to the small patio and out onto the lawn. He knew what it was now, but why was it here? Was it some kind of lawn decoration or what?

It certainly was huge, and Michael wondered just where the hell D. Duke had gotten it. Then suddenly he remembered where there were two others just like it and he realized that he didn't know why they were there either. It was, by far, one of the oldest propellers he'd ever seen. It stood almost as high as his waist. He looked down at the ground. Hell, if it hadn't been sunk into the ground, it would probably come to his chest. It had a long a shaft attached to it. There were two just like it on Beach Drive. They sat side by side on an empty lot on the Intracoastal side, and he'd always wondered why they were there. Randomly covered with what looked like a greenish film, they were a light dirty brown just like this one. Bronze that had oxidized, he surmised. He looked back up at the deck and then at the angle of the propeller blade aiming up at the cloudless blue sky. Just maybe . . . it was not likely that you could fall right onto this, but if you were thrown or jumped out, you could conceivably hit this huge monstrosity on your way down.

He went back up to the deck and looked down again. It was about fifteen feet from the railing to the top of the propeller. Would that be enough distance to create the force needed to sever a man's head? Was the propeller sharp enough? He'd seen some field glasses on top of the refrigerator so he went inside to get them. Then he adjusted the focus until he had zoomed in on the propeller blade, magnifying the edge. He just couldn't tell. Hell, maybe the copper and tin alloy was still sharp enough. It had rained since the night of D. Duke's death, but maybe there was still some forensic evidence on the blade, if that was indeed the case. Heck, at least he had something to question. He went back inside and called the chief.

After the events on the island today, he shouldn't have been surprised that he couldn't hook up with him. So he called the coroner directly and agreed to meet him in an hour. He went over to lock the sliding glass door leading to the deck and out of the corner of his eye he could just make out the burned roof of the beach house where four people had died today. He shook his head and turned into the room saying out loud, "You helped do this D. Duke. You helped kill those kids. What do you have to say for yourself?" He stood there half expecting to get an answer before slamming out the front door. He didn't even bother locking the door figuring that nobody wanted that old man's junk anyway.

The station house was as somber as a tomb as everybody stayed around their own desks, trying to get their minds around the tragic events of the day. When it was time, he met the coroner and watched as he swabbed the propeller blade. As they both stood on the deck looking down they both agreed that it was possible for a man to be dropped onto it and have his head severed. If he jumped, the same thing could happen, but he would have had to go head first to hit right. So then what happened? Did the head roll down the sloping lawn into the Intracoastal while the body found its way to be buried on the beach?

Michael said he'd call for the test results in a few days and then locked up after the coroner left. As he went down the front stairs, he noticed a tabby cat sitting on the front lawn looking up at the house. He made his way to the cruiser without disturbing it and then sat in the car until the cat moved on. He followed it with his eyes as it lightly pranced down the twilight-lit street until he couldn't see it anymore, then he slowly drove down the street trying to see where it went. He lost it when it went between two houses and scurried behind some bushes.

This island, like all coastal islands, had more feral cats than it needed or wanted. It was a never ending battle. Twice a year as many as could be caught were taken to vets on the mainland to be neutered and then returned to the island. It helped to keep the population down, but there were still more cats than there were homes for them.

The journal entry had said, "Ask about the cats." *Who* was he supposed to ask about the cats? *What* was he supposed to ask about the cats? *Why* was he supposed to ask about the cats? Maybe there was a play on words about cats? Could she have meant Katz? Was there anybody on the island named Katz? Had anybody rented that week named Katz? Was he going crazy? Yes, he decided he was. He drove back to the station, checked out and went home. At least he had something to look forward to tonight. Cassie was going to be coming over and he couldn't wait to see her. When he realized that he was looking forward to talking to her and telling her about his day more than stripping her down and making love to her, he decided that he was indeed going crazy.

Chapter 15

It was almost nine o'clock when Cassie knocked on Michael's front door. He opened it and then they both silently reached for each other, sharing a big long hug that was more indicative of the horrible day they'd each had rather than their feelings for each other. Michael was the first to pull away, though he still kept his hands gripped on her upper arms. He pulled her into the house and kicked the door shut with his foot.

"You smell nice. Who cleaned you up?"

"Harley."

He gripped her arms even tighter, "Harley?" he asked with disbelief. The sudden rush of an emotion akin to jealousy surfaced and he had to mentally shove it aside.

"Oh, you said cleaned me up, not cleaned me out," she replied innocently.

"Yeah," he said, loosening his grip and eyeing her closely. "I said, who cleaned you up, not out."

"*I* cleaned myself up. And I also signed a contract on the townhouse with Harley's company, and then *they* cleaned me out. I gave them twenty-five thousand dollars as a down payment, so my savings account is pretty much cleaned out."

"Well, I sure am glad you clarified that. I wasn't very happy with the thought that Harley had been touching your body. You can give him all the money you want, just don't ever let me hear that you've given him this body." As if to emphasize the body he was referring to, he possessively grabbed her and pulled her

175

body in close to his as his hands roamed freely over her back, hips and buttocks. Then he bent his head and his mouth descended to hers, his lips full and warm as they searched out hers.

He kissed her deeply, letting his tongue have its way as it chased hers around the inside of her hot mouth. And instantly, his body wanted hers under his, his granite hardness pumping vigorously into her yielding softness. But he wasn't about to jump her bones the minute she came through the door, he respected her too much for that. He'd wait until he could at least maneuver her over to the sofa in the family room before he stripped her and plowed into her. But even as his body responded to his thoughts, his emotions took over and he realized that he wanted Cassie in a way that was more than primal, more than just physical. He wanted her to be close and comforting and nurturing. However, he had no idea how to get to that soft womanly side. Somehow, that part of a relationship had always been elusive for him.

Cassie, on the other hand, knew exactly what was expected of her. By now the whole town knew about the tragedy that had occurred on the beach and they were all trying to cope with their feelings. Certainly after Michael's direct involvement, he would be grieving even more. With an instinct as old as time, she took his hand in hers and led him over to the satiny, floral-patterned sofa. She sat down and pulled him down beside her. Then she directed him to stretch out and put his stocking feet over the edge while she forced his head into her lap. Softly, she combed his thick hair with her widely-spaced fingers, going over and over the same areas as she tentatively touched his face with the fingertips from her other hand, smoothing out the lines between his brows while she encouraged him to talk.

"How awful it must have been for you to hold that tiny lifeless baby."

"It was awful. But it was even worse to touch the four-year-old little girl. When I had to put her fingers on the ink pad and then press them on the paper, it was the hardest thing I've ever had to do. Her father was holding her and rocking her as if she were just sleeping, crooning over and over, 'My little moon child. I see the moon and the moon sees me. God bless the moon and God bless me. C'mon sweetie, say it with me.' Then he'd start it all over again, each time desperately listening for her to join in with him. They lost all three of their children. How are they ever going to survive this?"

"I don't know, Michael, but they will somehow. With time, and lots of tears, the memories will start to grow dim, and they'll either pull together and get through this or be torn apart by the guilt, blaming themselves or each other."

"It wasn't their fault!"

"No, of course not. But they'll never see it that way."

"It was the bridge! That stupid, stupid bridge!"

"It was everything. Circumstances just went against everything."

"Any little thing could've changed the whole scenario. If the barge had been ten minutes later or even earlier. If it had been low tide. If it had been raining up by the pier, keeping the parents inside."

177

"If the kids had wanted peanut butter and jelly," Cassie added as she bent low to kiss his forehead. "You can't keep dwelling on it, Michael. It's not going to change a thing. We just have to try to make sure something like this doesn't ever happen again."

He smiled crookedly up at her, "Which is your job. Just how the hell is that damned new bridge coming along, anyway?"

"Now, now, let's not be nasty, just because I didn't have it built in time to avoid all this. Heck, all the permits aren't even in place yet."

"Sorry. I don't mean to take this out on you."

"I know. When I saw the engines waiting at the bridge today, I knew something bad was going to come of it. The island has been spared from this kind of tragedy for a long time. You've really been overdue. Think about all the times you did make it over to save someone from drowning or dying from a heart attack. You've made all the difference in the world many, many times over the years. Your luck just gave out today."

"It's not my luck that gave out, it's those parents'. My luck is still going strong. I've got you here beside me, don't I?" he said as he curled his hand around the back of her neck and pulled her down for his kiss.

As soon as his lips touched hers, he forgot where he was and all that had happened that day. All that mattered now was that she was here and that she tasted like maple syrup. As he desperately devoured her lips and snaked his tongue around her mouth, he asked with gasping breaths if she'd by any chance had pancakes for dinner. When she murmured her positive answer against his lips, he reached up with his other

178

hand and pulled her even closer, eager to taste more of her. Then suddenly they were lost in each other. He sat up and pulled her onto his lap while with one hand he worked her shirt out of her jeans.

As soon as he bared her midriff, he bent his head and began kissing her stomach, making a long trail of kisses starting at her navel and working its way down as he bared her smooth flesh, one inch at a time as he slowly pulled off her jeans. When she was sitting on his lap in just her shirt and panties, he looked deeply into her eyes and ran his hands up and down her smooth shaven legs.

"Did you shave them just for me?"

"What do you think?"

"I think you did."

"I would've shaved them anyway."

"Tonight? Just before going to bed?"

"I like the way they feel when I rub them against each other when I'm in bed."

"I can't wait to find out how they feel when I rub them against my freshly shaven jaw." And without hesitation he picked her up and carried her into his bedroom. The lights were already turned down low and the bed covers had been folded down to the foot of the bed. Something about the confidence of his sexual prowess miffed her for a moment, but as he gently laid her down on his bed, she turned her full attention to the passion-filled eyes boring into hers.

"In fact, the thought of those smooth legs under my lips is not one I can ignore much longer." He went to the foot of the bed, took an ankle in each hand and pulled her down to the edge of the bed. He brought one slim ankle to his lips as he lowered his body down to the bed, situating himself between her legs. He kissed her instep and ankle bone. Then proceeded to kiss her calf muscle, her knee, and just as she was anticipating that he would start on her inner thigh, he abandoned that leg and took up with the other one. Again, he went as far as the knee before halting. He went back to the first leg, and using just the tips of his fingers traced fine lines up and down the muscles of her inner thigh, watching them contract and spasm to his light touch. After he had treated the other thigh to the same treatment, he knelt between her legs and ran his lips and tongue over the area where his fingers had just been. When he felt her thighs spread wider to better accommodate him and he heard her soft sound of surrender, he sat up on his heels and, taking the soft cotton fabric of her panties between his big hands, he tore them right off of her. The elastic snapped back against his hand and he tossed them to the floor.

She gasped but he didn't give her a chance to protest as his mouth captured this newly exposed part of her. He ravenously explored every part of her with his lips and tongue before gently spreading her satiny lips fully with his fingers and concentrating on her moist open folds with his curled tongue. He licked and lapped and lightly nibbled as he tried to discover what pleased her most. When her thighs dropped even further apart, opening herself up even more for him, he slid his tongue up to the slightly recessed little nub that was beckoning him with its tiny pulsing and throbbing movements. As Cassie spread her legs even wider and lifted herself up to meet his ready tongue, he felt the beginnings of her orgasm as her clitoris shimmied and blossomed and then retreated. As delicately as he could he sucked on her there and brought it back out of hiding for one more delightful spasm.

The sound of her ragged breathing and soft moans, as well as the incredible sight before him, was causing him to strain against his own jeans so he quickly discarded them and climbed on top of her. He reached over to the nightstand drawer and found a condom, tore the foil packet open with his teeth and with one hand propped on the pillow by her head, he deftly smoothed the ultra sensitive sheep membrane over his stiff member. As soon as it was in place, he thumbed his penis down to her opening and entered her. With one quick thrust he was fully sheathed by her and he groaned his satisfaction.

He stayed that way inside her for a few moments enjoying the feel of her tightening around him. He looked down into her beautiful face before beginning a slow retreating action followed by hard, reentering thrusts. Soon he had developed an incredibly fast rhythm combined with very forceful thrusts. Suddenly, an overwhelming feeling came over him, something consuming him with need, a desperate need he'd never experienced before. Never before had he wanted to possess someone the way he wanted to possess her and words spoken over a week ago flashed into his mind, "You don't own a woman, you don't possess her soul until you bottom-fuck her." And just that quickly, he lost control of his mind. Instantly, he withdrew from her and flipped her over onto her stomach. He grabbed her by the hips and positioned her with her backside up. With his thumbs he pulled her ass cheeks apart and found her light brown, puckered hole. He was kneeling on the bed between her legs, his rampart hardness poised at the opening when she realized what he was planning on doing. And, just as she moved to pull away, he gripped her hard and shoved himself fully into her. She had no lubrication there, only what was being provided by the condom, now coated with her vaginal juices.

Her high-pitched scream mingled with his guttural grunt. And then, with one final tug on her hips, accompanied with a sharp thrust that sent him deep inside her anal opening, he came, climaxing his body into the bowels of hers.

He shattered into a million pieces and soared into a black oblivion. But before he could make his way back to earth, she started to pull away from him. In his stupor he held her tightly to him, softly crooning into her ear, "Shh. Shh. Hold still. Just lay here for a minute. I know it hurts, I'll take it out in a minute, it won't hurt as much when I'm soft." He kissed the back of her neck and listened to her soft sobs and then, ever so slowly, he tried to ease himself out of her. She was having none of that. She moved completely away from him, causing more pain in the process.

"Owww. Damn you! Why did you do that? That hurt!" She jumped up and ran into the master bathroom and slammed the door behind her.

He fell down onto the bed and rolled over onto his back and then gingerly removed the full condom. Why *had* he done that, he asked himself. He knew it would hurt her and apparently it had. But God, that was wonderful, he told himself. Incredibly wonderful.

When she finally came out of the bathroom wrapped in a towel, he was propped up on one elbow waiting for her. "Before you say anything, I'm sorry. I don't know what came over me. I was suddenly possessed with the idea of taking you that way. I've never done that before. To anyone. I'm sorry if I hurt you. I won't ever do it again if you don't want me to."

"You're damned straight you won't! I won't be here to give you the opportunity! That was the most demeaning thing that's ever happened to me!"

"It wasn't meant to be," he said softly with a contrite voice. "I just wanted to make you mine, to own your soul. Don't you understand? I just wanted your soul."

"You had it before," she retorted.

"I didn't know that," he said softly.

"Well, now you do."

"Come here and kiss me."

"I'm not sure I want to get anywhere near you."

"I promise, I will never hurt you like that again."

She came over and put her knee on the mattress beside his arm and he pulled the towel off of her and dropped it onto the floor. "Promise?"

He grabbed her and pulled her down folding his arms around her and forcing her bottom to fit into the curve of his groin. "You really didn't like it, huh? Not even a little bit?"

"No!" she hollered as she tried to wriggle away from him.

He held her fast against him and whispered in her ear, "Then I'll never do it again, I promise." He kissed her just below her ear and snuggled her bottom closer while he inserted his legs between hers. "I do like the feel of your legs against mine," he said as he rubbed his legs up and down and then back and forth, trying to calm and soothe her. He then pulled her around to face him so he could kiss her over and over again.

"So, I own your soul, huh?" he asked between kisses.

"Well, maybe I was a little hasty there. Let's just say that if you keep giving me orgasms like the one you gave me with your mouth tonight, I'll be putty in your hands."

"You were putty in my hands."

"I know. It's a little unnerving to have a man have so much control over my body."

"Doesn't bother me a bit. I kinda like controlling you."

She reached out and thumped him on the shoulder. "Well, if nothing else, at least we've taken your mind off of the events of today."

"I think it was the events of today that made me want to experience life to the fullest."

"Does that mean that having conventional sex with me isn't fulfilling enough for you?"

"Oh, by no means, no! Sex with you is wonderful, any sex. I guess I was just curious and angry and I really am sorry that I took it out on you. Forgive me?"

"How could I not forgive the only man who has caused me to experience both a vaginal and an oral orgasm?"

"Really?" he asked with a big grin.

"Really," she replied with an equally big grin. "And next time we get together, we'll try your favorite position."

"Doggy?"

"Yeah."

"But that's not my favorite way anymore," he said with a crooked grin.

"Tough! We'll try it your second favorite way then."

He pulled her close and wrapped his arms tightly around her, "I have a feeling that with you, they're all going to be my favorites."

She smiled up at him and gave him a kiss on the nose.

"So how was your day today?" he asked her.

"Oh, just grand," she said with a big sigh. "I found out that the supplier isn't building the bearing plates to my specifications and now I have to raise all kinds of hell to get them built right."

He hugged her closer, snuggling her head under his chin. "Well, I'm sure that whoever it is that screwed up is going to hear all about it tomorrow."

"You're damn right!"

"Give 'em hell, darlin'. Meanwhile, let's get some sleep, shall we?"

"Michael, I can't stay here tonight. Jenny and Colin would be worried sick."

"So this is a 'Wham, bam, thank you mister?' "

"Sorry to have sex and run, but I can't stay."

"Jenny and Colin will know where you are. Hell, you can even call them."

"And tell them what? That I'm sleeping with you?"

"You don't think they know already?"

"No. Why would they?"

"Cass, C'mon. Surely you don't believe they don't know."

"Michael, is it so hard for you to believe that not all women can resist falling into bed with you?"

185

"Yes. You couldn't."

Cassie pushed against his hard chest muscles. "Ohhh! That was my mistake! And I won't make it again!" she said as she pushed herself away from him, propelling herself to the other side of the bed.

He leisurely reached out and grabbed her ankle and slowly dragged her back across the sheets to him.

"Oh yeah?" he asked as he ran his other hand up her thigh and began rubbing his thumb back and forth across the top of her slit, awakening the small, sleeping nub he found there. "Get back here," he said gruffly as he climbed on top of her prone body. "Let me see if I can find a place to put this that pleases you better this time," he said as he rubbed his fully aroused penis against her hip.

His lips took the soft moan from her mouth as his tongue plundered her sweet cavity and then a moan of his own mingled with hers when she returned his kiss.

Chapter 16

The next day, Cassie was up to her ears in problems. It was raining so hard that the little bit of work they'd been able to do after fixing the CAT, was being washed down the embankment they'd just built. And suppliers from all over were calling with excuses why their shipments were running late. Louie was interviewing workmen and there was a constant line in the hallway as the workers tracked mud everywhere. And for some reason no one could figure out, the power to the trailer kept going off and on. It was off for twenty minutes at a time, just enough to be a major inconvenience. While it was off, there was no air conditioning, and the humidity that built up made everything sticky. Cassie's mood was not improved by the untimely phone call from her dad. He wasn't happy to hear about their delayed status. All in all, this had probably been one of her worst days on a job site—until the roses showed up.

Michael knew a good thing when he had it, and to insure he stayed in Cassie's good graces, he stopped at Shady Oaks Florist on his way into work. He liked the women who worked there, they were always cheerful and helpful. And Sherrie, the owner, always gave him a good price.

He and Cassie had finally parted last night, albeit very reluctantly, clinging to each other while repeatedly bestowing one more final good night kiss after another. He wanted to make sure that his breech of bedroom etiquette was forgiven and to do this he was willing to send a token of repentance. Also, he knew sending flowers, especially to a woman's workplace, elevated the relationship to a slightly more respectable level. He was working on making this an exclusive alliance, at least for now. He didn't want to have to worry about Harley or anybody else horning in until he'd had his fill of her.

He was starting to wonder about that part, though. It seemed that the more he had her, the more he wanted her again. And it was a rare moment in the day when he realized that he wasn't thinking about her, wondering what she was doing and if she was thinking about him.

He sat down at a desk and pulled the file folder out on D. Duke. It was a rainy, dreary day, so he wouldn't need to continually patrol on the island. Everyone would be ensconced in their beach houses watching videos or playing board games. The summer season was over, but the early fall season still yielded quite a few vacationers. These were the people who didn't have kids in school, who could enjoy the off-season rates, and the old timers who didn't like the intense heat of the summer. It was an easier time for the officers, no teenagers and no traffic problems. After the Labor Day holiday, things settled into a nice little groove for this small beach community of two thousand residents.

Michael settled himself at a desk and picked up the stack of index cards that was tucked into the crease of the folder. There had to be something here he'd missed, he thought, so he started reading them. He'd left off with the card dated April 14, 1999, when he'd finally turned in that night at the Hope Mills Motel, so he reread it and then set it aside and continued with the next one.

"D. Duke's been doing it again! Damn him! Never has a man had a more appropriate name. It takes away all the joy I get coming here to find that he's still up to his same old tricks. And the police don't care! My renters call and they don't do a thing about it. It's only ten in the morning, and I already feel like I need a drink! May 12, 1999."

When he'd rewritten this one from the journal it had practically leapt out at him, showing great promise. But no matter how many times he read it, he got nothing out of it. She knew who D. Duke was, but he'd already known that. She was upset about something he'd done and was still doing, that was the same way half the people living on the island felt and the police weren't able to do anything about it—same old story. Unless they had proof or caught him in the act, they really had their hands tied. They knew he was the culprit for a lot of the complaints, but they couldn't charge him with anything. There were rarely witnesses and even when there were, it was usually renters who would hardly deem it worth their while to travel back from Greensboro, Raleigh, or even further to see an old man get his just desserts for taking an illegal wine cooler bottle out of their hand. Reading it again did establish that she, he really did feel certain that the journal writer was a she, was a homeowner who rented her unit out. That narrowed it down to a possible 450 people who were doing the exact same thing with their beach houses.

He grabbed his pad and added "homeowner who rents" to the list. He read over the page. So far, he'd figured out that Lady Kit was a walker in most any kind of weather; that she owned a rental home, probably on the bay side which would have put her in D. Duke's vicinity; that she liked to cook and drink; that she took pictures and came here almost monthly, and she was somewhat of a stickler for the rules of the island. He wondered if he went to the ABC store with this description and said he knew she drank vodka occasionally, if they'd be able to help him out. Yeah, they'd help him all right; they'd help him to the door.

He could take a list of the dates that he knew her unit was *not* rented to the seven or eight real estate rental companies and see what that netted. Maybe they could match it up to a few of their listings that hadn't been rented out on those days. He would probably get a dirty look and a few choice curse words he thought as he picked up the next card.

"It's hot but the sun feels good on my face. It's not even noon and the college kids across the street are already drunk. One girl has six pierced earrings, an eyebrow bar and a navel ring. For all I know she could have even more under her teeny tiny bikini. I don't understand why they insist on putting all those things through their bodies, do they really think it looks good? It is so nice to be here again, I've missed the sound of the ocean and the beautiful sunrises. June 9, 1999."

Aha! She must live on the east side! It's pretty hard to watch the sun come up on the west side unless you're up pretty high. The west side has the beautiful sunsets, the east side has the sunrises. But really, he'd pretty much known that all along. After all, college kids did everything in groups and they rarely rented on the west side. They were across the street. Did that mean she was second row or further back? The college kids who came here usually came from money. It was always the best for them. They would certainly be staying oceanfront. Well, he was narrowing this down. She could now be one of 420 people.

"Couldn't come last month or the month before. The rent money is just too good this time of the year, but oh, how I've missed my beach! Can't believe another season has come and gone. The time just gets away from me. My sister has breast cancer, a few years ago it was ovarian cancer. This time I don't think she's going to even bother with the treatments. It saddens me to know that she's giving up, but since her husband died, I don't think she really cares to go on anymore. The bank called me last week. The last one of Harvey's CDs matures this month. I hate the thought that I may have to sell the beach house to live. But it's either that or sell the farm, which the kids don't want me to do, even though it hasn't been a productive one for over thirty years. I hate not knowing what to do. Harvey always made these decisions. It's hard to believe he's been gone fifteen years now. Sept.15,1999."

A widow for fifteen years. With grown children. A dying sister. It all added up to the fact that Lady Kit was an older woman, but he'd kind of suspected that all along anyway. But Harvey, Harvey had been her husband's name or possibly a brother or something. How the hell could he use that little piece of information? He wouldn't even have bothered to think about it if it had been John or Robert or James, but Harvey, that was a little unusual. Maybe he could go to the NC Department of Revenue and check the deeds for property on the island in the name of Harvey something. It sounded like a lot of work that could amount to a lot of nothing if she'd bought the property after he'd died or if his name had been taken off the deed. Or . . . he could go to Cliff at the Sunset Beach Trading Company. He'd owned his store on the causeway for a long time. He knew all the locals and remembered most of the vacationers who came here year after year. After all, it wasn't a vacation if you didn't walk to Cliff and Lynn's for homemade fudge, a double-decker ice cream cone, and a souvenir postcard to send to the poor working stiffs back home.

He bundled the cards back together and secured them with a rubber band, tucked them back into the sleeve of the folder and stood up. He needed a break anyhow; his back was getting kinked. Something he'd done last night with Cassie had put a little strain on it. Remembering her and her sassy little bottom stuck up in the air caused him to burgeon below the belt. He smiled as he adjusted himself, too bad she hadn't liked that. Ray must have been wrong about all those women clamoring for more, unless it took more than one time to take. He shook his head at himself as he reattached his gun belt, as if she'd ever submit to that again. Not his Cassie. Huh . . . ? He wondered why he was thinking of her that way. His Cassie.

He got into his cruiser and rode over to the island. As he passed the deserted, muddy construction site, he looked over at the trailer. There were lights on at the end where her office was and outside a black Corvette was parked next to her Jimmy. He felt the temperature rise within him and his fists grew hard on the steering wheel. If that car was still there when he came back across the bridge, he'd . . . he didn't know what he'd do. But he'd do something, that's for sure.

"Damn it Harley! Just do something about it! The last thing I need to hear today is that there's a problem with the deed!"

"It could take months to straighten it out according to the people at the records department. Let's look for another unit."

"No. I want that one."

"Well then you'd better be prepared to wait 'til Christmas before you can settle."

"Work something out with the owners. They must be as upset about this as I am. Arrange for me to rent it until we can go to settlement."

"That might work."

"Good, let me know how soon I can move in," she said in a dismissive manner.

"What'll I get if I can get it done this weekend?"

"You'll get a commission."

"No, I mean, what will you give me?" he asked with a suggestive smile.

"What do you want Harley?" she asked with exasperation. She was standing up behind her desk now, running her tension-filled fingers through her hair.

"I want to take you to a NASCAR race in Charlotte. I want you to go away with me for the weekend."

Just as he was saying that, Michael came through the trailer door. If Michael thought he'd been angry before, it was nothing compared to how he was feeling right now. "Well that ain't going to happen," he said in a firm but quiet voice.

Harley spun around and gaped at him. Michael, who usually didn't wear his police hat, just stood there and rakishly tipped it back allowing the water to drip off the back of it and down his long, black raincoat.

He looked mean and sure of himself as he stepped into the room and closed the door behind him with his foot. Cassie could see the trouble brewing in his eyes, and she quickly ran around the desk to get between the two of them.

"I was just getting ready to tell Harley that I really don't care for racing."

Michael's eyes swung to meet hers, his steely dark eyes staring her down. "Is that the only reason you don't want to accompany him?" he asked, his voice low and menacing.

"Why, no," Cassie said trying to inject a bit of humor and a smile. "I don't particularly like Charlotte, either."

"Hey, what's going on here?" Harley asked, sensing the thick tension in the room.

"What's going on here, is that you're asking my girl to go out of town so you can bed down with her and I don't like it. One . . . single . . . bit," he grated out.

Harley turned and looked at him. "Your girl?"

Michael looked pointedly at Cassie. "Cassie would you care to fill him in?"

Cassie looked at Harley. "Harley, Michael and I we're uh..."

"We're uh what?" Harley demanded.

Michael looked at Cassie and filled in the blank for both of them, "A couple."

"A couple?" Harley bellowed, turning back to Cassie.

Michael raised a questioning eyebrow at Cassie as he waited for her to answer Harley's inquiry.

"Yes, Harley. A couple."

"You mean, you and he . . . you and he have . . ." he stammered.

Michael grinned broadly and cocked his head, "Yes, she and I have," he said with great satisfaction.

Harley stood there for a moment trying to take all this in. This was not what was supposed to happen. He wanted her. And he thought he was going to have her. He'd made plans for her, and him.

"Harley, I never said we'd be anything but friends," Cassie enjoined.

Harley's face turned crimson then he turned around and stomped out. A few moments later, they heard the corvette's tires spinning in the mud before he managed to get some traction and pull out of the space.

Michael and Cassie just stood there staring at each other. No one spoke for a minute, then Cassie stood up to her full height.

"You knew he was in here," she accused.

"Yes. I did," he said simply.

"Then why did you barge in here like that?"

"Just protecting what's mine."

"I am not yours!"

"Yes. Yes, you are."

"How do you figure?"

"Did you not tell me just last night that 'I owned your soul?' "

"I amended that."

"To 'you're putty in my hands.' "

"Well, does that mean that I can't be putty in anyone else's hands?"

"Yes."

"Well, I didn't know that."

"Well, now you do."

They continued staring at each other, listening to the rain hitting the roof and running down the gutters.

Then, he slowly removed his hat and holding it down by his side, he walked over to where she stood. With his other hand, he grabbed her around the waist and pulled her to him. He bent his head over hers and slanting it slightly, he captured her lips in one quick movement. While her arms found their way slowly to his wet shoulders, he moved his lips over hers, possessing her with his kiss. Then he abruptly pulled away and released her, almost sending her reeling before turning on his heel and exiting the trailer.

Cassie stood in the center of her office, her fingertips to her lips, knowing that something very important had just happened between them but not knowing why he seemed so angry about it.

Chapter 17

For the next few days, Cassie worked from first light until almost nine o'clock every evening. By Saturday, they had recouped the work they had lost and actually made some headway, but she was exhausted. Harley got over his hurt pride and finally returned her phone calls. She was pretty sure that Harley's father had had something to do with that. It had been arranged that she could rent-to-own while the title problems were being researched, and she was scheduled to move in on Sunday, her only day off.

Since there wasn't much to move, she agreed to go to the pool with Michael that afternoon after she was settled in. Her new complex had its own little pool, but Cassie preferred the one at the Maples Activity Center. The chairs were more comfortable and there was a well-stocked lending library.

She and Michael had not seen each other since that rainy day in the trailer, although they had spent many hours talking on the phone, late into the night when she should have been sleeping. They had both been very busy, Cassie with problems at the site, Michael with meetings and recertification classes, mostly at the firing range.

They agreed to meet at the pool at noon and have lunch there. Michael, of course, provided the food. They had finished eating a wonderful pasta salad and were sipping Michael's own version of a wine cooler: white zinfandel, pear juice and cranberry juice with a splash of citrus flavored soda.

Michael sat across from her on one of the lounge chairs. He had one leg out in front of him with his knee bent and his other leg thrown wide and he suspected that she could see something of his sizable manhood, if she'd bother to look. He knew the webbing on his suit was loose, but hell, he had to impress her somehow and most of the women he knew had been pretty impressed with his size. She was ignoring him and had been for quite some time. He kept his eyes on her face hoping to get a sign of her interest, but she just continued reading her book and every once in a while she reached over to the small plastic table beside her to take a sip of her drink. It was as if she was ignoring him on purpose and he didn't like it. He didn't like it at all.

Cassie was trying very hard not to notice the extremely virile looking man less than ten feet away from her, the dark, brooding man intensely focused on her. Not only did he have a muscular, heavily furred chest that would cause beauty queens to swoon, now he was blatantly displaying a rather large fleshy mass coiled in the dense black hairs just beyond his tensed upper thigh.

"Pretty good book, huh?" he asked nonchalantly.

"Yeah."

"What's it about?"

"Not something you would care to read."

"So, tell me anyway."

"It's a romance, if you have to know. The story takes place back in the twelve hundreds."

"Ah. Damsels in distress and knights in atrocious armor."

"Yeah, sort of."

"Why do you like that kind of stuff?"

"Because I like the way they treated their women back then. They were respectful and courteous and very appreciative of a woman's charms."

"Honey, I'm very appreciative of your charms. In fact, I would like to be able to appreciate them a little more. How 'bout letting that shoulder strap slide down your arm and baring one of your breasts for me?"

"You've got to be kidding."

"No. I'm not. There's no one around and I want to see your breasts."

"You already have and in natural sunlight, in case you've forgotten."

"Oh, I'll never forget that. I remember those firm mounds of tanned flesh topped with malt chocolate-colored nipples. They were perky and firm and luscious. And I want to see them again."

"No."

"Yes," he said, his seductive eyes staring into hers, daring her to deny him.

She met his gaze for several moments and then she slowly reached up with her right hand and with one curled finger, she pulled the strap down off of her shoulder, letting it fall to the crook of her elbow. The fabric attached to the strap had been stretched taut over her breast, it relaxed and fell away, baring her right breast to his hungry eyes.

He stared at her for the longest time before murmuring, "Now, the other one."

She flushed under his fixed stare and the nipple on her breast hardened just from the knowledge that his eyes were fixated on her there.

Silently, she reached for the other strap and let it fall.

"Mmmm. Like sweet Hershey's Kisses placed atop mounds of succulent flesh. I don't suppose you'd allow me to suckle you now, would you? Is that the way they would have said it in the thirteenth century?"

His deep, sultry voice paired with the words he was saying caused her to feel a flash of heat and wetness flowing down between her legs.

"They wouldn't have asked. They took what they wanted."

He knew a moment of weakness when he heard one and he quickly moved to the side of her chair and cupped her breasts.

"Oh God, Michael," she said in a high, squeaky voice.

The moment his tongue made contact with her nipple she gasped. He backed away from her for a moment to look into her eyes, "It's been a while for us, almost a week. Are you as horny as I am?" He bent back to his task and she replied by grabbing his head and holding it to her breast.

As his lips encircled her aureole and he sucked her nipple into his mouth she felt a warm rush of liquid pool in the area below her belly.

"Michael. We can't do this here, people will see."

"We'll hear them before they can see us," he murmured as he switched to the other breast. His hand moved under her bikini bottom and his finger quickly separated her slick folds and entered her. "Ahh, baby. You are so wet. You want me don't you?"

"Mmmm," she replied.

"Tell me. Tell me you want me," he said as his finger thrust in and out of her while he continued to lick her nipples.

"I want you."

"To?"

"To . . ."

"Yes, to what . . . " he prodded. "Say it," he commanded, "I want to hear you say it."

"I want you to . . . " Just then the door to the pool banged shut and behind the tall hedges they could hear people talking and kids laughing.

Michael pulled his hand out of her bathing suit bottom while she quickly pulled her top up. Then he laid back down on the lounge chair making sure the material was well away from his thigh so she could see his full arousal. "As you can see, I want you, too." With his forefinger resting on his temple, he held his long middle finger under his noise and breathed in deeply. "Ahh, the essence of woman. My favorite cologne."

She turned beet red and he laughed heartily at her obvious discomfort.

"Care to give me a tour of your new digs, starting with the bedroom?" he asked in a husky, sexy voice.

"Why fight it?" she asked. "Your displaying yourself in such a provocative manner has caused me to remember the answer to question number three in my notebook." She stuck her tongue out, stretched it to the center of her top lip and rubbed it back and forth.

You could hear his gasp from the other side of the pool and the new arrivals turned to the sound. She chuckled as she gathered her things together. "Meet you there," was all she said as she sauntered over to the gate.

It was lucky he was a cop. Anybody else would've gotten pulled over. Even though she'd had a head start, he met her just as she opened the door and walked into the small foyer. He took everything out of her hands, set it all on the floor, and closed and locked the door before picking her up and carrying her into the bedroom.

"Are we in a hurry?" she whispered in his ear.

"Yes," he hissed back at her. "We are."

He had her bathing suit and his stripped off almost before he reached the bed. Then as he dropped her onto the bed, he cursed, "Damn! I don't have any with me."

"None in the car?"

"It's a police car!" he replied testily.

"Don't worry, I've got some. Somewhere in one of these suitcases," she indicated with a sweep of her hand. They both looked down at the seven or eight cases.

"I imagine I could go to CVS and be back before you found them in all this."

"Well, never mind. We can do something else," she said as if she was suggesting a friendly game of checkers.

"Do something else?" he exploded as if that was the stupidest statement she'd ever made.

She pulled the covers down and slipped between them, stifling a put-on yawn, "I could take a nap right now."

"Take a nap!" he exploded again.

She watched as he started unzipping suitcases and rifled through them. She took pity on him and her clothes and got up and walked over to her purse on the dresser. She took a foil packet out and waved it back and forth. "Is this what you're looking for?" she asked demurely.

He gave a low growl and stood up and then he practically tackled her back down onto the bed.

Chapter 18

"This chicken is delicious Michael," Cassie said as she lifted another bite to her lips. They were sitting in her new dining room, enjoying their first meal together in her new townhouse. After Michael had slaved in bed practically all afternoon, he'd donned his jeans and headed for the kitchen. The incredible sexiness of him standing shirtless in just his tight jeans had caused her to drag him back to the bedroom one more time. He finally put his shirt back on—it was either that or order Domino's.

"It almost didn't make it to the table tonight. I thought you were going to chain me up in there," he said indicating the bedroom with his fork. He smiled his pleasure at her embarrassed blush.

"I'm sorry, if I took advantage of you," she said sarcastically. Then her tone softened, "But I never knew that sex could be like this. I thought it was just something that guys did to have fun and girls just went along with it because they didn't want to be alone."

"I cannot believe that no man has ever taken the time to satisfy you."

"Well, to be fair, there's only been two and I'm not sure they were all that concerned with me, to tell you the truth."

"Why the hell not?"

"They just weren't, I don't know why. Maybe they were just too young to know any better."

"Yeah, it does take some practice to figure you women out."

"And you? You've had lots of practice?"

"Let's not go there. Suffice it to say, enough."

"Apparently," she said dragging out the single word and giving him a big smile.

He looked around the room as he took a sip of his wine from the beautifully cut crystal glass. "I really like your place, it's just perfect for you. Well, except for the kitchen."

"What's wrong with the kitchen?" she asked with a frown.

"You don't need one. You should have saved the money and put it into a billiard room or something."

"Ha ha. Very funny," she said as she threw her napkin at his face. "Turns out, I do need the kitchen. Where else are you going to cook for me?"

"Hmmm. I think next time, I need to charge a fee for my services."

"Oh yeah, like what?"

"Like I cook Chateaubriand for you, and you sit topless in front of me while we eat it."

"You're not serious!"

"Oh, yes I am."

"Well, I won't do it."

"Oh, yes you will."

"How can you be so sure of that?"

"One taste and if I tell you to strip to the waist to have more, you will," he said confidently. "You'll see."

"Yeah, I'll see all right," she said unbelievingly. "I'll feed your Chateaubriand to Taffy, that's what I'll do."

"Ooooh," he said menacingly as he slowly stood up. Something about the expression on his face caused her to inch out of her chair, but before she could clear it, he had scooped her up and tossed her over his shoulder. "I think somebody needs to be put in her place." he said as he affectionately swatted her bottom.

"Oh, yeah? And where's that?"

"Here," he said as he carried her back into the bedroom.

"You can't possibly be serious!"

"Bet me!" he said as he laid her down on the bed and began unzipping his zipper.

"Aren't you full from eating?" she asked.

"Naw, I haven't even had dessert yet. We'll save that for later. Go find your notebook, I think it's about time we worked on question number three."

"Oh no!" she said as she tried to scramble off the bed.

"Oh, yes. Or are you one of those women who is happy to receive oral sex but not inclined to give it?"

"I'm not sure. I've never done it. I don't know how." Her words came out like she was speaking in staccato monotones as she continued to move away from him.

He smiled over at her and chuckled, but at the same time, he stopped undressing. He walked around the bed to where she was and gently took her by the arms. "C'mere and sit beside me," he said as he walked her out to the living room and sat her beside him on the sofa.

"You know that sex is very important to me, but so are you, and if there's something you don't want to do, then we won't do it. We have to find out what we like together. But I'm not going to let you say absolutely no to blow jobs until you've at least tried it. Whenever you're ready, I'll coach you. It's not that hard to do, in fact a lot of women love doing it and I can assure you there isn't a man alive who doesn't like having it done to him. So, whenever you're ready, just let me know and we'll try it. Okay?"

She looked up into his concerned face, his eyes searching hers as he tried to reassure her. "Okay," she said timidly.

"Good, now get in the billiard room and do those dishes while I clear the table!" he said as he pulled her off the sofa and pushed her forward. And together they cleaned the kitchen. Then Michael made some coffee and they took their dessert into the Carolina room. It was almost dark outside but you could still see the shadows on the golf course and some snowy egrets soaring by on their way to find roosts for the night.

"There's a hurricane in the tropics that may be coming our way," Michael commented between bites of his pie.

"I heard something about it on the news this afternoon."

"When did you watch the news this afternoon? I thought I had you pretty well involved."

"While you were showering, I turned it on. They say it could be here as early as Thursday, if it doesn't turn away."

"Still a category three?"

"Yeah, I think so."

"We haven't had one for a while. We're due."

"I've never been around for one. It figures that as soon as I buy my first house, one's on its way."

"Let's turn on the weather channel and see what they're saying, I'd like to know now if I'm going to be working next weekend."

"Why?"

" 'Cause there's a lot of stuff I have to do this week around the house if I'm not going to be getting it done next weekend."

She stood up and went to get the remote. "Like?"

"Trim some bushes, spread some mulch, treat the deck and generally winterize the house."

"You really like doing that stuff, don't ya?"

He thought for a moment and nodded, "Yeah, I do."

She switched on the TV and sat down beside him. He put his arm around her shoulder, squeezed it lightly and deftly took the remote from her hand. He found the weather channel and together they listened to the updated report on the hurricane that was heading their way.

"This could be a bad one," he said when the local report was over and the national weather came on.

"Just what I don't need right now," Cassie mumbled.

"Honey, nobody *needs* a hurricane."

"You know what I mean."

His fingers stroked her cheek, "I know. You're worried about the work on the bridge."

"A hundred and thirty mile an hour winds could blow away everything we've put there!"

"Well, then I suggest you spend this week taking whatever precautions you can, because it looks like it's going to be here this coming weekend."

Just then the phone rang and Cassie jumped up to get it. Michael listened to her end of the conversation, instantly keyed to her tenseness as soon as she knew who was calling.

"Yes, daddy. I heard. Yes. Yes. I know, I know. I will. No, please, you don't have to do that. I can handle it. Yes. I know what to do. You don't need to come down. Why can't you trust me on this? I'll take care of it. Yes, I'll call you. G'night, daddy."

"I gather that was daddy," he said with a cockeyed grin.

She walked slowly back to the sofa. It was obvious that his call had affected her greatly.

"Honey, what's wrong?" he asked, pulling her down beside him.

"He thinks he should come down to make sure we get the approaches set and the abutments poured this week."

"And you don't think you need his help?"

"I don't want his help. He never thinks I can do anything on my own. He still treats me like a kid."

"Well honey, he does have a lot of money invested in this, and after all, it is your first big job."

"No, it's not, I've been on lots of big jobs. I can do this. I know I can."

"Well, then, do it. Show him you can. You can, can't you?" he asked suddenly concerned for her psyche.

"Of course I can. I just don't need this hurricane right now."

"Anything I can do to help?"

"No, not unless you can buy me three or four more days to finish getting the approach ramps built and the

209

abutments ready to be poured and placed before the hurricane gets here."

"Sorry, I can cook, clean, comfort and cuddle, but I cannot make time stand still."

"Then what good are you?" she asked with a raised eyebrow.

"C'mere, I'll show you my special talent."

"I think I've already seen your *special talent*."

"Yes, but you've never seen it in the living room."

"Thank God, I didn't buy a thirty-room mansion."

"Then we would've had a real billiard room."

"Where's the phone book?" she asked distractedly as she looked around the room, "I need to call Carolina Crane."

"That's my girl, back to her Tonka toys rather than play with my big toy."

"Michael, I'm sorry. But you know what this bridge means to me."

He stood up and came to give her a hug. "I know. And I'll get out of your hair so you can get some work done. I had a wonderful time today," he said as he held her head against his chest.

She looked up into his face. "So did I."

He leaned down to kiss her and she wrapped her hands around his neck to steady herself as his lips moved over hers. It was a deep kiss, one of promise and commitment. And neither was eager for it to be over. She walked him to the door and watched as he got into his cruiser and left. He'd been on call all weekend and she'd been grateful that he hadn't been called out, but she had a feeling he was going to pay for the luxury of his idleness this upcoming weekend.

Chapter 19

The next week was very busy for Michael and Cassie as they both prepared for the coming hurricane. Cassie brought in huge stadium-type lights mounted on massive trucks and, splitting her fifty-man crew into three shifts, they worked around the clock so that they could have the concrete poured and set before the hurricane arrived. If not, they would no doubt lose three weeks of work when the hurricane blew all the layers of dirt and gravel off of the mainland approach. Some bridges are built end-to-end, some one section at a time working towards the center, and some mile-long bridges are built in stages, some parts near completion while other parts are just going up.

The new Sunset Beach bridge was being built end-to-end with the work for both the approaches and abutments being started before the tedious and arduous work of driving the pilings, building the footings, installing the pier columns, attaching the substructure and laying the deck began. The mainland approach required moving an intersection and building a road through parts of a golf course, around a water tower and between the right of way of two houses on the Intracoastal. Making the road was bad enough with all the traffic problems it involved. To have to redo a large portion of the job would be costly, and it sure would try everyone's patience at a time when they were already anxious to have things back to normal again.

Michael was busy assisting homeowners with evacuation procedures as well as securing his own home for the impending storm. From all appearances, it looked like it was going to hit just north of Little River, South Carolina, less than ten miles from Sunset Beach and it had all the components to make it a category three, possibly even a four. Merchants were closing up and sealing their windows and doors and all the hardware stores were selling out of their stocks of plywood and tape, as well as emergency supplies. The grocery store shelves were emptying faster than they could be refilled and there was almost a line at the Exxon station. In general, excitement and trepidation filled the air as everyone prepared to either hunker in or flee for the hills.

That was always a big question in the days preceding a hurricane, whether to stay or to go, whether to protect home and hearth or just grab the family, a few cherished possessions and head inland. Almost all the people on the actual barrier islands evacuate during hurricanes as the coastline takes the full brunt of the storms. The wind is devastating enough but the tidal surge during and after can cause massive flooding, especially if they are unfortunate enough to be in the lunar cycle of a full moon. Beach towns count on this happening. It's inevitable. That's why the houses are all on stilts and all the ground level enclosed areas are designed to break away to let the water flow as it wills.

On all barrier islands, the power is purposefully shut off before the storms to decrease the likelihood of fire and fallen, live power lines. It is also shut off to encourage both homeowners and renters to vacate. So, if anybody has the idea of stocking up on videos and beer for a hurricane party, they'd have to have a generator to do it. The prospect of no air conditioning, no television, and hot beer has most people booking hotel rooms or bunking with friends and family. The Red Cross also opens up several shelters, welcoming the displaced vacationers and the locals who have no other place to go or the money to get there. The police department is called on to install officers at each shelter to maintain order and to help with emergencies. None of the officers would be evacuating with their families. And once the hurricane had passed, there would be even more to do, depending on the damage it left behind.

The island of Sunset Beach had an all together different situation because of the bridge. The bridge had to be locked in position as soon as the winds reached forty miles per hour, so the officers had to practically go from house to house making sure everyone was gone. Or, if a homeowner insisted on staying, they had to be advised that they were not allowed to leave their homes at all; that they would be trespassing if they stepped one foot over their property lines. Then they would be given a toe tag, and if after all that, they still were determined to stay, policemen would record their names and the names and addresses of their next of kin. Once they were assured that no one else was leaving the island, the bridge would be closed to vehicle traffic and locked in position so that there would be less chance of damage to it. Boats could still head out of harm's way down the Intracoastal, but at this point, if you were on the island, you were stuck there for the duration.

Homeowners from all over the country were also calling, begging someone from the Town Hall or from the Police Department to go over to their beach house to secure patio furniture, flags, planters, bikes, you-name-it. One officer took a call from a woman in Germany asking if he would please get the keys from the rental company, go to her beach house and empty her refrigerator, because she knew from past experience that if you had food in the refrigerator and the power was shut off for several days, it could smell up the whole unit as well as encourage all manner of insects. Not being able to say no to such a desperate plea, he'd complied with her request after admonishing her not to leave food in the refrigerator again if she was going to be away during hurricane season.

There are also a lot of people, both on the mainland and on the island who are elderly or disabled that need help securing their homes and arranging to be relocated. There are thirty people in the Police Department's "Are You Okay?" program, a group of people made up of elderly widows and widowers with no family or relatives in the immediate area, who need to be called daily to be checked on. These people would need to be taken to the shelters and most of them would need to have prescriptions filled and medical supplies picked up first. It was an incredibly busy time for law enforcement and town officials.

Cassie was working with each shift, sleeping an hour or so at her desk with her head on her arms, trying to make sure everything got done. The hurricane was due to hit late Friday afternoon. The heavy equipment had to be secured or moved no later than Friday morning. She even had to arrange to have the port-a-johns picked up. One of the large cranes that had already arrived for the pier work had to be taken on its barge to a sheltered cove and tied down. The people from the NC DOT who had experienced this type of situation many times before, advised Cassie on this and she was relieved to hear that it had been finally secured somewhere near the Southport Marina. The trailer should have been moved, but there just wasn't time, so a contractor was hired to come in and brick underpin it to give it more stability. But the only thing really on Cassie's mind was getting the grading and the paving done and the concrete poured before they ran out of time.

Michael stopped by to see her a few times during his trips back and forth over the bridge. Not only did the homeowners have errands that needed to be done, the merchants on the beach needed some help, too. Each time, he found Cassie asleep at her desk, her black curls covering her whole head, making it look like someone had dropped a curly wig in the center of the disheveled desk. He was amazed at how she could sleep with the incessant noise of the beep, beep, beeping coming from the trucks as their back-up warning systems engaged over and over and over again.

He left her alone after softly caressing a blue-black tendril framing her partially hidden face the first time. But the second time, he couldn't resist kissing the exposed column of her neck and she awoke, softly moaning her pleasure at the thrills his lips were giving her. They spoke for a few minutes and then he left her so she could finish her nap. The next time he stopped by, he brought some Chinese food from China Garden, the restaurant at the Village at Sunset Beach.

"I figure we're going to be apart for several days, so you might as well have the curry and its morning after malodor. I had a hankering for General Tang's Chicken," he said as he placed the square boxes on styrofoam plates in front of her. "This could be your last hot meal for a while; the restaurants are preparing to close. All the employees are starting to evacuate and I'm not going to be around to cook for you. We should have everyone off the island by ten o'clock tomorrow. How are you doing?"

It was Thursday evening and they were nowhere near done. "We're almost finished with the framing. They just started pouring the concrete this afternoon."

"How long's it take for that stuff to dry?" he asked as he munched on a spring roll.

"Dry enough to use? Two weeks or better. Dry enough to withstand a torrent of rain, hopefully only twenty-four hours. We've got huge sheets of heavy duty plastic to cover it with, but I have no idea how that's going to work."

"You look real tired," he said giving her a soft smile.

"I believe that I am. I feel like I felt after taking my freshman finals—red-eyed, over-caffeinated and unsure of exactly what I've accomplished."

"Heard from your dad?"

"Oh, many times. Many, many times."

"Giving you a hard time?"

"Not in so many words. Giving me more advice than I need though and a lot of grief about staying."

"Speaking of which, which shelter are you going to?"

"I'm not. I'm staying home."

216

"Oh, no you're not. If you're staying, you're going to a shelter. Jenny's working at the one here at Sea Trail, I just saw her a little while ago when I dropped some people off."

"Michael, it's only a category three. Lots of people are staying in their homes."

"Lots of people who have substantial, *brick* homes. Ever heard the story of the 'Three Little Pigs?' "

"My house is substantial," she said indignantly.

"No, it's not. It is simple frame construction and there are trees all around it."

"All the more reason I should stay home. What if one crashes through the roof? I need to be there to protect my property, to cover the hole and move things out of harm's way."

"Cassie, you're going to a shelter."

"No, I'm not!" she retorted.

"We'll see," he murmured.

"What's that mean?"

"We'll see, that's what it means. How's your Chicken Curry?" he asked, trying to change the subject.

"It's good. It could stand to be a tad spicier. I like things spicy."

"I know," he said with a wink.

After they finished eating, Michael pulled her into his arms and gave her a deep, tender kiss. Then he hugged her extra tightly and said he had to get back to work, and that he'd call her tomorrow.

She went outside to see how the work was progressing. The wind had picked up and there was a delightful breeze that was slightly nippy, constantly cooling off the exhausted workers. As each shift was done. they were taking their tools and going home, joining families already packed and ready to head out. Most of the workers lived in mobile homes out toward Ash or Longs, so they were all going to shelters or motels on the other side of Interstate 95. There was very little traffic using the bridge now. Most of the people were already far from the threat of danger, entombed in motel rooms watching the never ending weather reports of the impending storm. Cassie looked around. With just a little luck they could have everything done by morning. That wouldn't allow much set up time for the poured concrete, but maybe it would be just enough, if they could keep it dry, and she certainly hoped that they could.

By 7 a.m. the big trucks started moving out and she was left alone with a handful of workers. They would wait as long as they could before covering the last sections that were poured with the heavy sheets of plastic. The cooling breeze constantly fanning everything should help, she reasoned. She decided to go home, check to make sure everything was secure and that she had what she needed and to take a much needed shower. Then she thought she'd do what some of the remaining locals were doing, driving over to the beach to enjoy the wild thirty-five mile an hour winds and to see the daredevil surfers who thronged to the beaches when hurricanes were imminent—the waves being the biggest, roughest and most challenging as the headwinds churned up the seas.

Freshly scrubbed and dressed in jeans and a light hooded sweatshirt, she made her way over the bridge, stopping to be admonished by an officer to make sure she was back over well before ten when the bridge would be tied back. Normally, they wouldn't let people who weren't property owners go over to the island just before a storm was to hit, but they were locals too and they knew that people wanted to see some of the power of nature just before it unleashed its full fury. And others needed to see their beach one last time, not knowing what they would be coming back to.

Cassie walked down to the water's edge and looked above her as the people on the pier were making their own preparations for the storm. It was closed now, so she couldn't walk out to the end, which would have been like being in the middle of a tempest. The waves were swirling and crashing high on the pillars beneath the pier, sending spray way up into the air.

Oh, this was magnificent! Exhilarating! And oh, so beautiful. She sat down in the sand on the lonely beach looking all around for a long time. The sand would have been blowing and stinging her in the face if it hadn't been so damp. The humidity of the storm was settling in and making the air heavy as the barometer kept steadily falling. She wondered where all the birds had gone; she hadn't seen so much as a plover the whole time she'd been here. They must have someplace special to go when the weather's bad, she reasoned. She forced her tired body up, smacked the damp sand off of her wet and numb derriere, and slowly walked back through the gazebo to her Jimmy and left the island.

The rain started at 4 p.m. They'd had a heck of a time securing the heavy sheets of plastic; but finally, everything was done and all the workers left. Cassie went into the trailer to lock up and shivered from the reaction of her rain-dampened body coming into the lingering effects of the air conditioning. The noise of the rain hitting the trailer was like a constant roar and the wind could be heard meeting resistance with everything. The trailer creaked and rocked and she was suddenly a little frightened and anxious to get home. She grabbed her keys and locked the door and was making her way to her truck when she noticed the trailing edges of some plastic sheeting flapping in the wind on one of the abutments. Damn!

She threw her purse and keys into the Jimmy and stalked over to the abutment. The tie downs they had devised weren't doing a damned thing to keep the rain off of the lower sections. Each time the plastic flapped up, water came in contact with the concrete and the plastic was inching up with each succeeding tug caused by the wind. What the hell was she going to do? If it came off, the concrete would be washed away and hardened into whole ribbons of rock-hard debris strung all over the place. What a mess that would be to clean up and it would put them lightyears behind. She stood there in the pouring down rain, blowing huge breaths of air out of her mouth, letting her bottom lip tremble from the effort as she racked her brain trying to figure out what to do. The rain was blinding; all she could see was gray. Everything was gray and it was getting darker by the minute. She was already drenched and shivering when she turned to face the trailer and remembered the underpinning they had hastily put up. With any luck, the mortar between the bricks would still be wet, or at least wet enough that she could break it up.

She ran over to the tool shed, found it locked as it should have been, and had to go to the Jimmy to get her office keys so she could get the key to the shed from its hook by the door. Finally, with shovel in hand, she attacked the neat rows of bricks that had been placed on one of the corners. Surprisingly, they came apart with minimal effort and pretty soon she had a pile of fifty or more. She threw down the shovel and started carrying the bricks over to where the sheeting was, placing the bricks all around the perimeter. She hoped and prayed that they would be just the added amount of protection needed to keep the rain from breaching the covering.

She was three quarters of the way around the perimeter when suddenly out of nowhere, hands wrapped around her waist and lifted her off the ground.

"What the hell do you think you're doing?" she heard Michael snarl.

"Leave me alone! I've got to fix this!"

"Like hell you do! We're in a hurricane!" He bent and grabbed her behind the knees and lifted her up into his arms. He was covered from his head to his knees in yellow rain gear and his hair was plastered against his face where the hood gaped open. Even so, he was still soaked to the skin underneath it all. She was also drenched, her clothes clinging to her rigid body. It was obvious that he was furious with her and now she was furious with him. She started kicking and thrashing all the while screaming for him to let her down.

"No!" he screamed back at her as he tried to keep his hold on her while she struggled wildly to get down. When she managed to get her legs out of his firm grip and part of her fell to the ground, she was stunned by what happened next. As she kicked out at him, he spun her around and spanked her hard on her bottom, six or seven times. Then before she knew what he was up to, he'd handcuffed her! Her buttocks were stinging as he bent down and picked her up, both hands gripping her firmly around the backs of her thighs. He tossed her over his shoulder and carried her to his cruiser. One hand moved to tightly grip her ankles as she kicked at him and he winced at the blows her handcuffed wrists were inflicting on his back. He had just reached the cruiser when her teeth sank into him. In response, his fingers curled punishingly like steel talons into the soft flesh of her backside. Then he opened the passenger door to the cruiser and threw her in.

"Give me your cuffs, Jeff!" he demanded of the officer sitting behind the wheel. Then he firmly held onto her slim ankles while he struggled to cuff them on her.

"Take her to the Jones/Byrd Shelter and give her to Jenny. Don't listen to a word she says about coming back here or going home and don't take those cuffs off of her until you get there and make sure they're in lock down before you leave her! Come back around for me when you're finished." He slammed the door so hard, she thought it was going to fall off. Jeff, never one to question a direct order and especially not one from someone as angry as Michael, drove her straight to the shelter, despite her protests. In his review mirror he could see Michael walking back to the pile of bricks.

Later that night, Michael stood beside Jenny looking at Cassie who was sound asleep on a cot in a little alcove at the shelter.

222

"She was so angry at you when she got here I had to threaten to have an officer put the cuffs back on if she didn't settle down," Jenny whispered, a slight smile turning up the corner of her mouth.

"Then, after a while, she cooled off and started helping out. She played with some kids, and helped serve dinner. She even took care of a little baby while a young mother ate her dinner. I don't think I've ever seen someone so careful with an infant as she is."

"How long's she been asleep?" he asked in a low voice as he stared at Cassie's sleeping form.

"About two hours."

"Good, she needs the sleep. She hasn't had much sleep this week."

"Yeah, I know. Her father even called me to check up on her when she stopped answering the phones."

"She sure is committed to that bridge."

"She's committed to anything she gives her heart to."

"Uh . . . where's Colin?" Michael asked, clearing his throat and avoiding acknowledging Jenny's pointed comment.

"He's at the house, minding the fort and taking care of Taffy. Paisley's here somewhere, playing cards with some elderly people from Seaside.

"It's really nice that Sea Trail does this."

"Yes, it is. They open this conference center up to employees and residents for every hurricane. They shelter and feed everyone for free and they also allow people with pets to stay downstairs in the golf cart barn. A lot of Sea Trail residents are on the Red Cross Disaster Services Team. They open five shelters locally. There are a lot of wonderful people seeing to the needs of this community."

"Speaking of which, I'd better get back to work. We've already got some badly flooded roads out there."

"She's going to be upset she missed you."

"Oh yeah, she's going to be upset she missed the opportunity to cuss me out or take another bite out of me."

Jenny laughed, "No, that's not why; she's been worried about you. I think she's over your little scuffle, she knows you were just trying to protect her. I'm sure she'd be relieved to know that you're safe."

"I'll come back later."

"I'll tell her."

"Thanks."

"Be careful out there," she called after him.

He came back at two in the morning and quietly asked the officer on duty if he'd seen her. "Yeah, she took a crying baby somewhere back in the kitchen area. It was keeping everybody awake."

"Thanks," he said as he removed his rain gear, shaking the excess water off before hanging it over a chair. Then he eased his way into the lounge area where people were sleeping on the carpet in little partitioned-off sections. He pushed open the double doors to the kitchen and walked into the dimly-lit room.

He saw her sitting at a table at the far end of the room, a little bundle nestled in her arms, her feet propped in a chair.

"Ah, I'm glad I found you when you can't cuss and scream or throw things at me."

"Don't bet on it," she said, her voice barely a whisper.

"I'm sorry about the handcuffs."

She nodded. "I guess I didn't give you much choice."

"No, you didn't."

"What about the spanking?"

He smiled widely, "Well, I'm not sorry about that, you deserved it."

She lowered her lashes in acknowledgement, "What's it like out there?"

"More water than I've ever seen."

"Great."

"Some trees down here and there. We've had to pull a few people out of their cars before they floated away. And of course, there's always one or two babies that can't wait to be born. A couple of deputies delivered a baby at West Brunswick. And get this, a nurse, the *only* nurse at Shallotte Middle, got a bad allergic reaction to some mold on an old Army cot and had to be taken to the hospital with breathing problems. Now the Sheriff and an Eagle Scout leader are the whole medical team for three hundred people.

"You must be very tired."

"I slept extra on Monday."

"You can't save sleep like that."

"You can't?" he asked with a grimace and then immediately feigned falling asleep against the door frame.

She laughed and it sounded so good, he laughed too. "So whose baby?"

225

"Mine. I want to keep her. She is such a good baby."

"That's not what the duty officer says."

"Well, she just needs somebody to hold her," she said as she softly stroked the sweet pink cheeks.

"You can't expect a mother to hold her baby all the time. She'd never get anything else done," he said as he walked over and looked down at the sleeping infant.

"Want me to hold her for a while?"

"No, I'm okay."

He saw a large pile of table linens in a darkened corner at the opposite end of the room. He took her hand and gently pulled her out of the chair then he lowered her to a sitting position on a few of the cotton bags that he'd plumped up for her. He settled himself comfortably against the rest of them with his back propped against the wall and pulled her beside him. With the sleeping infant in her arms she snuggled against his chest and he wrapped his arms around them both.

Chapter 20

The next morning everyone woke to a calm, beautiful, pale blue sky. Thankfully, the damage had been minimal. Trees were down all over the place, there was some flooding and a few trailers had been blown over, but surprisingly, no one had been hurt. No one was even missing; in fact, everyone was accounted for by 11 a.m.

Cassie made it to the site shortly after the sun had risen and was ecstatic to see that the plastic sheeting had held. As she walked around, surveying the concrete abutments, she noticed that there were bricks completely around the perimeter. She knew that wasn't possible, Michael had stopped her when she was only partially around the tied-down sheeting. She turned to look at the pile she had been taking the bricks from, and to her surprise it was gone. She smiled widely while her eyes shone with tears of happiness. Michael had stayed and placed the rest of the bricks by himself. He wouldn't allow her to stay and protect all their work while the hurricane was raging, but he had stayed and finished the job.

If she was not absolutely careful, she was going to fall madly in love with this guy, she told herself, knowing full well that that day had already come and gone. The icing on the cake had been when she'd awakened in his arms this morning with a soaking wet baby lying between them, the irregular circle of wetness staining his uniform shirt.

It took several days to clean up the debris, settle people back into their homes after the electricity had been restored, and clear the roads of downed trees. The water receded within two days and life got back to normal for everybody on the coast. Cassie got back to building her bridge, and Michael got back to trying to find D. Duke's murderer.

As Michael sat at the bridge waiting to come back across to the mainland, he kept thinking that he was missing something elemental, and it was driving him crazy. He asked himself, who would know the most about someone? He put the thought into a personal perspective and asked himself who knew the most about him. His mother? Yeah, but D. Duke's was probably dead. His father? D. Duke's was definitely dead. His wife or girlfriend? As far as he could ascertain, D. Duke had never had either. His best friend? He had no friends, so far as Michael could tell. Just a few neighbors who were acquaintances who had been warned about him by the locals the very day they had moved to the island. His attorney? Couldn't find one. There was no will; no legal papers had been found anywhere, just a few tax returns showing no income from interest, just social security. His doctor? His doctor! Of course! Michael's own doctor knew a great deal about him. He knew that Michael had stitches on his leg when he'd fallen off his bike into a bed of oyster shells. One particularly sharp one, impregnated in a rock, pierced his calf and they had been worried about infection for a while. He knew that he'd had mono once and that he hated the physical required every year to play football. He knew he'd had jock itch and German measles and frequent enough infected throats that the doctor had threatened to take his tonsils out. What did D. Duke's doctor know about him?

He turned around and went back over the bridge to D. Duke's house, found his address book in a kitchen drawer near the phone where he'd seen it before and thumbed through it until he found the name of a local doctor that he recognized. He remembered that it was the same name he'd seen on the emergency contact card in D. Duke's wallet. Dr. Hardison had been practicing in Brunswick County for close to thirty years, and if he was D. Duke's doctor, he might know something that would help. He took the phone from the wall and punched in the numbers beside the doctor's name in D. Duke's book. Then he asked the receptionist if he could make an appointment to talk to the doctor officially. He was put on hold while she went to talk to the doctor.

Idly, he twisted the phone cord and wondered how long it would be before the phone company shut off service. He flipped the switch on the wall and the overhead lights went on. As soon as the bills were overdue or someone notified them, he thought. Whose job was that anyway? He supposed when the company holding the reverse mortgage heard about the death, they would want to fix the place up as soon as possible. The unit, even needing some work, would sell quickly. As a possible crime scene, he could delay the sale indefinitely, but why bother—somebody should be enjoying this view.

The receptionist came back on the line to tell him that the doctor said he could see him in an hour if he could get there by then, so Michael left the island and headed into Shallotte. As he drove north on Route 179 past Ocean Isle, he thought that it must've been pretty hard on ol' D. Duke trying to get around without a car. There weren't any taxis in the area until a few years ago and there still weren't any buses. It was a good thing D. Duke liked to walk and surely people who knew him would have picked him up as they drove past. Sadly, Michael realized that he wasn't even sure D. Duke's closest neighbors would've stopped to offer him a lift. How awful it would be to be an outcast in such a small community. But, remembering the few times he'd talked with him, he knew that D. Duke was one of those people who didn't know that people were shunning him. He was one of those people who was seemingly oblivious to the rudeness going on all around him, even when it was targeted at him.

The doctor answered all his questions but hadn't been able to provide Michael with a single useful thing until Michael thought to ask him about cats. "What about pets, specifically cats? Did Mr. Ellington have any?"

"Lord sakes no! He was deathly allergic. And when I say deathly, I mean just that. Five cats in a room for ten minutes would be enough to kill him."

"Really?"

"Yeah. He had really bad allergies to cat dander. It would go right to his throat, cause it to swell six times its size and completely block his airway. He knew if he had another episode that it would probably kill him."

"Another episode?"

"Yeah. He had two attacks. Once, when he was just a little tyke. That's when they found out he was allergic. And then once again, as a teenager. I wasn't around then, but it's all in his file. The epinephrine

230

they gave him opened up his airway but it dangerously sped up his heart. With each attack more epinephrine was required. So eventually, the drug he needed to save his life, would cause a worse problem—an almost-always fatal heart attack. The heart gets going so fast it's like a car over revving."

"He knew all this?"

"Oh, yeah, sure. He was real careful around cats. Shame, too, he always liked 'em so much. It's as the old saying goes, 'Whatever it is you love the most, you can count on it not being good for ya.' "

"So, if someone wanted to kill Mr. Ellington, all they'd need was a couple of cats?"

"Yeah, I suppose so. If you knew about it."

"Who knew about it?"

"No idea. He may have talked with any number of people about it, or he may not have told a soul. I don't know."

"Did he wear a medical alert tag?"

"He could have. I don't know. Didn't you check?"

"Anything on his neck would have gotten lost."

"Oh, yeah. Right. I forgot about that."

Neither said anything for a minute while they both thought in silence. Then the doctor ventured, "So, if he was already dead from the cats, why'd they cut his head off?"

"I think he cut his own head off."

"Pardon?" the old doctor looked at Michael, his tired eyes bugging out of their sockets.

Michael gave him a tiny, sideways smile then he explained about the ancient, solid bronze propeller in D. Duke's back yard.

"Well, if he was dying from his reaction to some cats on his back deck, and he somehow managed to fall over the railing and chop his own head off, he certainly couldn't have managed to bury the rest of the body over on the beach."

Michael smiled over at the genial doctor who was suddenly getting outraged over the death of a long-time patient. "No, he couldn't have managed to do that, I'm afraid."

He stood up, shook the old gentleman's hand, and after swearing him to secrecy about his propeller theory—he didn't want to appear the idiot if it didn't pan out, he said good bye and promised to do what he could to solve the murder of the doctor's somewhat eccentric patient. As Michael made his way home he thought over everything the doctor had said. Allergic to cats, huh? But he was no closer to solving this crime than he'd been before.

Chapter 21

The following day, Michael got the results back from the coroner's lab proving that the propeller in D. Duke's back yard had indeed cut off D. Duke's head. D. Duke's blood was on the blade as well as minute pieces of matching tissue and hair. The pictures taken by Michael of the angle of the blade in relationship to the deck railing also coincided with the angle that D. Duke's head had been severed from his body.

The chief congratulated him on his discovery and listened intently to his other progress on the case. Then Michael drove to CVS, bought a small plastic ball and drove over to the island to D. Duke's house. From the back yard he looked up at the propeller. Then eyeing the path, he dropped the ball where he thought D. Duke's head might have landed on the sparse lawn. It immediately rolled downhill, down the sloping bank of the canal and into the coastal water. He followed it with his eyes for a minute and then, hopping backyard fences, he followed it to the end of the canal where it followed the currents and headed down the Intracoastal Waterway toward the bridge. He knew he didn't have to worry about polluting the waterway that he loved so much; a small boat would see the ball and claim it as theirs. Not so D. Duke's head that wasn't quite so visible or light on top of the water. And D. Duke's head had fallen into the canal at night when you could hardly see five feet ahead of yourself unless you had special running lights. It had probably bobbed its way slowly down the canal, taking most of the night to reach the waters of the Intracoastal.

He got back into his cruiser and left the island. The last he saw of his multi-colored bouncing ball, was a small glimmer against the water as it floated south of the bridge on its way to Calabash and the Little River Inlet.

Okay. That explained a lot, but not nearly enough. Somebody threw D. Duke over the railing, his neck hit the propeller blade and his head went rolling away. The other half of his body was picked up, put in his boat, rowed and or motored to the back side of Bird Island and buried. Who would do all that and why? Why didn't they just dump the rest of the body in the canal? Why go to all the trouble to bury it? Why chance being seen in D. Duke's boat going down the canal. Why? Why? Why? The area chosen for D. Duke's grave should have been remote enough that he would never have been found. Was the idea for him to be missing instead of dead? And what reason could there be for that? Sooner or later, he would be missed. Maybe not in a nice way, but people would finally notice if he just wasn't around anymore.

So, whoever the killer was, maybe he was stalling for time. Time for what? Time to vacate the island? Time for his trail to diminish? A renter maybe? Time to get home and be forgotten about? And what about the cats? What about the damned cats! He nearly screamed it aloud in the car, he was so frustrated.

Maybe there was evidence of some sort in the boat. He'd been promised a phone call by tomorrow. He already knew that they had matched some of the blood found on the bottom to D. Duke. But being a fishing boat, it wouldn't be all that unusual to have the blood of many fish as well as drops of his own here and there from gaffs with the hooks over many years. The most he could hope for were fingerprints they could identify, or hair that wasn't D. Duke's, or maybe some fibers that were somehow unique. Or better yet, as long as he was wishful thinking, a wallet with the I.D. still in it.

He drove by the work site for the new bridge and tried to spot Cassie's dark curls under a yellow hard hat among all the others. But he couldn't keep his eyes off the road for that long. The crew was getting larger now that they were getting ready to start working on the piers. He wondered how she was doing. The hurricane had set them back a few days as they waited for everything to dry out and arranged to have all their equipment brought back. Cassie knew that it could have been a lot worse, so she was in pretty good spirits. She had thanked Michael for placing the rest of the bricks for her by putting her sweet body under his. And, she had lamented what she'd done to his skin when her hand had found the crescent of her bite mark on his back. She had been upset with herself for her lack of control, but she had promised him the exact same treatment the next time he took it upon himself to spank her and truss her up like that. He remembered that he had laughed at her and thanked her for the warning, saying next time there was a hurricane, he'd put his Kevlar vest on under his raincoat.

Michael had planned a football party at his house on Saturday so he could introduce some of his friends to Cassie. It was also a tradition that whenever his alma mater played against his friend Trey's, that they would host their friends. Last year had been Trey's turn. so now it was Michael's. Trey's idea of refreshments differed greatly from Michael's. Whereas Trey served pizza, beer from a keg, and stale nacho chips with melted Cheese-Whiz, Michael served handmade wraps with his own Pesto-Garlic sauce, crudites with three home style dressings, gourmet potato chips and his ever so popular Gatorade wine. And, of course, a variety of local micro-brews.

So, while Cassie was working fifteen-hour days on her bridge, Michael was shopping, cleaning and cooking in preparation for his guests on Saturday. The irony of their role reversals was becoming a nagging thorn, but he dismissed it with the thought that he'd certainly rather not eat Cassie's cooking unless he had to. She'd made him dinner one night this week and he still hadn't figured out what she'd done wrong to make the Hamburger Helper Beef Stroganoff sauce lumpy, while the noodles were still crisp.

He checked back at the station and found that he'd finally gotten a reply back from Monica Cowell. He'd left her a message over a week ago and she'd finally called back and agreed to meet with him. She was on the board of the "Bridge Busters" as they were commonly called, the group that had spent so much time and money keeping the new high-rise bridge from becoming a reality for Sunset Beach. Michael wanted to talk to her because he knew that she'd had dealings with D. Duke in the past. Maybe she could shed some light on any enemies that D. Duke might have had.

He quickly phoned her back and pressured her to meet him now instead of setting up an appointment several days from now. She reluctantly agreed and he got back into his cruiser and headed back over the bridge. As he pulled over the center grating of the bridge, he looked to his right to see if he could see his ball, but it was nowhere in sight. A mental picture of two great white herons playing dodge ball in the marshes came to mind and he had to laugh at his own idiocy.

Monica Cowell's beach house was impressive to say the least. It was huge and lavishly decorated with fine polished antiques. It figured that a woman who wouldn't let go of the past long enough to plan for the future would be into yesteryear's furnishings.

The widow Cowell was a bit of an antique herself. Tall and reedy with the carriage of an over-cured debutante, she was generously rouged with dry, cracked lips bleeding from caked on pink lipstick combined with maroon lip liner. She smelled sickly sweet of some gardenia fragrance and had an orange hibiscus bloom pinned in her white hair. She was wearing a white gauzy top over tight, white capri pants. Her ensemble ended with her feet tucked into very dated white and gold Malibu slippers. If she'd had a cake in her hand, she could have walked off the page of an old Betty Crocker cookbook.

After refusing her gracious offer of sweet tea and a slice of pecan pie, he sat on the edge of her hard, puffy settee and opened his note pad. The first question Michael asked was one he'd been curious to know the answer to for a long time, "Why wasn't D. Duke in your association?"

"We wouldn't let him join," she said rather haughtily.

"Why not? He was a taxpayer, an island resident, and he sure was dedicated to your cause."

"Too dedicated. Our organization is concerned with preserving all the good things in our community. We simply couldn't condone his actions. Where would the good be in that? It certainly wouldn't have helped our image any. We want what is honorable and honest and straightforward. We have always played fair, no matter what you may have heard. Our goal has always been to give a voice to the people who have lived here for generations, as well as to those who moved here just yesterday. We didn't want Mr. Ellington to represent us—we didn't want to be known for underhanded tactics or intimidation."

"When was the last time you saw Mr. Ellington?"

"About a week before they found him, bless his soul. We were having a committee meeting at my house and he just came right on in like he belonged here. I walked him back to the foyer and told him we were having a budget meeting. That we were trying to figure out how we were going to pay our attorneys to continue the fight. He said he'd get the money we needed, not to worry. I told him that was nice, why didn't he just go do that. Basically I humored him and sent him on his way."

"Did he get you any money?"

"I never saw him again. But I don't think any of his money would have helped, even if he'd had any. As you know, they've already started on the new bridge. At this point, I believe it's hopeless for us."

"Yes. It appears so."

"Well, at least we held it off for over ten years. That's something to be proud of in itself."

Michael bit his tongue, curbing what he really wanted to say. Instead, he mumbled, "Yeah. That you did."

"Some of the old timers will never see the new bridge being built. My parents for instance, bless their souls, died three years ago. They outlived the idea of the new bridge. They never had to look out their deck and see that concrete monstrosity looming over the marshes."

Yeah, and they never had to see a tiny, lifeless baby whose blonde tufts were charcoal from the very smoke that had robbed her of her breath, he thought. "No, I guess not," was all he said. After a quick look down at his note pad, he asked, "Have you any idea who would've wished any harm to come to Mr. Ellington?"

"Now surely Officer Troy, you don't want me to sit down and list everyone who's ever been on this island, do you?"

He grimaced, "No, I guess I phrased that wrong. Is there anyone you can think of who would have taken the steps to do harm to Mr. Ellington?"

"No. I don't know anyone who would actually kill someone else, or at least I hope I don't," she said with some trepidation that the murderer could indeed turn out to be one of her neighbors.

"Well, I thank you for your time. If you think of anything that might help, will you please call me?"

"Certainly."

"One other thing."

"Yes?"

"Would you mind it I looked at the view from your deck?"

"Why? Are you looking for something?"

"No, I just want to see the view. You must have one of the most beautiful views the island has of the bay and the marshes."

She beamed with delight and with her bright red, lacquered fingertips, she indicated for him to precede her through the open French doors.

She did indeed have a magnificent view. Her home was situated on the east side of the island, almost at the end. You could see the Intracoastal all the way from Ocean Isle. You could see Tubbs Inlet, the bay, and the canals and looking in either direction you could see the ocean joining the coastal waters and rivers. It was a sunny day and many boats were out, leaving little white streaks behind them as they went on their way. A few jet skis were in the Intracoastal and you could hear the whine of the motors straining as the riders turned into wave after wave.

"That's my next project," she indicated with a tilt of her head. "Those blasted things make so much noise."

"Now that's a campaign I could get behind," he said with a smile.

Chapter 22

Michael had just left the Sunset Beach Trading Company, a quaint gift shop and ice cream store on the causeway. He stopped there often because he loved Lynn's homemade maple walnut fudge but also because he enjoyed talking with Cliff. Cliff and Lynn owned the neat little souvenir and sundry store and had for many years. Cliff was handsome in a rugged kind of way, with smart, intelligent eyes lighting up his face when he smiled. His smiles were genuine and frequent. And Lynn, who had just turned fifty the year before, had the sweet cuteness of a school girl and the unbridled enthusiasm of an ingenue, though as a retired school teacher, she was anything but. The neatest thing about Cliff though, was how he had a handle on just about everything, which was exactly why Michael had stopped at the store to talk to him. He was a good sounding board and he always saw things from several different perspectives.

Confronted with a dead end on this mystery, he asked questions of his friend and listened carefully to all his answers. But after debating with him back and forth for the better part of an hour, the only thing Cliff had said that stuck in Michael's mind was: "Remember, the predominant motives for murder all boil down to either greed, jealousy, fear or revenge. No one had reason to be fearful of D. Duke and certainly no one would be jealous of him. That leaves greed or revenge. Unfortunately, if it's vengeance, then you've got your work cut out for you. These days people do seem to commit murder at the slightest provocation."

Michael was just about over the bridge when the call came over his radio, someone was having a heart attack at the Sunset Beach Trading Company. Jesus! He'd just left there! He hit his lights and siren and quickly came off the bridge, made a circle around the little island in front of the Twin Lakes Restaurant, and headed back over the bridge.

The radio dispatcher said it was a man in his fifties. God, he hoped it wasn't Cliff. He pulled up in front of the shop, turned off the siren and ran inside. It wasn't Cliff. It was a man visiting from Ohio who had suddenly just dropped onto the floor in front of the glass fudge showcase. Cliff was already performing CPR and Lynn was on the phone trying to get the bridge on the phone, making sure they knew about the emergency on the beach. She was assured that the police dispatcher had already alerted the bridge tender and through the phone she could hear the ambulance coming from the mainland.

Michael relieved Cliff and within minutes the paramedics arrived and took over. A syringe was readied while the defibrillator was hooked up and positioned and several times they yelled clear before moving back. They finally detected a faint heartbeat and quickly readied him for transport. With sirens screaming, they headed for the bridge and Brunswick Community Hospital, twenty-five minutes away.

His heart stopped three times before they got him there. As soon as he was wheeled in, he was prepped for open heart surgery. He had massive blockages that had to be attended to right away, but despite all he'd been through, he was resting comfortably in his own room in the hospital late that very same night.

A few weeks later he made the rounds to all the people who had been instrumental in saving his life. Starting with the doctors in the hospital, he worked his way backward to the paramedics, then the police— Michael in particular, Cliff, the fire department that had been instrumental in procuring the defibrillators they'd had on hand, and the bridge tender who'd had to keep all traffic off the narrow, one-way bridge for half an hour as the paramedics kept trying to jump start his heart. Then he wrote checks to the police department and the fire department and a sincere letter to the Brunswick Beacon expressing his sorrow that nearly ten years ago, he had signed a petition as an island homeowner protesting the construction of a high-rise, fixed-span bridge.

He acknowledged that his name had been only one of many; but that didn't matter, he had played his part in putting people's lives in danger and he'd had no right. Yes, he was a homeowner, but he rented his home at least thirty-five weeks out of every year; the rest of the time it was occupied by friends or family or left empty. He'd only visited the island maybe five or six times since he'd owned the investment property. He'd had no right to determine the safety of those whose actually lived and worked on the island. At the end of his letter, he pledged a check to the city of Sunset Beach in the amount of $150,000 to be used for a huge festival, complete with fireworks, food and music to celebrate the day the new bridge opened.

A few days after the heart attack victim had been saved, and Michael was being commended for his performance by the police chief, a folder was handed to him by the desk sergeant. Michael opened it and walked with it to his desk. It was the report he'd been expecting about D. Duke's john boat. Blood, blood, everywhere. But very little of it tested to be D. Duke's. No prints on the oars, motor cover, or motor pull. None. Absolutely none. That could only mean one thing, they had to have been wiped clean. There should have been prints all over these things; but since there weren't, it meant that the murderer had probably touched them all and then wiped them clean.

The report said that there were fibers on the floor belonging to some light green fabric, maybe a blanket of some kind or a sofa throw. Michael remembered that the other bed in D. Duke's house had no bedspread. He wondered if there could be any fibers on the sheets that might match. He opened the small envelope containing the fibers and looked at them, then closed it up and stuck it in his pocket. He finished reading the report. There really wasn't anything in it that would help him, except, it had been noted that the oars still in the oarlocks were at an angle that could only be facilitated by someone tall, probably close to six feet.

A small golf pencil with an eraser from The Thistle Golf Club had been found in the bottom of the boat according to the report. No prints had been found on it either. It wasn't that unusual to find a golf pencil in a boat around here since there were well over a hundred golf courses within a fifty mile radius. What was unusual was that the short golf pencil had an eraser. Very few courses supplied pencils with erasers. Was there any significance? He opened the other envelope and looked at the pencil. Why hadn't it had any fingerprints? He slid it around in the envelope, the eraser had been used once or twice and the point was not newly sharpened, so it had been used. Where were the prints? Why wipe it off and drop it, why not just keep it? A red herring? He reread the whole report and then tucked it away in a desk drawer. He was getting sick of this whole case. He'd almost rather be sent to help funeral motorcades than work on this stupid case anymore!

He went home to make preparations for his football party the next afternoon. Cassie was coming over this evening to help. He knew it was because she wanted his secret recipe for Gatorade wine and that she was planning on watching him with an eagle eye to get it. He smiled at the thought of her. Well, maybe he could be coaxed into giving it to her. For the right price—the price of her warm, soft body, sliding silkily over his. He'd never wanted or needed sex so much in his life. Just the thought of her small, curvy body sent his blood south, making his penis go from flaccid to flagrant in mere seconds.

Cassie arrived on his door step two hours later, freshly scrubbed and eager for her next cooking lesson. She helped Michael make the pesto sauce from the fresh basil he had growing in his garden and then she peeped over his shoulder as he read the recipe for his kick-a poo-juice.

"Are you trying to sneak a peek at my secret recipe?" he asked, feigning shock at her lack of scruples and pressing the printed side of the card against his chest.

"Why, yes sir, I most certainly am."

245

"It's good stuff, huh?"

"It's great stuff."

"And you want the recipe?"

"Well, would ya mind?"

"It'll cost ya."

"Now, why doesn't that surprise me? What's it gonna be this time?"

"I don't know. This is a mighty good recipe. And so far I've kept it a secret from everyone. If I tell one person, I take the chance that that person will pass it on, and so on and so on until darned near everybody in Brunswick County knows it."

"I promise I won't tell a soul."

"Somebody'll torture it out of you first time you serve it."

"Okay," she said as she leaned into his chest and placed her lips beside his ear. She whispered a few words and his eyes opened wide. "Would that earn me the secret?" she asked as she slowly moved her hand from his muscled chest to his zipper.

"For that, I'll write it out in calligraphy for you," he hissed through clenched teeth as her hand slid into his pants and she found her target. Within seconds, she had his jeans pulled down to his knees.

Slowly she knelt before him and tentatively took him into her mouth. His hands clamped hard onto the edge of the counter and he groaned his pleasure. After tonguing him unmercifully, she repeatedly took as much as she could into her mouth. She reached down with her other hand and gently stroked his heavy sacs. She knew when he was almost ready, she'd read all about this in one of the Penthouse Forum stories one of the construction guys had left in the john. And even though she'd told Michael that she'd never done this before, she had actually been coerced into doing it on a couple of occasions, although she'd never actually managed to get the job done.

Cassie had never experienced the overwhelming thrill it was giving her to drive Michael so crazy. It was a powerful feeling having him so completely dependent on her for his pleasure.

From his heavy breathing and his frantic thrusts, she could tell he was right on the brink of coming. As soft as feather strokes, she touched him with the pads of her fingertips just behind his balls, one of her fingers barely touching his anal opening. His hands left the counter and he grabbed her head by whole handfuls of her hair as he shot his load into her straining mouth. She took it because he wouldn't let her back away and refuse it. Finally, having no recourse, she forced herself to swallow it.

Had she been able to see his face at the height of his climax, she would have seen his jaw firmly clenched and his face agonized, while a long throaty hiss issued between his clamped teeth. Slowly, he became aware of her discomfort as his body rejoined his mind. Ever so gently, he reached down and grasping her firmly by her elbows, pulled her up against him. Her hands splayed against his chest steadied her as he captured her mouth with his, taking her mouth in a possessive kiss of ardent appreciation. When he started kissing her all around her mouth, tasting every curve of her lips with his tongue, she heard him mumbling something. Listening intently, she heard: "One three-liter box of cheap red burgundy wine, one liter Wink soda, one can frozen peach juice concentrate and the juice from a jar of maraschino cherries along with the cherries, green ones if you can find them, refrigerate or float ice rings on top in a punch bowl." He continued murmuring and licking as he lifted her onto the counter, then one hand dove under her T-shirt and cupped a full, warm breast while the other undid the button and zipper on her jeans. As his finger found her moist center and entered her, he shuddered. "Ohhhh, Cassie. You are so so wet, darlin'. Does going down on me turn you on?"

She murmured her approval of his finger placement and then whispered against his lips, that surprisingly, sucking on him had lit a fire down there.

"Well, I think I'd better use my tongue to put it out." he said as he stripped her jeans and panties off of her in one swift movement, adding, "since my 'special talent' seems to have been sucked dry." Spreading her thighs wide he bent to place his mouth on her as he gripped her buttocks and brought her to the edge of the counter. Between his tongue lashings, the gentle nips with his teeth and his constant affirmations of her marvelous musky taste, she relaxed and completely let herself be pleasured by his mouth. Suddenly, something coiled tight and then sprung free as he greedily sucked on her fully engorged clitoris. She spent herself, allowing nothing of herself to be left behind. She gave herself completely and wholly to Michael in a way that she had never dreamed was possible between two people. She wanted this moment to last forever and she knew that in her mind, it would. She would always remember this moment, this cherished time when they had so completely satisfied each other; this moment in time when she realized that she was truly and desperately in love with Michael.

Michael stood up and hungrily kissed her on the mouth. "Can you taste yourself on my tongue?" he asked. "You are delicious, I couldn't get enough of you," he said as he lifted her off the counter and set her on her feet.

She blushed furiously at his blatant comment. What did one say to that? Thank you? I'm glad you like it? She retrieved her clothes, and together they cleaned the kitchen of the mess they'd made so far and set out the ingredients for the next item on tomorrow's menu. Cassie cut the fresh vegetables for dipping while Michael made his homemade dressings.

Then they talked about their day, the slowly developing unsolved case and the bridge. Her crew was getting ready to work on the abutment on the island side and that required moving the heavy machinery by cranes and barges across the waterway. The old bridge would not be able to take the weight of some of the heavier earth moving pieces and they needed the cranes on the waterway side anyway since another crew was going to start placing the pilings within the next few days. Michael never realized the logistics involved with each phase of the construction and that anything forgotten until the last minute could result in many days lost. The weather was still holding. It was in the sixties or seventies most days and since it was only early October, unless they were threatened by another hurricane, they should be able to work with no hindrance until January. Then there would still be some good days, sandwiched between cold and rainy ones.

"I think I'm going to enjoy being on the other side of the Intracoastal for a while. The wildlife seems a bit more abundant on that side. Even though it's quite a distraction to see the snowy egrets and the great blue herons in the marshes. I find I just have to take the time to stop and watch them, they are so graceful. I feel very peaceful when I see them going about their every day nesting and feeding habits while we make all that noise and dust around them. I'm surprised they're not all scared away; they must be getting used to us being there."

"This is a wonderful place to live if you like to watch birds. The whole island and most of the mainland is a bird sanctuary."

"What I don't understand, is why you see 'for sale' signs in front of so many houses. You'd think that once someone bought into a piece of this paradise, they would stay and enjoy it. It seems like it would be awfully hard to move away from all this."

"Well, some people don't have a choice, their jobs take them to other places. And a lot of older people relocate here and then find out that they have a serious health problem and they need to be close to a big university hospital, like Duke or the Medical University of South Carolina in Charleston. People who have cancer, generally have to go to Myrtle Beach or Wilmington for treatment, sometimes daily. And then, you have the people who come down, fall in love with the area, build a beautiful retirement home and then they realize that they can't stand to be away from their children or grandchildren, so they move back home to be with their family."

"Yeah, I guess. I just think that once you find a place like this, it must be so hard to pack up and leave it all behind."

"Does this mean you're staying after the bridge is done?" he asked, trying not to put too much interest into the question.

"I really hadn't thought about it. I have to go where daddy sends me. But I think, no matter where I go, I'll keep my little place here and make this my home base. My vacation spot when I'm between projects."

"Oh."

"And speaking of daddy, he's coming down," she said in a gloomy voice.

"Why so glum?"

"How often do your parents come to check up on your work?"

"Never. I mean they come to visit, but they don't check up on my work, but then I don't work for them."

"Yeah, well, you're lucky. That's the only thing I hate about this job."

"You hate your father?"

"No, dummy. I hate that he keeps checking up on me. It's like he expects me to screw up or something. I know how exacting he is, but he could trust me a little more."

"Why do you think it is that he doesn't?"

"Well, I have made a few mistakes."

"Like what?"

"I ordered box girders instead of plate girders once. But I realized my mistake in time to make the change."

"So what was wrong with that?"

251

"Well we had to pay to ship the box girders back. Ten truckloads of them. They're concrete, they weigh a ton. It cost a lot of money."

"Okay, so everyone's entitled to a little mistake."

"Daddy didn't see it that way. And then there was the time I put the coffer dam too close to a waterfall."

"What happened then?"

"The underwater currents eroded away the base and we almost had a breech which would have flooded the whole excavation."

"So what did you do?"

"I had to bring in some sandbags to secure it."

"So what's wrong with that?"

"Sixty-four hundred of them."

"Oh."

"And the divers to place them."

"Aha. I see. Another cost overrun."

"Exactly."

"And daddy doesn't like you wasting his money."

"No, he doesn't. But he especially doesn't like it when I do something dumb, something I should know better."

"Sounds like those things could have happened to anybody."

"Yeah, well, the last boner really put the nail in my coffin."

"I'm not sure I want to hear this one," he said with a grimace.

"Fine, I won't tell you."

"No, you gotta tell me, now that you've brought it up, you gotta share. That's the rule."

"The rule, huh?"

"Yeah, once you start something, you gotta finish."

"Okay," she said as she continued slicing carrots. "I met a guy, he seemed real nice. We went out a few times, he took me to a couple of parties to meet his friends. Then one night on the way to a concert, he gets pulled over for driving too fast. The cops go back to their car to check him out and while we're sitting there waiting for them to return, he starts cussing and fuming and then, before I know what's up, he pulls out and leaves."

"Well, naturally they give chase and finally after the scariest ride of my life, we get pulled over again. This time by four different police cars. We're handcuffed, arrested, booked and locked up."

"By the time my father gets there and bails me out, I have lice and a cell mate that wants me to be her girlfriend, hers alone, if you know what I mean. I was probably only twenty minutes away from finding out just what it is that lesbians do when they have sex together."

"Well, needless to say, he was preeetty furious. When he found out what I was being charged with, he went berserk. Resisting arrest, possession of narcotics—enough to qualify me as a dealer and send me away for thirty years, and abetting a criminal. He'd jumped bail in Indiana and was driving a stolen car."

"Wow!"

"That's not all."

"What! There's more? What else?"

"He was married."

"Cassie, honey, why were you seeing this schmoo?" he asked as he softly tucked an errant curl behind her ear. He saw the beginnings of tears starting

253

to form in the bottom of her eye lids, clumping her lashes.

"I didn't know! I honestly didn't know! I never knew about anything! And, yes, maybe I was a little naive, as my father's friend, Judge Casser, kept saying. But I trusted him, I had seen no reason not to."

"Did you have sex with this man?"

She looked down at her hands and he saw one tear let loose and slide towards her nose. "Yes," she whispered so softly that he almost couldn't hear it.

"Protected?"

"Yes."

"And you've been tested?"

"Yes. Every test there was. My father insisted on it. It was so embarrassing."

"Everything negative?"

"Everything was negative."

He turned her to him by her slim shoulders and looked into her now tear-stained face and smiled down at her. "And no more lice?"

She smiled up at him, "No, no more lice and no girlfriend, either."

"Well, I wouldn't have minded you having a girlfriend; the lice I would've taken objection to."

"What is it with you guys? Do all guys get off on the thought of two girls together?"

"Well, I personally can't vouch for all guys, but all the ones I know wouldn't mind a threesome now and again."

"I prefer one-on-one, and I like the one I'm with to have his own tool."

He leaned down and kissed the tears from her cheeks, "That's my girl, she likes to play with boy's toys." He kissed the column of her throat and then went back to her lips, kissing only the bottom lip with his lips as he worked his way around to the top one. "I think I need to be inside you now," he said simply before he bent at the knees and picked her up.

Carrying her to the bedroom, he marveled at her beauty. She was homespun and natural with the faint taste of carrots on her tongue. Her abundant black curls, that he'd already mangled many times tonight, had flopped back into place and she had that just tousled and nicely-loved look on her flushed cheeks. He laid her down on the comforter, undressed her again and stood back to admire her while he removed his clothes.

She was warm and inviting and fleshy in just the right places. Her dark, puckered nipples were sitting atop proud, full and nicely rounded breasts. His eyes followed the planes of her flat abdomen down to the dark, bushy vee and his favorite body part danced for her as he grabbed a condom from the night stand. He knelt on the comforter between her legs as he slowly rolled it down his thick penis, her eyes watching his movements.

His eyes met hers and he climbed on top of her, positioning himself at her opening. "Are you still wet from before or do I need to get you ready for me?"

"I've been ready for you all my life."

"That's a long time to wait."

"Well, what can I say? You're worth waiting for. Now take that incredibly hard prick of yours and put it deep inside me."

"Your wish is my command," he said as he thrust his hips forward and entered her. The minute his groin was flush with her mons veneris, something came over the two of them and they started grinding and arching and thrusting, so eager were they to be completely involved and enmeshed with each other. She met each of his hard downward thrusts with a matching uplift of her hips and soon the tempo they had established was knocking the headboard into the wall. With one hand he braceleted her wrists high above her head, with the other he cupped one of her jiggling breasts. When he knew he couldn't stand this wonderful torment much longer, he bent and took the nipple all the way into his mouth and suckled her. And just when he thought he would have no choice in the matter of bringing her to satisfaction first, she cried out his name, dug her fingers into his buttocks and held him tightly to her as her world tipped and emptied and she fell off. She continued throbbing against him long after her orgasm was over, and soon the incredible feelings caused by the residual squeezing action of her vagina, over took him. With one final thrust, the tip of his penis grazed her cervix and he exploded into her. Every color star imaginable was bursting in his brain while his body sought its release in hers. His groan was loud and prolonged, dying out just in time for him to hear the words she was murmuring over and over again, "I love you Michael. I love you. Love you. Love you."

For a moment, he wasn't sure of what she was saying or what he was hearing. He was, after all, still in a fog, he told himself. Maybe it just sounded like she said that she loved him. But leaning up on his elbows and looking down into her face, he confirmed by the starry look in her eyes, that this was indeed a woman who had just professed her love. And now she was expecting something back, some words similar in meaning. Shit!

Fall back on flattery was his staunch motto for times such as these. So he whispered in her ear, "Cassie, honey, you were incredible. It's never been this good before." Well that part was true, it *had* never been this good. "And just look at you, you are so beautiful. Gorgeous eyes, a sweet little nose, full luscious lips," he started kissing her neck, allowing his lips to continue on to the center of her chest, "and great tits with the most responsive nipples I've ever had the pleasure to taste." He gave each tight bud a long lash with his tongue.

"Much as I'd like to hear you describe all the other parts of me, did you hear me Michael? I said, I love you."

He kissed her lips and murmured softly, "Yes, I heard you." There was a little catch of sadness in his voice that she didn't miss.

"Oh," she said, realizing that he wasn't going to say it back to her.

Oh no. He knew the signs of a big storm brewing if he ever saw one, and he didn't want to get caught in this nor'easter. Think, think, think, he told himself. The best his brain could come up with was: *lie.* "Cassie, I feel the same way that you do, it just takes men a lot longer to express it in words. Give me more time, those three little words are hard for a man to say because they can lead to so much more than they're ready for."

Cassie's exuberant expression of love, so uncontrollable a few moments ago, was now embarrassing her to death. Her elation of just a few

257

moments ago was shattered and she just wanted to go away and crawl into herself. Buck up, she told herself, so he doesn't love you, big deal! But it was a big deal. It was a huge deal and she wanted to scream from the pain of it. Instead, she ran her hand over his lushly matted and finely sculptured chest, played with a hidden nipple for a few seconds and then pushed against him, trying to lift him off of her. He readily complied with her and lifted himself up, disengaging them at the same time. He looked down and discovered that the condom was missing. So before she could sit up, he pushed her down lightly and using one hand to spread her thighs, he felt for the end of the condom between her slickery folds.

Wonderful! she thought. Let's just be embarrassed all the way around tonight, shall we? Deftly, he gave a slight tug and the thin membrane came out of her. She quickly closed her thighs and rolled over, pulling the comforter on top of her to completely cover her. She wasn't cold. She was embarrassed, ashamed and extremely aware of her nudity. While Michael was in the bathroom, she dressed and went back to the kitchen where she washed her face and hands.

When Michael came back out to the kitchen she was drying her face with a paper towel. "As soon as I finish these vegetables, I think I'll go home. I'm starting to get a bit tired. It's been a pretty long day."

"Cassie, we need to talk."

"What's there to talk about? You said it and everybody already knows it. Girls mature lightyears ahead of boys. I'll sit on the side lines and wait for you to catch up, if you ever do catch up, that is."

"Cassie . . ."

"Michael, it's no big deal. Really, I'm fine."

"What's this about sitting on the sidelines stuff? What's that mean?"

"It means that maybe we've gone a bit too fast. As you've heard tonight, I have a tendency to do that. We should slow down or cool it for a while."

"Slow down? Cool it? What the hell do you mean by that?"

"What do you think it means, Michael?" she said, her tone taking on an air of one irritated at a stupid question. "It means no sex!"

"Cassie! Let's be sensible about this!"

"I am Michael. I'm being as sensible as I know how to be when all I want to do is crawl under a rock. Damn! I cut my finger!"

Immediately, Michael was standing beside her holding her bleeding finger between two of his. "Pressure, immediate and firm pressure," he said as he walked her over to the sink. Slowly he released the pressure and looked at the cut, it quickly filled up with blood again. "It's not too bad, I think a band aid will take care of it." He wrapped her finger tightly in a paper towel and told her to hold it firmly. Then he went to the bathroom and brought a band aid back. After running water on the cut and drying it, he wrapped the band aid tightly around her finger. Then he brought it to his lips and kissed it. "I think you need bed rest. Bed rest in my bed. Then you'll be all better in the morning."

"I think it would be better if I went home now. I'll come back tomorrow before the game and help you."

"You have to make the kick-a-poo juice. And if you don't remember the recipe, I'm afraid you'll have to bribe it out of me again," he said with a sly smile.

"I remember and what I don't remember you'll supply free of charge because I know you don't want your guests to be served anything inferior, anything less than the real McCoy."

Sensing the tension and knowing that there were still issues between them, issues he didn't want hanging over their heads tomorrow when he had company, he reached for her, "Cass, let's talk about this. I don't want you going home mad or even worse."

"Worse?"

"Feeling rejected," he said, bringing the major issue to the foreground.

Cassie picked up her purse, dug inside for her keys and stomped over to the door. "I didn't realize that I'd been rejected, but since that's apparently the case, let me tell you something. There's no harm in loving somebody and letting them know that you love them. The harm is when you don't recognize a good thing when you've got it. Because sure as shootin', when you finally figure out what it is you gave up, it'll be too late, 'cause somebody else'll come along and see what you didn't. I'll be here by noon to help out and meet your friends and if there's anybody I take a hankering to, I do hope you'll be a gentleman and bow out gracefully without compromising me." She opened the door and quickly closed it behind her.

He stomped over to it and brusquely opened it again. "Cassie!" he called out to her but she pretended not to hear him as she got into her Jimmy and backed out of the driveway.

He slammed the door shut. Women! They always want you to give more than you're ready for! He walked over to the liquor cabinet and poured himself a shot of Jack Daniel's. Then he tossed it down, enjoying the slow, mellow burn. Well, he'd just show her. Two could play this game. If she was going to shop around then so would he! Compromising her? What the hell did that mean? Kiss and tell? What kind of man did she think he was, anyway?

Chapter 23

Michael did not sleep well that night. He found himself tossing and turning all night, his naked body constantly entangled in the bed sheets. What was that woman doing to him, he thought as he ground some coffee beans for his breakfast. He'd had thoughts of her all night, thoughts of her with other men. Images of her naked on the beach, her welcoming arms reaching up to a faceless man followed by quick snapshots of her riding on her various life-sized Tonka toys, stripping off her clothes for a variety of men, smiling suggestively at them. He groaned at the recollection of those vile thoughts.

Cassie arrived at noon as promised and together they finished the preparations, their stilted silence a constant reminder of last night's discord. By one o'clock all the guests had arrived and Cassie was introduced to them all. The men sequestered themselves in the living room in front of the TV while the women busied themselves in the kitchen, fixing drinks and putting the final touches on the food before bringing it to the picnic tables in the back yard. As the game progressed, the women and children settled themselves outside on the chairs and chaises on the lower patio.

As the men wandered in and out of the kitchen and frequented the laden buffet, Michael noticed that Cassie was fitting in nicely. The women had taken her into the fold and they were all laughing hysterically at something one of them said. He went to get a beer from the kitchen, but instead of rejoining the group in front of the game, he stood at the open patio doors watching Cassie sitting at the picnic table. He'd noticed that almost every guy here had given her quite a bit more than a just a glance. And there she was now talking to Ray, one of his fellow policemen.

Cassie placed Ray as soon as he introduced himself, she remembered him from the walkie-talkie conversation she had so inopportunely overheard. She forced herself to be polite and friendly. Then, when she saw that Michael was watching her, she forced herself to vamp.

"So, Ray," she said as she batted her lashes and gingerly touched his arm, "what do you like to do in your off time? Are you into golf or water sports?"

"I like to play a round of golf, then go out on the town. There's a lot of great night life around here. Usually I go to Myrtle Beach to do some shagging, and I like to go to the concerts at the House of Blues at Barefoot Landing." He leaned in and whispered in her ear, "Maybe you'd like to go with me sometime?"

She smiled up at him and nodded, "I'd like that very much. I've only been shagging, once though, you'll have to refresh me on how it's done."

He grinned widely, "I'd be happy to. How about next Friday?"

Michael heard the last part as he walked over to get some chips out of the big bowl on the table. What a sleaze! He was making time with his girl at his party! And she was encouraging it, just like she said she would. Well, let's just see how she feels about me playing the field, he thought as he walked over to one of the Adirondack chairs. Jessica, a friend from

Raleigh, was relaxing in it. He walked over and started massaging her neck and shoulders. Her low moans and groans could be heard punctuating the conversations of those on the lawn.

Cassie looked over at Michael, frowned, and turned back to Ray. "I can't next Friday, my dad is coming into town. How 'bout the Friday after?"

"Sure. That would be great. I'll call you."

"Okay." Boy, did she feel guilty. Had she really just set up a date with this slime ball just to make Michael jealous? Yes, that's exactly what she had just done.

Michael continued rubbing Jessica's neck until he saw Cassie go back into the house, then he patted Jessica on the shoulders and offered to refresh her drink for her.

In the kitchen, Cassie and Michael exchanged wary glances, both of them raising their eyebrows to the other in challenge before parting again. For the next hour Michael was more aware of where Cassie was and what she was doing than he was of the status of the game.

He was sitting in a chair on the patio when he spotted some friends who were just arriving. The husband waved to Michael as he walked across the lawn and the wife smiled, her hands around a covered casserole dish, most likely some unique version of a Coca-Cola Jello salad. That was Violet for you, always bringing something to a gathering, in the good old southern tradition of hospitality. As he stared at her, he thoughtfully appraised her. She was the epitome of the southern wife. There she stood in her floor-length, flowered, silk dress with its vee-shaped collar trimmed with lace, her fashionably strapped sandals and her smartly styled long, flowing, blonde tresses secured with jeweled barrettes. Behind her were her two clean and smartly dressed children, the perfect picture of a family whose heritage and upbringing were unquestionably proper. That's what he wanted. That's what he had almost had. A true southern, stylish woman with class and breeding.

Jeanette had been perfect, southern born and raised, from a good family with impeccable manners and class. She'd graduated from a premier South Carolina college and was tall, slinky and cultured, a junior leaguer involved in the community, the church and the schools. She was a woman who would have, for all appearances, taken admirable care of her husband and family. Even if it wouldn't have been exactly true, she would have acted the part she'd been trained to, all the requirements fulfilled, except for her duties in the master bedroom. There, she wasn't at all what a southern wife should be—living to please her husband, tenaciously daring any other female to try to attract her man. Oh sure, dalliance was allowed, but a southern woman worth her grits was assured of her man's faithfulness, just as he was assured of hers.

The only problem with Jeanette was her overwhelming fear of sex. And as gentle as he was, as much time as he allowed, he could not get her to relax and enjoy his caresses. Taking her virginity had been traumatic for them both. Even after an hour of foreplay, she had been dry and unyielding. He'd hated to let her go, but it never would have worked, at least not for anything more than appearances.

As he continued to stare at Violet, Cassie watched the wistful expressions on his face. Without even meaning to, he was making her jealous all over again.

Just then, Michael turned to meet the eyes that were staring at him so hard. Cassie. She was nice. Hell, she was a lot better than nice. And he liked her a lot. But she didn't fit the image—his concept of a wife, the idea he'd always had that she be a fine lady of the south. He'd envisioned her many times over the years, and she'd always been slim and graceful, wearing a flowing, long dress with a big, floppy summer hat. He saw her now in his mind's eye, walking down a white carpeted path on a green velvet lawn under an arched white trellis, her hand extended to his as they went to stand before a minister on a beautiful, lazy summer day.

His mind focused back on Cassie and she gave him a quizzical look. How was he supposed to tell her that he couldn't love her? That she wasn't what he wanted. That she wasn't blonde and willowy. She didn't fit the bill: she couldn't cook; couldn't decorate; couldn't sit on committees deciding which color azalea plants they should put in front of the church, and she wasn't a gently-bred woman of the south.

She gave him a small smile and a sexy wink and it was then that he remembered what Cassie could do for him. She could keep him deliciously happy in their picture-perfect, "Southern Living" master bedroom. He envisioned her sitting atop a huge canopied bed, her tiny body almost lost in the huge tapestry hangings, her dark curls vibrant against her white silk pajama shirt as she knelt and provocatively beckoned with her curled finger for him to come join her. And that was where the real problem was, because as easily as he could picture himself with someone else for a wife, he couldn't picture anyone but Cassie in his bed, no matter how hard he tried.

"What are you thinking about?" she asked as she sauntered over to where he was sitting.

"Us," he answered honestly.

"What about us? Is there still an us?"

At that exact moment he made up his mind. He was going to lie. Rather than lose her all together, he decided he was going to lie. He had no idea whether he loved her or not. He didn't think that he did, but he didn't want to lose her, not just yet. And he couldn't stand the thought of her seeing anybody else. His dreams of last night came to the forefront of his mind and he gritted his teeth. No, nobody else would have her, the thought of her with somebody else was actually making him physically ill.

"Michael, what's wrong? You look angry."

"I am. I'm angry at myself. I've been stupid and I see that now."

"What do you mean?"

Just then they were interrupted by Trey, "Hey, buddy, you'd better get in there and cheer your team on. They're behind by two touchdowns. And we need some more beer."

"I'll be right there. There's plenty more in the downstairs refrigerator. I'll bring some up."

He stood to get up just as Violet came down the stairs and walked over to him. In her syrupy sweet, southern drawl she remarked, "Michael, I've been lookin' all over for you. I just love what you did to that deck. It's so nice and roomy now, perfect for these outdoor parties. Do you think I could get your recipe for that scrumptious Gatorade wine?" her sugary plea was almost a candy-coated whine.

Michael looked over at Cassie and winked, "I'm afraid, I only give that out in exchange for promises of carnal pleasure. Talk with Billy Joe and let me know what he says, ya hear."

She gasped and covered her mouth with her dainty hand, "Well, I'll be! Michael, surely, you're joshin' me!"

"No ma'am, I'm not." He put his arm around Cassie's shoulders and turned to walk away. While he was still within earshot of Violet, he said, "So, you didn't write those ingredients down, huh? Mighty darn shame, now we're gonna have to start all over again. There's a bedroom downstairs, let's just duck in there for a quick refresher. And this time, maybe you'd better write the recipe down!"

Violet gasped as she overheard his words, spun around and hurried back up the stairs, gently holding the hem of her dress just below her knees as she scurried away.

They both doubled over with laughter as soon as they were alone in the basement rec room.

"You should have seen the look on her face!" Cassie said.

"I'll bet it was priceless."

"Actually, I'm not sure she wasn't giving your proposition some thought."

"Really?" He turned as if he was now suddenly eager to rejoin her.

"Now, come on. Does she seem the type to fool around?"

"You never know. These southern women come off all refined and proper, but they have a wild side, too."

"Yeah, so do us northern women."

He wrapped his arms around her and pulled her into his chest. "Don't I know it. Hey, come here," he said as he pulled her over to a small love seat tucked into the corner of the basement, "I want to talk to you."

"What about?" she asked as she sat down next to him.

He sat on the edge with his thighs spread, his hands fidgeting between them. "I'm sorry about last night. I didn't realize 'til this morning how stupid I'd been."

"How were you stupid?"

"I let my instincts take over and I fought with you over something that temporarily scared me."

"Me telling you that I loved you?"

"Yeah." He reached over and grabbed her hand. "Remember that night I came to your bedroom at Jenny and Colin's?"

"Yeah."

"I told you then that I was falling for you. Yesterday, I thought that I still was, falling that is. I thought I was still in the process of falling in love with you. Now, I realize that I fell. In fact, I had already fallen before you even said anything. I just wasn't ready to admit it. I am now." He turned to face her and forced himself to meet her misty eyes. With steady hands, he cupped her face. "Cassie, I am in love with you." He lowered his head and took her lips with his, searing in his words. He moved his hand down to her neck and pulled her closer, his tongue savoring the feel of her lips as they opened for him. He had his tongue deeply in her mouth, plundering her sweet cavity and he was about to put his hands under her sweatshirt when they were interrupted.

They heard heavy footsteps on the stairs and then the booming voice of his friend, "Hey, buddy, what about the beer? And your team's not even covering the point spread anymore. Can I take over doing that for you while you entertain your guests?"

"I am entertaining one of my guests, if you don't mind. And no, nobody kisses my girl but me." He set her aside, stood up and walked over to the refrigerator. "Okay, okay, I'll get the beer. And don't worry, it's not even half time yet, there's plenty of time for a comeback. Come on sugar, help me carry some of these cans up, will ya?"

"Sure," she said brightly. She would do anything for this man, this man who had just said he was in love with her.

He patted her on the bottom and gave her a quick kiss on her nose. "You can stay after the game and help me clean up can't you?" His meaning was all too clear, he wasn't at all interested in her help cleaning up.

She frowned, "No, actually I can't. I have to get over to the new site and set up a few things, I've got a crew coming in for a few hours tomorrow."

"Tomorrow is Sunday."

"I know. And I don't like to work on Sunday, but we lost a day due to rain and with daddy coming next weekend, I have to get a few things done."

"Okay," he said, clearly disappointed, "but I want one afternoon and night this week to cook you dinner, one night when you're not all stressed out about your father's visit."

"Okay. I think I can manage that. Maybe Wednesday, how's that?"

"Perfect. I'll be over around 2:30."

"I can't leave the site that early!"

"Well then, just give me your house key so I can get dinner started."

"What are you making?"

"It's a surprise."

"Oh. That'll be nice."

He loaded her arms up with beer cans then took the top one and shook it real hard.

"Trey's probably on the rear deck. Take that one to him for me, will ya?"

She smiled, "Sure."

With each step she took up the stairs her heart sang out, he loves me, he loves me, Even the thought of her dad's visit next weekend couldn't put a damper on her spirits. She loved Michael and Michael loved her. Soon they would marry, she just knew it. Her name would be Cassie Troy. She was in such a state of euphoria that she forgot to step back after she handed Trey the can of beer and she ended up with just as much foam on her as he had on him.

It was just as well, she needed an excuse to leave early. She wanted to be alone with her thoughts. She wanted to take the time to savor the words Michael had said, over and over again. One minute you're falling, then before you even know it, you've fallen. He had fallen in love with her. It had sounded like he hadn't meant to, that maybe he didn't even want to, but still he had and that was all that mattered. Michael was in love with her.

Michael sat at his kitchen table fingering the case file on D. Duke. It was Saturday night. The mess from the party was all cleaned up and here he was sitting all alone feeling guilty as all get out. He'd lied to Cassie, he'd told her that he loved her when he didn't, and he was disgusted with himself. This was the lowest thing he'd ever done and he knew it.

Even when he was in college, he'd never stooped this low. He prided himself on the fact that he never left a bar without paying for his beer and that he never forced himself on a woman. And boy, the opportunities he'd had. There were many nights when he had found himself accompanied by a bombed-out-of-her-mind coed, who wouldn't have a clue what you did to her the night before as long as you didn't put her skirt back on inside out. Why was this bothering him so badly? It wasn't as if he was using her. He realized after pondering that over for a few moments, that that was exactly what he was doing. He was using her. Using her and her feelings for him to keep him sexually satisfied until someone better came along. A southern candidate for the role of his wife.

On top of all that, his team had lost, suffering the worst defeat they'd ever had. He grabbed the stack of banded cards and found his note pad. He had to find some way to divert his thoughts. Maybe Lady Kit would speak to him tonight and give him the clue he needed to crack this case. Then maybe he could become one of the department's permanent detectives.

"I think this may just be the prettiest time of the year to be here. The meeting was canceled, and had I known, I probably wouldn't have come, but I'm sure glad that I did. The sunsets are just gorgeous. I wish I could stay for the festival, but I promised to play the piano at church Saturday night and Sunday morning. October 13, 1999."

Whoa! That was something he'd missed before. Church on Saturday night and Sunday morning. She was probably Catholic. Although, a lot of help that would be, there were so many people attending Catholic churches these days that most police departments had a whole contingent of officers rotating weekly just to control the mass exodus when the services were over. Plus, she was playing back home, wherever the hell that was, so that was no help. What meeting was canceled? Did she come here for meetings? He wrote "plays piano" and "meetings?" on his note pad and flipped the card over.

"Went to Europe for the holidays. Ate way too much food. Now I'm forced to diet and exercise. God, how I hate to exercise! The only time I seem to enjoy it is when I'm here. Walking along the beach doesn't seem as tedious as that stupid treadmill! January 12, 2000. How odd it is to write that number."

Europe. So, she had a little money tucked away or maybe she used a credit card. In any case, there was no help there, either. A lot of people went to Europe; in fact, several people who owned houses on the island lived in Europe.

"It's getting harder and harder to get away. I just may have to resign as a volunteer. I have a new job at work, in fact, I have several. They've laid off four people since the first of the year, but have they laid off any of the work? No, of course not! I'd quit if I didn't have so much invested. Just how much do they think one person can do, anyway? The weather's been nice this week, but it hasn't been a particularly good visit. Had to call the police this week. Those damn college kids with their parties! It's a shame that I have to go home to get some sleep, usually I rest so well here. May 9, 2000."

Well, he already knew she wasn't overly fond of the college kids that visited the beach, but he hadn't remembered from reading these before that she had lodged a complaint. Now he had something else he could check up on. He could go back to the dispatch records for that week and pull all the noise complaints called in on the island. He'd concentrate on the east side. "This week" could mean the current week she had been in or all the way back seven days prior. Just to be sure, he'd pull the complaints going back ten days. Her lack of a pronoun before the word "had" could mean that somebody else might have called, not that she herself had called. Hell, she could've meant another homeowner had to call or even a vacationer had to call, but certainly somebody close to where she lived had called. That much he could investigate and maybe he'd get lucky and her name would be on a report. He rubbed his eyes and banded up the index cards again. First thing in the morning, he'd check out those complaints. Now, he needed to get some sleep.

As he undressed for bed, he thought how nice it would be to crawl under the covers and snuggle up to a warm, sweet-smelling body. A body that curved so perfectly into his. He wasn't thinking of sex, he was just thinking of sleeping. Sleeping with a woman with corkscrew curls and sultry eyes who played in the dirt for a living. He shook his head and smiled at his own foolishness. Sleeping? Who the hell was he kidding? He wanted to be banging that headboard into the wall again.

Chapter 24

Michael had already set the table and had dinner ready when Cassie got home. She quickly showered and threw on a halter top and some shorts before joining him in the kitchen. He walked her into the dining area and motioned for her to have a seat at the head of the table. His place setting was on the opposite end of the elegantly set table. Then he went back into the kitchen to serve.

"Everything smells terrific!" she called to him as she placed her napkin on her lap.

He put a plate of the Chateaubriand he'd prepared in front of her. They were at her house, having a somewhat formal dinner that Michael had been preparing for most of the afternoon. On her left side, beside her forks, he placed a box of McNuggets. She thought that was odd, but didn't comment on it. He then took her fork, skewered a slice of the succulent, sauced-coated beef and fed it to her.

She closed her mouth around the fork and chewed very slowly, savoring the exquisite taste. "Ummm. This is wonderful. What is it?"

"Chateaubriand."

"Oh, it is excellent," she said as she tried to take her fork back so she could get another piece.

"Would you like some more?"

"Oh yes, please."

"Take off your shirt."

"What?"

"Take off your shirt."

"Oh. Chateaubriand," she said, as it dawned on her that they'd talked about this once before.

"Yes."

"I'm not taking off my shirt."

He quite nonchalantly picked up the plate, put the box in front of her and walked with the plate to the end of the table where his dinner was waiting. He placed the plate beside his and started eating.

She sulked for a minute as she watched him eat his meal with relish. "I don't want this. I want what I've been smelling since I got home."

"Then take off your shirt," he said firmly.

"No."

"Then eat the McNuggets," he said unwaveringly.

"Would you do something despicable and degrading just because I asked you to?"

"If it meant you would get a feeling comparable to the incredible hard on I'm expecting to get when you bare your beautiful breasts to me while I eat my dinner, then certainly, I would oblige you." He picked up the plate and waved it around, "C'mon, bare yourself and I'll bring this to you. It's getting cold."

She gave him a dirty look, then slowly reached behind her neck and unbuttoned the halter straps of her shirt. She dropped the straps and the front of her shirt fell to her waist, baring her breasts. She reached behind her back and unfastened the closure there. Then she grabbed the shirt, held it to the side of the table and let it drop to the carpet. As soon as her shirt was off, he stood and brought her plate to her, his eyes never leaving her chest.

She was so embarrassed that she started eating right away, just to have something to do that was normal. As he settled himself back into his seat at the other end of the table, his eyes feasted on her. He slowly ate his dinner, totally focused on the woman at the other end of the table and the generous bosom that she was displaying for him. The view of her exposed chest was a little obscured by the center candle stand, so he deftly moved it off to the side, out of his way.

She was finding it hard to eat while she was so conscious of his eyes on her. His smoldering eyes drank her in as he fixedly stared at her and involuntarily, her nipples hardened and puckered.

"This excites you," he said simply as he took another bite of his food.

"It's good food."

"I don't mean the food, and you know it. You like this, displaying yourself for me."

She gave him a small smile, "I can certainly say that sex with you is never mundane."

"No, I never let it be mundane."

She took another mouthful and thoughtfully chewed it before commenting, "I think I'm going to need to reupholster this chair."

"Why?" he asked, as his eyebrow lifted in confusion.

"It's getting all wet and sticky," she replied.

He ducked his head under the table cloth and saw that she was seated on the chair, completely naked, just the napkin in her lap. Her tap shorts in a pile by her feet.

"When did you take your pants off?"

"When you were cutting your meat."

"You are so wicked."

"Isn't that what you want me to be?"

"Most definitely," he murmured huskily as he slowly stood and tossed his napkin onto the table. In two strides he was standing beside her cupping her breast. Then his hand dropped to her lap and he removed the napkin. His hand delved between her thighs, spreading them wide on the velvet seat before inserting his middle finger into her.

"Ahhh. You are so incredibly wet. You really like Chateaubriand, don't you?" he asked in a low voice, as he bent low and his lips sought the underside of a plump breast. Then, kneeling beside her chair, he pulled her off onto the carpet and covered her with his hard, needy body.

"One of us is overdressed for dinner," she said between sighs as his finger kept massaging her.

"I always dress for dinner."

"I always used to."

His lips took hers passionately as he tugged on his shirt trying to get it out of his waistband.

"Why do you want to do this here, under the dining room table, instead of in the bedroom?" she asked as she unbuttoned his shirt.

"Because it's somehow wicked, and I want you to be wicked for me," he said in a low growl.

Her hands moved over his thick chest hairs as she felt his muscular chest, then she bent and took his nipple into her mouth, saying, "Oh, I will be," as her other hand sought and found his zipper.

He quickly stood and removed his pants, then kneeling down he positioned her on her hands and knees, saying with his own wicked smile, "If I'm going to get carpet burns on my knees, then I'd just as soon they be from taking you in my favorite position." He

279

slipped a condom on that he'd removed from a pants pocket, and without hesitation, entered her from the rear. Grabbing her hips firmly, he pounded into her, oblivious to anything but the incredible sensation of his steely hardness being wrapped in her velvety tunnel.

Chapter 25

Michael sat at his desk staring at his notes and the reports in front of him. He was having a hard time concentrating this morning. Sex with Cassie last night had been awesome. He'd never had a night like that. They had finally gotten out of bed at three in the morning to go clean up the mess from dinner. Then they had taken their dessert, the homemade creme brulee, back to bed with them. They sat in bed talking while they spooned it into each other's mouths. After that, he had tenderly ministered to her knees that were raw in several places from the friction with the carpet in the dining room.

He could not seem to get enough of her. Every time they made love, he found out something new about her. Each time, it was like unlocking a treasure chest and finding a new bauble to hold up and admire. Last night he discovered she had a high-pitched scream that sounded like the indicator for worn out brake pads and he found himself doing everything in his power to hear that wonderful sound again.

Now, as he tried to organize piles of complaints from May of 2000, he couldn't help his wandering thoughts. She had invited him to the annual Sea Trail Christmas Dinner Dance to be held at the Carolina Conference Center on the plantation. Apparently, she thought they'd still be seeing each other by the time Christmas rolled around, and if that was the case, then she would be in contention for his longest running relationship since Jeanette.

Most of his friends were now married and raising families. Heck, a few were even on their second marriages. He knew that by agreeing to take her to the dance, he was committing their relationship to the exclusive status. Which didn't bother him so much when he thought about Cassie possibly going out with other men. But it did kind of tweak him a little to realize that he wouldn't be in a situation to ask out his princess of the south, if she should somehow make herself known to him. He'd stall Cassie as long as he could, he decided. After all, he didn't even know this far in advance if he'd be scheduled to work that night. Not that he wouldn't have been able to get out of it, if he'd really wanted to.

He flipped through the pages of sixteen noise complaints that they had received in the ten days prior to May 9th. It had been an unusually boisterous time for some reason. The colleges must have just ended their spring sessions. He drew a rough sketch of the streets on the island and drew boxes for each house, placing one at each address where the complaint had originated and another where the noise had been reported from. Ten of the sixteen complaints were on the east side; six of them were in the proximity of D. Duke's house. He didn't recognize the names of any of the callers, so they probably weren't homeowners, or if they were, they were only here part time. Three females. Now what? Did he call each one and ask them if they wrote in the Kindred Spirit journals? That seemed a bit ridiculous. What kind of responses would he get to that?

He sat back in his chair and thought for a minute. Then he sat up and grabbed the reports. He'd go to each house, show them the report, ask about the complaint and then steer the conversation to cats, D. Duke, and the mailbox. Then he'd get them to write something. Maybe he'd get them to write his name down as he offered them his personal follow up on anymore noise complaints. His name had an 'e' in it, he was sure he'd recognize Lady Kit's 'e'.

Four hours later, he was tired and discouraged. Eight of the sixteen beach houses were vacant, five assured him that at the time of the complaint their house had been rented, and the other three people, nice as they were, weren't any help at all. They were all permanent residents, knew about D. Duke, hadn't ever been to Europe, had never had Mulligatawny soup that they knew of, and their writing nowhere near resembled Lady Kit's. Interestingly enough though, they all had cats.

It was exhausting, steering conversations this way and that, without people suspecting what he was really after. Now that he'd whittled his list from sixteen to the eight vacant houses, he didn't know what to do. He'd left a card under the door at each residence. But it could be months, maybe even summertime, before the owners returned to their property so he could question them. He could have gone to the Register of Deeds to find out who the home owners were, or to the real estate agents that had the rental listings, but a telephone call to their primary residence wasn't what he wanted or needed, he needed handwriting samples.

He stopped at D. Duke's house and matched the fibers in the envelope to a few he found on the carpet by the bed, at least he knew that D. Duke's body had been wrapped in the missing bed covering. That meant he'd been thrown over the railing instead of carried down the steps. He wondered what the murderer had thought when he'd discovered his corpse had lost its head.

And his only link to whoever had killed him was that damned journal! He grabbed his notes and read down the list he had made of every organization he could think of that had volunteers. He'd stopped when he got to thirty. Everybody had volunteers. Frustrated, he flipped through the journal cards. If only there was a pattern, something he could tie to something else. Sitting down, he spread all the cards out. Then he listed the dates: September 9, 1998, October 14, 1998, December 9, 1998, February 10, 1999, April 14, 1999, May 12, 1999, June 9, 1999, September 15, 1999, October 13, 1999, January 12, 2000, May 10, 2000, June 14, 2000, September 13, 2000, October 11, 2000, April 11, 2001, May 9, 2001, June 13, 2001, August 15, 2001. Eighteen entries. He stared and stared and stared. All the dates seemed to be in the middle of the month, none in the very beginning, none at the very end. He wondered if the dates would all end up on the same day of the week. He pulled out his checkbook calendar and started circling the dates. He had to make a calendar for the last four months of 1998 as his checkbook register only went back to 1999.

Lordy! Would you look at that! They were all on Wednesdays! He sat up straighter in his chair. Now he was getting somewhere! He continued staring and searching for patterns, then he suddenly realized that they were all the second Wednesday of every month. Whoa, not exactly. September 15, 1999 was the third Wednesday and so was August 15, 2001. He highlighted those two dates and continued to stare until his head started to spin from the intense concentration.

Realizing that he had gone as far with this as he was going to today, he packed it in and went home to get ready for his dinner date with Cassie. They were going to the Grapevine in Calabash for dinner and he promised her that tonight, he'd let her finish her dinner.

They were going to meet at the restaurant because Cassie had to go back to work after dinner. She was way behind in her paperwork, and as her father would be here in a few days to check on her, she wanted to get it all done. When he arrived, she wanted him to find no fault with how she was performing her job.

The work on the bridge was being held up because of the progressively earlier sunsets. Pretty soon, they'd have the time change, and then they would lose the evenings altogether. They had lights they could use for some things, but it was too dangerous to have workers in the Intracoastal at night. It was hard enough for the boats to see where they were going without giving them something else to run into on the dark waters.

Cassie ordered the Santa Fe Pasta and Michael, the Bow Tie Shrimp. Together they enjoyed a bottle of Merlot while feasting on the delicious hot bread they dipped into the olive oil saturated with fresh garlic.

"Nobody's going to be able to stand the two of us," Cassie said with a smile.

"Doesn't matter. As long as we can stand each other, who needs anybody else?"

She smiled broadly at him and popped a garlic-soaked piece of bread into her mouth. "So what'd ya do today?"

He filled her in on his day, all the ups and downs of it. And after he told her about his discovery of the dates, she asked to see the calendar. He had his checkbook in his back pocket so he handed it to her. He was amazed, when just minutes later, she handed it back to him saying, "It's not the second Wednesday that's the common denominator. All those dates are the Wednesday after the second Tuesday, even September 15, 1999 and August 15, 2001."

He opened the register and checked the dates for each month, one by one. "My God, you're right. How the hell did you figure that out so quickly?"

"When you're an engineer, math is your life. Patterns like that just jump out at me."

"I could have stared at this for weeks and never seen that. Thanks."

"You're welcome. Now all you have to do is find out what groups meet every second Tuesday."

He quickly jumped up and hurried out the front door. A few minutes later he returned with the current edition of the Brunswick Paper he'd just bought at the General Store across the street. He took out the "Under the Sun" section and turned to the page that had the calendar of events. Each day of the week was listed for the next week with all the meetings listed for the area's groups.

"Alcoholics Anonymous, Weight Watchers, Empowerment Support Group, More the Merrier, Parenting Classes, AL-ANON, Bingo in Leland, Senior's Bridge Club, Bingo at the Elks in Calabash, Bolivia Fire Department Auxiliary, Firefighter Training at the Tri-beach Fire Department, A.A. Women in Recovery Group, A.A. Midway Group,

Lower Cape Fear Jaycees, Calabash Commissioners, Shallotte Planning Board," he read.

"Wow, that's a lot."

"And that's only the ones who call in their events to the Community Coordinator."

"Well, you can take out all the A.A. ones. From the journal entries you've read to me, I gather she drinks a little now and then. And you can probably rule out anything that's out of the immediate area. And there's bingo everywhere, she wouldn't have to come here to play bingo."

"There are still too many organizations to check out, especially with the limited information we have. But I do have an idea."

"Really? What?"

"A stake out."

"A stake out? Where?"

"The mailbox. Two Wednesdays from now is the Wednesday following the second Tuesday of the month. I'll go to Bird Island and wait for her."

"She doesn't come every month you know. And she's been coming a lot less frequently lately," she said, pointing to the calendar for 2001 with its red circled dates. "Only four times out of ten this year."

"Well, maybe she'll make it this month."

"How will you know if it's her?"

"I'll check the journal every time somebody writes in it. I would know her handwriting anywhere."

"Then what'll you do?"

"I'll talk to her, find out what she knows about D. Duke's murder. Then I'll get her recipe for that Mulligatawny Soup."

"What if she won't talk to you?"

287

"Then I'll arrest her and take her in for torturing. We'll whip it out of her." He wiggled his eyebrows up and down at her, "Anything sound interesting?"

She shook her head vehemently, "No, I'll probably get an old-fashioned whipping from my father this weekend, and you've already spanked me once, you know!"

It was poor timing that the waitress chose that exact moment to arrive with their entrees. She quickly served them, and not saying a word, hastened away.

Michael laughed uproariously at Cassie's surprisingly reddened face, then reached across the table to squeeze her hand, "And let's hope, I never have to do that again."

"Spank me?"

"No," he said with a mischievous grin, "spank you in the pouring down rain."

"Why do guys get off on the idea of spanking a woman, anyway?" she asked as she idly twirled her spinach fettucine.

"I guess it's the thought of making a woman submit to them," he said in a low husky voice as he leaned across the table so she could hear him.

"Don't I submit to you?" she asked.

"Yes, honey, you sure do. Lean over here, I want to tell you something."

She did as he asked and after a few moments of waiting for him to speak she said, "Well?"

"Nothing. I just wanted to look down your shirt. You sure are showing some mighty fine cleavage tonight."

"Oh!" she said as she sat back hard and threw a piece of bread at his face.

"Temper, temper. I wouldn't want to have to spank you and deprive your father of having your unblemished cheeks all to himself." If it hadn't been for his sexy wink, she wouldn't have known if he was teasing her or not.

She took a large gulp of her wine and sighed deeply. God, the thought of this man spanking her was actually turning her on, what the hell was the matter with her? Taking another deep breath, she said, "Back to Lady Kit. If you're hanging around the mailbox all day, won't that scare her off?"

"She won't even know I'm there. I'll take a little tent and set up down the beach, I can use binoculars to see who writes in the journal. Then, after she starts walking back up the beach, I'll go check out the journal. If the writing's hers, I'll follow her home. It's as simple as that."

"That Wednesday will be November 14th. It might be too cold."

"Ach! I've sat in duck blinds and on tree stands for days in much colder weather than we ever have in November."

"Not for you, stupid! For Lady Kit!"

"Oh. Well, we'll just have to hope it's a nice, sunny, warm day on the beach. According to the dates in the journals, she's been here in December, January and February, the cooler weather must not bother her too much. How's your dinner?"

"Excellent. And yours?"

"They sure do it right here."

"You know you can ask for less garlic."

"What would be the point in that?"

"Well, with the amount of garlic they use, Lady Kit may get asphyxiated."

"Lady Kit," he said dreamily, "I wonder, does she have golden wheat colored hair, fair blues eyes, long, limber legs and strawberry kissed lips?"

"She's old."

"Maybe not."

"She'll be ugly."

"I don't think so."

"She won't do number three."

He shook himself as if he was welcoming back reality and chuckled, "Well, then I guess I'll just have to keep you. You seem to have mastered that little piece of knowledge."

"Dessert?" she asked coyly.

"You know, I'd love to eat you, if time would permit," and again, the waitress was privy to the hot, heavy words this man was speaking to his date.

It was Cassie's turn to smile at his reddened cheeks. "Just coffee please," she said to the wide-eyed waitress, "I don't have time for dessert."

"What a shame," the waitress muttered as she left to get the coffee. They both laughed and Michael said, "It is a shame." It hadn't taken him long to overcome his slight embarrassment and join in her reckless banter. "I always liked that kind of pie."

Cassie almost spurted out the sip of water she had just taken. She had forgotten the expression he was alluding to: a muff pie or a hair pie, the words from her college days being so replete with sexual vernacular. The only one that had ever really made sense to her was mustache ride, and even that had to be explained the first time she'd ever heard it.

290

"I have to get back to the trailer. Thank you for dinner. By the way, you never did say whether you wanted to take me to the dinner dance or not."

"Let's wait 'til after your father's visit. He may forbid you to see me. I just may not be what he has in mind for his little girl." He stood and helped her with her chair, "You're not getting away from me without a good night kiss. Where do you want it?"

She thought for a moment and stood on her tiptoes to whisper in his ear, "On the tush."

"I didn't mean where on your body. I meant where as in—in front of the restaurant or in your car."

"Oh."

"Never mind, I like your idea better. I'll stop by the trailer in an hour or so."

She gave him a big, bright smile and scampered off. He stayed and paid the bill wondering just how in the hell he was going to ditch her when the time came. No one ever kept his mind and his body going quite like she did.

When Michael came by the trailer later, he found her on her hands and knees in front of a file cabinet, bent almost half way into it, trying to find something crammed into the very back of it.

"Now, that's a most provocative pose. Should I come down or are you coming up anytime soon?"

She mumbled something he didn't understand about not being able to find a permit as she struggled to her feet. He reached down and helped her up, pulling her up against his chest.

"Maybe you should just call it a night and come home with me."

"From my experience, I get more rest working than I get *resting* with you."

He smiled down at her and said, "Well, you do have a point there. If it's rest you need, you probably won't get it at my place."

"You'd think that after last night, we'd both be satisfied for a while."

"What can I say?" he said as he softly stroked her neck and chin, "I'm addicted to you; can't seem to get my fill of you." His lips caressed hers as he softly kissed all around her mouth. Then, using his fingers, he gently pulled her bottom lip away from her teeth and inserted his tongue into the crevice created. The sensuousness of his tongue stroking her teeth while his fingertips gently worried her moist underlip was so erotic. The things this man thought to do to her.

His hand grasped the side of her head and he pulled her face closer to his as his tongue thrust deeply into her mouth, chasing her tongue and running the tip of his along the slick underside of hers. Then his tongue became forceful and rough as it plunged repeatedly in and out of her mouth, creating a wild and frenzied tempo. Cassie felt the heat of his fevered kisses and heard the rapid pounding of jungle drums in her ears.

When he finally disengaged his lips from hers, it was to allow a loud moan to escape his lips, "God, Cass, I had you every way I could think of last night and now I want you even more."

"I know. I want you, too," she said on a deep sigh.

He went back to the trailer door and threw the lock, flimsy though it was, then hit the lights and walked back into her office, shutting that door also. The faint light from the desk lamp illuminated her office with its silver white light. He pulled a straight backed chair away from in front of her desk and unzipped his pants, then he sat in the chair and motioned with his finger, "Come here, I've got something I want you to sit on." As he unwrapped a condom and put it on, he watched her remove her jeans and panties. "But first, turn around for your good night kiss on the tush." She saucily paraded the naked bottom half of her body as she walked over to him. Then, just as she reached his chair, she presented him with her backside. He chose a smooth cheek and lavished it with his lips and tongue, her soft sighs delighting him. Then he swatted the other one and spun her back around and helped her straddle his thighs. He positioned her and then with one firm and well-placed thrust he was deep inside her moist cavity, feeling her encompassing him.

"Ahhh . . . ," he groaned as he savored the feeling of her tight walls surrounding his pulsing penis. "You feel absolutely wonderful." He grabbed her hips and lifted her slightly and then he thrust hard back into her. Realizing that her feet could touch the floor, she placed her hands on his shoulders and leveraged herself up and down, riding the length of him with every downward stroke. Her thighs were getting the workout that his usually got, but the pleasure she was receiving from his hard shaft going in and out of her took her mind off her burning inner thighs muscles. She felt his hand move down and start caressing her as he entered and retreated over and over again. And just about the time she came to the conclusion that she couldn't do this as long as he was accustomed to doing it, she felt a fierce melting sensation deep in her lower groin. It was followed by her own spasmodic jerking and then instantly, she was compelled to collapse against him, her legs muscles all but useless while her throbbing clitoris continued its pulsating as his fingers masterfully massaged it.

He allowed her a few moments to recover herself before he gripped her hips tightly. And, using both hands, he pulled her in to him as close as he could, and even she could feel the recurring pumping action as he spent himself into the cavern of her body. She watched his handsome face as it contorted into a painful grimace and then he groaned his pleasure of her through his gritted teeth. "Ah, honey, I don't think I'll ever get enough of you. I love you." Damn! Where had that come from!

She wrapped her arms around his neck and kissed the side of his face. It was scratchy now from the growth of his heavy beard. "And I love you. It makes everything just perfect, doesn't it?"

"Mmmhmm," he simply replied. He couldn't get over the fact that he'd just professed his love to her, right out of the blue like that. Obviously his body was quite a bit more appreciative than his brain. He'd have to be careful what he said in these moments of passion. Soon she'd be expecting a ring and he didn't want to get into that!

"How exactly, do we get out of this?" she asked as she looked down at his lap where they were joined.

"Not without some difficulty," he replied as he gingerly lifted her off of him. The mess that ensued was fortunately all his to attend to. Cassie found her panties and pants and put them back on while he was in the bathroom.

"What time is your father due in tomorrow?" he called through the door.

"It's not 'til the day after tomorrow. He's flying in. I have to go get him and then we have a meeting in Wilmington with some of the people from DOT."

"How long's he staying?"

"Four days, I think. You want to meet him?"

"Do I have to?"

"No. It just would be nice, though."

"Okay, okay. Set it up, I'll meet him," he said, obviously reluctant.

"Well, gee thanks."

"I'm sorry. It's just that meeting the fathers of the girls I'm dating is always so awkward."

"Dating? Is that what we're doing?"

"Well, you know what I mean," he said as he opened the door and stepped out of the bathroom.

"Actually, no, I don't think that I do."

"Well, we're more serious than just dating."

"How serious?"

Uh oh. Here it comes. Trying desperately to avoid the confrontation he saw heading their way, he scooped her up into his arms and nuzzled her neck. "Very serious. I said I loved you, didn't I?"

"Yeah, but now you don't really sound like you mean it."

"How could you doubt me?"

"Michael," she said looking him full in the eyes, "tell me honestly, do we have a future together?"

"A future? You mean like hanging out, having great sex all the time, sleeping together and maybe even living together someday?"

"No. I mean like dum dum de dum," she said humming the first few bars of the bridal march.

"Oooooh. You mean like marriage?"

"Yeah, I mean like marriage. Happily ever after and all that."

It was definitely do or die time. He thought he'd have a lot more time than this before things went kaflooey. Time to keep their relationship honest and not lead her on. Time to let her know that a commitment from him wasn't going to be in the offing. But now, he wasn't at all certain how she would take it, but there was no avoiding the truth. "No. I don't see a future like that for us," he softened the blow by adding, "at least not now."

"Let me get this straight. You say you love me, that you've fallen in love with me, but yet, marrying me is definitely out of the question."

"I didn't say definitely."

"You didn't have to, I could tell that's what you meant."

By now, they were facing each other, both of them with their hands on their hips, their voices escalating as they continued the discussion that was breaking her heart.

"Just what is it about me that makes me such a poor candidate to be your wife?"

"It's not that."

"Stop pussy-footing around, Michael. Tell me! I want to know what's wrong with me!"

"Cassie there's nothing wrong with you, baby. Nothing wrong with you at all."

"I want to know why!" she was almost screaming now, "Why am I not in the picture to share your future! Why Michael? Tell me!"

He took her arms and gently shook her, trying to calm her down. But that only infuriated her more. "You're not leaving until I know why you won't ever be marrying me! I have to know. Are you still in love with Jeanette?" she asked on a sob.

"No," he said softly, "I'm not still in love with Jeanette. But in a way, I'm in love with the type of woman that she was."

"And just what kind of woman was that? Other than frigid I mean?" she said snidely.

Well, that did it! Now he was angry, too. "She was gentle and proper and graciously southern. She knew how to cook and entertain. She was a genuine lady who was always impeccably dressed and carried herself with more than a modicum of grace. She had the very best manners and, she was utterly charming!" he shot at her.

Cassie just stood there staring at him, her eyes incredulous. Then she whispered just loud enough for him to hear, "You want a southern belle for a wife? Are you still living in the days of the grand old south? This Yankee isn't good enough for you?" Her voice was getting louder but it was wavering and before she could check them, a hot torrent of tears overflowed her eyes.

She spun around as she brushed her eyes with her sleeve and grabbed her keys. Stomping to the door, she turned and flung out the only words that came to her mind, "Well, I know how to make buttermilk!" before opening the door and then slamming it shut and leaving.

Michael stood there staring after her. *She knew how to make buttermilk?* He shook his head. He had known this was going to be bad, just not quite this bad. Here he was standing in the middle of her work trailer, all alone. He was miserable and he knew that it could be a long time, if ever, before he had such exceptionally good sex again. Even if Cassie cooled off, it was highly unlikely that she would ever allow him to touch her again.

Chapter 26

Cassie sat in her bed alternately crying and sipping wine. He only wanted her for her body. Nothing else. And even he wasn't sure how long he wanted her for! That must've been why he was so reluctant to commit to going to the Christmas party with her. All those words about "never getting enough of her;" "the best lovemaking he'd ever had;" "how wonderful they were in bed together;" he probably said that to everybody! She almost screamed from her frustration. He'd really played her well. Well, let him have his syrupy, sweet southern belle! Who needed him!

About four o'clock in the morning, she finally admitted to herself that she needed him. She needed him almost more than she needed to breathe. Popping m&m's one right after another, she realized she probably hadn't handled this all too well. After all, they'd only known each other for a short time, she shouldn't have been pressuring him to decide his future with her. Maybe if she'd just let things follow their proper course, he would have eventually mentioned marriage—despite her northern status. She really hadn't given him a chance.

This was not a good time to be so emotionally upset, she acknowledged to herself. Her father would be here soon. She was waiting for the inspectors to pass her work and approve the next phase of the construction. And now, she was miserably unhappy, probably in no shape to deal with any unexpected problems on the job. Her father would see her losing her determination and drive as she succumbed to her feminine depression over her lost love. And, before she knew it, she'd be taken off the project.

Well, that wasn't going to happen! She'd show her father she could cut it. And she'd show Michael that she could live without him. Even if it killed her, she'd show him that he hadn't meant a thing to her, not one damn thing! She rolled over, ate the last three candies and punched the pillow. She had to get some sleep or she'd be irritable on top of everything else. She forced her eyes closed and saw Michael's face as it had looked just before he came inside her tonight. A face filled with sublime ecstasy, a man so deeply in the thralls of love making that he hadn't shielded the love she'd seen in his eyes. He did love her, she just knew it.

Tomorrow she'd go to the Pelican Bookstore at the Village of Sunset Beach and see if she could find a book about relationships. There had to be something she could do to fix this.

Six months! Six months was the earliest a woman could expect a man to start leaning toward a permanent commitment. Six months! She'd hardly even given him six weeks! Oh, the poor man. No wonder. Cassie kept reading the chapter on the "Commitment Shy Male," —apparently Michael had a lot of company. But actually she had no proof that he was against committing to marriage. Actually, it was to the contrary, he'd already been engaged once before. He was just against committing to marrying *her*. But, with the knowledge she had gleaned from this book, she felt sure she could change all that, given some time. And time was what she was going to give Michael. And apparently that's what he was giving her, too, because he hadn't called or come by once, since their argument. She slumped back against the pillows and dropped the book into her lap.

The wind was whipping her curls in front of his face as she stood in front of him while he turned the big wheel on his boat. His hands were on top of hers and she was smiling up at him. He took one hand and skimmed her shoulder, giving it a soft caress before stroking his fingertips along the length of her arm. When he moved his fingers from her wrist to her shoulder and then back again, he felt her shiver slightly at his faint touch. The next time his fingers touched her shoulder, he moved the strap of her bikini just enough down her arm to allow the taut material covering her breast to fall and expose her. His hand moved to cup her and he gently squeezed her warm, soft flesh. He palmed her and felt her nipple rise under his hand, going from a silky soft cap to a tight hard bud in mere seconds.

He averted his face from hers, checked the traffic on the waterway in front of them and then let his eyes fall to her chest where he caressed her bared breast with his hungry eyes. As his hand squeezed and his thumb and forefinger probed her lengthening nipple, his other hand, over top hers, steered them.

"Take your top off," he ordered huskily.

"But someone might see . . . "

"Now." His voice was commanding and she could tell he was dead serious about her doing his bidding. "If *I* have to take it off, I'm tossing it overboard."

She had no doubt that he'd do it and then she'd have nothing but a towel to go home in. She reached behind her and untied the strings, then let it fall to the deck where she figured it was safer. At least she'd be able to find it later. And then, she was topless, standing at the helm on his boat while he steered them through the inlet.

"These nice big globes could stand a little sun on them. and I could stand getting a little appreciation for them from our local fishermen."

She gasped as she saw him heading right toward a group of boats anchored just ahead.

"No!"

"Yes," he hissed as he brutally squeezed the newly exposed breast. Then, he roughly pinched her nipple and laughed, "Let's give the hard working fishermen a little thrill."

She cringed as he slowed the boat down and it drifted into the midst of the small gathering of fishing boats. She tried to turn into him to shield herself, but he gripped her shoulders and turned her body to face the men on the boats. "Hey, guys, take a gander at these. some nice stuff, huh?" he asked as his hands moved to cup and lift her breasts like he was displaying them on a shelf.

Her own deep sobs woke her and she realized that she was only dreaming. Dreaming about Michael and his obsession with her breasts. Her pillow was soaked as well as her face and she reached for a corner of the sheet to wipe it. What an awful dream! And what had caused her to have it?

The bed sheets were tangled all around her and her nightgown was pulled down off her shoulders, sagging down to her waist. Great! Now she was having erotic nightmares with Michael in them! He couldn't escape her mind for a waking minute and now he was controlling her even in her dreams!

She knew Michael would never treat her so badly. But dreams were weird. They had a strange way of taking a little bit of reality and infusing fear until it became terror. She had a healthy mind, and she knew she wasn't paranoid, but she probably was experiencing a little shame and some guilt over the sex and sex games she and Michael indulged in. This all probably boiled down to her father's upcoming visit. Yikes! That was today, she realized. There was just something about her father knowing she was being intimate with a man that caused her to feel so very, very naughty.

Maybe it was a good thing that she and Michael weren't speaking to each other right now. Michael wouldn't have to meet her father and her father wouldn't have to see the proprietoral look on Michael's face. It was a look she was sometimes proud of, but that scenario on the boat . . . whoa. Where did these awful dreams come from? Things that would never even occur to you in a million waking hours, somehow came together all too easily in your subconscious.

Well, for now she wasn't missing Michael, not a single lick. How dare he do such a thing to her! And he'd better think twice about taking her out on his boat again, too!

But she could still feel his hands on her breasts as he'd cupped them and ripened the nipples. Hell, she could almost feel the sunburn on them! The mind is an incredible organ, she thought as she rolled over onto her stomach and tried to settle back into sleep. Speaking of organs, he did have an incredible one . . .

Michael was tossing and turning in his own bed ten miles away, but he wasn't having the same kind of dream that Cassie'd had. In his dream, Cassie was walking down the aisle on her father's arm and his subconscious mind followed her slow and steady progress down the aisle. He felt slightly euphoric until her father handed her off to a man who closely resembled Harley.

His sudden plunge into despair provoked a loud groan that actually woke him up. As he sat up and ran his fingers through his thick hair, he shook his head. He hardly ever had dreams, or if he did, they were never tantamount enough for recall upon waking. What was that woman doing to him?

He got up and paced around his room as he tried to shake off the feelings of dread that the dream had left him with. Suddenly, he turned back to face the empty, rumpled bed and he realized that he was lonely. Not just lonely for companionship or for someone to warm the sheets, but lonely for someone to share his life with.

Images of children running in and out behind trees, himself tossing a smiling, drooling cherub of a baby up into the air, and a dark-haired baby sleeping peacefully in a white, lacy cradle came to his mind. And he knew he was ready, more than ready to settle down with a wife who would have his children.

That must be why he had that dream about Cassie getting married. She wanted to get married, just as he did. It was just that time in both of their lives for them to consider it. He sat in his over-sized club chair in the corner and stared at nothing as he tried to envision the southern bride of his dreams, the woman he had conjured up in his mind so many times in the past. As he sat there and concentrated, he found that he had a hard time bringing her forward in his mind. *Just where the hell was she anyway,* he said aloud as he banged a fist on the arm of the chair.

Well, he didn't know who she was or where she was, he told himself, but she sure as hell better make herself known to him in the next few months if she wanted to get this thing on the road and fulfill her destiny to be his bride. He didn't want to wait much longer for her to show up. If she knew what was good for her, she'd better get her ass into her car and get herself here. His patience was about running out. And then, in his mind, he envisioned a tall, blonde-haired woman with pink lips and cheeks wearing a long flowing gown swirling around her smooth, tanned legs, as she ran down the steps of a university sorority house. Her long, silky blonde tresses fanning out from her beautiful face as she turned to wave to her friends behind her on the steps. She was running for her car, her blue eyes eager and full of hope and promise. His eyes were closed and he had his head resting on the back of the chair, and then he smiled, a great big smile. She was on her way. He just knew it. It was only a matter of time now.

Chapter 27

Cassie met her father at the airport in Wilmington and together they made their way to the DOT offices. She filled him in on their progress to date, informing him that they had finally signed on the amount of men the project would need and that they were ready to start driving the pilings. All the equipment was in place, the permits had all been obtained, the work up to now was approved and they were ready for the serious part of building this bridge.

They met with the structural design engineers, the NEEPA Consultants, the project development people and the Environmental Analysis Branch of DOT. On a wetlands project there could be any number of things coming along to stall its progress or halt it all together, most of them having to do with the wildlife living in the wet lands they would be building over. There were microscopic darters to worry about, spawning shortnose sturgeon, several varieties of turtles and birds, and even alligators in some places. Even the most unseasoned construction worker knew that the frailty of the coastal environment was of paramount importance to the taxpayers. All of the workers knew of stories where denizens of the air and water had permanently halted multi-million dollar projects in mid phase.

In the last few years, it had become standard practice to build a temporary bridge beside the real bridge. The reason for this was to minimize the damage done to the wetlands. In years previous, construction crews would have thought nothing of filling in the wetlands and building up the areas as needed to allow navigation for the huge 225-ton cranes required to lift the heavy materials.

But now, thanks to the marine biologists and the conservationists, they knew that the temporary causeways they created using rocks and dirt, compacted the soil, leaving the wetlands dry and devoid of oxygen. Irreparable damage was done each time the moisture and oxygen was squeezed out by the weight of not just the newly erected elevated causeways, but the added weight of the heavy machinery moving across them.

Loose, well-oxygenated soil is what makes the wetlands fertile. The organically rich, marsh muck needs to stay loose at the bottom and not be compacted or misplaced. Hence, the temporary bridge, built with hollow pilings to allow the soil to remain loose and able to quickly revert back to its preconstruction content once removed. Even barges, with their extreme weight from the cranes, caused the soil to compact far below them through the added pressure on the water.

The environment having the ability to recover quickly once the construction was over, was what the new construction agendas were all about. The temporary bridges allowed for the tidal waters to continue flowing under them instead of the fabricated causeways creating unnatural dams and interfering with the water currents. So all in all, they could leave the wetlands pretty close to the same way they found them, with the exception of the new structure. Anyway, that's the goal and you have to be more than just knowledgeable about design, stresses, and materials to build a bridge these days, you also need to know all about the area and all the little creatures that live there.

Since the area where the Sunset Beach bridge was being built was considered a jurisdictional waterway, not all the same criteria applied to it. And, it was determined that barges would be allowed to assist in the construction, a temporary bridge running alongside the new one to allow the cranes to move, would not be necessary. The necessary elevation needed to be achieved for the approach would all be on land so they wouldn't have to disturb the wetlands.

It would be up to the designer and foreman to determine if this bridge would be built end-to-end or both ends to the middle. Cassie had opted for building it end-to-end. She hoped that this would allow for steadier progress with fewer repositionings and less men. She hoped she was right. He father had nodded his approval at her answer and her reasons for it. This was not going to be a very long bridge compared to some currently being built in North Carolina. There was one being built in Manteo that was five and a half miles long. It was being built in many different stages, all of them going on at once; some sections were practically finished, while others were just in the pile driving stage. That kind of construction required several complete crews, different foremen, a whole team of inspectors and large bottles of aspirin dispensed daily. Cassie wouldn't be ready to tackle that kind of bridge for several years to come, if ever. It would be like writing off ten years of her life.

During the meeting, the list of suppliers was approved, the materials discussed, and the levels of salt in the water that they would be dealing with were analyzed. The question of whether they could get by with one or two less piers than the original plans from ten years ago called for due to the improvement in materials was brought up and discussed and the problems anticipated with the substructure were also covered. They met with the bridge construction engineer, the resident engineer, a representative of the Army Corps of Engineers, someone from the Department of Water Quality and three professors from UNCW doing a study with CAMA.

All in all, things had gone very well, but Cassie was still nervous because of her father's presence and wasn't as cheered by the proceedings as she normally would have been. They had basically approved all her work to date and given her the go ahead needed to proceed to the crucial pier building phase. And more than once, she questioned her attitude and wondered if her depressed state of mind was more a result of her emotional upheaval over Michael, or her fear of not meeting her father's approval on everything.

On the long drive from Wilmington to Sunset Beach, her father reached over and squeezed her hand. "You did good. I'm very proud of you. Looks like I don't have to stay on top of you quite so much anymore."

She turned and looked at him, her eyes huge in her surprised face, "Really?"

"Don't you think you did a good job?" he asked, with one heavy brow raised.

She chuckled and turned back to face the road, "Yeah. I do."

"Jenny tells me you have a boyfriend. One who's a cop."

"I wish she would mind her own business! She sure is a busybody!"

"Please don't speak like that, Jenny's only trying to make sure you don't get hurt."

"Well, it's too late. We've already broken up."

"My, that was pretty quick."

"Yeah, well . . ."

"So it's just you and me for the next few days?"

"Naw, Jenny wants you to come over for dinner tomorrow night and we thought we'd all go to a show. You'll like Colin."

"No, I don't think I will."

She turned and gave him a queer look, her face scrunched up with confusion. "Pardon?"

"I don't think I'll like Colin at all."

"Why not?"

"He's got Jenny."

"So?"

"There was a time I thought about making a play for her after your mother died."

There was silence in the truck for several minutes then she asked, "So why didn't you?"

"I wish I knew. Afraid to ruin our good friendship I guess. That and I thought I might be a little too old for her."

She glanced over at her father sitting erect in his bucket seat. He was quite a handsome fellow for a man close to fifty and Jenny might well have been taken with him, if he'd tried for her, but she just couldn't imagine Jenny without Colin.

"Dad, why haven't you seen anybody since mom died?"

"Well at first, it was just unthinkable. Then I had you to worry about. Now, it's just too late."

"Nah! Look at you. You're in great shape. You dress nicely, you have impeccable manners and you've got that great Andrews smile that knocks 'em dead."

"I'm losing my hair," he said as he patted the balding spot in the front of his head, "and I wouldn't even know what to do to get started even if I saw someone I liked."

"So what? You're losing a little hair, big deal. And if you saw the right woman, you'd remember exactly what to do. You've got a few things that give you an advantage over other guys your age."

"Like what?"

"Well, for one thing, you're rich."

"I'm not interested in a woman who's only interested in that."

"Okay, you're a good cook."

"Yeah. I do kind of make some nice dishes."

"And you're funny."

"Oh yeah, everybody's always laughing at what I say," he said sarcastically.

"Well, they would if they weren't all your employees who are scared to death of you. You need to get out—away from the business. Meet other kinds of people, not just people in the construction business."

"How am I going to do that? You know what my schedule is like. It took quite a bit of finagling just so I could make this short trip."

"Dad, you don't have to take so many jobs. You don't have to be the biggest and the best anymore.

Take it easy. Delegate more. Overbid a few things. And if you get 'em fine, then hire somebody to help. If you don't, so what?"

"Yeah. You're probably right. I guess I should start winding down some. I mean, I'm getting so old and all," he said with sideways glance and a big grin.

"Now, I didn't mean it that way and you know it. I just meant that you've worked so hard all your life, don't you think it's time to step back and enjoy it a little? You've never been to Hawaii or the Bahamas, the Greek Islands or even Sunset Beach for that matter."

"Well, I'm here now," he said as she turned left at the light beside the highway sign for Sunset Beach, off of Route 17.

"Yes, you're here now and if it's all the same to you, I'd just as soon show you the bridge tomorrow, I'm about talked and inspected out for right now."

"You do look a little tired. Why don't you show me this wonderful townhouse you're buying, then after a little rest, I'll take you out to dinner somewhere nice."

"That would be nice, Dad. I'd like that."

She couldn't remember when she'd had such a nice conversation with her father. And he'd actually said he was proud of her. Why had she been dreading his trip down so much? She just didn't have any confidence right now, that was the big problem. This thing with Michael was all her fault. She'd blown it. She'd tried to pin him down way too soon, and in doing so, she'd lost him completely. And her book said she couldn't call him, he had to call her first. As she turned the Jimmy into Sea Trail, she wondered if he was thinking about her and got even further depressed when she decided that he probably wasn't.

Chapter 28

Michael sat at his desk staring at the lists in front of him: Lists of piano players for Catholic churches; lists of organizations that met on the second Tuesday of every month; lists of people making noise complaints. It was driving him absolutely bonkers. He slammed his fist down on the desk and abruptly stood up. He didn't know if he was more upset about the dead ends he kept running into, or the fact that he couldn't go five minutes without thinking about Cassie, wondering what she was doing and if she was thinking about him as much as he was thinking about her. He went to the kitchen to get a cup of coffee that he really didn't want. It was just something to do to keep his mind from his problems.

There were several other officers in the hallway, and as he moved to one side to step past them, he heard Ray telling them that he had a date next Friday night with that hot, new lady bridge builder. He quickly spun around, his flashing dark blue eyes piercing Ray's as he jabbed him in the chest with his finger.

"Like hell you do! Cassie is my girl and don't you forget it! She's not going to be one of your one-night stands!"

Ray's own narrowed eyes took on a hateful glare as he pointedly pushed Michael's hand from in front of his chest. "If she's your girl, then why did she accept a date with me?" he sneered at him.

"We we're having a fight that day, that's all. She was just trying to make me jealous."

"Well, we'll just see about that. She hasn't called me to cancel."

"I'm canceling for her!" Michael said, his voice raising enough to command the attention of the other officers in the kitchen. He gave each person a glare that said "don't anybody dare mess with me," as he slowly turned and stomped back down the hallway.

Damn! He'd really let his temper have full rein that time, he told himself as he drove over the bridge to the island. Without really knowing where he was heading, he soon found himself parked in D. Duke's driveway. He didn't know why, but lately whenever he had something on his mind, this was the place he wanted to be. It had somehow become a solace to him.

Well, he could take care of business while he was sulking. He had wanted to check something out anyway, and just yesterday the stuff he had ordered from the lab had been dropped off at the station. As soon as he had put together in his mind the scenario that D. Duke had been wrapped in his own bedspread and tossed over the deck, he realized that D. Duke had probably been killed somewhere inside his own house. He had ordered some luminol to spray around the house to see if there were any blood splatters that had been cleaned. If there had been any blood in the area, its residue would show up as phosphorescent in the dark, even long after the obvious stain had been cleaned. He grabbed the bottle from the trunk and climbed the steps. Using the key that he had now added to his own key ring, he opened the door. Instantly, he knew that someone else had been there.

There was a heavy perfume scent welcoming him instead of the familiar masculine smell to which he had become so accustomed. He looked around for any sign that would identify the source, and his eyes honed in on the lone white business card that had been left on the kitchen counter. He closed the door and walked over to pick it up. Betsy Harlevas with Century 21. Ah, the bank was preparing to list the property for sale. An immediate sadness washed over him as he realized that his days of coming here for a few minutes of solitude would soon be over. A property like this, even as dated and disastrously decorated as this place was, would sell quickly. It was all about the view and the proximity to the beach, everything else could be fixed or replaced. In fact, some people bought premium lots like this one, tore down or moved the existing house, and built a more modern one in its place.

He looked down at the spray bottle in his hand and randomly sprayed a few squirts here and there. Then he went over to the blinds and adjusted them. There was still too much light, so he closed the drapes as well. When he turned from blocking the sunlight coming in through the deck door with a beach towel, he was stunned to actually see the phosphorescent glow of blood splatters in the dining area.

Damn! He walked over and stared down at the carpet and then over at the ones on the wall. There weren't many, but there were enough to see a slight pattern. It was almost as if D. Duke had been sitting in this chair, he thought to himself as he gingerly touched the heavy, old wooden chair tucked beneath the table.

Mentally, he formed a picture in his mind of D. Duke sitting in this chair while someone came from behind and bashed him in the head. He slowly turned and his eyes followed the direction his head took as it incrementally rotated. He examined the room carefully. He tried to make himself detached and to see things as if seeing them for the first time. When his eyes focused on the big brass American eagle, his head stopped its slow perusal, and he stood stark still staring at the heavy patriotic sculpture.

Yes, that could certainly be it. He walked over and sprayed some luminol on it. Almost immediately the glowing slivers of light illuminated the bird's wing span. Eureka. The murder weapon.

He walked into the kitchen and picked up the phone. Then he smiled as he heard the recording announce that this phone was no longer in service and that it could only be used to dial 911. Well, what the heck. He punched in the numbers and identified himself. Fifteen minutes later, the chief showed up followed by the crime scene guys who were a little sheepish about not having discovered all this weeks ago. He was congratulated by the chief while they both watched the officers brush the eagle for fingerprints, not surprisingly, there were none.

"The prints were wiped off, but the blood residue still shows even after cleaning. We'll take it back to the lab and see if we can get anything else from it. Someone had to have gripped this pretty tightly if they were swinging hard. Maybe we can still lift something from it." They carefully wrapped the eagle statue and packed it up before taking it with them.

"Any closer on the journal writer?" the chief asked.

"Yes. I think I can find her. I've plotted the dates that she goes to Bird Island, I figure she'll be there sometime next Wednesday. So, I'm going to sit and wait and watch for her."

"A stake out on the beach, huh? You mean I'm going to be paying you to spend the day relaxing on the beach waiting for a woman to show up?" he said with a sideways grin.

"Yup!" Michael replied with his own big grin. "Not bad duty if you can get it."

"Well, let's just keep this to ourselves, shall we? If this gets around, I'll never hear the end of it."

After the chief left, Michael proceeded to lock up and leave, but not without first going out on the deck and enjoying the view. With any luck, it would still be beautiful next week and he'd have a nice day lazing on the beach while he waited for Lady Kit to make her appearance.

Looking over toward the Intracoastal, he could see the heightened activity of bigger crews as the work on the bridge began in earnest. There was a huge crane mounted on a barge as well as several smaller ones and both sides of the Big Narrows Channel, as the Army Corps of Engineers refered to the small waterway alongside the causeway, were now spilling over with crews of their own as the approaches were filled to the right height and then graded. The piers would definitely be ruining the view for a while, that and the cranes. What little elevated skyline there was, would be offset by the jagged-topped piers until the columns and beams were added. Then the huge white monoliths would dominate the horizon from any place near the Intracoastal. It would be beautiful when it was finished, of that he had no doubt. But until the spans were added to give it the graceful curves and connecting lines—it would be an eyesore. And people would complain. Long before it was open for use, its detractors would smugly point out the tall monstrosity that was ruining their beautiful beach, just as they'd told them it would.

He got the binoculars off the top of the refrigerator and trained them on the mainland. His eye spotted one of Cassie's trailers. There were several of them now. Automatically, he scanned the immediate area for her. He missed her. His gut hurt from it and he didn't know what to do about it. He could have avoided all this if he'd just agreed to go to the dinner dance with her in the first place. Why hadn't he? Then he remembered what Ray had said, and his stomach clenched even tighter. He simply could not allow that to happen. He'd rather think of her in a coma than under Ray's horny body. He put the binoculars back, locked up, and went down to his cruiser.

He hit the steering wheel with the heel of his palm. Hell, he didn't want her under anybody's body but his! He backed his cruiser out of the driveway and drove off the island, pulling right into the construction yard. Her Jimmy was there, but he didn't see her anywhere. He saw Louie and asked him where she was.

"She took her dad over to the other side with a few of the inspectors."

He had forgotten about her dad's visit. Maybe he'd wait a few more days before groveling. He backed up his cruiser and pulled back onto the newly-detoured road. He drove past the station on his way to the McDonald's at Grissettown. He was not normally a fan of the fast food restaurants, but today, for some reason, he had a hankering for a Big Mac with lots of greasy fries, maybe even a chocolate milkshake, too.

Driving down Route 179, he spotted a sign advertising Thistle Downs, the new development being built on the Thistle Golf Course. It reminded him of the golf pencil the forensics team had found in the bottom of D. Duke's boat. What could be the significance of that, he wondered. Just why would a pencil that had been used, have no prints on it? If it had no prints, then it had either never had any, or they had been wiped off, he mused as he drove. If they had been wiped off, then someone had wiped them off and left it on purpose as sort of a . . . sort of a what? A clue? If that's what it was supposed to be then he was obtuse, because as a clue, it didn't mean a thing to him. So, more than likely, it had never had any prints. Which meant that whoever used it, had been wearing gloves at the time. Hell, it *was* a golf pencil—golfers did wear a glove sometimes. So you put on your glove, smack someone in the head and then you grab a pencil to write something down? A pencil that had never been used by anybody else before, never even picked up by anybody else before? So, it was still in the box, put there by a machine in the assembly and packing process. So where was the box? Where were the rest of them? This was nuts! He pulled into the line for the drive thru and pondered all this while he waited his turn.

Around four o'clock, as he sat at his desk rereading the rest of Miss Kit's journal entries, he had an inspiration. He picked up the phone and called Cassie at the trailer. It surprised him when she answered the phone, he'd half expected her not to be there.

"Cass? It's me, Michael."

"Michael?" she sighed and then, remembering that she was supposed to be indifferent or hard-to-get according to her book, she corrected herself, "Michael who?"

"Exactly how many Michaels do you know that cause you to sigh their name?"

"I wasn't sighing, you caught me on the end of a yawn."

"Yeah, right."

"Is there something you wanted?"

"Yeah, there was," he said gruffly and she was sure that whatever it was that he had in mind, she was quickly talking him out of it by her attitude. Time to eat a little crow.

"I did sigh your name. I've missed you."

"I've missed you too," his voice was now low and husky.

"I'm sorry about the other night."

"Me, too. If you still want me to take you to the dinner dance, I would be honored to take you."

"Really?"

"Sure."

"That would be great."

"The reason I called was to see if you and your dad would like to go out on my boat tonight. I thought we could go to The Fish House on Oak Island for dinner. They have the best shrimp and grits you've ever tasted."

His boat! She almost choked on the water from the water bottle she was sipping from. Vivid images of her awful nightmare came to mind and she had to tell herself that Michael wasn't like that, that he'd never treat her that way, that he'd never share her body with any man like that. Still, if the invitation hadn't included her father, she would have been more than just a little hesitant to accompany him. She cleared her throat to keep from coughing.

"I've never tasted shrimp and grits," she said. Then, fearing that she was making it all too plain that she was not from the south, she quickly added, "but that sounds great. I'll ask my dad and see what he says. I know he doesn't want to be stuck with me cooking dinner. Last night we went to Umberto's at Coquina Harbor and he ordered two meals just so he'd have something in the refrigerator to reheat in case I decided to pick up a pan and cook."

Michael laughed and she almost sobbed with the sensuous thrill it gave her to visualize his head thrown back with his chiseled jaw open in genuine laughter.

"I don't blame him one bit. I'll be sure to put a cooler in the boat that he can use to bring back tonight's leftovers."

"Very funny."

"What time are you closing up shop?"

"That depends on what time the crane operator's union says he's finished for the day."

"What time did he start?"

"Eight."

"Then he'll be through at five."

"Then we'll be through by six."

"Well, just come on over anytime. It'll take about twenty-five minutes to get there."

"Do you need to make reservations?"

"Nah. Not this time of the year. Although, we may have to wait a few minutes to be seated."

"Okay, we'll probably see you close to seven."

"Bundle up."

"Why? Will it be cold?"

"Yeah, it will be on the way back. But that's not why I want you to bundle up."

"What's the reason?"

"I don't want to be tempted to touch you in front of your father. Wear something ugly."

"You, too." she said as she slowly cradled the phone.

Michael showed his mastery in more ways than one that night. First, he impressed her father with his knowledge of fishing and hunting. Then he expertly maneuvered his boat into the only open slip in the crowded marina. And finally, he displayed his extraordinary skill of being able to keep his impetuous daughter in line. Several times he had seen the looks exchanged between the two of them and he was impressed with the powerful aura Michael had as he simply raised an eyebrow or stared pointedly as he exerted his will over hers, forcing her to do his bidding. From silently directing her to use the proper utensil, to chastising her for slurping her soup, it was obvious that Michael was a man in charge when it came to her in public. He wondered who ruled the roost in the boudoir though. By the gentlemanly but arrogant way he treated her, he had most definitely possessed her. But it wouldn't surprise him in the least to know that it was his daughter who took command in the bedroom from time to time.

Later, on the way home, as he held his shivering daughter in his arms, he marveled at the changes he had seen in her. From what he could see, she was confident at work, more than capable with the inspectors and suppliers, and fiercely protective of her crew. She was getting better with her paperwork, though he suspected that Louie was doing more of it than he should, and her attention to detail was beginning to please him immensely. For the first time since she had cajoled this job out of him, he was somewhat assured that she could actually do it. He looked down at the woman with the blue-black curls blowing in the wind and was reminded of the little girl she had been. The little girl who had managed to get herself stuck sixty feet up in a tree when she was eight, who stole a horse from a visiting circus when she was twelve, and cried all night when her momma died when she was fifteen. Was it only a few months ago that he'd had the scariest night of his life when his lawyer had told him that she could go to jail for the next thirty years just as easily as not. Prayer, and friends in high places, had come to her rescue. As he smiled down at her, and alternately looked at Michael, so comfortably at ease on the water, he realized that maybe soon he'd be turning the job of her protector over to somebody else who loved her.

When they got back to Michael's dock, he handed his wrapped bundle to Michael. "Here, you two can say good night in private. I'm going to smoke this cigar out here, if you don't mind."

Michael eagerly took her into his arms and walked her up the hill and into his house. Once inside, he helped her remove the blanket she'd been wrapped up in. He kissed her wind-chapped cheeks and then stood back to look into her velvety blue eyes.

With her hair in loose curls all over her face, her cheeks and lips reddened by the cool night air, and her eyes alight with something indefinable, she was without a doubt, the most beautiful woman he'd ever seen.

"Cass, you are so lovely." She looked up into his rugged face, saw the passion in his blue-as-the-heavens eyes and her lips parted. Her tongue made a swipe across her lower lip to moisten it just as he bent to take her lips with his. You never get to have the first kiss over, but for them it was as if they were kissing each other for the very first time. Only the dark silhouette of a man walking on the deck, with a red ember where his mouth was, kept them from having more.

"Good night sweetheart," he said as he held her door for her. "It was nice meeting you, Mr. Andrews."

"Same here. Call me Gene."

"Good night."

He watched her pull out of his driveway and head up the street. Gene was an all-right kind of guy. He fished, hunted, knew a good cognac when it was served to him and he smoked cigars. But most importantly, he had raised a hellion who was also an incredibly beautiful and sexy woman.

Chapter 29

The next day was Friday and Jenny and Cassie took it upon themselves to call a few of the single women that Jenny knew were close to Cassie's father's age. The plantation had more than its fair share of widows; quite a few of Jenny's friends had husbands that had died just in the few years since she'd lived here.

"Jenny," Cassie said as she sat at the kitchen counter watching Jenny go through her address book, "don't you think it's a mistake to have dad get involved with a woman living all the way down here?"

"Oh, not at all! You know as well as I do that as soon as he gets back to Virginia, he won't even think about going anyplace where he could meet any available women. It'll be all work, work, work."

"Yeah, but a long distance relationship from here?"

"It's not all that far and besides, Gene's ready. He's more than ready to get involved again."

"I'm not sure I want him involved with a woman down here! He'll be coming down all the time—driving me crazy."

"If he's coming down all the time because of a woman, you'll probably never even see him. Just think about it. Since you and Michael started getting so hot and heavy, just how many times have you come over here to visit with us?"

"That's not all because of Michael and you know it. I do have a job that keeps me very busy. Plus, we had a hurricane to contend with!"

"I know. But I also know how it is with a new love. You want to be alone."

"I can't imagine my dad with a woman romantically, if you know what I mean."

"No one can imagine their parents being *romantic*."

"Did you know dad thought about asking you out once?"

A wistful look came over Jenny's face, "I thought at one time that he was getting pretty close. Then one day, we had one of his new trucks blow an engine on the beltway. When GM refused to honor the warranty because it was so heavily overloaded, he and I really got into it. We didn't talk for almost two months."

"What happened to get you guys talking again?"

"He tried to take his business someplace else and found out how good I'd been treating him all along. Something he'd known, but just forgotten."

"No one could touch your price?"

"Oh, it wasn't that so much, though I did treat him more than fairly. Building heavy duty trucks of that caliber requires a great deal of specialized knowledge. Not every car salesman can spec out a truck, get it ordered, have it approved by the factory, and deliver it in compliance with all the state and county codes. He almost ended up with twelve trucks that wouldn't have been able to lift a wheelbarrow, never-the-less the heavy generators, machinery and materials they'd be required to carry."

"Oh really?"

"Yeah, I had to intervene with GM to keep them from forcing him to take delivery of those very oddly equipped trucks."

"What did you do?"

"Well, you know how your dad refused to accept any truck that had air conditioning?"

"I seem to remember something about that."

"It wasn't a problem when we had time to custom order, but every once in a while, he'd call and say he needed a truck by the end of the week and I'd have to scramble around looking for one in stock at one of the other GM dealers on the east coast. Several times I found exactly what he wanted, only they always had air and he flat out refused it, even if I told him we wouldn't make him pay for the option."

"Why was that?"

"He felt that if he had a truck with air conditioning, his employees would spend more time in it than they needed to and less time outside on the job doing their work. And he said he didn't want to go through the bickering first thing in the morning as the men fought over the one or two trucks that had the air. He really is a very astute business man. Anyway, so here he had these twelve vans on order through another dealership that were so far along in the ordering process that they couldn't be stopped, when he discovered they wouldn't be heavy duty enough to haul a third of their normal load. Of course, he'd already found out just what could happen when they were overloaded. I'll never tell who managed to let it be known about the payload deficiency, but let's just say the salesman from the other dealership couldn't help bragging and I couldn't help reading the zone rep's specs on incoming orders for the zone. It wasn't hard to spot those twelve road-paint yellow vans."

"Well, then what happened?"

"He tried to get the orders changed but the chassis had already been built and they wouldn't let him cancel. He finally called me for help and I got him off the hook."

"How'd you do that?"

"Well, the chassis couldn't be changed but the options could. I called the zone rep, told him to add air and arranged to sell them to a florist who had several locations around the beltway."

"So, you saved his ass, and he came back to you."

"In a manner of speaking, yes."

"So, which one of those women do you think he's going to latch on to?" Cassie asked as Jenny thumbed through the list of homeowners.

"Probably none if he figures out what we're up to."

"Well, he doesn't know that we don't always go to the TGIF get together at the Pink Palace every other Friday night. Let's make it sound like it's a must-do kind of thing and insist he come along."

"Okay, all we can do is try."

Colin came in through the connecting garage door just then and put a couple of bags on the counter. "What have you girls been up to? I smell entrapment in the air."

Both women looked stunned as they stared at him, their eyes agog.

Jenny finally managed to stammer, "How the heck did you know?"

"Easy. I ran into several of our divorced and widowed friends at the ABC store and Food Lion. Seems a little birdie has let it be known that there will be an unattached male at tonight's TGIF. I believe the deli is being sold out right now as I speak; women are scrambling to make some kind of platter to take to share. And I understand that *we're* also bringing some hors d'oeuvres to the Pink Palace this evening."

Jenny shook her head and marveled at the coincidences that continually occurred around here. You really had to be careful with this small town living. "Amazing. I hadn't even finished making the phone calls yet."

"I think you can stop now, the word's getting around on its own. By the way, who's the poor unfortunate schmuck?"

Both women simultaneously turned their back on him and made their way around the counter, quite obviously meaning to leave his question unanswered.

"Uh oh, I have a bad feeling about this." Colin took the liquor out of one of the bags and went to put it in the pantry. "Jenny, are you matchmaking again? Because if you are . . ."

"I'm not. It was Cassie's idea."

Cassie spluttered and balked, "I beg your pardon, whose idea?"

"Well, you're the one who brought it up."

"Brought what up?"

"The conversation you had with your dad the other night."

"You're setting up Gene?" Colin exploded.

"We're not setting him up," Jenny explained, sending Cassie a sharp look. "We're just trying to get him to meet some people here on the plantation."

"He's going to hate this. He won't go."

"Well, we're not going to tell him about this now, are we?" Jenny said as she took Colin's arm and walked him outside to the back deck where they could have some privacy.

"Jenny, you really need to stay out of other people's business. Gene's a good looking guy. He can find himself a woman when he's ready."

"He's ready. And no, he can't. He doesn't even know where to look anymore. Just how many women in their fifties or sixties do you know that hang around construction sites?"

"Well, you do have a point there."

"Does this mean that you'll go along with this?" she asked with a coy little smile as she traced circles on his chest.

He looked down at her and gave a big sigh, "I feel like I'm being a traitor to my own side."

She quickly kissed him on the lips, spun around and made to go back into the house. "We won't ever let on that you were involved," she said over her shoulder.

"Just wait a minute," he said as he grabbed her arm and flung her back into his chest. "If I'm going to be an accomplice to this matchmaking travesty, I want to get something out of it for me." His lips sought hers and his hand went to the small of her back as he forced her body tightly against his. After a searing, bone-melting kiss, he leaned back and looked down at her wet, pouty lips, "I want to know what's in it for me if I don't warn him off."

Jenny smiled back up at him. "What it'll cost me?"

He took her hand in his and walked her through the house and into the bedroom as he said, "I don't know yet, but I think you'd better say good-bye to Cassie for now."

331

Jenny called over her shoulder to a curious and confused Cassie, "See ya tonight at the Pink Palace. Remember you have to bring an appetizer to share and it's B.Y.O.B. and don't you dare forget your father! I'm having to pay for our misdeed in advance!"

Cassie smiled as she got off the barstool. "I'll be there. And don't suffer too much on my behalf," she said sarcastically.

Jenny laughed and Colin chuckled and then she heard their bedroom door as the handle clicked closed.

Cassie went out the front door and got into her Jimmy and headed back to the construction site. She had taken an over-long lunch hour as she'd needed to take a break from her father. Today he was reconciling accounts, checking invoices for shortages or incorrect billings, and double checking to make sure all the payroll taxes were being paid on time. He wasn't fun to be with when it was all work, especially the dreaded paperwork.

She thought about Michael and was saddened to think that she wouldn't be able to see him tonight because of this TGIF thing, another reason for her to have some trepidations about Jenny's rash plans.

Chapter 30

Michael drove over the bridge to the island to clean out the refrigerator at D. Duke's house. The police department had received a courtesy call from the electric company notifying them that they were going to shut off his electricity for nonpayment of his electric bill. Since D. Duke was cross-referenced with the "Are You Okay?" program, his name was on the energy share list. They were calling to see if he needed some assistance paying his bill before they shut off the power. Well, since he was deceased and no longer able to pay his account even with assistance, they were turning off the power today.

Michael remembered there was Kool-aid, baloney and a few other items in the refrigerator, so he decided to go over and chuck them out. When had he become so custodial about D. Duke's house, he asked himself.

Driving down Dolphin, he spotted a lot on the end of the street, on the opposite side, being staked off for construction. He hadn't even known that there'd been a lot for sale there. He shrugged, maybe it was the original owner finally deciding to build, he surmised as he got out of the cruiser and walked across the yard. He could see the familiar colored flags of the utility companies that marked off their respective lines as they fluttered in the breeze. He didn't recognize the name of the builder though. Even squinting, it was hard to read the writing, but there was a logo under the name that looked very much like a lightning bolt.

He discovered that the power had already been turned off when he opened the refrigerator and there was no light. But it was still cool inside, so the power had probably been turned off in the last hour or so. He gathered up all the food and put it in a trash bag and placed it by the front door. Then, he did his obligatory walk around and found himself out on the deck scanning the horizon.

After watching the ships on the ocean and the waves lapping against the bulkhead and the dock, his eyes honed in on the immediate area around the house. His eyes locked onto another lot also in the beginning stages of construction, and again, there was that same builder's sign with the lightning bolt logo. What the heck? Were they experiencing another building boom?

His eyes searched the whole block for any other signs of activity, but there were none. So after a few minutes of dilly dallying, he locked up and went down to his cruiser. Just as he was getting ready to make a left turn at the end of the street, he spotted another lot already staked out down to the right. He changed the direction he was heading mid-turn and went off down to the right. What the hell was going on, he said out loud as he recognized the now too-familiar logo. He drove up to the lot and stopped the cruiser. He read the sign pronouncing Jared Jenrette Jenks as, "The builder who gets things done with lightning speed."

He opened the door and stepped out into the deep sand. This lot was across the street from the majestic live oaks he admired so much and just a hundred yards or so from an informally-made, rutted boat ramp hidden between some tall bushes. Only the local kids knew about it. It was where they put their jet skis in instead of using the often crowded public ramp down by the bridge.

There was an old black man kneeling by a stack of cinder blocks, measuring some heavy-duty twine by wrapping it from his elbow to his wrist over and over again. He looked up as Michael approached and Michael could tell by his instant stiffening that he was expecting trouble. His uniform was going to be a detriment to getting some information unless he could ease some of the fear he saw in the old man's rheumy eyes.

"Hi! Your company sure has a lot going on in this section. I didn't even know there were lots here that were available for sale."

Realizing that he wasn't in any trouble and that the policeman accepted his right to be here, he warmed to a conversation with him, "They was sold all together to my boss as a parcel."

"They're not sold?"

"Nah. He's buildin' three spec houses."

"Wow, that's some chunk o' change!"

"I heard him tellin' my supervisor that he's 'specting to git close to two million for 'em."

"Wouldn't surprise me a bit." First row duplexes commanded over half a million each. These beach houses were center island by the canal, except for this lot that was bay side and close to the access to the Intracoastal. They should fetch between $450,000 to $600,000 easily. "I never heard of this Jared guy. Where's he from?"

"Whiteville. The whole crew's from Whiteville."

"Man, that's going to be a lot of driving for you guys."

"Don't I know it. Gots ta get up at 4:30 to make it here by six."

"Six? You better tell your boss that we've got noise ordinances. No construction noise until after seven."

"Well, hallelujah! I sure am thankful to be hearin' that!"

Michael smiled at the suddenly elated, weathered old man as he turned to go back to his cruiser. Halfway there, he turned back and called over to him, "Can you use some baloney and cheese and some bread? The bread's frozen but it'll thaw by lunch time."

"Sure, ain't never been one to turn down free food."

Michael went to the cruiser and got all the food he had taken from D. Duke's refrigerator and freezer. He himself had put the bread from the refrigerator into the freezer to keep it from spoiling that first day, as if by some strange reasoning, he thought D. Duke would be back to eat it some day. He wished he hadn't thrown all the Kool-aid down the sink now, but he saw that the old man had a big water cooler strapped to the back of his beat up pickup truck to take care of his thirst.

"Thanks," the man said as he reached for the bag Michael was handing him. His genuinely appreciative smile showed an almost toothless mouth. What a shame. The man building these luxury beach homes would net well close to a million for his financial investment, while the men like this one, who were up well before the sun, working in the extreme heat or the numbing cold, would probably net less than five grand for all their efforts.

Michael waved to the man, then called back to ask him his name before getting back in his cruiser.

336

"Washington Jenkins," he told Michael, "but you can call me Wally, everybody does." Just what was it about the long-dead patriot so many black people admired that they chose to name their children after him, or maybe the better question was why didn't any white people esteem him in the same way?

Driving back over the bridge, he looked to see the progress they were making on the new bridge, off to his left. What a slow tedious job bridge building was. They were now involved in the pile driving stage and since most of the work was being done under the water line, it didn't look like they were doing much of anything except occasionally moving the crane. But he knew from Cassie's almost complete absorption, that they were plodding along, and gradually getting the foundations poured.

He'd spoken to her this morning for a few minutes, but she'd had to get off the phone in a hurry when one of the workers had come into the trailer with what was obviously a broken arm acquired from a fall.

He hadn't found out if he could see her tonight. And, Lord, how he needed to see her. Every naked inch of her.

When she called him later that afternoon, he was crushed to learn that she had other plans that she couldn't get out of. And even though he wasn't happy about it, he acknowledged that she had to spend time with her father while he was here.

Chapter 31

Things didn't go exactly the way Jenny and Cassie had planned that night. Cassie got her father to the Pink Palace with minimal effort, but even though he was unfailingly polite to all the women who approached him and introduced themselves, it seemed he was much more interested in talking to the men.

Colin broke apart from the small circle of men, including Gene, who were avidly discussing this week's upcoming football games. He walked over to where Jenny was standing in the kitchen behind the tall counter, cutting more carrot and celery sticks.

He surreptitiously grabbed a handful of her soft derriere and squeezed it as he leaned into her and whispered in her ear, "I think you ought to get out of the matchmaking business. All you've managed to do tonight is get a bunch of women all hyped up with no end to their wildly over-revving libidos."

"These women aren't like that. Not every unattached woman is looking for a man for carnal purposes, you know."

"Oh yeah? Look around you. They're practically drooling over him."

"They are not! They're just being friendly. These women are attractive and sophisticated. They all take good care of themselves. They're well educated and fun to be around. They are very nice people!"

"Well, there you have it," he said as he softly stroked her hip. "Gene's probably not looking for nice; more like naughty would probably suit him better.

Somebody vivacious and a little cantankerous, not somebody who's so obsequiously willing to please. A cross between Doris Day and Mata Hari with a little Betty Crocker thrown in."

"Now where am I going to find someone like that?"

Just then, Mary Murphy Matthews Meadows came through the front door, hurriedly side-stepping the groups of people deep in conversation as she made her way to the kitchen.

"Ah, the Merry Widow arrives," he whispered in Jenny's ear. "Did you call her, too?" he asked incredulously.

"Don't be ridiculous! Of course not! And don't call her that!"

"Why not? She's the most cheerful person I know of who's buried three husbands."

"Just because she has a positive attitude after life's dealt her some pretty bad blows, that's no reason to hold it against her."

"That's what you say. You're a woman."

"What's that mean?"

"Simply that you're siding with her, while I'm siding with the men who've loved and lost."

Mary made it through the crowd and into the kitchen. She went straight to the refrigerator, stretched as tall as she could and just managed to get her fingers to reach a tall, insulated water sipper that was on top of it. But even though she could touch it, she couldn't manage to get it down.

Colin moved to stand behind her and easily lifted it down for her.

She turned and gave him her bright, mega-watt smile, "Thanks, Colin. I really appreciate it. I left this here this morning after my aerobics class. I've grown pretty attached to this old water bottle. My first husband gave it to me."

She spun around and turned to leave. Colin was surprised that she knew his name, since they'd never really met. He'd heard all about her from some of the guys he golfed with.

So this was Crazy Mary, he thought as he quickly appraised her up and down. Everything about her screamed spitfire, hellion, and vixen. She had the most unnatural shade of red hair imaginable, but as it corkscrewed out of her head and bounced around, it looked surprisingly good and somehow youthful, and there sure was plenty of it. Her complexion was smooth; her skin almost alabaster. Here was a woman who probably wore a heavy Turkish bathrobe down to the beach and didn't remove it until she was under a large umbrella and smeared with enough SPF 75 to create a film on the ocean. Her eyes were a vivid wildflower blue and her lips were full and Lucille Ball-like because of their glossy crimson coloring and their prominent cupid's bow shape. Her body was tall and only slightly more womanly than manly except for her breasts, which were more than ample as they strained against being confined in the tight sports bra she wore under an unbuttoned over shirt. Nice mammaries, as the guys would say. There was a large expanse of pearly white skin under her bra before her tight biking shorts began and Colin found himself wondering just how old this three-time widow was. She didn't look a day over forty, judging by her face and her body, but he knew from Jenny that she was in her early fifties. White and blue Reboks completed her totally athletic look and that's when Colin noticed that the colors red, white and blue were incorporated throughout her entire outfit. She looked like she just finished biking, running, and walking down a runway for Gear on the fourth of July.

Then he looked over her shoulder as he heard a familiar voice say, "Hi, my name is Gene Andrews, I understand you do hair and give facials. Do you have any appointments open for tomorrow?"

"What time can your wife come in?"

"Oh, I'm a widower. My wife died a long time ago."

"Well, I'm a widow myself, so I know how hard being alone can be. It's only been a little over a year for me. What time do you want to *come* tomorrow?"

Colin thought that maybe he hadn't actually heard that extra-soft inflection on the word 'come.'

Gene smiled down at her and said, "You tell me when you *want* me and I'll be there."

This highly provocative play on words wasn't getting past Colin or Jenny, although Jenny wasn't sure Mary was purposely involved in the spirited repartee until she heard her answer in a put-on twang, "I reckon I'll *want* you . . . to *come* . . . just as soon as I can get there, too." Then all serious and business like, she smiled up at him and said, "I open at nine, you can be my first appointment or better yet—my last, I close at four."

"I think, I'd like to *come* last," he replied as he winked at her.

Spinning around and marching toward the door, she sent her quivering mass of abundant crimson hair free as she one-handedly undid the large clip at the nape of her neck and shook her bouncing, spiral curls loose. It was an impressive cascade of vibrant, silky colors and not one man or woman in the room missed the show. It was flagrant, showy and sexy as all get out.

As the door shut after her, Gene could be heard chuckling while Jenny and Colin just shook their heads.

"I told you, he'd be looking for someone spicy," Colin whispered to her as he watched Gene rejoin the group he'd been talking to.

"Okay, so what part was Doris Day?"

He thought for a moment, "You know, I'm not quite sure she had that part."

"No kidding," Jenny replied with a crooked smile. "You'd better go find Cassie and tell her to start buying all her clothes in black."

Colin pulled her up against him, "Just because he's getting a facial and having his hair cut, doesn't mean he's getting married."

"Does his hair look like it needs cutting to you?" she asked, indicating the back of Gene's head with an upward and sideways tilt of her chin in his direction.

"Now that you mention it, no."

"And you know how a facial's done don't you?"

"No, can't say that I've ever had one."

"He'll be put in a reclining chair and she will be bent over his face."

"Bent over his face? How far?"

"Let's just say he'll be getting quite an eyeful with his facial."

"You know, maybe it is time I had one of those."

Jenny reached between them and cupped him firmly. "If you're looking for anyone spicier than me, then maybe I need to start working on my own widow's weeds."

"Honey, I can't imagine anyone spicier than you."

"Are you just saying that because I've got you by the balls."

"No, I'm saying that because of what you do to my balls," his voice suddenly got husky and her hand was no longer was able to contain all of him as they stood side-by-side, secreted behind the tall counter.

"Well, my mission's accomplished. Want to take me home so I can get started on my next project?" Jenny asked.

"Which is?"

She stood on tiptoe and whispered in his ear, "I had to pay an up-front penance for involving you in my matchmaking scheme. I think it's only fair that you reciprocate since you conjured up Mata Hari Mary instead of letting Gene find a nice girl to go out with."

"Reciprocate? You mean . . . "

Jenny smiled and nodded her head.

"Lead the way, Spice Cake."

Chapter 32

Cassie had been talking to a woman named Marie about her recipe for potato salad when she noticed Jenny and Colin making their way out the door. She excused herself and made a beeline for them, "Hey, where are you guys going?"

"I'm going to get laid," Colin said. Jenny jabbed him hard in the ribs.

"We're leaving now, I can't possibly explain the conversation we were just privy to, but your dad's got a sort of date for tomorrow."

"Really?" she asked her eyes all alight with surprise. "With who?"

"Believe me, you don't want to know," Jenny said. "Just be thankful he's leaving the day after tomorrow to go home."

"I don't understand. You sound disappointed. Isn't this what you wanted?"

"Not exactly."

"Well, I want to meet her."

"Okay," Jenny said, as a brainstorm came over her. "She'll be working at Mary's Beauty Shop on 179 tomorrow at 4:30, I'm sure she'd be delighted to meet you."

"What's her name?"

"Just ask for the lady who does facials."

"Jenny . . . " Colin admonished.

Jenny started pushing him out the door as Colin called behind him, "Go at 4:00. Do not go at 4:30."

When they were in Colin's car, he turned to her, "What the hell's the matter with you Jenny? Do you really want her walking in on her father when he's doing who knows what with Temptation Mary?"

"You're right. I don't know what I was thinking. I'll call her tomorrow and explain everything."

"Well, you'd better. I don't think Cassie's relationship with her father would be improved if she walked in on him while he was 'being serviced' at the beauty parlor."

"I don't really think that's going to happen."

"Didn't you hear their sexual bantering?"

"Yeah, but that's just posturing. It was all for show. She's probably really shy."

Colin choked but managed to say, "Okay, Jenny, believe what you want. Just make sure Cassie doesn't go there to meet Mary tomorrow, okay?"

"Okay."

"C'mon," he said as they pulled into the garage, "let's not forget what we left the party early for."

"Yeah? I forgot, just why was that again?"

"Something about penance I believe. And now you have something else to repent for. Just what is the penalty for a royally botched up job of matchmaking?"

"I think it has something to do with champagne in a hot tub."

"I don't think so." He took her hand and led her into the house, "I'll show you what punishment *I* think you deserve." He led her into their bedroom and shut the door behind them, then he took her mouth in a bruising kiss as he leaned her up against the door and hiked her skirt up to her waist. The thin strip of nylon between her legs was already soaked when his fingers entered her.

"If you keep getting this juiced up every time I punish you, maybe I should invest in a few bullwhips," he said against the throbbing pulse in her throat.

"You own me, but you'd better never mark me."

He chuckled as his pants fell to the floor and he leaned into her. Pulling the crotch of her panties to the side, he thrust himself into her. They both made the exact same sigh of satisfaction as he completely filled her.

The door shook in its casement as he rammed into her over and over again. "Had enough yet?" he panted.

"Not nearly," she answered between gasps.

"Tough, I don't think I can punish you anymore, it feels too damn good." He gave one more thrust that flattened her whole body against the door and she vaguely remembered hearing him groan, "Arrghhh," as her body caved into the liquid, hot feelings that leapt through her veins, sending her pulsing nerves on a wild psychedelic ride that turned her thighs into loose rubber bands.

Chapter 33

Michael sat at his kitchen table looking through the file that had been beckoning him from the other side of the room the whole time he'd been trying to watch TV. Lately, the more he thought about this case, the more baffled he was. The motive was the problem here. This wasn't a hopped up, drug-infected city. Murder was serious business here. Would one of D. Duke's stupid little shenanigans be enough to send someone over the edge enough to do him in? Hell, road rage wasn't even an issue down here, unless you counted the times someone sounded off with their horn because they'd just missed the light at the bridge.

He picked up the stack of banded cards from the center crease and thumbed them from the side, listening to the sound they made as they flapped one against another. He smiled at the one on top, his sentiments exactly.

"The world is going crazy—every single person in it! Except me, of course. I'm the only sane person left on the planet. Just before I left home, I grabbed my mail and tucked it into my luggage. Big mistake. I should leave the problems of my real life at home and not bring them here to my ideal life. After breakfast this morning I made the mistake of opening it all. Can you imagine the gall and the deviousness of these charge card companies? Two of them actually sent me notices with my statements, notices that I surely wouldn't have noticed if I hadn't already been burned by them before with their hidden "notices of changes to your account," that are shoved between the flaps of the perfume advertisements. Anyway, these new notices are informing me in the tiniest print possible that they are changing my rates unless I send them a letter asking them not to. I am still floored by it all. Really! What do they expect people to say, "Please raise my rate, I surely would love to pay more of my money out to higher interest charges?" No. They figure that less than one or two percent will even see the notice, others won't understand it even if they read it, and still others will be too lazy to reply by the deadline to avoid the higher charges. Why oh why, did I bring my bills here to pay? This is paradise. I come here to get away. How stupid of me to bring my problems with me instead of leaving them where they belong. June 14, 2000."

Well, she had a point there. He'd received a few of those stupid notices too and of course, he'd hurriedly written out the letters with the prerequisite information. He wondered if she'd read the notices completely, because the act of writing and refusing their higher rate, closed the account for future purchases. He always tried to pay his balances off monthly to avoid paying any interest, but sometimes financing the work on his house couldn't be paid off in one installment and how he hated to waste his money on interest. He knew exactly how she felt, probably the same as millions and millions of other indebted-to-plastic Americans.

"There's talk of hurricanes, but so far nothing has come close to us, not since Dennis and Floyd at the end of last season. The beach house has had a good rental season so far and if we don't get a bad hurricane, maybe the insurance rates won't go up again this year. It is so beautiful here. I can actually see some kids playing in the water. I think their family has one of the boats moored on the other side of the jetty. Ah, to be so young and carefree again. To splash and splash and not care if your hair gets wet! I have a hankerin' for some good music and some good seafood. I think I'll go to Crab Catchers tonight. The paper shows Harlequin's going to be there. September 13, 2000."

This lady may be a bit younger than he had envisioned. He'd been to Crab Catchers in Little River on the waterfront many times and generally they had a pretty young crowd. But she sure was right about the food and the music; Harlequin was a husband and wife team and they were really very good. Lots of good music and good seafood. He wondered if Cassie had ever been there. It occurred to him then that he and Cassie had never danced together. Strange to live in a century where you could make love to someone before you even danced with them. Michael set that card aside and picked up the next one.

"Went to Cheney's today to buy a few gifts. Claire has beautiful merchandise at the most reasonable prices. I've heard her husband sing at a few of the local church gatherings. It must be nice to have a God-given talent such as that. Claire told me that his group is coming out with their own CD soon, she's so excited about it. Then I went to Pelican Books on the other side of the Village at Sunset. Ann was working and I picked up a few books written by North Carolina authors that she recommended. It's so nice to come here, everybody takes the time to talk to you and share something of themselves. And it's not all about the selling, 'cause many times I just go in to browse and I still leave with a new friend. Tonight I'm going to eat at the Sugar Shack in Ocean Isle. I've been thinking of those delicious Johnny cakes and the spicy jerk chicken for weeks now. I read in the Brunswick Beacon that the Museum of Coastal Carolina is having a guest speaker, he's going to talk about the history of the Brunswick Islands with a special emphasis on Sunset Beach. It should be an interesting lecture and I'm really looking forward to learning about the community as it was back in the fifties and sixties. Of course, the beach has always been the same. We're blessed with an east/west beach that never has to deal with the problems of erosion. In fact we get a build up of new sand with almost every hurricane. What another beach loses, we collect. That's one of the reasons our property values are so high. Oh, I'm just a little chatterbox today aren't I? October 11, 2000."

I'll say. That was the longest entry by far. He could go and talk to Claire and Ann, women he knew, but what would he tell them? He didn't think he knew enough to place her in their minds. They dealt with so many locals and tourists. He'd been to a few of the Museum's bimonthly meetings, so he knew that they generally garnered thirty or more people. He did know the exact day she was at both stores though and that she used charge cards. It was a long shot, but maybe her name would be on one of the credit card slips. Maybe either Claire or Ann would recognize the name. A project for Monday anyway. He flipped to the next card. There were only four left to reread, April 11, 2001. May 9th, 2001, June 13, 2001 and August 15, 2001. The last one she'd written to date, he'd practically memorized. It was the one Cassie had first seen, September 12th, 2001. The one where she mentioned D. Duke and knowing something about what happened the night he was killed.

As he sat back in his chair and slumped his body into a more comfortable position, he heard a soft knock on the door. Who the hell could that be? He looked up and saw just the very top of a black, curly lock in the uppermost diamond of the small glass grouping on the old-time cottage door. And he smiled. He smiled from ear-to-ear as he stood up to welcome his unexpected visitor.

Chapter 34

"Hi," Michael said as he opened the door for her.

"Hi. Everybody abandoned me. I thought we were all going to dinner after TGIF, but Jenny and Colin went home to fool around and dad said he had to go rest up for a haircut."

She seemed a little down and he wasn't quite sure what to say to cheer her. "I'll take you out for dinner if you want, but I've already eaten so I'll just watch if that's okay," he said as he motioned for her to come in.

"Thanks, that's okay. I'm not all that hungry anyway. They had a lot of hors d'oeuvres at the Pink Palace."

"Well, come on in and I'll fix you a drink."

"No, I've already had a few of those, too."

"Well, then come on in and let's just head for the bedroom," he said with a grin.

She gave him a wan smile that immediately alerted him that she wasn't in the mood. He took her hand in his and walked her over to the sofa. "Then just come sit by me and tell me what's on your mind."

"You can read me like a book, can't you?"

"Sometimes. Tonight, I'm just not sure what kind of book you are."

She dug down deep into her oversized handbag and brought out the book she had been reading on relationships. "Maybe this will help," she said as she passed it over to him.

He looked at the cover, then flipped it over to read the back jacket. Then he read the table of contents that highlighted all the chapters and finally he slowly flipped through it. "This tells you how to live your life?"

"It tells you how you can make the biggest mistake of your life."

"And what would that be?"

"Doing the wrong thing and letting the man have control of the relationship."

"I thought men were supposed to control the relationship."

"That's what you're supposed to think, but no, they just think they do. Actually, it's the women who orchestrate everything."

"And exactly how is it that they do this?"

"That's the part I'm not really sure of, but I think that's the part I've already screwed up."

He put the book down on the coffee table and sat back with his arm around her shoulders. "Honey, I've heard about this book—most single guys have. All this book does is teach you how to manipulate men and use sex as a bargaining tool. It takes all the spontaneity out of dating and usually stifles a budding romance because it sets the couple at cross purposes from the very beginning."

"It's a book for women who want to get married. It tells women how to trap their man."

"Sweetheart, I hate to tell you this, but men have been marrying women for centuries without the help of this book," he said as he hefted it.

"Yeah, well . . . they've apparently been doing it all wrong."

"Okay. Cut to the chase. How is that book going to affect our relationship?"

"We can have sex, but it has to be absolutely incredible and we positively cannot ever live together."

"Okay, I can agree to that."

She gave him a sideways half smile as she lifted her perfectly sculptured brow, "Oh, I'm sure you can."

"There's more?"

"There's more."

"Give."

"I can't return your phone calls right away, and I have to turn you down two times for every three that you ask me out."

"Cassie, if this is going to be your plan, I don't think you're supposed to tell me all this."

"Oh. You're probably right. I've blown it again," she said dejectedly as she slumped down into the cushions.

"Speaking of blowing, let's get back to that incredible sex part."

"I say when. I have to call the shots on sex or I lose all my advantage. Tonight's the 'refuse to give in night.' "

"Am I allowed to coerce, beg or intimidate to change your mind?"

"That's the crux of this whole strategy. I cannot give in or all is lost."

"Well, let's just see how good you are at playing this game," he said as he pulled her closer and turned her to face him. His lips softly settled over hers and he ever so gently moved them over hers. He didn't rush anything as he slowly savored her moist, soft petals. First he took her top lip between his and drew his tongue along her full bottom one, as if he had all the time in the world. When he finally let his tongue tentatively search out hers as he parted her trembling lips to his, it was welcomed with great enthusiasm. He smiled beneath her lips as he felt her melt into him. No matter what her agenda, his was going to be the one that they followed.

Her hands went to his rough jaw as she cupped his face to hold him closer. She left his tongue licking the air between them as she pulled away to comment, "You didn't shave this evening."

"I didn't know you were coming over, baby doll, or I would have," he said as he reached for her again, "I'll be careful. Promise."

"I'm afraid you won't be given the opportunity. Tonight's an 'off night' remember?" she purred as she flicked the metal teeth on his zipper.

Instantly he sprang up as if to meet her fingertips. "Ahhh. Cass. Surely you're not going to torture me like this."

"I think that's the whole idea."

"What about the incredible sex part?"

"That's not tonight. Or tomorrow night, either."

"Just when the hell is it then?" he asked, his voice raised in frustration.

She stood, picked up the book and moved to go. Then she turned and gave him a wry smile, "I'm not exactly sure, I'm only on chapter 4. I have to finish the book first."

"Like hell you do!" he said as he grabbed her by the waist and pulled her back down onto his lap. He had his hands under her sweater unfastening her bra before she could stop him, and then as soon as she felt his warm hands caressing her fleshy mounds and his thumbs stroking her pebbly nipples, she was forced to surrender to his touch. Soon she became aware of only one thing, that it would be incredible.

As he laid her down on the sofa and covered her with his body, he smiled to himself. If she thought she was going to control him with sex, she had another think coming. That was almost laughable, he thought as his hard body moved over her soft, yielding one. He had a few things to show her and tonight was not going to be an "off night."

Chapter 35

Cassie lay in bed the next morning staring at the ceiling in Michael's bedroom as she listened to him in the kitchen making coffee. She had a cat-just-ate-the-cream look as she stretched her much used and slightly abused body. God, what a night! And then a thought came over her and she sat straight up, roughly running her fingers through her disheveled locks. Damn! She was not supposed to spend the night! Ever! It was against all the rules! And she had a sneaking feeling that he knew that!

When he came into the bedroom carrying a tray with coffee and homemade sticky buns, he wore a knowing smile on his face. She'd fallen under his spell and succumbed and he knew it. He was secretly gloating over his success and she wished she had a way to put him in his place.

"The sun's getting ready to come up on the river. Want to get dressed and go watch it? We've got about twenty minutes to get going if you do."

"Sure. Mmmm, those buns sure smell good. When did you find time to make them?"

"I keep dough ready in the refrigerator. It only takes a few minutes to pour the pecan glaze on and bake them."

"You're going to make somebody a pretty good wife some day."

"So are you, angel," he said. Then as he made his way to his closet across the room, he repeated his words to himself. *So are you, angel.* But the thought of her belonging to someone else, the thought of her waking up in another man's arms, took the spring out of his step.

As Cassie pulled her jeans on, she realized she couldn't be angry with him. He was playing the game just as she was, and he certainly had a lot more experience at it than she had. This was the first time she felt this way, the first time she wanted something more than just dating, the first time she wanted something so badly that it almost consumed her with the need to have it. Pragmatically, she was coming to her senses though and beginning to accept the fact that Michael had other ideas about his future. Whether this was because she felt unworthy to be his bride, or because things just never worked out for her this way, she didn't know. She just knew that she wasn't the girl Michael was looking for, and as wonderful as being with Michael was, she knew it was time to protect as much of her heart as she could and get out of this.

When he came back into the bedroom and found her using his wide-toothed comb to untangle her curly locks, he smiled. She certainly was beautiful first thing in the morning. No smeared mascara under her eyes, no lashes clumped together with liner and shadow, no lipstick stains under the gloss that had been kissed off. He'd never known a woman who was so beautiful naturally. The women he had dated had all relied heavily on cosmetics to enhance their looks, and not a one had ever thought to remove it before going to bed. Didn't they know that stuff rarely came out of his pillowcases?

He went over to stand behind her, placed his hands on her hips and pulled her back against him as he kissed the back of her neck. "You taste and smell so good all the time. What is it about you? You don't even wear perfume."

"Must be the shampoo," she said as her eyes met his in the mirror.

"I don't think so. It's something about your skin," he said as his lips nibbled all the way down to her collar bone. "Damn you taste good!" he said as he pretended to gnaw off a big chunk of her shoulder.

She met his eyes in the mirror and she smiled back at him. "Maybe it's all the mud baths I get at work. They say mud does great things for your skin."

"Well, whatever it is you're doing, don't stop. I don't think I'll ever get enough of the fragrance of you."

Why did he say things like that when he knew that they weren't true? Why was he teasing her and making her feel like there was hope for them when she knew that there was not? He was just leading her on, letting her think he was caught up with her when he wasn't. Well, she couldn't let him keep doing this. Ultimately it would get them nowhere. He was still going to find that southern epitome of a woman that he had in the back of his mind, and she, good time Cassie, would be put out to pasture. This fun-loving, time-filling, place mark of a relationship he'd had in his life while waiting for his one true love, the magnolia queen of his heart, would be over. And Cassie would be hurt. He'd promised her once that he'd never hurt her, that she'd only be hurt by herself. How prophetic he'd been.

Well, she wouldn't be here hanging around waiting for the axe to swing. She'd get out while she still could. She put the comb down on the counter and turned around. "Well, the sun's not going to wait for us, so we'd better get out there."

He took her hand and together they went out onto the deck and down the steps to the long wooden walkway leading to his boat. At the end of the dock was a built-in bench and they sat side-by-side snuggled against the brisk morning chill as they watched one of the most beautiful sunrises she'd ever seen.

It was appropriate, she thought. End everything on a good note. A wonderful night of stimulating, wild sex, followed by a glorious display of light signifying the start of a new life. A life for her that would not include Michael.

She sipped her coffee as she sat nestled under his arm and relished this last time with him, a quiet time when she could reflect and clear her mind. This was the best course, it would be the best for him also. Miss Tabor City or Miss Greensboro or Goldsboro or Charlotte or whatever, would never find him if she was hanging on his arm. This would be the best for them both.

After the sun was fully risen, they walked back to the house and she gathered her things so she could go to work.

"I'll call you later."

"I'll be busy all day with inspectors and engineers."

"Then I'll call you tonight."

"It's daddy's last night. We'll probably go out."

"Okaayyy. Then I'll call you tomorrow."

"I'm going to be very busy."

"Cassie . . ."

"Look, Michael, this may not be the best time to talk about this, but I think we should see other people."

"Other people! What are you talking about?"

"I just don't think it's going to work out for us."

"Is this some kind of strategic maneuver your book is advocating? 'Cause if it is, it's not going to work!"

"It has nothing to do with the book. Nothing whatsoever. I need to get out and meet other men. Lately, I've had these overwhelming feelings that it's time to settle down with somebody and raise a family. Maybe it's because of you, that it all looks so good to me now. I'm not getting any younger and I've already discovered that I'm pretty choosy, so I'd better start now if I want to be married before I start pulling hairs out of my chin."

His hand cupped her cheek as his face slowly lowered to her lips. "You're just being melancholy right now, we'll talk later. And no matter how old you get, you'll never have more hairs growing out of your chin than I do." His lips softly caressed hers and she savored the feel of them, knowing that this would be the last time they grazed against hers. Suddenly, she reached up and pulled him closer, coaxing him into her mouth. His tongue sliding against hers had never felt better or so right. With a soft sob, she broke away and turned from him, running clumsily down the front steps and to her truck. She was at the stop sign at the end of the road before she realized that she was crying and shaking from the anguish caused by saying good-bye to the man that she loved so much.

Michael shook his head as he watched her back out of the driveway and go down the road. What in the

361

world was wrong with her today? They'd had a fabulous night. The most fabulous night of sex that he could ever remember. She'd been his plaything, his wanton, his slave. She'd been everything and all that a good lover should be. She was playful and pouty and willing to try it all. And he'd pleasured her. Pleasured her until she'd begged for mercy. Two people just didn't make love like that over and over again without bonding tightly to each other. And now she wanted to break all the bonds they'd built together, sever the cords of their passion and see other people!

Nah! There was more here than that! It must have something to do with that damned book! He went back into the house, saw the book on the coffee table and impatiently snatched it up. Grabbing another cup of coffee, he sat at the kitchen table and started reading it.

Chapter 36

The bridge was really coming along well. Cassie stood with pride staring down at the rows of pilings being driven into their foundations. Seventy feet down in some places, close to eighty in others. She was in the crane talking with Jasper, one of the best crane operators she'd ever worked with. They were going over the afternoon's workload and she was asking him questions about the next placement of the barge. Sometimes she didn't feel very secure on these things, especially if they were floating on water, but this was different. The crew had done a wonderful job of stabilizing the equipment.

She looked off at the horizon and marveled at the view, wondering just how much more magnificent it would be from the top of the crane. Oh, to be a piling or a section of rebar for just a few minutes as it soared through the air, way up high, on its way to be placed. The forms for the piers were being placed at the first pilings and pretty soon the concrete would be poured into them. As they continued on, moving from section to section, molding the steel forms to shape and pouring the piers, it would look more and more like a bridge.

Back in the trailer she read the notes one of the engineers had left about the relatively new Arco panels she'd read about. There were many reasons to consider using them, but she felt comfortable with her decision to stick to the prestressed, precast panels they had already selected. She called the manufacturer and ordered them to be made to her specifications, spending more in that thirty-minute phone call than she would probably spend in her entire lifetime.

It was late when her dad came by to cancel their dinner date. He begged her forgiveness, but he'd met someone that he wanted to take out to dinner. Would she mind getting a burger or something on her own? Two nights in a row he'd changed their dinner plans. Didn't he even care if she ate anymore? Had he even noticed that she hadn't come home last night?

She looked up into his eager face. "Of course I don't mind. Go. Have a good time. Get home early though, you've got a long day ahead of you tomorrow."

"I will." He bent down to kiss her forehead as she sat at her desk looking up at him.

He had a date. Her father actually had a date. Unbelievable. She tried to look at him through the eyes of a woman, a woman who wasn't his daughter. He was really a very handsome man. Hardly any gray, a few small wrinkles along the rugged deep crags on his perpetually tanned face, and eyes that saw right through you. She ought to know, he'd always seen right through her.

"Cass," he said as he stood with his hand on the door knob, "You're doing a remarkable job. I am extremely proud of you. I don't think there is a seasoned man on our payroll who could do a better job than you're doing."

Her eyes misted as she listened to the praise he was giving her. Words that she had yearned to hear from him for as long as she could remember. "Thanks, Dad.

That means a lot coming from you. I won't let you down."

"I know you won't. Oh, and Cass?"

"Yes."

"I think that's a fine man you've found, that Michael. You should hold on to him."

"Yeah. Okay, Dad. I'll try." He didn't need to know that just this morning she had ended her relationship to the only man her father had ever approved of.

When he had closed the door behind him, she dropped her head into her arms on the desk and had a good cry. Then, deciding that she wouldn't be able to swallow any dinner even if she could find something to fix, she headed over the bridge to the island. The journal on Bird Island was calling out to her. She needed someone to talk to, a way to express how she was feeling. Like thousands of others before her, she would find some solace in the spiral notebooks left in that mailbox by the sea. She parked at the end of the road on the west side so she could use the 40th Street beach access to get to the island, then she wouldn't have nearly as far to walk as it was rapidly getting darker. She grabbed a pen and her flashlight while she tugged on her heavy fleece jacket.

She quickly walked down the decking of the long wooden access, listening to the heavy thud of her work boots as she walked. The dunes were very wide at Sunset Beach, she reflected as she clomped along, wider than anywhere else she'd ever seen. That was because Sunset Beach faced south instead of east. And that's why the main street, which paralleled the ocean, went east to the left and west to the right at the stop sign that ended the causeway coming from the bridge.

They never had to worry about beach erosion here. Not only did they not lose any of their sand to the storms, they usually collected the sand that spilled away from the neighboring beaches. Sunset Beach is the only accreting beach on the North Carolina coast, one of the very few on the entire Atlantic Seaboard, in fact. It's one of the reasons that the real estate is so valuable.

She'd heard the stories from people who had visited the island in the sixties, stories about the Confederate blockade runner, the Vesta. It had run aground off the shore of Sunset Beach during the Civil war. With no hope of righting it, the crew made it to shore and abandoned the sinking ship. The years of ceaseless, battering tides took its toll and the ship fell to ruin, but even as late as 1967, its rotting timbers could still be seen through the water from the Sunset Beach pier. What's left of the Vesta now resides under the dirt of the pier's parking lot, a testament to how much sand had built up in thirty years, sand that had once belonged to another beach.

There was always some type of beach renourishment project being proposed, planned or executed on the long Carolina Coast. These are very expensive propositions that sometimes even the homeowners are forced to participate financially in. And, sad to say, the sand that is brought in is not always as nice as the sand that was swept away. Ocean Isle Beach found that out two years ago when their fifty-year project started. The two million cubic yards of sand that were dredged out of the Shallotte River

Inlet and deposited on the beach at Ocean Isle were nothing at all like the smooth, soft, fluffy white stuff the islanders and tourists were used to. The new sand was hard and crusty and filled with jagged pieces of shell, making it almost unbearable to walk in some spots without shoes. Holden Beach, although fortunate enough to get sand from the Cape Fear River, SeaScape and Oyster Harbour development projects, would never be quite the same. At least a million dollars is required annually to provide the ongoing renourishment to solve their problems of erosion. The Sunset Beach residents were very fortunate indeed to have such a wide beach and the even wider set back of dunes to protect it.

Cassie left her shoes and socks by the bottom step of the beach access. The sand was cold and wet, but it felt wonderful as it made contact with the soles of her hot, burning feet. She walked at a steady pace down by the water's edge to Bird Island. Midway down the island, she started walking diagonally up to the dune line, to the mailbox. Using her hands she swiped enough sand away so she could sit comfortably on the bench. She grabbed both spiral notebooks from the mailbox and after ascertaining which one was the full one, she replaced it. Taking the newer one, she sat on the bench and read the last few entries. It seemed she would be the only one telling a sad tale as several of the previous pages were filled with wonderful accounts of time spent here and the joyous events happening in people's lives. She took out her pen, found the first blank page and started writing as if she was on the clock with a highly paid psychologist.

"Boy, he was right. He said he'd never hurt me. And he didn't. I've done it to myself. But man, oh man, does it hurt. I feel like I tore my heart out of my chest and threw it into that churning ocean I see raging before me. Feeling as badly as I do now, I cannot imagine the pain I would be in if I had let this go on. If I had stayed with him, loving him and getting to know more about him, until six months from now when I'd happen to see his eyes search out another's across a room. I could not have stood it if I'd been there when Miss Raleigh-Durham showed up on the scene with her sweet southern drawl and cheesy, artificial smile of perpetual optimism. The sight of Michael's own eyes lighting up as he finally met the woman he has worshipped all his life, would certainly have done me in. What am I saying? I feel like I've been done in already.

"I've read about unrequited love before and it's always sounded so romantic. Even when I knew how tragic the circumstances were, I always thought it was better that at least one person had love. After all, love is wonderful, isn't it? A splendored thing according to song. Well that's bull shit! Love is not wonderful or splendid. It's not even good. Love only works when it's returned, and when it's not—it's just pain. Lots and lots of pain.

"I know I'll find someone wonderful to share my life with. There must be thousands upon thousands of wonderful men just waiting to meet me. Yeah, right! Well, even when I meet the right guy, Mr. Perfect-for-me. I'll never love like this again—I won't ever let myself.

"Michael, if there's one thing I'd like to say to you, it's this: You will never find anyone who will love you more than I do. You may find your southern belle soul mate, the woman who will believe as you do about all things southern, but you'll never have the love of a woman as thoroughly as you had mine. You owned my soul, Michael and it hurts so badly that I can barely stand it. C. November 12, 2001."

Cassie closed the notebook and replaced it in the mailbox. She flicked off the flashlight, preferring to walk back in the dark. The wind was picking up a little and as it blew her hair across her face, it wiped her tears.

On the way back home she stopped at Jenny and Colin's because Jenny had left a message earlier and Cassie hadn't had the time to return it. Now she wondered what Jenny had wanted.

When the door opened, Jenny took one look at Cassie and she reached to enfold her in her arms. "What's the matter Cass?"

Colin, hearing Jenny's words from his seat on the couch, came to stand behind Jenny. "Who do I have to kill?" he asked, his face stern.

Cassie swiped at the new onslaught of tears with the sleeve of her jacket, but she managed a slight smile. "Michael. But don't kill him, just beat him up a little."

"Uh oh," Jenny said as she turned and looked at Colin, her deep concern mirroring his. "Come on in, we'll talk about it. And have I got news for you! Your dad's smitten!"

"Well, your news sure sounds a lot more upbeat than mine. Let's have it," she said as she took her work boots off at the door.

"He went to get his hair cut and to get a facial. They were the only ones in the shop. Millie Vanderveer went into the shop to make an appointment and couldn't find anybody, so she opened the door to the back room and guess what she saw?"

"I can only imagine. Dad having a facial?"

"He was having all right, but he wasn't having a facial. He was having sex!"

"Sex! He wouldn't!"

"Well, according to Millie, he was! He was reclining back in the chair and his pants were down around his ankles and Mary was sitting on his lap with her skirt all spread out around her. Needless to say, Millie quickly closed the door and forgot all about getting an appointment for next week."

"I can't believe Dad would do that! Especially if this was his first date with her."

"Yeah, well, Millie is not known to prevaricate. So you can take this as gospel."

Cassie rubbed her forehead, her thumbs pressing down on her eyebrows as she massaged them back and forth.

"You got any thing for a headache? Mine is splitting."

"Sure. Sure," Jenny said as she went into her bedroom to get her something for it.

Colin was back on the couch and now he looked over at her with his lips pursed in sympathy. "The tears aren't because your dad's gone, I trust?"

Cassie smiled over at him and shook her head. "No, the tears aren't because of dad leaving."

"Michael?"

"How'd you guess?" she said sarcastically.

"The big tears are for family and friends, the little ones are for love."

"What? I never heard that before."

"It's true. Big ol' crocodile tears—cause you're mad or sad, little tiny ones when your heart's breaking."

"Why is that?"

"I guess because you're gonna need so many more that they'd better be smaller or you'll plum run out."

That made her laugh and by the time Jenny brought her some Tylenol and water she was happy she'd stopped by, regardless of hearing that her father was acting like a lovesick fool. "Does dad even know about safe sex?" Cassie asked.

"Why are you asking me?"

"I don't know. Who's supposed to have the safe sex talk when it's your father getting back into the dating world after so many years?"

"Don't look at me!" Colin called out from his position on the couch. "I just met the man this week."

"I don't know him *that* well," Jenny said.

Cassie went over to the door to put her boots back on. "I guess I'll have to mention something when he calls to tell me he made it home safely. I'm taking my headache and going home now."

"Have you eaten, Cassie?" Jenny called after her. "You know it's real easy to get headaches if you don't eat."

"I'm fine. I'm not hungry."

"Here, I made some turkey sandwiches for your dad to take on the plane, but he didn't make it back by here. Take them home and eat. We need that bridge desperately, so please don't get sick on us."

Cassie took the sandwiches Jenny thrust at her and then trudged out to her truck.

"Cheer up honey," Jenny called to her, "things will look better by morning."

"Sure they will," Cassie muttered to herself as she put the keys in the ignition and started the truck. The drive took all of forty seconds and she pulled up alongside a car that looked exactly like Michael's. Her heart sank. Why the hell wouldn't he just leave her alone? He wasn't in it, but it would be just like him to find a way to break into her house.

She opened the front door and went inside. She could see Michael sitting outside on the patio past the dining room, the living room and the Carolina room. He turned to look at her and smiled. Her head throbbed and all she wanted to do was go to bed. She threw the sandwiches on the counter and walked into the living room to close the drapes, thereby effectively screening everything in the Carolina room and beyond from her view.

Michael started pounding on the door. "Cassie, let me in!"

"Go away or I'll call the cops!"

"I am the cops!"

"I'll get more, I swear I will. I have a very bad headache and I don't want to talk to you!"

"Promise you'll see me tomorrow night and I'll go."

"No!"

"Cassie!"

"Your hollering is going to wake up my neighbors. Go away!"

"Not 'til you promise I can come over tomorrow night."

"Sure. Come over tomorrow night." No guarantee that I'll be here, but you can certainly come over, she thought. Knock yourself out, she silently added as she made her way to her darkened bedroom and closed the drapes on his troubled face.

She stripped off her clothes and fell naked into bed, pulling the cool comforter over her heated body. She never came home from the job site without taking a shower, but she just didn't have the energy tonight.

The phone rang at six the next morning and woke her. It was probably a very good thing it did, because she hadn't bothered to set the clock the night before.

"Hello?" she mumbled.

"Hi Punkin. It's me, I'm home. I had a safe trip, got in around four this morning."

"Four? What time did you leave yesterday?"

"Oh, sometime late in the afternoon," he said evasively.

"Like what time exactly?"

"Eight."

"Why did you leave so late?"

"Got tied up."

"Yeah. I heard."

"What did you hear?" he asked with a touch of concern in his voice.

"Let's see, just how was that again? Oh, I remember," she said sarcastically, as she prepared to lambaste him. "Something about your pants down around your ankles, and Mary. Mary, Mary, without her cherry, sitting on your . . . Well, you get the picture."

He gave a great big sigh, "It wasn't the way it looked. But I'll admit, it must've looked pretty bad."

"Yeah. So if it wasn't the way it looked, what was it?"

"You know, I'm your father. You're not supposed to question me. I'm an adult. Hell, I don't even question you anymore." *You* didn't even come home the night before last."

"Humor me. If it wasn't the way it looked, just what were the two of you doing?"

"You're not going to believe this, even if I tell you."

"Try me, I could really use a good laugh."

"Okay. I went in to get my hair cut."

"Dad, your hair didn't need cutting."

"Well, I wanted a facial, too."

"This is already a strange story."

"Just listen, will you? Mary was busy when I got there. One of her regulars had a kid that chopped off the hair of a little neighbor girl she'd been watching. Mary was trying to make it look somewhat presentable before the mother came to pick her up. So Mary talked me into using one of the tanning booths."

"A tanning booth! Dad you always have a tan!"

"Yeah, but not all over. Just my arms, head and neck. I kind of agreed with her that I should tan my chest and back. Then she said why didn't I just tan all over. Well, thank God I kept my underwear on, because I burnt the hell out of my legs. So after the hair cut, I told her I had to go. I couldn't stand having my pants on top of the burn. She talked me into using this goopy stuff that came from an aloe plant she had on the windowsill. Well it worked real well, the burning stopped. She insisted on giving me the facial, but I couldn't put my pants on until all the aloe stuff was dry. So I got in the chair in the back room with just my underwear on to wait until it dried. Next thing I knew, she just came right on in and started the facial as if the man in her chair had his pants on."

"Are you making this up just to cover up for what you did?" she asked suspiciously.

"No, dammit! Just listen to me. I was enjoying the facial. I was enjoying it very, very much. Too much, if you know what I mean."

"I think I'm getting the picture."

"Well, she had this really low-cut top on and her boobs were practically in my face as she bent over my head. So I asked her if there wasn't a different position we could be in while she did this. One where I could open my eyes and see her face instead of her chest. Well the next thing I knew, she had straddled the chair and was leaning over me, still rubbing some gook on my face. A lady burst into the room. Mary, in her shock, abruptly sat on my lap and the rest is history."

"Dad. That is the most asinine story you've ever told me. Would you believe all that if I was telling it to you?"

"Probably not. But I swear Cassie, it's the truth."

"All right, if you say so, I guess I have to believe you. I can't figure what you could be gaining by making up a story like that!"

"Anyway, Mary knew who the lady was. She knew it wouldn't be long before this lady, Millie something or other, spread it all around and she started crying. Seems Mary is always getting into crazy situations like this that people misinterpret. Then people start talking bad about her and it upsets her. Things just keep happening to her, mostly bad things. Nobody seems to understand. She says some people even think she did away with her husbands. Anyway, she was pretty upset, so I couldn't just leave her like that."

"Wonderful. What did you do? Give her half the company?"

"Cassie! This women needs a friend, not people who continually bash her!"

"Okay, what did you do—as her friend?"

"I took her out to dinner and listened to her whole life story. She's had a very interesting life. You just wouldn't believe it. I sat riveted to my chair until I realized I had missed my flight. That's why I left at eight."

"Whew! Well, I'm sure glad you're home, safe and sound. And everything's all right, right?"

"Yeah, everything's fine. Just fine."

"Why do I get this feeling that there's something you're not telling me?"

"Well, I'm coming back down in two weeks."

"What!"

"I got a date. Mary wants me to take her to this wine festival at a vineyard down by you."

Cassie groaned then muttered, "Belle Amie."

"Yeah, that's it. It's in Little River."

"Dad, are you sure this is for the best?"

"Well, Cass, Mary sure could use a friend."

"Yeah, but does it have to be you?"

"I kind of like her."

"Dad you live ten hours away. She's GU."

"GU?"

"Geographically undesirable."

"Well, maybe, but she very desirable in many other ways."

"I don't want to hear it. Listen, I'm sending you a little booklet and I want you to promise me that you'll read it. Every single page."

"Cass is this the booklet I gave you that talks about condoms and Saran wrap?"

"Dad!"

"Honey, please don't worry about me, I know it's been a long time since Mom, but things haven't really changed all that much for the generation that believes in abstinence until marriage."

"Dad you cannot marry her! Have sex with her if you want, but don't you dare marry her!"

"Thank you for your permission—I never thought you'd come around. Now get up and go build my bridge."

She heard a click and she turned her head to stare at the receiver as if she suddenly didn't recognize the strange object she held in her hand. Slowly, she pulled the covers away from her body as she continued to stare at it. When it started making the high-pitched squeal signifying a phone off the hook, she gently laid it back in its cradle.

Since moving to Sunset Beach, she'd found a man's head, fallen in love, poured her heart out to a notebook and threatened a cop with arrest. But this conversation with her dad topped it all. Crazy Mary and Doofy Daddy, falling in love. God help her.

Chapter 37

Michael spent most of the day at Cheney's Gifts and Pelican Books looking through old receipts dated around October 11th, in hopes that Lady Kit used a charge card instead of paying cash. Claire and Ann were wonderfully organized but it still took longer to find the records than to go through them. Both owners kept them at their shops, but they were not filed by the date the customer charged, but by the date submitted for payment. After several hours of work, he had a handful of names of local people. After another hour of work, he had crossed them all off the list. Only one person lived on the island and he knew who that person was. She had a lovely home on the west side that was rented out most weeks of the summer, the rest of the time she lived in Asheville with her mother. Definitely not Lady Kit. Lady Kit's mother had died many years ago.

He went back to the station house where he ran into Ray.

"I hear you pulled some easy duty this coming Wednesday. Imagine, doing a stake out on the beach, waiting for the Kindred Spirit to show up," he chided.

"Who told you that? It's supposed to be hush hush."

"The chief himself. I guess he couldn't stand to hold it in any longer and had to rant a little about your ridiculous stake out. How 'bout letting me take your duty. I could use a little more sun."

"You can't get much of a tan this time of the year," Michael answered as he tried to move past him.

"I don't know why you're wasting so much time on this case. Everything's leading to a dead end, you're probably never gonna solve it. Besides, why do you care so much? He was a just a mean, old, crotchety man and nobody's gonna miss him."

"I'll work on the case until the chief takes me off of it. And, for your information, D. Duke has just as much right to a thorough investigation as the next man, regardless of his demeanor. Just because he was eccentric and a bit of a wacko at times doesn't mean he deserved to be murdered."

"Yeah, yeah, I knew there was no talking to you. By the way, I still haven't had a phone call from Cassie canceling our date this Friday, so I guess it's still on." There was a smugness to his tone that brought an instant sneer to Michael's lips.

"If you so much as . . . "

"Hey, buddy," Ray said as he grabbed Michael by the shoulders, "If you say lay off, I'll lay off. If it's that way with you, you just tell me. I wouldn't let a woman come between us. We go back too far for that."

Michael relaxed and gave a big sigh, "Yeah, it's that way with us." Or at least it was, he thought, but he knew better than to mention that to Ray.

"So, fill me in on this stake out. Sounds very mysterious," Ray said with wiggling eyebrows.

Michael gave him a sketchy idea of what he'd found out and what he was hoping to do on Wednesday. The more he talked about it though, the more ridiculous it sounded. He found himself just a little embarrassed and he began dropping his head to

379

stare at his shoes. He noticed Ray was continually rubbing his hand up and down on the outside of his right pocket. It was a nervous gesture, similar to the one many people have of jingling their coins in their pocket. After watching him for a few minutes while he wound up the progress he was making on his investigation, it finally got the better of him. "What the hell is in your pocket, and why are you doing that?"

Ray put his hand into his pocket and pulled out a golf pencil. He gave Michael a big grin and held it up, "It's a place marker. A butt place marker."

"A what?" Michael asked.

Ray looked down the hallway and then behind him into the kitchen. Apparently not sure of their privacy, he gestured for Michael to walk with him outside the side door.

"I slip this," he held up the pencil by the lead point, and that's when Michael noticed it had an eraser on the end and the words "Thistle Golf Club Sunset Beach" with a phone number etched on the side in gold, "into a woman's crack and make her wear it there as a reminder where I intend to be next time I see her."

"What?" Michael exploded, unable to believe what Ray was telling him.

"It's sort of like a way to build the excitement, you know?"

"No, I don't know," Michael said in disgust.

"Don't be so righteous. They like it, Michael, they really do. They find me very powerful and it's incredibly sexy to have them pull their panties down and bend over for me so I can carefully place it in their crack before we part. One girl wore hers for over a week. That was the week of the hurricane. I couldn't get back when I'd originally said I could, so she wore it the whole time. Every time she sat, she remembered me. Every time she went to the bathroom or took a shower, every time she had to remove it and then replace it, she was reminded of me. It's awesome to have that kind of power over women. And it makes them incredibly ready for me. Hell, they practically open the door with a tube of KY jelly in their fist."

Michael didn't think that he had actually ever known a pervert. Now he was acknowledging to himself, that he did indeed, truly know one—a very deviant one. And the thought that he had meant to keep to himself, he said, just because he had to know the answer. "They found a pencil exactly like that one in D. Duke's boat."

"I wondered where that went to, I must've lost it when I bent over to help them get it off the sandbar. I always keep one in my pocket," he said as he leaned conspiratorially towards Michael, "never know when you need to mark your place."

"You know the county'll pay for counseling for you. Why don't you get some help?"

"What for? The women love me. I'm telling ya, you gotta try this kinda stuff. It's amazing what you can get a homely woman to do for you. You're the one who needs counseling, I think you're becoming a prude."

Michael just shook his head and walked away. If he only knew the things that he and Cassie did to and for each other, he wouldn't think that. His mind replayed some of the times they'd been together. Quick images of their first night on the beach, the night they had kayaked to the island, the night he'd insisted she

381

dine topless, all those racy images flipped through his mind and he felt his body harden with desire. He snorted, a prude indeed; but then a lot of what they felt for each other was because of the love they shared.

It was that quick, that revealing. Just like that, he had told himself that they had great sex together because they loved each other, and he knew right then that he was in love with Cassie. He didn't have to lie when he said it anymore. It was true, he loved Cassie. And now he couldn't wait to tell her.

Chapter 38

"Michael, I really don't want to see you tonight. I just said that last night so you'd leave me alone."

"Cassie, I have to see you tonight. I'll come to the trailer, or to your house or you can come to mine, but I have to see you tonight. I will not take no for an answer."

She sat in silence for a few moments and then said, "Okay, come to my house. I'll fix dinner."

"That's not fair."

"How bad do you want to see me? If it's not bad enough to eat my cooking, then I guess you don't need to see me."

"Fine. I'll be there. What time?"

"How long does it take to make fried chicken and potato salad?"

"Cassie, making fried chicken is not for the novice."

"Okay, I'll bake it. I can do that. How long for the potato salad?"

"Well, after you make it, it needs to get cold, so you're probably talking three hours total."

"Okay, I'll get home around six, so you can come over at nine."

"I forgot, I like mine hot not cold."

"Okay, eight."

"Can't I just come over and help you?"

"No!" she yelled into his ear.

"Why not?" he yelled back.

"Because northern girls can cook, too!"

"Okay. Eight. Can I bring anything?"

"No. And if you change your mind about coming, I'll understand."

"I'll be there, don't you worry."

Michael got off the phone and shook his whole body. Cassie's cooking. God, he really did love this woman.

Cassie hung up and smiled. Maybe that book was right. Keep telling them 'no' and they'd finally come around. She swore to herself right then that she would not let Michael touch her, not so much as a simple kiss or even the brush of his hand against hers. He'd have to understand that. He'd have to promise her that he would respect her wishes before she even let him through the door tonight. Tonight would be a test for them both. But first, she had to plan dinner. She had that recipe for the potato salad Jenny's friend, Marie, had given her that night at the TGIF gathering and she could open a can of green beans. After all she didn't have a garden like Michael did. But the chicken, it really should be fried, that went much better with potato salad, she thought. Then she had an idea, a brilliant idea.

After work she quickly ran into the Food Lion and grabbed the ingredients she needed. Then she got in line at the Hardees Skat Thru. Chicken was chicken, nobody could tell one bird from another. She'd take eight pieces home, put them in a skillet, throw away the telltale container and claim them as hers. No one would be the wiser.

She was as excited as a little kid as she laid the ingredients out on the counter. She had written the ingredients on a napkin she had carried in her purse and she hoped that she had read them right. But not having a lot of confidence in her cooking skills, she called Jenny and read all the amounts to her just to make sure: ten large potatoes unpeeled, one medium white onion, chopped, ten dill slices, diced, one teaspoon salt, half a teaspoon pepper, and celery salt to taste. It was a good thing she'd called Jenny or she would have used ten whole dill pickles, about five times more than she needed, and when she had put the celery salt on a spoon to taste it, she had decided not to use it at all—it wasn't to her taste. Jenny had convinced her to use one teaspoon, that it would taste better with the potatoes and mayonnaise.

"What mayonnaise?"

"Cassie, potato salad has to have mayonnaise. I've never heard of one without it."

Cassie flipped the napkin over, "Yup, there it is, mayonnaise to taste. How do they expect people to make something if they want you to taste it before it's even done to decide how much to put in it?"

"Do you want me to come over?"

"No. I'm going to do this by myself if it kills me."

"Let's just hope it doesn't kill Michael."

"Very funny."

She boiled the potatoes whole as recommended, then drained the water. She let them sit in the pot for twenty minutes while she got the rest of the ingredients ready. Then she gingerly peeled off the skins and diced up the potatoes. What a messy job this cooking was, she thought as she rubbed her eyes which were irritated by the onion. When the potatoes were cubed, she mixed them with all the other ingredients and then

385

tasted it. It wasn't half bad, but she thought it needed just a teensy weensy bit more mayonnaise. So that's what "to taste" was all about. It was close to seven and she didn't know if it would cool enough in the refrigerator, so she put it in the freezer. Then, thinking that still might not be enough time, she boosted the dial to the coldest setting.

Then she put the chicken in a skillet. It didn't look like she'd actually cooked it in the skillet so she poured some oil in bottom of the pan and let the chicken sit in it on a burner. There, that looked much better. Then she went to take a quick shower. She dressed in a soft, floral, floor-length gown then piled her wet hair on top of her head and secured it with an elastic band. If there was one thing she knew about cooking, it was to keep hair out of the food. Soft, floppy curls would eventually spring out all over her head after it dried giving her a delicate feminine look. Unwittingly, she was making herself look southernly proper and sexy as all get out. When Michael arrived at exactly eight, she was ready.

"Is that you Michael?" she called through the door.

"Yes. Let me in."

"No, I can't just yet. We have to have an agreement."

She heard his sigh of exasperation, "And what's that? If I don't eat your dinner I can't stay?"

"No, but that's a good one. You have to agree that you will not touch me tonight."

"What!"

"You heard me. You cannot touch me. No kissing, no hugging, no anything."

"I have to eat your dinner *and* I can't touch you?"

"Right. We're just talking and eating tonight."

Michael was sorely tempted to just turn around and go home, but he really had something important to tell her tonight."

"Okay."

"And you have to promise."

"Do you get to touch me?"

"No."

"Okay, then I promise. Can I come in now?"

He heard her unlock the door and then it opened. "Well, gee, wasn't that an interesting conversation for the neighbors," he said as he closed the door behind him. She jumped out of the way, afraid his hand would touch hers on the knob.

"God, Cassie, I said I wouldn't touch you. You don't need to be so jumpy."

"I'm sorry Michael, I'm just afraid."

"Aw, sweetheart," he moved to hold her and as she backed up, then he remembered his promise and raised his hands, palms forward. "What are you afraid of?"

"That if we just barely touch, that if we graze each other's skin somehow, that we'll both lose control."

"And just what, pray tell, would be so bad about that? Wait don't tell me, it's an 'off night,' right?"

"Don't make fun of me, Michael. I just think that we can talk things over better if we don't let our attraction for each other get in the way."

"Well, I have to agree with you there. It seems we do need to talk. Can I help you get dinner ready?" he asked as he walked into the kitchen.

"It's all ready." She spun around and took the potato salad out of the freezer and set it on the table.

387

"Your recipe calls for freezing the potato salad?" he asked nonchalantly.

"Well, no. I just thought that putting it in the freezer would cool it down faster."

"Oh, I see." Michael took a serving spoon out of the drawer and tried to insert it into the bowl. When it wouldn't go in and instead his hand met very firm resistance, he didn't say a word, he just laid the spoon across the top of the bowl. He watched as Cassie carried the skillet over to the table and set it down in the middle of the table.

"Don't you need something to protect the table from that hot skillet?"

"Oh, the pan's not hot. Not anymore," she quickly added, remembering that it was supposed to have been cooked in that pan. Michael looked at the fried chicken sitting in the oil and simply nodded, cocking one eyebrow as he tried to understand. It looked like Hardees fried chicken. The chicken was too evenly browned to have been cooked by any method other than pressure cooking. But he sure wasn't going to be the one to call her on it.

"Well, let's eat, I'm starved," he said as he took his seat.

"Just let me get the green beans from the microwave and we'll be all set."

She placed them beside his plate and he was relieved to see that they looked normal, even though they did have a familiar sweet smell to them."

"I thought they looked a little plain, so I spiced them up with some nutmeg and cinnamon."

"Oh, that sounds good," he said, wondering just how he was going to survive this meal and assure her that she could cook as well as any southern-bred woman could, without choking on his words.

"Here, have some chicken," she said as she handed him the tongs. He put his plate close to the skillet and picked up a piece of chicken. He watched it drip for as long as he dared before putting it onto his plate. "This sure looks good," he said as he smiled over at her. She gave him the most dazzling smile, and at that moment, he would have eaten monkey droppings if it would have made her happy.

"Potato salad?" she asked as she handed him the bowl.

He held it between his warm hands as he distracted her by asking about her day, hoping that by doing this, that at least a portion on the side would thaw enough so he could at least get some onto his plate. He patiently waited as she chatted about her day while he concentrated on transferring his body heat to the bowl while the bowl passed back its frigid coating of frost to his splayed fingers.

After he managed to get a semi-frozen clump onto his plate, he generously piled the steaming green beans right up against them. With any luck, but the time he cut the top half of the chicken up, he'd be able to eat everything else.

He watched her as she served herself and noticed that she seemed unaware that anything was abnormal. It was not until he watched her put a bite of the oil-soaked chicken into her mouth that she balked. He quickly looked away and ate the chicken that he had carefully carved from the center of the breast. She had taken a leg and didn't have that luxury. He smiled to himself as she continued to talk and alternately eat as if everything was just as it should be.

The potato salad turned out to be delicious once it was thawed, and he praised her lavishly. Watching her beam with pleasure, he realized just how very much he loved her. The green beans were a little different, but still palatable. He ate all the beans on his plate just to show her how much he appreciated her effort, and then because it made her so happy, he reached for the bowl and took some more.

"Everything was delicious, Cass," he said as he got up to help clear the table.

"I made dessert, too!" she bubbled, and he felt his stomach do a little lurching action. "Really?"

"Yes. Tapioca pudding."

Please God, tell me she cooked it all the way, he prayed as he put the dishes into the sink.

She took the custard bowls out of the refrigerator and put them on the table, one in front of each place setting. "Some of it stuck to the bottom of the pan and I was afraid that it might be the good stuff, so I scraped it all up." And sure enough, there in the congealed gelatinous mixture were brown and black chunks, seemingly swirled throughout.

"Well, let's get to it then. Bring me a spoon," he said with feigned enthusiasm.

They ate their dessert in silence then she looked at him with what he could only imagine was devotion. "You really are a good sport, you know."

"I beg your pardon?"

"You. You ate everything."

"Wasn't I supposed to?"

"You may not have noticed, but even I wasn't able to get much of the stuff down," she said with a sheepish grin.

He laughed heartily and moved to cover her hand with his. He backed off when he saw her move back in her seat. "I almost forgot, forgive me. I do so want to touch you though. It is okay if I tell you that?"

"Oh yes, that's allowed."

"Well, then," he said as he sat back in his chair drinking the coffee that he had thankfully thought to start before they sat down at the table. "Let me tell you exactly how I'd like to touch you. I would like to take my fingers and caress the back of your neck. I would like to outline your delicate little ear and feel the smoothness of your tiny little suckable lobe. My tongue yearns to lick and lap at your whorls while my fingertips make their slow journey to your jaw . . ."

"Wait! Hold up! I change my mind, that's *not* allowed."

"Okay, then let's play strip poker. I, at least, want to *see* you tonight."

"Why don't you tell me what you wanted to talk to me about. Why you insisted I see you tonight."

"Oh, that's simple. Very simple. I just wanted you to know that I'm in love with you. Unequivocally and totally in love with you. Or to use the words from your questionnaire, 'madly, passionately, and irrevocably.' Cassie, I love you, and this time I mean it with all my heart." The heat in his eyes attested to the truth in his words and it was hard to keep from swooning from the pleasure hearing them gave her.

Instead, she quickly stood up and flew across to where he was sitting, throwing herself into his lap. As her arms went around his neck, she sobbed against his neck. "Oh Michael, you don't know how happy that makes me. I love you so much, I thought it was all over for us. I thought you didn't love me, even though you said you did."

"We're just beginning, sweetheart," he said as he stroked her hair. "But you're going to have to get off of my lap now. No touching, remember?"

"Oh, Michael, it's different now."

"I gave my word. You made me promise, no matter what, that I wouldn't touch you."

"Oh, I did, didn't I?"

"Yes, you did. And if you're ever going to believe anything I say, I have to keep my word."

She slowly lifted off of him. "Okay, I understand," but it was quite obvious that she was crushed.

He sat back and looked at his little imp. She looked for all the world like a little child who's favorite toy was in time out. He bent his arm and pulled up his sleeve to look at his watch. "I'll tell you what. Let's get the dishes done, play a few hands of gin, then a game of strip poker where you're going to lose all your clothes. By that time, tonight will be over—it'll be tomorrow, and I can ravish you like a man's entitled to after he has just declared his undying love."

She instantly perked up, but then just as suddenly deflated. "I can't. I just remembered I have some paper work to do tonight. I have schedules and projections and reports to read."

"It's just as well. I have to get up extra early and get to the beach so I can wait for Lady Kit. Since I have no idea when she'll get there, I'll have to be there from sun up to sun down—I can't afford to miss her if she shows up. It could be months before she comes again."

"I forgot all about that being this week."

They were both silent for a few minutes as they looked into each other's eyes from across the table. The desire smoldered in his as he raked his eyes from her lips to her breasts and back again.

"I'm sorry I made you promise," she said tentatively.

"Me, too."

"It'll be so nice when we're married, and nobody has to go home."

"Married?" he coughed.

Instantly she regretted what she'd said. But she needed some clarity here, so she'd ventured into the forbidden zone, the zone a man could speak of, but a woman dared not, "You said you loved me."

"And I do, but one does not necessarily lead to the other."

"Oh. I'm afraid I misunderstood." She stood awkwardly and walked into the kitchen.

"Cass, I just realized yesterday that I was in love with you. Give me a break here. You tie my hands so I can't touch you. You're pressuring me to make a lifetime decision when I'm not ready to, and I think I just ate something that didn't quite agree with me. I have to go home now. Let me know when I can talk to you when there aren't so many rules I have to abide by." He was up and out the door before she knew what had happened.

Cassie stood there staring at the door Michael had just run out of. He was right. He was absolutely right.

About everything. And on top of it all, her cooking had made him sick.

She walked dejectedly over to the sink and started washing the dishes. Tears overflowed her eyes and she found herself staring at a sinkful of bubbles through blurry eyes. She carried the skillet to the trash can and dropped the oily chicken into it. Then, before she could even carry the skillet over to the sink, she had to make her own frantic run to the bathroom. Poor Michael, he truly did deserve to have a more domestically competent woman than she could ever hope to be.

Chapter 39

It was very late but Michael couldn't sleep anymore. He was finally feeling better and that was a blessing because it would have been damned near impossible to spend a day at the beach feeling the way he was. At four o'clock, he realized that he was not going to get back to sleep, so he fixed a cup of tea and sat down at his kitchen table to review his notes.

He had already set out his gear and packed the few things he would need: a small portable tent, a folding chair, a beach towel, a book to read, a mini cooler, binoculars, some warm clothes in case it was cold and even a bathing suit in case it was warm enough to actually sunbathe, and both breakfast and lunch. He decided not to bring any fishing gear. It would just be too much to carry all the way down there. He wanted to be in position by the time the sun came up. For all he knew Lady Kit could be an early riser and one of the first walkers to hit the beach.

His thoughts kept reverting to Cassie and how forlorn she had looked when he had expressed his displeasure on the subject of marriage. If he hadn't been feeling so badly, he probably wouldn't have been so rough on her, but Jesus! Where he came from, it was the *guy* who brought up marriage, not the woman!

He forced his thoughts to the folder in front of him. He reviewed what he thought he knew about Lady Kit. Then he crossed out the things that were suppositions, leaving only the things that he absolutely knew for certain about her. He was pretty certain that when she started walking down the beach toward the mailbox that he would know her right away.

The last few index cards that he hadn't had a chance to review, were on top of the small pile. He flipped through them—April, May, June and August. Then the one for September, the one that had set this whole investigation going. She hadn't been back since then—she was due, unless she was scared. That was something that certainly had to be considered. If she were culpable, it would be better to stay away. If she didn't show up today, he would be at a dead end. D. Duke's killer would be home free—there was nothing else he could think of to check.

He pulled out a card and read: "Ah, the rites of spring. Even the highways are filled with budding flowers. The azaleas are about to pop at home, but here, they are in magnificent full bloom already. It turns out that this was a great week to come. I went to the Ocean Garden Buffet last night. It was superb. They have the best Chinese food. I don't believe I have ever seen a Chinese buffet the likes of this one. It was so good I may even go again tonight! Don't tell anybody, but I walked out with a few almond cookies in my napkin! They will be an excellent snack for my afternoon tea today. This bench is getting more hidden by the sand with each visit. I should remember to bring a shovel and dig it out, but I don't think I even have one anymore. April 11, 2001."

The lady definitely likes her flowers and it is colder inland so the flowers are about a week or so behind those on the coast. She could live anywhere west of here. She likes Chinese food and it seems she can tell quality from just quantity. He'd eaten at the buffet she'd mentioned and he had to agree; they had the largest variety he'd ever seen. But he hadn't tried the almond cookies. He made a mental note to do that the next time he was there. Tea in the afternoon? Was she British or did she just like tea in the afternoon? His mother did, he knew that, and she was far from British. He wondered momentarily what his mother would think of Cassie. He had to remind himself that he was not going to think about her today. But he knew his mother would like her, except for the fact that she couldn't cook. That would be a major disappointment to her, and it would considerably limit the scope of things they could talk about together.

"The waves roll in, the waves roll out. A never ending cycle that has gone on since the beginning of time. A cycle that will never cease. Sometimes I wonder what the bottom of the sea looks like. If all the water were miraculously sucked up into the heavens, how many ships would we see at the bottom? Ships made of gopher wood and cypress, ships made of teak and mahogany, ships made of steel, all of them lying on the bottom with the lives taken by the sea in them, thousands upon thousands of them. I wonder what the true number is? Maybe it's 36,473; maybe it's 78,956. Well, whatever the number is, surely, somewhere in the world another number will be added to it today. It is so sad to think about—all those lives lost at sea. And planes, too. John Kennedy Jr.'s plane, planes from World War II, Korea and Vietnam. I think Desert Storm lost a few too, and didn't they have planes in World War I? Why am I looking out to sea and seeing death today? Actually, I see a man in a kayak way out there. I hope he makes it back to shore. The greedy sea doesn't need anymore lives. May 9, 2001."

He'd forgotten that one and how maudlin it was. Maybe she knew someone who was lost at sea. He thought a moment about all the ships that had sailed since time had begun. The ancient Greeks, the Vikings, all the early adventurers and explorers, the Spanish Armada, the whaling ships and generation upon generation of fishermen, and he thought even her highest number might be quite low.

"The season is in full swing. There's just something about summertime at the beach. As long as the sun is shining, everybody's full of energy and life. It's a time to escape, a time to abandon your responsibilities and be young again, a time to gather your thoughts and a time to dream new dreams. I have a new dream. I think I will add my name to the list as they suggested at last night's meeting and go wherever they send me. It will be a wonderful way to meet new people. I already have my passport and I've taken all the classes, and they wouldn't dare turn me down for the time off at work for something like this. June 13, 2001."

This was the strangest puzzle he'd ever worked on and he couldn't wait to unravel it all. Maybe today. So whatever meetings she goes to, they send people out of the country to do something she'd had to learn. It must be something worthwhile and humanitarian for she isn't concerned about her job refusing her the time off. Was she a missionary? A teacher for the Peace Corps? Well, at least he had a few new places to check if things didn't pan out today.

"There's a lot of talk going around about the new bridge. You'd think we'd be resigned to the idea of it by now, but we're not. I'll miss the old one, that's for sure, but I can't help thinking that it's time for some action. We've argued long enough—the community has experienced intense bitterness over this issue; it's time to move on and forego the sentiment. I kind of equate the Town of Sunset Beach asking D.O.T. for a new bridge to a teenage boy asking his father for a new car. It's truly up to the one providing the new car to decide what it's going to be. Whether he's just going to fix up his old jalopy to get him through a few more years or whether he's going to go hog wild and buy the best thing on the showroom floor, concerned for his son's safety and being adamant that he's not going to have to buy him another one for many more years to come. You'd think the son would be happy with a brand spankin' new, up-to-the-minute model, but he's not . . . he wants his '66 Mustang restored instead. Well, it's Daddy's money—and he's gonna do what he chooses. That's how I feel about the bridge. D.O.T. thinks it's an antiquated relic; the federal government and the state of North Carolina want to buy us a new one. So it's time to let the old bridge go, to remember it in pictures and in our hearts. You can see the signs of the impending construction, the detour signs are already up, even though they're covered; survey markers are everywhere and huge dumpsters are being placed beside the roads. It's inevitable now, and it's a cinch that they're not going to spend a dime fixing up the old one, so we ought to just accept their generosity and hope that the old one will last until the new one is opened. Que sera sera. August 15, 2001."

399

Boy, wasn't that the truth! Well, it was all academic now. Cassie, his Cassie, was building the new bridge and he was very proud of her.

He replaced the cards, closed the folder and stood up and stretched. It was almost time, time go over to the island. He poured what was left of his coffee down the drain and washed the cup.

Thirty minutes later he was in a cruiser parking at the west end of Main Street by the 40th Street beach access. It was still dark but you could see the faint light breaking across the horizon as he made his way to the beach and then on to Bird Island. He positioned his tent so it was about fifty yards beyond the mailbox, close enough so he could see what was going on from the tent, but not close enough to intimidate anyone and scare them off. The way he was dressed, and with the things he carried, he hoped to appear like any Joe Shmoe taking a day off from work to relax on the beach.

His small, round, pop-up tent took just minutes to open and secure and soon he found himself all set up with nothing to do. It was still too dark to read, too early to eat, and not a walker in sight as far as he could see. He was tempted to catch up on some of the sleep he'd missed, but he was on the job now—he'd mentally clocked in when he'd left the cruiser. So, in his first outfit of the day, his jogging suit, he did his first undercover order of the day—he jogged. To the jetty and back, to the jetty and back, to the jetty and back. He did this until he had worked up a pretty good sweat and he could see the sun coming up from the opposite side of the island. It was going to be a clear, warm, sunny day. That would be good for his purposes. Lady Kit wouldn't likely come out in pouring down rain.

He stripped off his jacket and sat down in the chair to have a cup of coffee from his thermos. Then he pulled out a homemade blueberry muffin, praying that his stomach was back to normal, because if it wasn't, he had no idea what he was going to do. Then he took out his book and started to read as he munched and sipped. This was all well and good, except that he couldn't relax. He was too wound up. He could feel how tense he was all the way down to his toes, which were now cramped in his sneakers. He unlaced them and removed his shoes and socks. The sand felt cool beneath his feet, but somehow, it relaxed him. He breathed a deep sigh and stretched out even farther in his low-slung beach chair. The air was nice, a little nippy, but nice. Sunset Beach did not have a fishy or salty tang in the air. It always smelled clean and empty; no recognizable smell. Except for the occasional days when sixteen different things lined up just right, and the wind blew the factory smells from the Georgetown paper mill, eighty miles away, up the coast. Thank God, this wasn't one of those days.

He finally saw a group of walkers making their way toward him. He got out his binoculars and focused on the small group. Six women, all carrying hand weights, power walking to beat the band. An exercise class no doubt. He scanned all the women, checking them out and was particularly fascinated with the leader's cute little ass when they all turned around to head back at the sand bridge separating the two islands. She was cute, but he'd never seen an ass as nicely rounded and as firm as Cassie's.

He allowed himself to think about her for a few minutes because it was just too hard not to. He smiled as he thought about all the trouble she went to, to make dinner for him. Then he laughed out loud when he thought about the Hardees chicken floating in a cold pan of oil. The potato salad showed promise though, once it was unfrozen. She was certainly a dichotomy. A beautiful woman who was incredibly smart in many, many ways, but not so smart when it came to beguiling. Well no, that wasn't actually true, she certainly had beguiled him. She just didn't know that there were some things you were supposed to keep hidden in a relationship, some things you were supposed to pretend you didn't know—when you actually did, and some things you were supposed to manipulate to the outcome you wanted. He guessed he should be grateful that she wasn't that way, that she was more open and above board about what she wanted, but dammit! That just wasn't the way things were done!

Then he thought about himself. Why was it so important? Did he really want to be put together by a silly little twit whose only aim in life was to lasso him in? A woman who's main claim to fame was that she could make Hoppin' John or a Red Velvet Cake? Hell, he could do all that, why did Cassie have to know how to?

He suddenly sat upright as images of Cassie came into his mind, an image of Cassie holding a sleeping baby in a darkened kitchen, the same Cassie who had fought like a wildcat to protect something she had built, something she cared passionately about. Cassie with her questionnaire. Cassie sitting at the end of a formal table, topless. Cassie, vigorously meeting each of his downward thrusts with an equally powerful upward one. Cassie, Cassie, Cassie . . . As all the images of Cassie came careening in and out of his head, he was overwhelmed with it all.

Cassie, his Cassie. His beautiful angel-devil. And he knew then that he'd rather have his Cassie with her grease-smudged nose and burned tapioca pudding than the Queen of the Azalea Festival.

His search was over. He'd found his southern bride. What difference did it make that she was from Northern Virginia? So she'd never make a co-cola salad or preside over a meeting of the junior league? She could drive a Mac truck, and it seemed that she had driven one clean through his heart.

He was suddenly, deliriously happy. And now he was anxious to find her and ask her to be his wife. He chuckled at the thought. She'd already made it crystal clear that she was applying for the job. He just couldn't wait to tell her that she got it! That she'd beaten everybody else out—all those mythical southern belles he conjured up and held on to over the years. Cassie Andrews, from Virginia, was going to be his wife!

He couldn't tell her until tonight. And now, the question in his mind was how to tell her. It should be done in a special way. A proposal, especially one as hard-fought as this one was, deserved something special. She deserved something special, he thought, as he paced around the tent. And then it came to him. He looked up and saw an elderly couple walking across the sand about two hundreds yards away. He calculated that he had time before they got this far down. He quickly strode over to the mailbox, grabbed the top spiral notebook and a pen. Searching for the last page that was written on so he could flip it over and use the first clean one, he accidentally came across the page where Cassie had just recently written her tearful entry. He recognized her writing right away because of the hand written questionnaires, he sat down to read it.

"Boy, he was right. He said he'd never hurt me. And he didn't. I've done it to myself. But man, oh man. does it hurt. I feel like I tore my heart out of my chest and threw it into that churning ocean I see raging before me. Feeling as badly as I do, I cannot imagine the pain I would be in if I had let this go on. If I had stayed with him, loving him and getting to know more about him, until six months from now when I'd happen to see his eyes search out another's across a room. I could not have stood it if I'd been there when Miss Raleigh-Durham showed up on the scene with her sweet southern drawl and cheesy, artificial smile of perpetual optimism. The sight of Michael's eyes lighting up as he finally met the woman he has worshipped all his life, would certainly do me in. What am I saying? I feel like I've been done in already.

"I've read about unrequited love before and it's always sounded so romantic. Even when I knew how tragic the circumstances were, I always thought it was better that at least one person had love. After all, love is wonderful, isn't it? A splendored thing according to song. Well that's bull shit! Love is not wonderful or splendid. It's not even good. Love only works when it's returned, and when it's not—it's just pain. Lots and lots of pain.

"I know I'll find someone wonderful to share my life with. There must be thousands upon thousands of wonderful men just waiting to meet me. Yeah, right! Well, even when I meet the right guy, Mr. Perfect-for-me, I'll never love like this again, I won't ever let myself.

"Michael, if there's one thing I'd like to say to you, it's this: You will never find anyone who will love you more than I do. You may find your southern belle soul mate, the woman who will believe as you do about all things southern, but you'll never have the love of a woman as thoroughly as you had mine. You owned my soul, Michael and it hurts so badly that I can barely stand it. C. November 12, 2001."

Michael looked up to see the couple down by the water picking up shells. With his eyes misted from blinking back his unshed tears, he fumbled through the pages to the next blank one.

"Cassie, you own my soul, too. Will you marry me? Michael."

He closed the book and replaced it in the mailbox. Then he went back to wait for Lady Kit. Sometime tonight, he'd find some reason to bring Cassie here and get her to open the book. He'd have his grandmother's engagement ring in his pocket, if he could get to his safety deposit box where he kept it before the bank closed. Then he'd have Trey arrange to have a bottle of champagne and a Roberto's pizza delivered by Matt's four-wheeler and they'd dine in front of the mailbox, staring out at the ocean while they thought up names to call their kids. Now how romantic was that? He was pretty proud of himself coming up with all that on such short notice, so proud and distracted that he almost didn't notice the little lady with a floppy straw hat walking toward the mailbox.

From his shielded position on the other side of the tent, he watched her through the binoculars. He watched her take a notebook out of the box, go to the bench and brush some sand off, and gingerly seat herself.

It looked like she was reading back quite a few pages, so Michael went around to the other side and dragged his chair around. He was careful not to let her see him and mindful of the reflective glare binoculars could have if they were aimed improperly.

After a while, she flipped back a page, took the pen in hand and started writing. It was a little after ten and Michael could feel his heart racing with excitement. This could be Lady Kit. Pretty soon, with her help, he would solve the mystery of D. Duke's death. He would hunt down and arrest the murderer and the chief would give him an award and make him a detective. Then he'd grab Cassie, run back down here and propose. How perfect a day was this, he thought, as he adjusted the focus on the binoculars.

The lady replaced the notebook, stood back, and taking a small camera out of her pocket, she took a picture of the mailbox. Up until then, he'd really thought she was Lady Kit, but now he wasn't so sure. That was more something a tourist would do, than something a local would do. He waited until she was a respectful distance away, then he quickly ran up to the mailbox and grabbed the journal.

With the very first glance on the last page, he knew it wasn't her. The writing was no where near the same.

He read what she'd written just the same:

Michael, I hope she accepts, but it sounds like you might have waited too long. The best of luck to both of you. Jeannie from Stowe, Ohio.

What did she know! It wasn't too late! Cassie was in love with him. She made potato salad for him just last night. She was thrilled to pieces when he professed his love for her. It was not too late!

He went back to the tent, took out his lunch and grabbed a handful of grapes. He hadn't realized how hard he was chomping on them until he found one with a seed, which caused him to bite into the side of his mouth. Damn! That hurt. And the tomato juice he'd brought to drink was going to hurt even more. He put it back in the cooler and grabbed a bottle of water. He watched people come and go. He even watched a man go up into the dunes and come back out without his suit on. Man! Go to the other end of the beach! he screamed in his head. We certainly don't need that to drive Lady Kit away! Hell, the man didn't have much to show off anyway.

He looked down at his own physique and smiled. He could go nude tonight if he wanted to. He and Cassie could eat their pizza in the buff if they wanted to. Hell, this was Bird Island. It wouldn't even be breaking the law.

Well, it wouldn't be, until the money got appropriated for the sale of the island to the state and the island became a coastal nature preserve. Then the state could ask the town to annex the island, expanding the town's ordinance banning public beach nudity.

407

That was at least a year or two away the way things were going, he thought.

The thought of Cassie lying with him naked on this beach tonight brought back the powerful image of her lying naked while he'd zoomed in on her the first day they'd met. He felt his groin tighten and he groaned. He had never met a woman who kept him so aroused all the time and thoughts of a midnight tryst on the beach looked very promising indeed.

It was starting to get pretty hot. The sun was high and blazing. The winter sun was not as intense as the summer one, but it was still very bright as it steadily beat down on him. He'd already stripped down to a T-shirt and shorts, but after a while, even that was too hot. He went into the tent and put on his bathing suit with the thought of wading into the water and taking a quick dip to cool off. It was mid-November so the water would be quite cold, but the air temperature felt like it was in the high seventies. The sun was full and high and his brow was sweating. The breeze he'd had earlier had died away and now the air was still. He came out of the tent to discover someone over by the mailbox. He looked at his watch, it was almost 3:30. God, he hoped this was her. She was wearing chunky red capris and a black shell sweater. He thought her hair was a salt-and-pepper gray, but he couldn't be sure, she had a folded scarf tied around most of it.

He grabbed his chair, picked up his binoculars and watched her as she took out a journal and sat down to write in it. Before he knew it, she was up and off, walking briskly down the beach back toward Sunset. He waited a few minutes, then sauntered over to the mailbox, trying to feign disinterest in case she looked over her shoulder.

He grabbed the journal, flipped the pages to the back of the notebook and gasped. Eureka! Lady Kit! He quickly looked up and then back down at the page. She was walking so briskly that he didn't know if he'd have time to read it now and still catch up with her. But he thought it might contain something important, so he quickly scanned it. Only stuff about the fine weather and a painting class she had enrolled in. He looked up and was astonished to see that she was barely more than a red speck with a black dot on top of it. The lady sure could move!

Shit! He started to sprint. And he kept that up until he had closed the gap by all but a hundred yards or so. Man, she was walking fast! He held a hand on his side as he caught his breath, but he still kept walking and after a few minutes he realized that with his longer stride he would overtake her if he didn't slow down. He wanted to keep her in view, but he didn't want to approach her until he knew at least where she lived since he had no way to know how hostile she would be to his questions.

He followed her as she walked the entire west end of the beach, then walked under the pier and continued on to the east side. He nodded a few times to people who recognized him and pretended that he was out for a briskly-paced stroll at the water's edge. He kept Lady Kit's slightly-wide, red-covered backside in sight at all times, all the while pretending not to even notice that she was there, briskly walking thirty or forty feet ahead of him.

They walked for ten minutes more before she left the beach at the 10th Street access. Then, at the end of the access, she turned right and started walking on the road. Michael knew instantly that this was not going to bode well for him. He was barefoot. The sand wasn't too bad, but even it had abraded his feet somewhat and he knew he couldn't handle walking on the street very well. The street was full of small pebbles, gravel pieces and prickly spurs in lots of places. There was no sidewalk. It was the street or the grass in front of someone's house—one hardly better than the another on his bare feet.

He knew the names on most of the front row beach houses. Trying to keep his mind off his tender feet, he tried to recall as many names as he could from the center stop sign. Safe at Home, Outta Gear, SeaOats, Paradise West, Charlie's Place, Interlude, Starthrower, Gray Gull, Windrift. And now, the one he was in front of, the spiffy-clean, gray, Sandollar. Next, Plum Nelly, the duplex with the nice brick trim. Then, Mixed Nuts- sounded like a fun place to be. Followed by, the Magic Box—a name that could mean so many things.

They continued on past the beautiful, black and white Victorian dubbed Seychelles and then the Purple Cow, which was more mauve than anything else.

He could see her up ahead pulling away. So he turned on the steam and gritted his teeth against the constant jabbing of something into his heel or his sole. Ouch! Ewwch! Yipes! Eeeks! he muttered as he high- stepped his way past the obvious obstacles, but still landing on the minuscule pieces that found just the right tender spot to penetrate.

Her slightly matronly form was a block away and she was still walking very briskly—of course, *she* had shoes on! He could see her as she stopped to look at a pretty flower bed or waved to someone, but from this far, he couldn't tell if he knew her or not. A Sunset Beach police cruiser drove by and Michael tried to flag the officer down, but he wasn't able to get his attention, even though he thought that the officer should have easily been able to see him in his rear view mirror. Certainly he should have been able to hear his voice calling, "Hey! Hey! Wait up! I need a lift!" Whoever it was though, was going to hear it from him whenever he made it back to the station, if he ever figured out who it was. From the way he sat and the fleeting glance of a somewhat dark hair color, he thought it could be Ray, but he wasn't exactly sure.

There was a stretch of soft grass for the space of one yard and he silently praised the people who lived in the tan Mediterranean–style stucco with the elegant, curving front stairs, for the upkeep and excellent care of their yard. The grass felt cool and spongy on his hot, aching feet. He should have thought to go back for at least his shoes when he'd had the chance. As it was, he was going to be approaching this woman, whoever she was, at the door to her house in just his bathing suit, without even his badge to properly identify himself.

She stopped to talk to a man and a woman standing in their yard and he was able to get within half a block of her. He continued to watch her as she nodded her head and then waved as she continued on. Then, just as he was patting himself on the back for making it this far, she crossed the street. He looked at the black, pebbly asphalt and knew that it would be hot. Not as hot as it got in the summer, but it would be hot enough on feet that now felt as if he'd sandpapered them smooth before making a hundred tiny slits in them. He cursed himself for not going barefoot more often to toughen them. Then, as he watched, she backtracked on the opposite side of the street to 11th street and then turned onto it. She walked down the quaint side street that was on a canal. A minute later, she turned onto a little path created by shell-shaped stepping stones. Up the pathway she went, up the center steps and into the door on the right side of a large duplex. Her house was just two lots down from D. Duke's.

Hobbling along as best as he could, he managed to catch up to her a few minutes after she'd closed the screen door behind her. Just as he reached the top step, he noticed another police cruiser patrolling the street. It was too late to be of any assistance. He'd made it this far on his own and now he wasn't so thrilled with the idea of partnering up with an officer who was properly dressed for an interrogation. It would just make him look even more unprofessional than he already was. He raised his hand and knocked briskly on the wooden door frame and saw her turn and look down the darkened hallway as she removed her scarf in front of a hall mirror. She peered at him as if she ought to be able to recognize him, but clearly she did not. "Who is it?" she called in a strong voice meant to intimidate.

"I'm officer Michael Troy from the Sunset Beach Police Department. Unfortunately, I don't have my I.D. on me, but you can call the station and they'll verify it for you. The number's 555-2151."

She scrutinized his face for a moment and then seemed relieved that she didn't recognize him. "Oh, that's okay. I believe you. What can I do for you, officer?" she asked as she walked down the wooden hallway to open the screen door.

He wiped his feet on the beachy welcome mat and stepped inside into the cool interior of the beach house. The smooth firmness of the cool, wooden floor felt wonderful under his feet. But he felt awkward standing there in his bare feet and bathing suit getting ready to discuss official business. "It's about D. Duke, Ma'am. I think you might be able to help us solve his murder."

She gave a big sigh and he visibly watched her slump. Resignedly, she turned around and started to walk back down the hallway. "Well, we might as well have a cup of tea and sit down to talk about it. I'll actually be glad to get all this off of my chest."

Now, in addition to feeling awkward, he also felt insecure and was immediately aware of the fact that he was completely unprotected. His gun, his radio, his night stick were all in the cruiser at the end of the street on the other side of the island. But despite the dangerous position he might have put himself into, he felt sure that she wasn't the murderer. She just didn't seem the type. A profiler might have reminded him that looks meant absolutely nothing when it came to homicide.

"That sounds nice, ma'am. By the way, just what is your name?"

She smiled at him, "It's Gladys, Gladys Covey. How is it that you've come to talk to me without knowing who I am?" She asked as she indicated a chair at a large honey oak table.

He pulled the chair out, and while she fixed their tea, he filled her in on how he had been alerted to her

413

journal entry, his subsequent trip to Hope Mills and his consistent dead ends trying to find her.

She chuckled as he related his attempt to pinpoint the day she would go to Bird Island to write in the journal.

"I've tried to figure out which organization you could possibly be with that met on the second Tuesday of every month, but I'm sure I haven't touched on the one that it is. What meetings do you come here for? If you don't mind my asking."

She gave him another of her full, grandmotherly smiles, "The local Red Cross Chapter meets in the community meeting room of the electric company the second Tuesday of every month at 7 p.m. I'm on the Disaster Services Team. I come back for them whenever I can. I've just joined the national delegation registry to be sent anywhere in the world when there's a disaster. I'll work wherever I'm needed for a few weeks each year as a volunteer damage assessment specialist."

"The Red Cross," he said as he scratched his jaw, "well, that explains your last entry, the one where you talk about having a passport and being able to leave your job."

Instantly she bristled, "I still don't know how they're going to react when they find out I'm going, but I simply don't care anymore. They treat me like a dog there. I've a good mind to quit if they give me any guff!"

He chuckled at her attitude, "I remember reading about your work. You're really not very fond of the place where you work are you?"

"No, I certainly am not! Over twenty years I've worked for them and do you think just once that they could remember my birthday like I remember everybody else's? No, siree. If I want a birthday cake, I guess I'll just have to bake it myself!"

He smiled as she blew off steam. "Speaking of cooking, do you think I could get your recipe for Mulligatawny Stew. The way you wrote about it, it sounds delicious."

"Oh, dear boy, it certainly is. I would be delighted to get it for you." She got up to get it but he stilled her with his hand. "Later. First tell me why you wrote what you did about D. Duke."

She sat back down and sighed. "I know I killed the poor man. It was all my fault, I'm sure. I don't know what happened exactly, but I'm sure if I hadn't called the police, D. Duke would be alive today."

"Whoa, slow down. Start from the beginning. Called who?"

She sat back, crossed her arms over her chest and recollected the night that D. Duke died.

"I was tired of it. I'd talked to him about it several times, but it did no good."

"What did you talk to him about?"

"Those cats! Those damned cats that he loved so much."

"Ah, yes, your reference to the cats. Okay, I'm asking about the cats. What about the cats?"

"He fed them. Every night, he fed them."

"I'm missing it here. Why are you so upset that he fed the cats every night?"

"He fed them here! Right here!" she pointed out the back door. He could see a deck and beyond that other houses on the other side of the canal.

"He fed them here?"

"Yes, every night he'd walk over here with two bowls. One was filled with water; the other he filled with cat food. He'd put them down a few yards from the bottom of the stairs near the patio. Well, naturally, the cats think this is their home now and they're here all the time! Whining, crying, trying to get in, sometimes actually getting in whenever somebody doesn't pay enough attention when they open the deck or the patio doors. My renters constantly complain about the cats; some won't even rent out my house anymore. There must be at least seven or eight cats now and who knows how many kittens. They're a big nuisance, whining at the doors to get in when it's cold or raining, screaming that awful wail that sounds like a little baby crying all night long when they're in heat, using all my flower beds for litter boxes! I'm telling you, there were many times I thought about killing D. Duke myself!"

"Why didn't you call the authorities?"

"I have. And so have my renters. Many times. All they do is tell me that he's not breaking any laws by feeding the cats. He's trespassing if he comes onto my property, but he never does. He feeds them just a few yards from my concrete patio, which is somebody else's property. That empty lot next door. I've tried to find out who owns it, but nobody seems to know. Now, that 'J.J.J.' company is building a house on it. I'll bet my new neighbors are going to be just thrilled when they find out on moving day that they've inherited a whole passel of cats!"

Michael stood up to go look out the glass sliding door that led to the back deck, which led down stairs to the patio, also accessible from the garage level below. Sure enough, that was one of the three houses that the new builder, Jared Jenrette Jenks, was building.

"No idea who owned it before?"

"No. It was one of the original pieces of property that Mr. Gore, Sr. owned when he bought the whole island. He gave it to somebody for doing some work for him years ago. The deed is a fee simple deed of conveyance. It was just signed over, no mention of the new owner, much like signing over a title to a car."

"Doesn't the new owner have to register it?"

"No. Not unless it's financed and apparently it never has been. Whoever owns it just has a piece of paper saying it's his now. The only one who could contest it, is Gore, Sr., if he says it's not his signature. But it was pretty common back then to pay people by giving them a bit of land."

"What about the taxes?"

"I guess somebody's been paying them or else the county would have slapped a lien on it and sold it for satisfaction, but they never would tell me who was paying the taxes—I'm not sure they even knew. They were always paid in cash so far as any records they could find."

"Curious," Michael said.

"It's more than that. It's the reason I haven't been able to do a thing about the damned cats!"

"So what do the cats have to do with D. Duke's death?" his frown and furrowed eyebrows attesting to his bafflement.

"I called the police the night he died. I just couldn't take it anymore. I saw him feed them around eight o'clock that night, then he did something I've never seen him do."

"What's that?" he asked completely mystified and getting just a touch impatient.

"He took the wrapper that the cat food was in and put it in my trash can."

"Boy, he really went for broke and stepped over the line that time," Michael said sarcastically.

"He did! That's exactly what he did!" Obviously she hadn't picked up on his sarcasm.

"He broke the law! He came onto my property to dispose of the trash. The trash left over from feeding his precious cats!"

The lady had developed some strong venom on this subject and Michael suddenly couldn't reconcile her to the Lady Kit he had become so fond of. Without really thinking it through, he wanted to say something to make her feel bad about herself and her selfishness. "Did you know D. Duke was allergic to cats?"

"What?"

"Did you know that D. Duke was allergic to cats?"

"No. No I didn't know that."

"Well, he was. Deathly allergic."

"Then why did he have so many?"

"They weren't really his. They were strays. He couldn't feed them anywhere near his place, it would've killed him. And I'll bet when he did feed them here, he didn't stay long enough to do more than throw the food into a bowl."

"That's true. Many times I ran out to talk to him, but he just kept walking briskly away ignoring me completely."

"He probably wasn't ignoring you, he just had to get away before he took a breath or allowed one to rub up against him. But he loved cats, always did, ever since he was a little child."

"I didn't know any of that," she said somewhat contritely and Michael was relieved to learn that he hadn't misjudged her so much after all.

"He didn't tell people, I found out from his doctor after he died."

There was a moment of silence between the two of them and then Michael resumed his questions. "So you called the police and told them you had a trespasser. What happened next?"

"Well, they sent an officer. When he came here, I explained the whole thing to him. I even took him down to my trash bin and showed him the cat food packet that was lying on top of my trash in the trash bin."

"Then what?"

"He said he'd go speak to him."

"And?" he prompted.

"I watched him go. He walked over to D. Duke's and went inside. They say D. Duke died that night, sometime around ten. The police officer didn't come back for his cruiser that was parked in front of my house until well after midnight."

"Hmm. That's a little odd. What was the officer's name, do you remember?"

419

"No, I don't. I remember seeing his name badge, but for the life of me, I can't remember what his name was. I've been trying to remember it since that night. You look a little like him, only you're a little taller, more broad chested and a good deal better looking."

"Well, thank you," Michael said as an embarrassed flush crept up his neck.

"His coloring was very much like yours."

Well, that could have been several of the guys, he thought. "Can I borrow your phone?" he asked.

"Sure, it's right there over on the wall." He punched in the number for the station and waited for it to be answered. Then he asked the duty officer, who thankfully was a woman and out of the loop of suspicion, to check the duty log for the night D. Duke was murdered to see who was sent out on the call to Mrs. Covey's. For some unknown reason, the officer's name had been whited out and the date had been written there as if someone were correcting a mistake and then accidentally inserting the date in the wrong column. This was not looking good, one of their officer's had been implicated and now it looked like there was some kind of a cover up. "Jody, you were one of the officers sent to help retrieve D. Duke's boat weren't you?"

"Yeah. I think I still have a few of the mosquito bites from that day, in fact."

"Who else was there?"

"Let's see, there was, Pete, Randy, Jeremy and me along with a few guys from the forensics lab."

"Ray wasn't there?"

"No."

"Are you sure?"

"Absolutely. I would've remembered if he had been. I went out with him once and I avoid him like the plague. I would have remembered, if he was there."

Ray had lied about dropping the pencil then. "Where is he now, do you know?"

"Somewhere on the island. I thought he was going to go relieve you, at least that's what he said."

"Shit! Get the chief for me, will ya?"

"He's not here. He checked out for a few minutes, said he'd be right back, had a hankerin' for one of Duffer's Reubens."

"Well, track him down, tell him I need some back up on Bird Island." Then, not trusting the bridge, he held his hand over the mouthpiece and spoke to Gladys, "Do you have a car you could use to drive me to my cruiser at the other end of Main Street?"

"Sure."

He moved his hand away and spoke back into the receiver, "And see if you can find Matt or whoever's on beach patrol duty and have them meet me at the 40th Street access in five minutes."

"Okay. Michael, is everything okay?"

"No, it's not okay. I think I know who murdered D. Duke and the chief's not going to be very happy about it," he quickly hung up.

"Where's your car?"

"In the garage. This way," she led him through a door and down the stairs to the garage. Using the wall mounted panel she pushed the button for the door to open. They both hopped into the car and he told her that he'd like to come back and talk to her some more and to get that recipe.

421

She smiled and told him that he would be welcome any time, as long as it was before Saturday. She would be leaving to go back home on Saturday.

She let him off at his cruiser and he quickly ran to open the back door, momentarily forgetting about his sore feet until they sharply reminded him of their tenderness by almost buckling his knees under him. He had purposely left the rear driver's side door unlocked because he knew he would be leaving the keys in his uniform pocket. He quickly put his uniform on over his bathing suit, grateful for the socks and shoes to protect his feet. Strapping on his gun while he walked over to the beach access, he called out his thanks to Gladys.

He just could not believe it! Ray, the murderer! Was it really possible? What other reason would he have for lying about being there when the boat was salvaged? The pencil. It had to be the pencil. How else could he have explained it being there? And it made sense that it had no prints on it; he was forever rolling those pencils back and forth, his hand moving over the outside of his pocket. It must have slipped out of his pocket unnoticed, when Ray was in the boat with D. Duke's body—or part of D. Duke's body.

He wondered if Ray had even known at that time that D. Duke had lost his head and he didn't have the whole body with him. Well, he'd certainly found out when it had come time to bury the body! He tried to remember back to the day that the head had been found to see if he could remember Ray's reaction. But the only thing he could remember about that day was Cassie. Cassie, the woman he was going to marry. Cassie, the woman he was going to propose to tonight if he didn't get shot, killed, or make a complete ass out of himself.

Matt was there with the four wheeler waiting for him when he ran down the steps of the beach access and Michael immediately hopped on behind him. "Seen Ray?" he hollered in Matt's ear so he could be heard over the roar of the engine.

"Yeah, he went down to Bird Island about twenty minutes ago. A few minutes before that, some really nice chick stopped me and asked if you were still down there. I told her I thought you were and she turned and walked away. Man, she was gorgeous: moppy black curls and violet colored eyes."

"Cassie?" he asked, suddenly in a panic.

"I didn't get her name. There she is though, way down there near the jetty with Ray."

"Awww shit! Drop me off here, then go get some back up, we might even need a boat in the water at the jetty. Ray's backed into a corner and who knows what he'll do. Looks like we could easily have a hostage situation here. This is good right here," he said as he hopped off a hundred feet from where his tent was. "And hurry!" he yelled as Matt turned around to head back up the beach.

Chapter 40

Cassie had been thinking about Michael all day long. These games they were playing were for the birds. She was going to tell him that. She was going to tell him that she was going to throw away that book and just be herself and let him be himself and let whatever happens, happen. She didn't want to be at odds with him. She wanted to be with him, and she didn't want an author she didn't even know dictating when she and Michael could have sex.

They had fallen in love without the help of a book, they could manage their relationship without one. She wanted to see him tonight, but she couldn't call him on the beach so she decided to take a few minutes to go over to the island to talk to him. She was also very curious to see if he had spotted Lady Kit yet.

She saw his tent and made a beeline for it. No one seemed to be on the island, which seemed a bit odd, since it was such a beautiful day. Then she remembered that it was a weekday, way out of season, and that this was fairly normal for this very exclusive beach. It was why so many people loved it here this time of the year.

She was only five feet from the tent when Michael came out of it. At first, she thought it was Michael, but it wasn't. It was that awful man, Ray.

"Well, well, Cassie. It's so nice to see you. Coming to remind me about our date for Friday night?"

She had completely forgotten all about that impulsive foolishness she'd participated in on the day of Michael's football party. No time like the present to set matters straight. "Actually, no. To be completely honest, it slipped my mind. See, Michael and I were having a . . . well we weren't getting along . . . and I guess I was using you to make Michael jealous when I came onto you. I'm very sorry, that was not a nice thing to do."

"No, it wasn't," he said as he moved menacingly toward her.

"Hey, no reason to get angry. It was just a misunderstanding. I'm really sorry that I didn't think to call you right away and cancel."

"Well, I think you need to be punished," he said in a very serious, matter-of-fact tone.

She started to back away from him, but he quickly grabbed her hand and pulled her towards him. "And I think I know just how to punish you," he said as he reached behind his back, grabbed his cuffs and with a flick of his wrist he imprisoned her slim wrist in one of the shiny silver manacles. The other one he deftly flicked open and closed over his own wrist.

"Now we're together. Locked to one another," he said with a salacious wink. "Let's walk and talk while we get to know one another better," he said as he led her over toward the dunes.

"No! Let me go! Michael will be furious if you don't let me go right this minute!"

"Michael will be furious anyway."

"What does that mean?"

"It means he's about to find out something I didn't want anybody to know, and once he realizes it's true, he's going to be pretty hard to control."

"What the hell are you talking about? Where's Michael?" she screamed as she jerked her hand away from his, sending a shooting pain along her arm as the handcuff sliced into the tender skin of her wrist.

He glared at her and grabbed for her forearm, dragging her toward a tall dune covered with sea grass. "When I found out he was coming here to wait for that bitch to show up, I thought he was just being stupid. How many days did he think the chief was going to allow him to sit on the beach and wait for some nameless woman to show herself?"

Cassie was starting to get an uncomfortable feeling about what Ray was talking about. She had thought at first that he was simply mad at her. Then, when he had started dragging her to the dunes, she thought that maybe he intended to molest her and tell everybody she'd asked for it. Now she wasn't so certain. What did Michael and Lady Kit have to do with Ray? Apparently Ray hadn't known that there was a reason for Michael waiting for her on this particular day.

"Why do you care?"

"Why do I care?" he asked insolently. "Why do I care?" he repeated, his voice almost too soft now. "I guess you could say, I care . . . " he said drawing out his words, "I care because she knows that I killed D. Duke."

"What!" she jumped back, heedless of the handcuff and how it was tearing into her skin.

He seemed to enjoy watching the shock as it registered on her face. He continued to propel her forward, further into the seclusion of the dunes. "Yup. I killed D. Duke," he said smugly.

"You? Why would you have killed him?"

"Because he had something I wanted."

"What could D. Duke possibly have that you wanted?"

"Land. Undeveloped land on one of the most beautiful islands in the country."

"You killed him to get some land?"

"Yup. Funny that. Nobody even knew he owned any land, 'cept the house he lived in, that his daddy willed to him. But there he was when I came to talk to him about the cats, sitting at his dining room table getting ready to deed three lots, completely free and clear, over to that ban-the-bridge group. Prime real estate just right for developing. Well, as he talked, I listened. He was quite eager to tell somebody how he was going to give the properties over to them to pay the attorney's fees so they could keep fighting the new bridge. Stupid old man. Couldn't he see they couldn't stop the damn thing anymore?"

"I asked him about the deeds. I'd never seen any like that before. He said they were fee simple. Blank titles to land, ancient paperwork from when the island was originally sold. D. Duke's father had done a lot of work for the senior Mr. Gore. He helped him with the ferry. He carted bricks and stone and lumber for him and he helped him clear the first lots for the very first houses on the island. Instead of money, he'd been paid with land, land that would be worth a fortune half a century later. D. Duke's father had said the deeds were like money in the bank and he refused to sell them. All these years, they'd lived at nearly poverty level when they had those parcels with absolutely no liens. His father had told D. Duke to hold onto them as long as he could, not to sell them until it was the right time. Well,

D. Duke figured, now was the right time, time to sell the land to preserve his precious island.

"Well, I just couldn't stand to see him do that, waste all that money like that. So I told him that he'd better sign a blank piece of paper near the bottom to go along with the blank deeds, just in case someone questioned whether he'd actually given them the land, that they weren't simply stolen deeds or something. Well, he bit. He pulled out a clean, white sheet of paper and signed his name to the bottom. And there I had it, three blank deeds of conveyance and a last will and testament confirming that they were mine."

"Last will and testament?"

"Well, I wrote that over top of his signature later."

"Weren't you afraid somebody would question how you got the property, how you happened to be his last 'best friend.' "

"Nobody knew he owned the properties to begin with. Nobody anywhere. And, I'd actually planned on him being simply missing for a while. That would've given me some time, and no suspicions—but when that didn't work out, I simply took the paperwork, paid the current taxes to get my name on the receipts and became partners with a developer in Whiteville. After the houses were built, we were gonna sell them and be in fat city."

"So why are you telling me all this?"

"Because it doesn't look like it's going to turn out that way anymore. Your boyfriend had a little more smarts than I gave him credit for. He found the bird that I knocked the old man out with, figured out about the boat and then he had phenomenal luck when that stupid man on the beach had to build his sand sculpture right where I'd buried the body. Well, most of it," he shook his head and gave her a wry grin. "I didn't even know until I'd dragged him from the boat over there," he pointed with his hand, bringing hers up with his, "that his head had been chopped off! I had a hell of a time figuring out how the hell that happened. But Michael, Michael figured that out, too. Should of just dragged him down the steps instead of throwing him over the side of the deck."

Unable to absorb all he was telling her, she shook her head in disbelief. "You killed a man for the land his father had held his whole life for his son?"

"Honey, it's all just about money. And now your boyfriend's on to me. I saw him following that bitch home. I knew she'd remember. As soon as I read that journal thing Michael had in that file folder asking about the cats, I knew she knew. I tried to get to her, too. But the damn woman was never home! I should've looked her up in Cary, taken care of her there instead of waiting for her to show up here. Well, now you're gonna get me out of here. But first, I think we've got time for some fun."

He took his free hand and shoved it up under her work shirt, "Let me see those nice titties Michael's getting so fond of," he whispered as he felt around under her shirt and bra, trying to get to her breasts.

"No!" she screamed, pushing hard against his chest. She had forgotten how attached they were and she ended up falling on top of him as she knocked him into the sand. "Well, if you're in that much of a hurry, baby, let's just get your pants off."

"Don't you touch me!" she hollered as he started unbuttoning her jeans. She swatted at him with her free hand, trying to keep him from untucking her shirt when the button and zipper gave way. Just then, Ray tensed. His whole body went rigid. "Damn! I thought we'd have a lot more time than that!" he said as he stood up, pulling her up with him by jerking on her elbow. She heard the low drone of a four wheeler coming from way down the beach. As it approached, it got louder and louder.

"Now, if you do exactly as I say, we'll get out of here. If you don't, we're both going to die, I promise you that," he hissed as he pulled her out from behind the shelter of the dunes.

They could see the four wheeler with two men on it, one wearing the uniform of the Sunset Beach Police Department. Cassie prayed that it would be Michael. Michael would know what to do. Ray jerked her hand hard as he pulled her alongside him. She gasped from the pain of his brutal manhandling. "Either keep up or get more of the same," he growled as he led her farther and farther down the island toward the jetty with its massive slate-colored rocks.

She looked over her shoulder as she was being dragged away and she saw that it was Michael. He hopped off the four wheeler and then he was alone as the four-wheeler made a tight circle and headed back in the direction it had come from. Michael had a fierce look on his face as he stalked toward them. His face conveyed that he was hell bent on rescuing her from this madman and confronting a cowardly murderer.

"Here he comes, baby doll, white knight to rescue his fair damsel. Well, black knight's going to have the victory here, one way or another, it's gonna be my checkmate." Michael now had his gun in his hand as he walked briskly towards them, closing the distance. Ray was careful to keep Cassie in front of him as he turned to walk backward toward the jetty. Ray had also unholstered his gun and was waving it in front of her face, reminding her who was in charge. As he hugged her tightly to him, he dragged her with him, mindful never to give Michael a clear shot.

Cassie slumped to her knees, willing to suffer the punishment to her hand to allow Michael the extra time he needed to catch up and the opportunity to fire his weapon, but Ray saw through this gambit right away. He shoved his gun into his waistband and simply scooped her up and carried her, forcing her hand behind her as his manacled hand gripped the back of her thighs. As she grappled with him, trying to get away, he stuck his other hand way down inside her pants and under her panties. Her zipper was still undone and he had plenty of room to feel up her buttocks. He gripped her tightly, securing her to his shoulder by grasping a firm, now exposed cheek. "Nice, nice, nice. It is a shame I'm not able to stop now and have a piece of this. But once we get on that boat, I'm gonna have it. Count on it," he hissed into her ear.

She gave one great sob as his hand delved between her cheeks and a cruel finger separated her cheeks. His finger rimmed her hole then he shoved it in as far as it would go. "You're going to like my cock here much better than my finger, I assure you. Just you wait and see."

Cassie screamed out as she strained with all her might to lift her body away from his finger, but he held her tightly to him as he laughed. At Cassie's scream,

431

Michael raised his gun and took aim, but Ray lifted her body higher and shielded himself while he removed his finger from her, took his weapon from his waistband, and aimed it at her head. The message was clear, you shoot—I shoot. They were at the rocks now, the sharp, gray granite rocks that led the way into Little River Inlet. The long line of rocks jutted out of the sea at an eighty degree angle from the beach. They were wet and slippery and they would be brutal if you fell on one, even more so if you fell between them where smaller versions waited to impale you.

"Start climbing," he said as he jammed the barrel of the gun into her back, "and these are your options: we get to the end of the jetty where they'll have a boat waiting for us or we both go into the ocean. And believe me, I'll drag you down to the very bottom with me. They won't find your body until every sea creature around has had a bite out of you. Now, get movin'!"

They had gone about thirty feet when Cassie heard Michael's voice call out from behind them. Looking back, she was able to see that he had followed them out onto the rocks and was slowly making progress towards them. Out of the corner of her eye she saw two boats heading toward them coming from the inlet. Their purposeful beeline right for the rocks was a sure indication these were not pleasure boaters.

"Well, well, my cohorts are bringing me a boat, imagine that!" he said smugly as he pushed her along ahead of him. She struggled to climb from one large boulder to another as her jeans threatened to come off her hips, she tried to pull them back up with her one free hand. Ray jerked her back against him and hollered back over his shoulder to Michael, "Cassie and I are going for a boat ride. She says she'd rather be with me than you!"

"Bull shit!" Michael hollered back.

"I had her. I had her virgin ass over there in the dunes!"

"No, you didn't! And it isn't virginal!"

"I did too have her!" Ray shouted back at him.

"No, no you didn't," Michael said calmly, almost too calmly.

"Just what makes you so sure about that?" Ray yelled, getting angrier by the minute.

"I just know that's not true, Ray," Michael said as he scaled a large boulder and now stood only fifteen feet away. "I'm the only man that's had that dubious honor and I believe she'd kill a man or herself before she'd let that happen again. And, my Cassie's meaner than cat shit. She'd bite off a man's penis before letting it go in there again."

"You're not getting her back!"

"Oh, yes I am!" Michael answered as he continued climbing the last few remaining rocks that separated them.

The rocks were rough and unyielding and one slip would crack a man's skull. They all knew it, as the three of them inched their way to the end of the jetty, crawling like ants with their backsides up in the air as they scrambled from one rock to the next.

Arduously they moved along. The officers on the shore, poised with rifles watching and waiting for the chance to shoot, the officers in the boat waiting for the same opportunity. But Ray was smart. He knew what they would do in any given situation. And right now the girl was his most valuable asset, so he kept her as close as he could while they moved to the end of the jetty. He kept her bottom tucked into his body as he half lifted, half dragged her from one rock to the next.

Michael was catching up, but Ray didn't care. His mind was made up. He had the girl, one way or the other—they were inseparable. She would get into the boat with him or she would drown with him, of this he was totally committed. He felt pretty confident that they'd let him get away. The chief was in one of the boats, and he would be calling the shots.

Then they were at the end, and there were no more rocks above the water level. "Bring the boat over!" he yelled to the officers in the water.

"No!" Michael yelled at them, his eyes never leaving Ray's. From this moment, his mind would be focused on exactly where Cassie was every single second, but his eyes would be intently watching every move that Ray made. He had to be ready. For Cassie's sake, he had to be ready for anything.

"You're not getting her back!" Ray hollered at him as he held Cassie tightly against his body. He knew the men on the shore were too far away for a clear shot and the men in the boats were being rocked so hard that they couldn't even begin to take aim, so he wasn't worried about keeping his head protected until he heard Michael's stony reply.

"Oh, yes I am."

They stood that way staring each other down as the boat pulled back in response to Michael's order. Cassie saw the hard look in Michael's eyes and knew that they would never be getting on a boat. Ray saw it, too.

She looked into the water churning all around them. If they all went into the water together, she'd have no chance with Ray's weight pulling her down. Even if Michael was strong enough to swim in this very strong current, she knew that once he was underwater, he wouldn't be able to see to find her much less pull them both up together. She didn't have much longer to think about what the possible outcomes could be, because Ray suddenly brought his service revolver up to his head and with no hesitation, pulled the trigger.

Michael screamed Cassie's name, then with deadly accuracy he aimed and fired. He shot Ray's hand off right at the wrist as Ray started falling backward into the ocean, allowing Cassie to break their connection just as the momentum carried her forward and she slipped and fell into the water right behind Ray.

Cassie had heard Michael's voice scream, "Cassie!" just as she heard the loud explosion. Then instantly, she heard another and seconds later she felt the frigid coldness of the water as it enveloped her.

Anticipating her fall, Michael dove in after her, aiming his body right at hers as it hit the water, allowing him to grab her pants leg as he followed her into the turbulent sea. The force of their fall together sent them both fifteen feet under before he could right them and start propelling them back up. On the way up to the light shining through the dark layers of the water, he saw the splayed out body of Ray as it sank slowly into the ocean, red streamers of blood making long ribbons out of his head and from the place where his hand used to be. He wished that Ray could still see out of those open, unblinking eyes, because he wanted him to see Cassie clutched tightly in his arms as he carried her back to the surface. There had been no way in hell that he was going to lose her, he'd always known that.

Chapter 41

Using all the strength he could muster, Michael sent Cassie high over his head to break the surface first. He had no air left. After firing his gun and instantly diving in after Cassie, he hadn't taken a good breath. But he was more concerned for her than he was for himself. She just had to be all right, he prayed. He felt light headed and suddenly incredibly weak when he felt her hand grip the material of his shirt and jerk his head to the surface. And then he was gasping and flailing to stay above the surface. His first cognizant thought was of her as soon as he realized that he wasn't drowning. She was there, alongside him, catching her breath and making sure he didn't go under again.

He shook his head to clear it and to get rid of the majority of the water running into his face from his hair. "You okay?" He gasped.

"Yes. I'm okay."

She held up her hand with the empty handcuff attached to her wrist. Thankfully the limb that had once been encircled in it, had fallen out into the water. "Pretty sure of your shooting, aren't you?"

"You're lucky I'm the best shot in four counties."

She smiled over at him, her tears of relief mingling with the salt water streaming down her face, "I sure am. That was quick thinking on your part. Most men wouldn't have thought to do that or had the balls to do it."

"I'm not most men, I had a lot to lose," he said with earnestness as his hands cupped her face. "I knew from the moment I saw him dragging you down the beach, that I wasn't going to lose you. God, I love you," he said as he took her lips with his.

The next few minutes were a blur as the men in the boats hauled them over the sides and raced them back to shore. Two more boats had joined the others and a diver was preparing to go into the water to retrieve Ray's body. Someone handed Michael back the gun he had dropped between the rocks before taking his plunge into the inlet and slapped him on the back. Blankets were thrown over both of their shoulders and Cassie was being whisked away by the paramedics. The chief had pulled him aside to talk to him, and the next thing he knew, she was gone.

"Where are they taking her?" he asked in a panic.

"She's okay, don't worry. The skin on her wrist has been cut pretty badly. They're just taking her to get a few stitches."

"Did somebody get the cuffs off of her? I don't want her being treated like an inmate!"

"Yes, yes, we got 'em off. The paramedics thought she might go into shock, so they wanted to take her to the hospital, just to be sure."

"I want to go with her."

"We can follow in my car," he signaled for one of the officers in the four wheel drive truck, "Give me the keys to your truck, I'm going to take him to Brunswick Hospital. Here's the keys to the Harley. Take it back to the station for me will ya?"

"Sure chief," the eager rookie said. It wasn't often that the station's Harley police motorcycle was driven by anyone other than the chief.

The chief patted Michael on the back as they walked to the truck, "You did some mighty fine shooting there. Mighty quick thinking, too."

"I just did what I had to, to make sure he didn't take her with him. If he hadn't shot himself in the head, I might have done it for him."

"I wouldn't have faulted you for that."

They got into the truck and drove down the beach, now deserted except for a few curious onlookers.

"Got your message about the back up, but I had no clue what the hell was going on until I got there. Then, I almost couldn't believe what I was seeing."

"I'm sorry I couldn't fill you in a little more, but once I figured out it was Ray who had murdered D. Duke, I knew he wasn't going to come in on his own. I actually thought he might grab a few hostages to get away from here, but it never even occurred to me that one might be Cassie. I don't even know why she was on Bird Island in the first place."

"Well, it won't take long to sort all this out." When they got to the wooden emergency services ramp beside the gazebo, they saw that the paramedics were just pulling out. The chief flipped the siren and let it make one little wail to let them know to wait up. "Go on, go to the hospital with her. Then bring her back to the station and I'll get everybody's statements. By then, I'll have the necessary investigators there to clear you."

"Thanks. I'll need someone to bring my cruiser from the end of Main Street," he said as he threw the chief the keys.

"No problem, I'll get someone to bring it to you. And Michael?"

"Yeah?" he said as he ducked his head down to see him through the open window.

"Good job."

"Thanks," he said with a big smile. Then he ran over to the waiting ambulance and was let in through the back doors.

Cassie was on a stretcher, half sitting, half reclining. Her beautiful face lit up in a bright smile as soon as she saw him. They were both still wearing their drenched clothing and she was beginning to shiver. Her hand was bandaged so all he could see was her fingertips. He looked over at the paramedic and asked. "How bad is it?"

"Not too bad, she's not bleeding anymore, but she's got some deep gashes there."

"You shouldn't have fought him so much, Cass. Didn't you know that I'd come get you?"

"Actually, no, I didn't. I just couldn't let him take me away. You know what he would have done to me don't you?"

"Yes, I know, but there's no way in hell I would have let him. Pray tell, why were you on the island to begin with?"

"I came to see you. He was in the tent. I thought he was you until he came out of the tent."

"Why did you come to talk to me?"

She looked up at the paramedic monitoring her blood pressure. "We'll talk later, I just had to see you that's all."

"Well, we need to get you some dry clothes."

"You, too."

"I'll be fine, I'm just worried about you," he said as he bent down to remove her soaked work boots. "God, no wonder you were so hard to lift out of the water! These weigh a ton!"

He stripped the sodden socks off her feet, and massaged her toes. She sighed, "Ah, that feels so good."

He leaned down and whispered in her ear, "If you think that feels good, wait 'til I get you home tonight."

When they arrived at the hospital, one of the nurses found some scrubs for them to wear and while the doctor cleaned her cuts and stitched her up, Michael held her other hand. Then, after assuring the doctor that they would come back if there were any signs of infection, they left in the car that two officers had brought for him. He stopped by his house to pick up some clothes then he drove Cassie to her house where they showered and dressed. He insisted that they take turns using the bathroom instead of showering together. He had plans for her tonight, and technically, he was still on duty. Then they called the construction site to see if Louie could handle things on his own until tomorrow since they needed to be debriefed by the chief and a team of investigators.

After the chief had been introduced to Cassie, Michael motioned the chief aside and whispered something in the chief's ear as he placed a small silver key in his hand. The chief smiled and nodded, then looked through his rolodex for the card for the bank manager at BB&T at Ocean Isle. He went into another office and called her home number, found a duty officer and handed the key, along with a signed note from Michael, to him with some very specific instructions.

"So," he said as he settled himself down in the chair behind his desk, "I hear Ray confessed to killing D. Duke to you before taking you onto the jetty. Is that right?"

"Yes sir . . . " And for the next two hours Michael and Cassie answered questions by both the chief and the internal investigators who had temporarily relieved Michael of his gun, as procedure dictated whenever an officer discharged his firearm. When everyone was satisfied and the whole story had been detailed for everyone, Michael was given his gun back and he and Cassie left.

Hand in hand, they walked to his cruiser. "Well, we have to go back to the island to get your truck, he said. And I doubt that anyone thought to get my tent and my gear, so would you mind walking with me to get them? Then, we'll go get something to eat. I'm starving."

"That sounds like a good idea. I could use something to eat. I could use a drink too!" she said with a laugh. "It's not everyday that a man wants to abduct you for nefarious purposes."

"I want to abduct you for nefarious purposes," he said huskily into the side of her neck. She felt the stirring of his lips and breath on her skin all the way to her toes.

"Yeah, but I *want* to go with you."

Suddenly Michael straightened, and looked her solemnly in the eyes, "He didn't do anything to you, did, he?"

She hung her head and then quickly looked back up. "He touched me. He fondled my bottom and poked between my cheeks as he told me what he was going to do."

"Damn! Honey, I am so sorry that I wasn't there to protect you."

"You were when it counted. I can get over a few rough gropings. It would have been harder to get over him raping me."

"I wish I'd shot him in the balls!"

"Then I'd be dead. He would've taken me to the bottom of the inlet with him. You shot him exactly where you should have and you know it."

"Yeah, I just wish I'd had time for two shots!"

She laughed and reached over to fluff his hair through her fingers. "He's history. Tell me all about Lady Kit."

They walked arm-in-arm from the 40th Street access to the tent they could see in the distance as he told her about Lady Kit.

When they got close to the tent, he steered her over to the mailbox, "Before we take the tent down, come over here and see what she wrote in the journal today."

They walked over to the mailbox as they admired the magnificent sunset stretching out for as far as you could see, the colors spreading all the way to the other side of the island, beyond D. Duke's house.

"This is just about where I saw you naked for the first time."

443

He'd seen her naked many times since, but she still blushed. "One day soon, Bird Island may be within your jurisdiction and nude sunbathing won't be allowed."

"I'll always have the memory of you lying naked on the sand. Then yelling at me while you tried to get that towel to cover you." He patted her fingers that were wrapped around his arm and they both laughed at the memory.

When they got to the mailbox, he grabbed the journal from the box, walked over to the sand-covered bench and cleared a spot for her. He lowered her onto the bench and handed her the journal.

She flipped through the pages until she got to the first blank page and then peeled the page back to reveal the last page with any writing on it. Using her finger she read through the two entries at the top of the page that were written by tourists and then her eyes fell on the one written by Michael and she read: "Cassie, you own my soul, too. Will you marry me? Michael."

With tears flowing from her eyes, she looked over at Michael, who was now kneeling, his arm extended to her with the palm up. Sitting in the middle of his palm was an opened box. Nestled inside the small, black box was a silver filigreed ring with a big, brilliant cut diamond in a high-mounted center prong.

She looked from the ring to his handsome face and to the sincere, pleading look in his blazing blue eyes as he wordlessly communicated his love for her.

"Yes. Yes. A thousand times yes!"

He removed the ring from the box and gently eased it onto her finger. Then she hugged him fiercely around his neck and kissed his throat. He felt the heat from her lips and had an overwhelming desire to feel them against his own. He took her arms from around his neck and placed them on his shoulders. He heard her mumble, "I guess the book worked!" And he laughed out loud, "I guess you could say that! But I'm the only one who read it!" Then he took her face between his hands and kissed her thoroughly, giving her the tongue lashing that she very much deserved.

When he had kissed her so thoroughly that she was limp in his arms, he picked her up and carried her over to the tent. Lifting the flap with his elbow, he ducked and carried her inside. And there, waiting in a plastic bucket was a bottle of champagne on ice. Next to it were two glasses lying on a towel and a big flat box still in its sliver pouch, proclaiming the contents to be a Roberto's pizza.

She looked at the blanket spread out that could be either a bed or a table and smiled. Then she raised her eyebrow in question, "Hey, hey, hey! What's this about having glass on the beach?"

"I guess D. Duke would be extremely disappointed with me."

"No, somehow I don't think he would. Pour me a glass and let's drink to the man who brought us together by losing his head."

Michael chuckled as he set her on the blanket and poured them each a glass. "I love you, Cassie," he said as he clinked his glass with hers.

"And I love you, Michael," she said as she lifted hers in salute. "And I promise to be the kind of wife you've always wanted. I'll even learn how to cook."

He let out a loud groan, "That's okay, honey. Just concentrate on the other thing I want from my wife."

"And what's that?" she asked.

He set his glass down on top of the cooler, then took hers from her hand and set it beside his. "Incredible sex. Absolutely, incredible sex," he said as he leaned in to softly kiss her while his hand went to the buttons on her shirt. "Let's have the pizza naked, shall we? And would it be all right with you if I didn't use a condom tonight?"

"Michael, I don't really want to get pregnant right away. I'm building a bridge, remember?"

"Yeah, it just means you'll be relegated to the sidelines for a while—no riding your Tonka toys. You'll manage," he said as he kissed the side of her neck.

"Are you sure we're ready to have a baby?"

"I know I am. I'll tell you what, I'll wear one every other time and we'll see who wins."

Epilogue

Michael and Cassie went to visit Gladys Covey, a.k.a. Lady Kit, before she left to go home to Cary on Saturday. She had already written out her recipe for Mulligatawny Stew to give to Michael and was delighted to learn that he was engaged to the lady bridge builder. She hadn't met Cassie before, but as far as she was concerned, anybody who had a hand in building the new bridge was all right in her book. The faster she could get onto her island, the better. She was shocked to learn that D. Duke had been the owner of the lot next door to hers, the place where he came to feed his beloved cats.

Michael brought the stack of index cards with her entries, the ones he had copied from the Kindred Spirit journals. They went through them, one-by-one, and he found out that: Harvey *had* been her husband; next to Grapevine, Crab Catcher's and Ocean Garden Buffet *were* her favorite restaurants; and no, she hadn't used her charge card that day in Pelican Books or Cheney's; and yes, she did play the piano, but only occasionally. The time she had written about it in the journal had been the time she'd had to go back to Cary to play for a friend's wedding. And the time she'd written about the shipwrecks, had been just after she'd found out her cousin had died in the Persian Gulf after a helicopter he'd been in, crashed into the sea. They both talked about how much they missed Madd Inlet, how they hated the charge card companies and how they were already missing D. Duke.

The three properties that had belonged to D. Duke that were now in the process of being developed, reverted back to the state. D. Duke had left no will, and there was no next of kin to be found, so his estate was surrendered to the state. All four of his properties were sold and the proceeds garnered by the state. And that's how D. Duke became one of the largest contributors to the new bridge project. Ironically, the bridge that he had fought against all his life was now being funded indirectly by him.

Gladys lobbied for a portion of D. Duke's estate to be used to fund a memorial project to supplement the county's program to neuter, spay and vaccinate the feral cats on the island. The locals were happy that at least some of D. Duke's money would go to something he had really cared about.

Cassie's dad, bought D. Duke's beach house when the state held its auction. And together, he and Michael were renovating it. Gene had seen the investment value of the property, and he needed a place to stay on his now frequent trips to the beach.

Michael and Cassie were married at the Sunset Beach gazebo where she threw her bouquet into a balmy breeze. Mary Matthews Murphy Meadows caught it, but that's another story.

Mulligatawny Soup

Sauté in 1/4 cup butter in a deep kettle or Dutch oven:

    1 medium onion, peeled and sliced
    1 medium carrot, diced

1 stalk celery, diced
1 green pepper, seeded and diced
1 medium apple, pared, cored, and sliced
1 cup cut-up cooked chicken

Stir frequently until onions are tender.
Stir in gradually:

1/3 cup flour
1 tsp. curry powder
1/8 tsp. mace
2 whole cloves
1 sprig parsley
2 cups White Stock (Consommé)
1 cup cooked tomatoes
salt and pepper to taste

Simmer covered 1/2 hour, then serve.
6 servings.

About the Author

Jacqueline DeGroot lives in Sunset Beach, North Carolina. She lives with her husband, Bill and daughter, Kimberly. Her son Jeff lives in Calabash and her step-son James lives in Watertown, N.Y. She loves walking on the beach, cooking exotic dishes and decorating lavish cakes. *The Secret of the Kindred Spirit* is her third book. This edition is its first reprint. Her first book, *Climax*, she fondly refers to as her dirty, trashy, sleazy, romance, mystery-thriller. Her second book, *What Dreams Are Made Of*, is a collection of love stories. Since *The Secret of the Kindred Spirit*, she has written and published *Barefoot Beaches*, *For the Love of Amanda*, and *Shipwrecked at Sunset*. Reading has always been a large part of her life. Her idea of paradise is being able to sit on the beach with a good book and a plastic glass of champagne, listening to the waves perpetually washing up on the land. Check out her website (www.jacquelinedegroot.com). Her next book, a dark, erotic thriller set in Wilmington, N.C., will be out next year.

CPSIA information can be obtained
at www.ICGtesting.com
Printed in the USA
FFOW04n1126190615
14343FF